# "OKAY MARINES. TAKE 'EM DOWN!"

There was a silent flash, gasses spewing from the vents around the Wyvern's load tube, and the SAM streaked vertically into the sky, arcing to the south to close with the huge, gray globe of the Chinese lander. From the opposite side of the crater, a second Wyvern soared into the night; the Marines out on work detail when the raid had begun were emerging from their crude shelters now and joining the fight.

White-yellow flame blossomed against the lander's stern . . . and then again. There was no change in the craft's course; it continued drifting across the sky, from west to east, chasing its own shadow now as it grew closer to the ice.

It took several seconds before Lucky realized . . . *it wasn't slowing down!*

The 1,200-ton orbit-to-surface shuttle impacted on the ice nearly half a kilometer beyond the crater's east rim, well to the north of the first craft. It drilled in tail first, landing gear deployed . . . but when the landing struts touched the surface they appeared to crumple as the rest of the craft mashed on down into the ice. There was no flame, no blast, not even the boom of an impact.

If there had been any sound, though, it would have been instantly drowned out by the cheers of the watching Marines.

And Lucky cheered with them, half rising to punch a gloved fist into the black sky. Victory was sweet . . . even if it *was* only temporary.

*Eos Books by*
**Ian Douglas**

STAR CORPS: BOOK ONE OF THE LEGACY TRILOGY

EUROPA STRIKE: BOOK THREE OF THE HERITAGE TRILOGY
LUNA MARINE: BOOK TWO OF THE HERITAGE TRILOGY
SEMPER MARS: BOOK ONE OF THE HERITAGE TRILOGY

# ONE

**15 SEPTEMBER 2067**

*U.S. Navy Deep Submersible*
  *Research Center*
*AUTEC, Andros Island*
*Bahamas, Earth*
*1055 hours (Zulu minus 5)*

"Incredible," Major Jeffrey Warhurst said, his face pressed against the forward viewing port like a kid experiencing his first visit to a seaquarium. "It's like a whole different world!"

Golden light exploded, a shower of drifting sparks. In the inky blackness, a line of blue-green lights rippled through the water beyond the port, a spectacular display of deep-sea luminescence. Close by, something like a translucent shrimp exhaled a cloud of yellow fire like a tiny rocket's exhaust, scooting off through the night, while in the distance, silver hatchet fish glowed with ghostly radiance.

"It's all of that," Mark Garroway said. The cramped DSV bridge was almost in total darkness, so that their eyes could remain sensitive to the light show outside. The two men were lying face-down on narrow, side-by-side couches so they could see forward. The sub's pilot occupied a closed-in, padded seat above and behind them. "You see some of the weirdest damned things down here. Bill Beebe called it 'plunging into new strangeness,' until 'vocabularies are pauperized and minds are drugged.' "

7

"Beebe?"

"He helped develop the bathysphere, back in the 1930s, with Otis Barton. The first true deep sea exploration vessel . . . if you can call a steel sphere dangling at the end of a thousand-meter cable a vessel. He was the first scientist ever to see some of these deep forms . . . alive, at any rate. He made his dives off of Bermuda."

"And he saw creatures like these?" Jeff asked. Something collided with the port, exploding in a storm of drifting sparks and leaving behind a pale, iridescently glowing smear. "Wow! Marvelous!"

The third man on the DSV control deck shifted in the pilot's seat, both hands on the attitude-control joysticks ball-mounted on the arms of the padded chair. "Time, gentlemen," he said. "We should be getting back to the surface." He was a stocky, powerful man with a body-sculptor's muscles. His square-jawed face was all but covered by the bright red VR helmet he wore, which fed him a constant 3-D and 360-degree image of the submersible's surroundings.

"I thought these subs had a thirty-day endurance," Jeff said.

"They do," Mark said, "when they're fully supplied, which this one is not. Even so, we have expendables enough to stay down for three or four days, at least. But that's not what's affecting our deadline. General Altman's scheduled to arrive in another hour, and we should be topside to meet him, don't you think?"

"Damn," Jeff said, continuing to watch the soft-glowing fireworks beyond the port. "I could stay down here for days!"

Mark chuckled. "Yeah, I know exactly what you mean."

Jeff Warhurst glanced sideways at the older man, at the rugged face in profile faintly illuminated by the red-hued glow of the bridge lights. Mark Garroway was seventy-one years old but showed no sign at all of slowing down, and his face was alive now with pleasure and wonder. He looked as excited as Jeff felt, for all that he was thirty-two years older.

The man was a legend in the Marines—"Sands of Mars" Garroway, the then–Marine Corps major and electronics expert who'd led a small band of Marines across 650 kilometers of the Vallis Marineris back in '41 to defeat a UN garrison at Mars Prime and go on to recapture the U.S. xenoarcheological base at Cydonia.

Jeff had been a Marine since 2050—seventeen years now—and had all but worshipped Garroway as his personal hero for longer than that. It was still a little hard to realize that he was lying next to the hero of Garroway's March . . . in an environment even more alien, in most ways, than the frozen surface of Mars.

"I guess this is all pretty old to you. You probably get tired of this after awhile, huh?"

"What?" Garroway said, startled. "Tired of *this?* When I do, I'll be tired of life!"

From what Jeff had heard, the elder Garroway hadn't slowed down much at all in the past quarter-century. Shortly after his return from Mars, he'd worked as a consultant with the Japanese, helping to make sense out of the flood of new technology arriving from the ET finds on Mars and the Moon. After that, he'd retired here, to the Bahamas, to open his marina, but even then he continued to work as a government consultant. AUTEC—the big U.S. submarine testing and research station on Andros Island—was only a few kilometers down the coast. With the building of the Bahamas seaquarium next door at Mastic Point twelve years ago, Mark Garroway had become both moderately wealthy and something of a public figure. Garroway's marina had been offering both realworld and virtual commercial submarine tours of the reefs for tourists for years now; his undersea tour service was a part of the Oceanus Seaquarium's exhibits and one of the most popular tourist attractions in the Islands.

*This* submarine, though, was not one of the tourist boats, not by about five thousand meters. Nicknamed Manta, the boat was a blunt, stubby, cigar shape eight meters long melded smoothly with rounded wings that gave it an elongated saucer look. Her hull was jet-black carbon-boron-Bucky fiber weave, or $CB_2F$, a process back-engineered from ET finds on the Moon, and stronger by a factor of five than anything based on purely terrestrial materials processing. The boat was driven by a magnetohydrodynamic jet, an MHD drive that compressed water drawn through intakes forward and expelled it aft like a rocket's exhaust; the craft's flattened shape, complete with upswept stabilizer tips on the ends of the circular "wings," was that of a lifting body designed to literally fly through water as an aircraft flew through the air. Originally developed by the U.S. Navy for abyssal trench research and exploration, the Manta could dive to depths in excess of ten kilometers, enduring hull pressures of well over a ton over each square centimeter of its hull. Mark Garroway had been asked to earn his consultant's pay this month by evaluating the Manta for use as an undersea transport for Marine raiding parties. And Jeff was here because of Project Icebreaker.

As the sub's pilot pulled back on the joystick controlling the vessel's attitude and increased thrust with a shrill, whining hum, the Manta began rising through the darkness. Something like a golden, shell-less snail flew past on undulating wings, leaving in its wake a faintly phosphorescent trail. The life here, Jeff thought, just a few hundred meters beneath the surface of the Atlantic Ocean, was as alien as anything that humankind might one day encounter among the stars.

"This is why you retired here, isn't it, sir?" he asked. "To be able to play with the Navy's high-tech toys? Maybe keep doing a bit of exploring . . . new worlds, and all that?"

"Oh, in part, I guess. Though I never did much in the way of exploring, even during my deployment with the MMEF. When I got out of the Corps, mostly what I wanted was to run my own marina. Oceanus and the rest just sort of happened." He grinned. "But I'm damned glad it did."

"Hey, Mr. Garroway?" the pilot said. "We've got company."

Mark frowned, rolling sideways on his couch to look up at the pilot. "What is it?"

The helmeted man touched a control on the arm of his chair, and a monitor on a console beneath the forward port lit up with a rotating, computer-drawn view of a small, twin-outrigger submarine with a large, high-pressure viewing bubble.

"Reads as a commercial teleoperated job. Looks like one of the Atlantis remotes."

"Anyone ever tell those jokers these are restricted waters?" Mark growled.

"It *looks* like a commercial job," the pilot repeated. "But it could be our friends again."

"What friends?" Jeff asked.

"Someone's been *very* interested in our activities down here," Mark explained. "Now, Carver here is a Navy SEAL and suspicious by nature. But sometimes it pays to be paranoid. We think it might be the *Guojia Anquan Bu*, keeping tabs on our deep-submersible work."

Jeff frowned. "China's overseas intelligence bureau? Why would they be using a commercial teleop drone?"

"Probably because Atlantis is close by, with remote drones that can innocently stray into government-restricted waters 'by mistake.' And they can link in from anywhere, remember."

Atlantis was another seaquarium resort, much like Oceanus but located in Florida, just south of West Palm Beach. Three hundred kilometers wasn't exactly "close by," but it was close enough that teleop drones could operate comfortably for extended periods.

"Range?" Mark asked Carver.

"Seventy meters." The whine of the Manta's jet drive increased as the SEAL sub driver boosted the power. "Sixty. We're closing."

Outside, all was still in complete blackness, save for the constellations of luminous deep-sea life. According to the readouts, they were at 495 meters depth now, with an out-side pressure of nearly fifty atmospheres squeezing at the hull. A tense minute passed as the Manta climbed through the high-pressure dark.

"They're running," Carver said. "They know we're on to them."

"Run 'em down!" Mark said.

"Range ten meters," Carver said. "I'm gonna hit the lights."

"Do it," Mark replied. A harsh white glare stabbed through the sea outside, turning drifting bits of detritus into a blizzard of glowing flecks. Ahead, a bubble-topped vessel less than a meter long, with twin outriggers and a yellow and red paint scheme, twisted in the Manta's beam.

"That's an Atlantis boat," the pilot said.

"It's *tiny*," Jeff said.

"Unmanned," Carver told him. "Someone's linked in through its cameras and other sensors and is piloting it from somewhere else. I'm picking up two blue-green laser relays between here and the surface. Chances are, whoever's steer-ing that thing isn't even at Atlantis. They could've linked in through the Net."

"Damned tourists," Mark growled. "Can you take him?"

"Working on it. He's slower . . . but a lot more maneu-verable." As if to demonstrate, the other sub twisted sharply toward the Manta, ascending, passing out of the field of view from the tiny forward port.

"This thing has torpedoes?" Jeff asked.

"She can," Mark told him. "She was designed to release remote drones for deep exploration . . . but it's easy enough to plug in a warhead instead of an instrument package. We're not armed today, though. Have to do it the hard way."

"Huh. Competition between all the new seaquariums must be pretty fierce," he observed.

Mark glanced at him, as if to see whether or not he was joking. Jeff grinned and shrugged. It *was* a bit surreal. Throughout the last century, by far the largest sector of

American business had been the entertainment industry, and theme parks like the big seaquariums and their space-park cousins had proliferated the way movie theaters had the century before. Competition between them was stiff . . . but this was the first time Jeff had ever heard of a war between rival theme parks.

The Manta surged, rising sharply, then banking right into a tight, tight turn that felt like the boat was hovering at the shuddering brink of a low-speed stall.

"That's screwed him," Carver said. "I've just interrupted the BG-laser link with our own hull. The target is dropping into wait-and-see mode."

"That means it will circle," Mark told Jeff, "trying to reacquire the comlink beam."

"It means," Carver added, "that for the next few seconds, it will be *predictable*."

"Martin 1150." Mark tapped the screen showing the rotating schematic. "Pretty stupid, actually. No AI. No anticipation. It needs a human remote-driver to do damn near anything at all."

Jeff still couldn't see the other sub, but the Manta was falling now. A moment later, there was a sharp, hollow-sounding *clunk* from port, transmitted through the hull from the Manta's left wing. "Got him!" Carver said, bringing the Manta's nose high once more. "He's going down, boss. Crushed his starboard flotation tank."

"Good job."

"Do you and the Atlantis seaquarium often take out one another's subs?" Jeff asked.

"These *are* restricted waters," Mark pointed out. "Part of AUTEC's test range. If Atlantis loses a few of their tourist-ride drones, maybe they'll be more careful about keeping track of where they're at. It's not like GPS receivers are *expensive* or anything."

"But you think it might've been the Chinese actually piloting it."

"Almost certainly," Mark said. "They tried getting in here first with drones off one of their big nuke subs, but the Navy chased them off. Lately, we think they're using the commercial teleops to keep an eye on us."

"Why? The Manta is new, but there's no radical technology, no antimatter, no ET stuff. What's their interest?"

"That," Mark said, "is an excellent question. I wish I knew the answer." He glanced at Jeff again. "It could be they know something about Icebreaker."

"That's not good."

"No, Major, I wouldn't think it was."

"I've sent a message to the surface," Carver said. "They'll send a salvage boat down to collect the BGL relays. I doubt they'll be able to collect the wreckage, though. Depth's almost three thousand meters here. Pretty steep for the salvage boys."

"They wouldn't learn anything from a damned commercial drone anyway," Mark replied. "We'll have Intelligence check out the user logs at Atlantic, but whatever they find'll be a front anyway. S'okay. I doubt that they saw anything worthwhile."

" 'Grains of sand,' " Carver said.

"I know."

"What's that mean?" Jeff asked.

"Chinese intelligence services work somewhat differently than we're used to here in the West," Mark replied. "They operate on a philosophy as old as Sun Tzu's *Art of War*, and they can be incredibly patient. They don't rely on spies or moles or intelligence coups as much as they do on many thousands of discrete, tiny, apparently unrelated bits of information all being funneled back to Beijing by Chinese tourists, government workers, scientists, businessmen. The image is of millions of termites, each with a grain of sand, patiently building a mound two or three meters high."

"Hell, sir, I thought all spy work was like that," Jeff said. He'd spent three years of his Marine career working a desk for Marine J2 in the Pentagon and knew something about military intelligence. "Forget the cloak-and-dagger stuff. You piece together a fact here, a probability there, a statistic, a photograph . . . and you end up with a detailed report on why the Uzbek Republic is going to have a civil war next year."

"Sure, but the way we go about it is a pale, pale shadow of how the Chinese do things. Intelligence operations in the West tend to go from fiscal year to fiscal year and extend just as far as the current budget allows. For the Chinese, doing something, doing anything with an eye to the future is standard procedure. They can afford to take the long view and make decisions that won't bear fruit for twenty years."

"I've heard stories about that," Jeff admitted. "When they targeted our nuclear weapons program back in the last century, they did it a little bit at a time. But they *did* have a lot of help from greedy politicians and short-sighted bureaucrats."

"They are . . . opportunists," Mark said. "Opportunists with a very clear idea of where they want to go and how they need to go about it. *And* the patience to get there."

Forty minutes later, the Manta broke the surface, exploding into dazzling, tropical sunshine and riding a gentle swell. A kilometer ahead, a Navy subcarrier was just visible, her black, stealth-canted upper deck, sensor suite, and aft housing rising from a main deck that was completely awash, completely bare of masts, railings, or other radar-catching protuberances. A lot of the newer Navy warships looked more to Jeff's eye like the original U.S.S. *Monitor* than a modern surface vessel. Most attack vessels had even less visible above the waterline than the subcarrier *Neried*.

Though the *Neried* could launch and recover her submersible offspring underwater, the Manta was still undergoing sea trials and was scheduled this day for a surface docking. The subcarrier was broader than she looked in profile, with dual catamaran keels embracing a central wetbay facing aft. Carver brought the sub about to line her up with *Neried*'s stern, slowly guiding the DSV "up her ass," between the big ship's keel-mounted MHD propulsors.

Mark slithered backward off his couch and stood behind Carver's position. A touch of a button opened the Manta's hood, exposing her topside bubble canopy and allowing sunlight to flood the cramped space with light and warmth. The space directly under the navigation bubble was the only spot on the bridge where a tall man could stand upright.

Jeff stayed where he was, however. He was fine underwater, but once the Manta reached the surface, the boat became ungainly, wallowing heavily with each swell despite the broad reach of her wings. He felt the first sharp twinge in his stomach and throat.

*A fine thing,* he thought, both angry and bemused by the weakness. He swallowed hard and clung to the padding of his couch, trying to shut out the lateral shift and yaw. *A seasick Marine.*

He'd been violently ill his first time afloat, back at the Naval Academy during small boat evolutions. It had been all the worse because Jeff Warhurst was the son of a Marine officer, the grandson of an officer and former U.S. Marine Commandant, the *great*-grandson of a Marine who'd won the Medal of Honor in Vietnam.

And *that* Marine's father had been a Marine as well, a gunnery sergeant who'd watched the raising of the flag over Suribachi and five years later had frozen to death at a miserably desolate place called Yudam-ni.

All those Marine ancestors. And *he* got sick in small boats.

He didn't suffer long, however. Carver guided the DSV into *Neried*'s wetbay, a wide, low-roofed cavern that closed off astern of them once they entered. A docking crew on the walkways to either side jumped aboard and secured lines to her retractable deck cleats. Her wings folded up, like the wings of an aircraft aboard a Navy strike carrier, as the working party hauled her by hand into a berth nestled alongside three identical craft.

Carver released her dorsal hatch, and a few moments later, Jeff was clambering up the ramp, onto the brow, and out into the relatively open space of the subcarrier's wetbay.

Captain Matheson, *Neried*'s CO, and Marine Colonel

Haworth were waiting for the three as they stepped onto the walkway. "Permission to come on board," Mark said.

"Granted, granted," Matheson replied, grinning. "How'd it go?"

"Well, except for our unauthorized intruder, fine," Mark said. "That's quite a boat you people have there."

"Come on up to the plot room," Haworth said. "We'll talk. The general will be here in a few minutes." He glanced at Jeff. "What's the matter, Warhurst? You're looking a mite green."

The lighting in the wetbay was poor enough that the colonel couldn't possibly have noticed the color of Jeff's skin, so the comment had to be a joke. It hit near enough the mark, however, that Jeff suppressed a wince. "Squared away and shipshape, sir."

"I'm relieved to hear it."

In fact, the large ship, with her broad, outrigger construction, was remarkably steady even in rough seas, so he no longer felt the pronounced roll of the ocean's swell. By the time he'd followed the other officers up a level to the O1 deck and forward to the plot room, he was feeling somewhat better. A crushed ice machine in the wardroom along the way provided him with something cold and wet to hold in his mouth and thin his rising gorge.

General Altman arrived less than ten minutes later. They watched the approach of his UV-20 Condor on one of the plot room's PLAT cam monitors as it swung in over *Neried*'s landing pad, hovered a moment on furiously howling tilt-jets, then lowered itself to a gentle touchdown. Altman and three members of his staff disembarked from the craft and were led below through a deck hatch, as a team of sailors rolled the aircraft forward into the upper deck hangar, one of the few above-deck structures on the carrier.

"I don't know whether to be honored or terrified," Jeff observed. "Generals don't usually give briefings. And they sure as hell don't fly out to meet you. They make *you* come to *them*."

"Altman's a decent guy," Mark said. "He's a rifleman."

Jeff chuckled. In the Corps, it was said that every Marine—whether recruit or general, computer maven or tank driver or pilot or cook—was an infantryman, a *rifleman*, first. As with all aphorisms, there was some truth in the saying—as well as some wishful thinking. The every-Marine-a-rifleman concept sounded fine, but as with any large organization, the idealism tended to be lost after a while within the accretions of bureaucracy and daily routine.

But the saying was a popular one, and high praise indeed for a general.

"It is possible," General Altman told them, an hour later, "that Icebreaker has been compromised. Two days ago, the Chinese government formally filed a protest with our embassy in Beijing, demanding that we stop all attempts to recover ET artifacts on or in Europa, pending the arrival of a PRC transport."

Altman was a big, bluff man, a twenty-eight-year veteran of the Corps who'd won the Silver Star at Vladivostok and the Navy Cross and Purple Heart in the Cuban Incursion in '50. An African American, he rejected all labels or political euphemisms as they applied to race; if the subject ever came up, he referred to himself only as a "dark-green Marine." He had a reputation for bluntness—and for being willing to talk to his men and hear their gripes.

They were seated around an electronic table in the plot room, using the big, flat-screen computer monitor on one bulkhead to display graphics. One of the general's aides had used his PAD to link into the room's computer and put up a blurry vid-image of a spacecraft, obviously shot at extremely long range. It was a typical A-M drive ship design, a long, central spine with multiple reaction mass tanks, a heavily shielded drive unit aft with enormous heat radiator fins, a complex arrangement of slowly turning spin-gravity modules forward for the crew. Smaller craft, dwarfed by their huge consort, drifted in her shadow.

"Reconnaissance drones and tracking satellites have been keeping an eye on their two A-M drive ships in geosynch,"

Altman went on. "The *Xing Feng* and the *Xing Shan*. They appear to be making preparations to get under way. In the past two weeks, cargo and manned launches from Xichang have gone from one a week to one or two a day. They also appear to be loading supplies aboard the research vessel *Tiantan Shandian*. Everything seems to indicate the Chinese are taking a much stronger interest in their political and military presence in space. Coupled with their ultimatum yesterday, their activities in space are taking on something of a sinister connotation."

Jeff looked up from his own PAD, where he'd been studying the Chinese ship in detail. "Question, sir?"

"Go ahead, Major."

"Why would Beijing be so hot about space now? They're still recovering from their war."

And it had been a nasty war, at that. Greater China had split into North and South after their civil war earlier in the century, with Tibet going her own and independent way. North China had fought on the European side during the UN War, mostly in the hope of settling old claims to parts of Siberia and Russia's East Maritime Provinces, while Canton had sat the war out as a watchful neutral. Stopped cold at Vladivostok, she'd refused to sign the Treaty of London, but she'd also pulled her forces back behind the Amur. Within fifteen years, North China had invaded the south. The fighting had been vicious and fratricidal, including chemical and biological weaponry, though no nukes, thank God. The war had lasted twelve years and cost an estimated one and a quarter billion lives and uncounted trillions of yuan in damage. Since most of the fighting had been fought with Maoist guerrilla tactics, there'd been relatively few major battles in all that time, but vast parts of the South, especially, had been completely wrecked, and several major cities, including both Shanghai and the South China capital of Kuangchou, were now uninhabitable ruins.

General Altman considered Jeff's question for a moment. "A good question, son. There are two answers, really. The first is that a fight with outsiders will make the job of politically unifying the country easier. The people are always willing to tighten their belts and endure privation if they're faced with an outsiders-versus-us crisis."

"Ah, xenophobia," Mark said from his side of the table. "The glue that binds us together . . . against 'them.' "

"The second is more critical to Beijing's leaders, though," Altman went on. "They're afraid we're going to grab all the juicy e-tech for ourselves."

E-tech, originally "ET-tech" or "altech," was the term now applied to the new technologies flowing to Earth from the alien ruins on Mars and the Moon. New materials, new manufacturing processes, a hint that nanotechnology might be possible after all, the possibility of new power sources . . . the practical benefits were only just beginning to emerge from the xenoarcheological digs.

"So . . . just like the UN War," Jeff said. He glanced at Mark. That fighting, precipitated by a UN attempt to stop the United States and Russia from opening the ancient alien ruins on Mars, had led directly to Garroway's March and the Battle of Cydonia.

"In simplistic terms, yes," Altman's senior aide, a lieutenant colonel named Montoya, said. "What we've found on Europa might well prove to be the key to all of the other ET discoveries we've made. *Something* is down there beneath the ice and still operating, possibly after half a million years. It may help us make sense out of everything we've learned—about ancient humans living on Mars, the An enslavement, the Hunters of the Dawn, all of it. And the promise of new technologies, my God! Most of what we've been able to recover so far have been bits and pieces and scraps. Some of the stuff from the underground complex in Cydonia is still operating, of course, but we haven't figured out how to read the Builders' records yet. And the An base we found at Tsiolkovsky is still almost a complete mystery. It's going to take decades, maybe *centuries*, to learn the languages well enough to know what we're looking at. Unless, of course, the Singer can give us some clues."

"The Chinese are facing their own version of the Geneva

Report," Altman added. "Like us, they're counting on technology to hold the Long Night at bay long enough to get their feet under them. E-tech might give them a shortcut, might even solve all their problems, *if* they can crack the language and engineering problems."

The UN had used the Geneva Report's infamous computer projections to justify their attempt to bring the U.S. and Russia to heel in '40 . . . and to grab the Martian e-tech. The report had predicted a complete breakdown of civilization by the year 2050 if *all* of the world's nearly 10 billion people were not immediately brought under a single, unified system for distributing food energy and the world's limited resources.

There were those who pointed out that the Geneva Report had, in fact, come true. The wholesale slaughter in China over the past twelve years might be just the proverbial beginning of the end.

The United States and her closest allies, Russia and Japan, had been counting on new materials processing, new industries, whole new technologies from the xenoarcheological digs to render the Geneva Report moot. It might still happen . . . *if* civilization could be held together just a little longer.

"The damnable part of it is," Mark said, "they're not doing anything to help themselves by trying to stop us on Europa. Dog in the manger, you know?"

"Maybe they don't like depending on us and the Japanese for handouts," Jeff suggested.

"It probably does come down to a question of control," Altman said. "The military regime in Beijing has been on shaky ground ever since the end of communism and their Second Civil War. They can't afford to let the people have unrestricted access to the new technologies, not without risking falling out of power. They need to be seen as the saviors of China, and they need to control how fast the e-tech comes in—which is probably a lot faster than we've been able to provide it ourselves. The IES doesn't like releasing their findings prematurely."

The Institute for Exoarchaeological Studies—the foundation in New Chicago coordinating e-tech research—was notorious for its cautious advance into unknown territory ranging from advanced materials processing to nanotechnology to faster-than-light communications.

Considering the fact that many of the e-tech findings were of a scope and power guaranteed to utterly transform all of human civilization into something quite new, Jeff had always felt that that caution was more than justified. No one had any idea what lay around the corner in the near future; there were bound to be surprises, and some of them might be unpleasant ones.

"Regardless of the political pros and cons," Altman continued, "our interests on Europa must be protected. If the Chinese are planning on intervening there, it's up to us to stop them. Washington is cutting the orders now. One-MSEF's deployment has been moved up by five weeks. The *Roosevelt* will boost on September 29. And you *will* be ready."

Jeff looked up, startled. "Sir, that's two weeks!"

"Do you have a problem with that, Marine?"

"The scheduled boost was in seven weeks. The men are still in their training cycle—"

"They should be ready to go, anytime, anywhere. That's what the Corps is all about."

Jeff wanted to say that training and equipping a Marine Space Expeditionary Force to the frozen wastes of Europa was a bit different from hitting the beach in Borneo or Iran or Cuba or any other LZ on Earth. Instead, he said, "Aye, aye, sir."

"They should be familiarized with the Mark II armor by now."

"Yes, sir. They won't have time for training with it on the Moon, though."

"You'll have to hope that Earthside practice is enough. We're going to want to start shuttling them up to the *Franklin D. Roosevelt* as soon as possible."

Practice on Earth, with one G and a full atmosphere of

pressure, could not possibly replace training with the new suits in vacuum and Luna's one sixth G. Again, though, he knew better than to argue. Marines learned how to carry on. *Improvise! Adapt! Overcome!* No matter what.

"You've had a chance to evaluate the Manta."

"Today was my first day, General. It looks like a beautiful craft. I don't know yet how well it'll serve as a transport on Europa."

"Frankly, Major, that's not your job. Mr. Garroway here will make sure the Manta is up to Corps specs. You just have to have your people ready to board ship and boost."

"Yes, sir."

"In one week. With boost a week after that."

"Aye, aye, sir."

"Good man." Altman seemed to relax a bit. "I know it's asking a lot of you and your people, Major. And . . . in the long run, we don't even know if you'll be needed up there. But we *have* to be ready, just in case."

"We'll be ready, General. It'll be tight, but we'll be ready."

"You were selected for this command, Major, because we know you can deliver the goods. Not because your grandfather is a former Commandant. Not because of political connections. You have consistently demonstrated superior skills, training, and knowledge throughout your Marine career, and especially since you were selected for the Marine Space Force. We know we can count on you."

"Thank you, General. That means a lot, coming from you. I'll do my best."

But later that night, as he rode the hypersonic transport from Nassau to Los Angeles, he thought about General Altman's pep talk and wondered if he *could* deliver.

Major Jeffrey Warhurst was a peacetime Marine. Although the United States had been involved in several nasty little skirmishes around the globe since the end of the UN War in '42 and the breakup of the old UN, he had never been in combat. His family's heritage of service in the Corps had not yet been seriously tested. Packing two companies of the 1st Marine Space Expeditionary Force up in an A-M drive transport and shipping them off to a place as implacably hostile as Europa with him second in command under Colonel Norden could be an easy way to lose almost three hundred men—even without the possibility of a shooting war with China. Quite frankly, he wondered if he had what it took to take on a job this size.

A hundred kilometers above the northern Gulf of Mexico, Jeff broke out his PAD and opened it up. He would have to talk this one over with Chesty.

# TWO

**18 SEPTEMBER 2067**

*Mr. Virtuality*
*Lompoc, California*
*1750 hours*

The sign above the place on Highway One, just outside
of Vandenberg Air Force Base, read "Nude Girls! Girls!
Girls!" and Corporal George Leckie had to admit that they
did deliver. He and his buddy Tony were stretched back on
piles of oriental cushions, naked, completely surrounded by
nude women. He had seven attending to his needs alone,
each and every one of them paying full and sensuous attention to *them*.

The room was decorated with appallingly bad taste in
something that possibly resembled an adolescent boy's idea
of what a Near Eastern harem might look like. One woman
cradled his head on her lap, her more than generous breasts
undulating with her movements just above his face; another
offered a bunch of green grapes; three more ran their hands
up and down his torso while a sixth massaged his feet and
the seventh slowly kissed her way up the inside of his right
thigh toward his groin, the tantalizing touch of her lips
making him gasp and shudder.

"Oooh," the one with the grapes said. "You're so *big*,
Lucky! I don't know if there are enough of us to take
proper care of you!"

"S'all right, Becka," he replied, grinning. "Just take improper care of me. It's getting a bit crowded in here, and I wouldn't want any of you to feel left out!" She placed one grape in his mouth and he savored its cool, wet flavor. There was a faint alcoholic bite to it . . . one of the gene-tailored varieties of fruit that included a drop of brandy in their chemical makeup. He'd been hitting the tequila and beer pretty heavily before coming to this back room, and the grapes were adding to the pleasant buzz.

The best part was knowing there'd be no problems with performance, and no hangover later.

He raised his head slightly, turning to see what Tony was doing. He couldn't see the other Marine at the moment, but a crowd of blondes—Tony *really* liked blondes—was huddled together on the cushion pile a few meters away, and the way one of them was sitting upright in the middle of the group, back arched and mouth agape as she bobbed happily up and down told him that Tony was already getting into the scene in a serious way. "Hey, Tone!" he called. "Howzit goin' over there?"

"Every . . . thing . . . *uh!* . . . go . . . for . . . *uh!* . . . launch . . ." the other Marine called back.

"Was I right? Huh? Is this a great place or ain't it? I . . . *ohhh!* . . ." The woman between his legs had reached a particularly and exquisitely sensitive spot, and one of the women working on his torso had joined her. For the next few moments, Lucky George could say very little coherent at all.

He was hoping to get off seven times tonight, once with each of them. Theoretically it was possible, but sheer exhaustion had overcome him each time he'd tried it in the past. But tonight he was feeling pretty good, and maybe . . .

"Leckie!"

The voice boomed from the pink and purple curtains draping the harem chamber's vaulted ceiling, echoing as though from speakers with the volume cranked up high.

It was a voice he recognized. "Oh, shit. . . ."

"Leckie! This is God speaking! Liberty's been canceled for all hands."

"Aw, Sergeant Major! Have a heart, will ya? We just got here!"

"*Now,* Leckie. Come out of there before I crawl in and pull your plug myself!"

And *that* conjured visions Lucky didn't even want to try imagining.

"Hey, Lucky?" Tony called. "Did Sergeant Major Kaminski just—"

"Yes, goddamn it, he did." He sighed. "Sorry, girls."

"Aw! You have to leave so soon?"

"Safeword 'bail-out,' " he said. Instantly, the boudoir, the grapes, the naked women, all faded out into the purple-charged blackness one sees with closed eyes. A moment later, he blinked, and he was staring at the inside of a grungy-looking metal sphere just barely roomy enough to hold a synthleather-padded couch.

A quarter of the sphere's shell, to his left, was missing, a large, circular hatch. Sergeant Major Frank Kaminski was standing there in his khakis, fists on hips as he glared belligerently into the virtuality capsule. "*So* sorry to interrupt your pleasant dreams, *Mister* Leckie," Kaminski said. "But your presence *is* required back at the squad bay!"

Lucky sat up and swung his legs out of the sphere. He was wearing nothing but a terry cloth wrap and a number of skin attachments connected to slender feed cables, gently adhering to five places on his scalp, and on his chest, wrists, back of the neck, and groin.

The wrap was to keep him from making a mess on the couch. The cold, sticky spot he felt against his skin on the inside told him it had already served its purpose, even though he hadn't been inside for very long. "Jeez, Sergeant Major!" he complained, starting to pull off the skin connectors. "It couldn't have waited another couple of hours?"

"No, it damned well couldn't!" He turned to glare at the half-naked man crawling out of the virtuality sphere next to Lucky's. "And you, Tonelli! Get your ass in gear! *Both* of you!"

Mamasan Koharu, the manager of the Virtuality, all prim

and proper in a conservative woman's business suit, held out a hot, warm towel with a slight bow and a smile. "You have good time, yes?"

"I want a refund, Mamasan! We paid you one hundred dollars each for four hours! That was the deal, see? We ain't been inside there thirty minutes!"

Her eyes widened. "Oh, no! No refund! Cost same, you thirty minute, you four hour!"

"No! I want my money back!"

"It cost same! Still must program computer!" She pointed at the couch. "Still must clean you cum off equipment! Cost same!"

He snatched the towel from her. "Christ, what a gyp!" He tossed the terrycloth wrap on the floor and began toweling off his legs. "I got rights! You can't rip us off this way. I'll get some of my buddies together an'—"

"Corporal Leckie!" Kaminski snapped.

"Yeah?"

"Put a cap on it. Get your clothes on, both of you, and muster with me at the entrance. You've got ten minutes. *Move* it!"

Lucky entertained the notion of arguing for all of perhaps two seconds. It wasn't *right*, getting taken for a ride that way! He and Tone had spent twenty minutes in the virtual bar with the tequila and beer, and had only *just* gotten down to the good stuff deeper in. Damn it! He'd wanted to go with all seven women! Man oh man, what a barracks story *that* would have made! While his physical body had—um—responded almost at once to the sensations he'd been experiencing inside the sphere, the interactive AI program running through his brain should have easily let him experience seven orgasms in a row in his head.

And now they were dragging him back to base, out a hundred dollars and nothing to show for it but a wet crotch and a semen-soaked wrap!

Yeah . . . he *thought* about arguing. But there was something about Sergeant Major Kaminski's bearing—not to mention the pressed-and-tailored perfection of his khakis

and that incredible splash of colored ribbons on his shirt—
that made even a veteran griper like Lucky Leckie think
twice, then back down. It didn't help that Kaminski was in
full uniform while he was stark naked.

The *real* problem was that Kaminski was a lifer. Those
campaign ribbons—for Mars and Garroway's March and
Cydonia, for Luna, Picard and Tsiolkovsky, for Vera Cruz
and Cape Town and Havana, not to mention the Silver Star,
the Bronze Star with cluster, the Purple Heart, Expert Rifleman—together they created a truly formidable barrier no
mere corporal with nothing but a National Defense Ribbon
and an SMEU qualification badge could stand against.

Hell, Kaminski would drop-kick him clear back to V-
burg if he even tried.

"Aye, aye, Sergeant Major," he said. Tossing the wet
towel on the floor, he turned and followed Tone into the
locker room, where they'd left their clothes. Koharu, who'd
modestly turned away at his nudity, was already fastidi-
ously scrubbing at his couch with a disinfectant spray.

Hell, he thought, it wasn't like she hadn't seen naked
men before. Everyone knew you could get real girls at Mamasan's, not just the computer-programmed ones. He'd
even tried them a time or two, and they'd been okay. It
was just that the fantasies made possible in the virtual reality spheres were so much better than anything any flesh-
and-blood whore could possibly conjure for you. Especially
with the newer equipment that let you experience full, all-
body sensation without having to have surgically implanted
jacks, gimmicks that had never been all that popular except
with the most passionately devoted computer jocks. Better
than the real thing.

Besides, linking in to an orgy with a roomful of
computer-generated women guided by an entertainment AI
was the absolute ultimate in safe sex.

Dressed in their civvies, he and Tone returned to the
lounge at the building's entrance, where several pleasant-
looking hostesses sat at tables or at the bar. Kaminski was
waiting for them.

"Here, you two," he said, extending two plastic credit slips.

"What are these?" Tone asked.

"Your refunds. I talked Mamasan down to half price for ~~both of you.~~"

"Shit," Lucky said. "How'd you manage that?" Mamasan Koharu had the rep of a polite and civilized female dragon who didn't back down on *anything* where her girls, her boys, or her business was concerned.

"I talked to her *nice*, Leckie. Something you wouldn't know about." He grinned. "And I told her it would be a shame if word spread among the personnel on the base about what happened to you. I guess she felt that losing a hundred was better than having her business go flatline."

"Well, hey! Thanks!" He took the credit slip, unholstered his PAD, and slid the data strip end through the reader. His account credited him with fifty dollars as the plastic slip turned from green to black. He tossed the dead slip on the floor.

Kaminski stopped him with a twenty-kiloton-per-second look. "Pick it up."

"But Sergeant Major—"

*"Pick it up, shithead!"* As Lucky obeyed, Kaminski growled, "Maintaining decent relations with the civilian population in the area is tough enough, asshole, without you vandalizing the neighborhood with your fucking attitude. Now shitcan your garbage and let's get back aboard!" He nodded to the watching women. "Ladies."

Outside, Kaminski's car, a gray Ford-Toshiba Electric from the motor pool, was parked in the Virtuality lot, tapping a charge from the contact posts. Beyond, traffic whizzed by on Highway One. Tone's car, a neon-red bubbletop Zephyr, was in the recharge slot nearby.

"So, what's all the rush, Master Sergeant?" Lucky asked as they trotted down the steps. "Are we on alert?"

"Affirmative. They just passed the word. The launch date has just been moved up. We're boosting, boys, probably late next week."

"Holy shit!" Tone said. "I ain't got any of my shit together."

"Then you'd better take care of it ASAP, Marine. It's a long way to Europa. The long-distance comlink charges'll kill you!"

Europa! Lucky still found it hard to believe. He'd always dreamed of going to space; that was why he'd volunteered for the Space Marines, after all. He'd been hoping to get a chance to see Mars, or at least be posted at one of the naval orbital facilities now sprouting up in Earth orbit.

But Europa! Why anyone would want to attack such a place—or defend it from attack—was beyond him. The briefings he'd had so far emphasized the unbearable hostility of the place—an environment where the temperature never crawled higher than 140 degrees below zero, with no atmosphere to speak of, and intense radiation delivered by the far-flung magnetic fields centered on giant Jupiter. The word was that a small scientific outpost was there, and there were rumors that they'd found something in the ice. Something important.

It was hard to imagine just what could be so damned critical in such a God-forsaken place.

From the way the scuttlebutt was flying, though, the scientists had found anything from one of the ancient ET visitors to a working faster-than-light starship to God Himself. Lucky, a bit jaded by his two years in the Corps, knew better than to pounce on any single rumor and absorb it as fact.

Meeting aliens wouldn't be so bad, he thought. Hell, it'd be a short ticket to fame and fortune for everyone on the expedition who pulled it off. But he didn't for a minute believe that there actually were aliens at Europa. Scuttlebutt, pure and simple. The *real* action in the solar system was on Mars, where scientists from a dozen nations were sorting through the relics left by the enigmatic Builders. *That* was where he'd been hoping to go.

Shit. He'd joined the Marines to see Mars, and here they

were sending him to a radiation-drenched ball of ice in the
cold and dark of the Outer System.

Tone swung the Zephyr into Vandenberg's Main Entrance. The usual demonstrations were under way, and
Tone had to drive slowly through a corridor in the road
kept open by police and Air Force MPs. IT'S BABEL AGAIN!
one prominent sign read. MAN WAS CREATED IN GOD'S IM-
AGE TO TEND THE EARTH! read a long banner held aloft by
six scraggly-looking youngsters. Many waved miniature
palm trees, the unofficial symbol of the Keepers of the
Earth. An enchantingly bare-breasted young woman with a
laurel crown sat astride a miniature woolly mammoth gesturing with a sign that read HEAVEN ON EARTH *NOW*. The
better-dressed members of the congregation wore helmet
cams and recording gear. It looked like the newsies were
out in full force.

Despite the chanting, jeering mob, the sentries looked
bored, and Lucky had the feeling this was all pretty routine.
Another day, another back-to-the-Earth demonstration.

At the gate, past the lines marking the secure perimeter,
they handed over their pads for a security check and pressed
their thumbs against DNA reader screens proffered by the
Air Force Blue Beret sentries. Security at the base was very
high; Vandenberg was one of only three primary launch
centers in the United States, and there were entirely too
many people about, both foreign nationals and U.S. citi-
zens, with reasons to sabotage America's space access capability.

Lucky turned in the seat for another look at the woman
on the dwarf mammoth. Funny how the antitechies were
always so selective about the technologies they wanted
banned. This bunch obviously didn't mind cloning frozen
mammoth carcasses, but they wanted humankind out of
space. There were others who didn't mind space travel, but
who thought tampering with genetics was blasphemy. You
could usually find them demonstrating outside major theme
parks that maintained genetically tailored and resurrected
herds.

He wondered what would happen if both groups tried demonstrating on the same day at the same gate. Might be amusing.

Through the gate, then, and into the base. Vandenberg was still officially an Air Force base, even though the U.S. Navy seemed to have positioned itself as the principal builder and operator of deep spacecraft. Congressional and intra-Pentagon warfare continued over funding and jurisdictional disputes, but in general, the Air Force controlled airspace up to the 100-kilometer mark, and operated the military shuttles carrying men and materiel to Low Earth Orbit. The Navy, with its long history of procuring, building, and operating large ships at sea for long periods of time, had responsibility for everything beyond the 100-km line. The Marines—the Navy's police force, as one misguided former U.S. president had called them—had followed the Navy into deep space, despite ongoing attempts by the Army to establish an Army Space Operations Group.

There were rumblings, as always, over the possible creation of a military space arm independent of all of the older armed forces. Lucky didn't think that would ever happen, though. Too many high-rankers and politicians had too much invested in too many past decisions to yield on such a politically charged and expensive issue. The arguments would continue, nothing critical would be decided, and Lucky would get to go to space.

If only it wasn't a damned tech-null hole like *Europa!*

The Zephyr swung into a curve, then crested a long, low ridge. Beyond, almost at the horizon, Launch Center Bravo sprawled across 8,000 hectares of scrub brush and rock. Their timing couldn't have been better. Seconds after they came over the ridge, an intensely brilliant strobe of blue-white light pulsed from one of the dozen launch towers bristling from the landscape like thick, white whiskers. Tone pulled the car over so they could both watch.

The strobe winked rapidly, ten times a second, a fluttering pulse of light from the base of the tower. A cargo transport rose into the sky, a squat, white cone with a broad and oddly flared base. As it cleared the tower, four more strobes began flashing at widely separated points scattered across the landscape. The effect was a warning, not the glare of the lasers themselves.

The sound, a far-off roll of thunder, didn't reach the two Marines for a number of seconds. The transport, its circular base now glowing white-hot, accelerated rapidly into the clear, deep blue of the early evening sky.

"Whee-oo!" Tone said, excited. "What a ride! What you think, Luck? They're pulling maybe eight Gs?"

"Cargo launch," he replied. "Betcha it's unmanned and pulling twelve Gs, easy!"

The hurtling transport began arching overhead as it slid into an easterly launch path. When Vandenberg had first been converted to launch operations in the last century, all launches had been into polar or high-inclination orbits, since an east or southeasterly launch path would take the vehicle over the dangerously crowded urban areas of Greater Los Angeles. Low-inclination launches from V-berg had become possible—if not exactly politically acceptable—with the development of single-stage-to-orbit boosters and, later, the Laser Launch System, or LLS. Launches routinely passed over Greater LA every day now . . . though that, too, was yet another cause for periodic demonstrations.

The cargo transport was now nothing but a star, brighter than Venus, sliding rapidly down the eastern sky. The ground-based lasers, playing their steady, invisible tattoo against the water reaction mass in the transport's plasma chamber, could boost it to orbital velocity in less than 120 seconds. Downrange lasers, at Edwards and San Clemente, would pick up the vehicle when it passed beyond Vandenberg's laser-launch horizon and see it safely past LA. Once it was in orbit, conventional on-board engines would kick in and guide it to its final destination—almost certainly the U.S. Deep Space Orbital Facility at L-3.

It was a bit eerie for Lucky, imagining himself riding that invisible laser fire into space in another few days.

Space. Yeah ... even if it *was* Europa, he would be in space at last.

**19 SEPTEMBER 2067**

*Space Tracking and Navigation
    Network (STAN-NET)
Widely Distributed, Earth and
    Near-Earth Space
0238 hours (Zulu)*

They called him Stan, although, like most artificial intelligences, he never thought of himself in terms of names or self-identity. Even the pronoun *he* wasn't appropriate, though it didn't matter to him one way or another. It was simply part of the persona assigned him by his human handlers for their own comfort and convenience.

"He" could not even be said to have a particular location in space. Like all AIs, he was the product of software—interconnected programs running on over three hundred different pieces of hardware, and those machines were scattered across space, from the TCC-5000 still coordinating space tracking operations from Cheyenne Mountain to the fifteen different Honeywell-Toshiba IC-1090s aboard each satellite in the TrackStar Geosynch constellation. His primary task was to monitor all spacecraft, satellites, and orbital facilities in cis-Lunar space; his secondary tasks changed periodically, but frequently involved alerting other AIs in the Global Network of specific events within his purview.

Such an event, linked to such a task, was occurring now.

One of Stan's remote trackers, a twelve-ton Argus-Hera satellite in high Earth orbit, had just registered an unscheduled burn and funneled the observation through to all of Stan's extended and massively parallel processor sites.

The source was KE26-GEO, the Chinese industrial/construction park in geosynch, at 108° East.

There were many such parks—in LEO, HEO, GEO, and

in the various LaGrange points of the Earth-Moon system. Most had started off as small space stations for research, communications, or small-scale microgravity industrial sites, then grown, often haphazardly, into collections of fuel tanks, pumping apparatus, construction shacks, solar cell arrays, habitat and lab modules, and spacecraft. A few—like the U.S. facility at L-3, or the Chinese KE26 station in geosynch—included the high-energy processing and containment facilities necessary for the manufacture and storage of antimatter.

Stan knew the location of each spacecraft within his sphere of attention—from 100 kilometers above the Earth to the orbit of the Moon—whether they were in orbit or under thrust. His primary programming had him functioning as a kind of space traffic controller—not that collision was a major threat; usually, the only times ships were in danger of collision was during approach or departure from a space station or other orbital facility, and at those times, ship vectors and delta-V burns were the responsibility of the ship and station personnel and AIs.

Still, there *was* considerable danger from the cloud of debris released by human activities in space since the beginning of the space age over a century before, everything from spent boosters and payload protective fairings to flecks of paint, which could be deadly if they impacted with, say, the visor of a pressure suit at several kilometers per second. Stan couldn't track individual paint flecks, but his database of stray objects included things as small as two-centimeter bolts and a stray canister of exposed infrared film. Stan's warnings of potential vector conflicts had resulted in 408 minor course corrections in the 12.37634912 years since his initialization. Spacefaring powers nearly always queried Stan on the possible outcome of specific boosts, vector changes, and time-distance-acceleration problems.

The Chinese had stopped making such requests three months ago. Technically, by treaty they were required to announce all launches in advance, but the requirement was strictly one of courtesy, not enforcement.

In fact, it was possible that they were operating their own deep-space tracking network. Stan was interested, however, in the politics of the situation. He did not understand the current tension between the Chinese and the newly created Confederation of World States, a loose trade and defense organization headed by the United States, Russia, and Japan that included all of the other space-capable powers. That such tension existed was self-evident from the news broadcasts of both sides, and from the fact that Stan's secondary program tasks had increasingly involved surveillance of Chinese space assets for DODNET, the complex of AIs running much of the U.S. military's command, control, and communications networks.

There were, at the moment, no fewer than nineteen spacecraft of various types at KE26-GEO . . . most of them cargo craft boosted from Xichang. Two were the antimatter-powered cruisers *Xing Shan* (the *Star Mountain*) and her sister ship, the *Xing Feng* (the *Star Wind*). A third was a research vessel, the *Tiantan Shandian*, which DOD-NET translated roughly as the *Heavenly Lightning*.

Stan had received numerous requests for updates on the *Star Mountain*'s status in the past few weeks, and he'd dutifully passed on all observations. There had not been much to report; the huge spacecraft remained inert, though thermal and radiation readings suggested that its fusion power plant was being brought to full output, probably in anticipation of a launch. He could make out little detail, however; the Argus-Hera tracking satellites, of all his assets, came closest at periodic intervals to the Chinese facility—but that was never closer than some 20,000 kilometers.

Still, standing orders required that any change in the status of either the *Xing Shan* or the *Xing Feng* be reported to the Pentagon *at once*.

Now, though, three of his Argus-Heras had picked up the bright, hot flare of a burn at KE26-GEO. Interestingly, it was not the *Star Mountain* that was accelerating, but the much older *Heavenly Lightning*.

The *Lightning* was listed as a deep space research vessel—415 meters long, massing 25,300 tons. The vessel was currently mounted on a two-stage stack, with a heavily modified *Liliang* ground-to-orbit booster as a strap-on first stage.

Stan monitored the burn for five seconds before arriving at any decisions. His orders did not explicitly mention the *Heavenly Lightning*, but he had considerable discretionary flexibility—a large part of the reason for artificially intelligent systems, after all. He noted that the *Liliang* booster's flare included high levels of gamma radiation—a sure sign that the vehicle's thrust had been upgraded through the simple expedient of adding a small quantity of antimatter to the reaction chamber, increasing the specific impulse of the booster's hydrogen-oxygen fuel mix.

After five seconds, Stan had assembled enough data to make a good guess on the craft's intended vector—a close pass of Earth to achieve a gravitational slingshot onto a new course. The ultimate vector could not be determined now, of course; he wouldn't be able to estimate that until he'd measured the *Lightning*'s perigee burn. But it appeared, with 85 percent certainty, that the *Heavenly Lightning* was bound for a retrograde solar orbit—one that seemed to be going nowhere in particular.

The information was not what DODNET and the Pentagon were most interested in at the moment, but Stan felt sure they *would* want to know.

He linked into the Global Net and began uploading his observations.

# THREE

*The Palace of Illusion*
*Burbank, California*
*2130 hours (Zulu minus 8)*

*Why,* Colonel Kaitlin Garroway asked herself, *do I come to these damned functions?*

The answer was obvious, of course. *Because the Corps wants well-rounded, well-balanced, socially* ept *officers and it wouldn't look good if you turned down too many invitations.* She had to ask the question nonetheless. She always felt so damned out of place at these affairs; at least the proverbial fish out of water had managed to evolve legs and lungs after a few million years. She held no such hopes for herself.

Once upon a time, social gatherings of this sort had been held in private homes—well-to-do private homes, to be sure, but homes all the same. If the guest list was simply too big for the living room, a reception hall might be rented for the occasion.

Nowadays, an entire minor industry thrived to provide suitable ambiance for the evening. The Palace of Illusion was run by a major area theme park to cater expressly to formal social events. She wondered how much all of this had cost—the lighting and special effects, the live music, the endless tables of food, the sheer *space*: the grounds and gardens outside on a hilltop overlooking the dazzling horizon-to-horizon glow of Greater Los Angeles; a Grand Hall so large the walls were lost in the artificial mists and play of laser holography designed to create a sense of infinite space; and elsewhere, private rooms, conversation bubbles, or even private VR spheres designed to accommodate social and conversational groupings of every size and taste.

Several thousand people were in attendance. Kaitlin felt completely lost. She wished Rob, her husband, was here, but the lucky bastard was on the other end of the continent right now, CO of the Marine Space Training Command at Quantico, and he'd been able to plead schedule and a meeting with the Joint Chiefs to duck the invitation. It was harder for Kaitlin. Her current assignment had her in command of the 1st Marine Space Regiment, which consisted of the 1st and 2nd Marine Space Expeditionary Forces, and various support elements. Normally, she was in Quantico too, but for the past month she'd been stationed at Vandenberg, commuting by HST on those few weekends she had free.

All of which had left her without an acceptable excuse for being here tonight.

She wandered the fringes of the Great Hall, looking for someone she knew. She had her personal pinger on, set to alert her if she came within fifty meters of any other pinger broadcasting an interest in things that interested her: the Corps, recovered ET technology, science fiction, programming—especially cryptoprogramming—chess, anything involving Japanese language or culture. It was also searching for any of a handful of people she knew who might be here. So far, no luck. Senator Fuentes was here, of course; it was her party. Twenty-five years ago, *Colonel* Carmen Fuentes had been her CO in the desperate fight for Tsiolkovsky on the Lunar far side. Unfortunately, the senator was surrounded five deep just now by well wishers, sycophants, politicians, and social climbers. Kaitlin didn't have a chance in hell of breaching *those* defenses.

She wandered through the crowd, amusing herself by observing the variations in dress and social custom. Kaitlin was wearing the new formal Blue Dress Evening uniform—long skirt, open jacket with medals and broad red lapels over ruffled white blouse, and the damned silly gold braid epaulets that made her feel like she was walking around with boards balanced precariously on her shoulders. And heels. She hated heels. Heels had been abandoned by progressively thinking women fifty years ago. All she needed to feel a perfect fool was a sword and scabbard.

There were quite a few of those in the room. Most of the male Marine officers were in full Blue Dress A uniform, with swords—the famous Mameluke blade first presented to Lieutenant Presley O'Bannon for the capture of Derna in 1805—at their sides.

Corps tradition. It was everywhere she looked. Those red stripes on the legs of their pants, for instance, symbolized the bloody Battle of Chapultepec in the Mexican War, the "Halls of Montezuma" immortalized in the Marine Corps Hymn.

Most of the people at the gathering, however, were civilians, and Kaitlin found herself feeling quite out of place with the creatures—as alien to her way of thinking as the Builders or the An or any of the myriad species glimpsed from the Cave of Wonders at Cydonia. Their dress ran the colorful gamut from full traditional formal to almost nude; complete nakedness was still frowned upon in most social circles in all but small and informal gatherings, but donning nothing but footwear, suitably fashionable technological accessories, and skin dyes or tattoos was customary for larger parties, if still mildly daring.

The creature confronting her now was a case in point. He was clad in the new technorganic-look, half hardware appliqué, half dyetooed skin. He wore a visible pinger on his right shoulder which was pulsing orange light at the moment, an indicator that he was interested in sexual diversions of any kind. Orange dyettooes covered half his body in what looked like Sanskrit characters, including his genitals—just to make sure that everyone knew he was available for play.

Kaitlin preferred the old days, when there'd always been a hint of mystery, even suspense, with any new and casual meeting.

The times, the culture, were simply changing too damned fast.

"Blue stellar!" the dyed apparition said. "You're Colonel Kaitlin Garroway, First Marine Space Force! Your pat was Sands of Mars Garroway, your—"

"I *do* know who I am," she said, a bit more sharply than she'd intended. She still couldn't get used to the new habit people had of announcing themselves by announcing you . . . an ostentatiously irritating means, basically, of proving they had a good Farley program running in their PAD assistants.

"Tek! Been progged to 'face with ya, Colonel. Saw you on the list when I dunelled it and nearly maxed."

Kaitlin blinked. She had the general idea that the kid— he couldn't have been older than his early twenties—was glad to see her, but she still wasn't sure why. He had a decided technological edge on her. He was wearing some pretty sharp-edged tech, including a partial sensory helmet—it covered only the left side of his head, leaving the primitive right half free and "natural"—with a flip-aside monocular for his data HUD. He was probably tapping all the data on her that he could find at this moment, while she had nothing to query but the AI secretary resident in her PAD. She was damned if she would let herself appear interested, though, by opening her personal access device just to electronically query the local net server for a Farley on this guy's name, background, and interests.

"And you are?" she asked, her voice cool.

"Oh, vid. Handle's Hardcore. Wanted to link with ya on some prime throughput. Like what the milboys are runnin' landing on Jupiter. I run, like, the Masters might get the wrong feed, c'nect?"

Kaitlin was abruptly conscious of just how many people in the room around her were wearing sensory communications gear of some sort, from appliqués like Hardcore's to full helmets with darkened visors and internal HUD displays. Resident AIs with the appropriate dialect and slang interpreters made talking cross-culture a lot easier than trying it null-teched.

"To begin with," she said slowly, trying to sort her way through the tangle of techculture slang, "the Marines aren't landing on Jupiter. A Marine Space Expeditionary Unit is deploying to Europa. That's one of Jupiter's moons. As for the Masters . . . I suppose you mean one or another of the A-Squared cultures?"

"Absopos, cybe! Like, I run the An made us what we are, linkme? And, like, I run they might not log our peaceful nature with the mils goosestepping into their domain."

A-Squareds. Thank the newsies for that bit of cuteness, meaning Ancient Aliens. There were two known, now, and a third inferred, thanks to xenoarcheological digs on Mars, the Moon, and even, lately, on Earth, now that the diggers knew what to look for. The Builders had left the enigmatic structures and fragments on Mars half a million years ago, and presumably had tinkered with human genetics at the same time, creating archaic *Homo sapiens* from the earlier populations of *Homo erectus*. The An had been something else entirely, a nonhuman spacefaring species that had enslaved a fair-sized fraction of humanity ten thousand years ago, and left their imprint in human myth, legend, and architecture across the Fertile Crescent, in parts of Africa, and in both South and Central America before being annihilated by the presumptive third Ancient Alien culture, the Hunters of the Dawn.

"The Builders have been extinct for half a million years," she told Hardcore. "The An appear to have been wiped out ten thousand years ago. If the Hunters of the Dawn are still out there, we haven't seen any sign of them. I can't see that any of them would mind us going to Europa. And the Marines are going there to protect American interests." *As always. First to fight. Too often, the first to die.*

"But that runs totally null, cybe. Like, they upgraded us,

so we have to be jacked in tight and one-worlding it when they return. . . ."

Kaitlin at last was beginning to take the kid's measure. An Ancient Astronut.

There were literally hundreds of new cults and religions about, spawned by the recent discoveries elsewhere in the Solar System that were continuing the ongoing process of displacement for humankind's place in the universe begun by Copernicus so long before. The Builders had tinkered with human DNA, and a few civilized members of that new species had died on Mars when the facilities there had been attacked by unknown enemies. The An had established bases on the Moon and colonies on Earth, enslaving large numbers of humans to help raise their monumental and still enigmatic structures at Giza, Baalbek, Titicaca, and elsewhere, before infalling asteroids deliberately aimed by another unknown enemy had wiped most of the An centers away in storms of flame and flood. Twice, it appeared, humans had narrowly escaped the fates of more advanced, alien patron races.

So much was known now, a revelation at least as stunning as the knowledge that humankind predated Bishop Usher's date of special creation in 4004 BC. But so much was still unknown, and in the mystery, in the undiscovered, there was plenty of room for speculation . . . and for radical new forms of faith. From the sound of it, Hardcore was a member of one of the new denominations that actually gloried in the knowledge that humanity had once been engineered as slaves. It certainly made the question of existence simple: Humankind was here to serve the Masters. Obviously, the Masters weren't about right now, but when They returned, they would expect an accounting of their faithful servants for the world they'd left in the servants' care.

Kaitlin wondered what Hardcore would do if she posed as a member of one of the other cults and political spin-off groups—a Humanity Firster, say, who'd vowed to venture forth to the stars and eradicate the alien scum who'd once tried to enslave Mankind, and failed.

She decided that the Senator would probably prefer that she keep a low profile. In any case, members of the U.S. Armed Forces weren't allowed to express political or religious opinions of *any* kind while in uniform.

"I can't share your view of the aliens," she told him, blunt, but as diplomatically as possible. "We do know that there might be . . . people out there we're going to want to protect ourselves from. Isn't it reasonable to want to find out all we can about them, as far from Earth as we can manage?"

"Hey, I can't 'face with that, cybe. I mean, we can't run different than our progamming, right? And we were made to serve the Masters."

A tiny chirp in her left ear told her that her pinger had just detected one of the people on her tell-me list. "Who?" she subvocalized.

"Dr. Jack Ramsey," her earpiece's voice whispered. "He has just entered the palace of Illusion."

"Thank God."

"Sorry?" Hardcore said, puzzled. "I don't 'face ya."

"And a good thing it is, too," she told him. "I've got to go. I'm meeting a friend."

"But, like, we gotta 'face on the issue, cybe. Don't log me off!"

"Please. Excuse me." She turned and started to walk away. "Which way to Jack Ramsey?" she asked her pinger.

"Five degrees left, now sixteen-point-one meters, closing . . ."

"Like, we should clear this." He was following her, matching her stride for stride.

"Hardcore!" another voice said. "Hey, you found her!"

"Found but not downed. She won't 'face, Slick-Cybe."

The newcomer was more conventionally dressed in a two-tone green tunic with a stiff, tight collar, but he sported many of the same technical accouterments Hardcore wore. He stepped in front of her, blocking her way. "Hey, Colonel. My des is Slick. We were hoping you'd give us a few moments of your time."

"Who is 'we'?" she demanded. She was losing patience with this crew.

"C'mon in," the newcomer said, grinning . . . obviously speaking for someone else's benefit. Kaitlin saw with alarm that several people were detaching themselves from various parts of the crowd around her and walking her way.

*Ambush* . . .

She couldn't help but think of it in military terms. They'd pinpointed her location with a scout, called in a blocking force, and now the main body was closing in.

And, damn it, she couldn't run in heels. She would have to stand and fight it out.

Their dress ran from Hardcore's stylish nudity to an elaborate Elizabethan ball gown that looked heavier than the man wearing it. One woman had her head shaved, wore golden, slit-pupiled contacts, and had dyetooed her entire body in a green scale pattern that gave her a vague resemblance to an oversized and rather too mammalian-looking An.

The oldest of them was conservatively dressed and appeared to be in his late thirties.

"Colonel Garroway!" that man said. "I'm Pastor Swenson, of the Unified Church of the Masters. I was hoping to run into you this evening!"

"You must excuse me," she told him. "There's someone I have to meet." She wished she was wearing a comlink right now, or at least a full-link-capable pinger. It would have been nice to punch in Jack's ID right now and call for help.

"This will only take a moment, please! We're afraid that the U.S. government and the CWS Planning Committee are making a serious mistake, one that could have the most serious repercussions for our entire species!"

"If they are, there's not a damned thing I can do about it, Pastor. I'm just a soldier, not a politician or a government planner."

"But the young men and women who are going to Jupiter are under your command, after all. You must have *some* say in how they're being used. And the news media would listen to your opinions. We believe these are extraordinarily critical and dangerous times, you see, and we—"

"As I told *this* gentleman, Pastor," she said, nodding at Hardcore, "I don't agree with your opinions about extraterrestrials. I certainly don't believe that something that happened thousands of years ago to tribes of primitives living thousands of kilometers from here requires us to somehow surrender our minds and integrity and will.'

"Ah, well, Colonel," Swenson said with an ingratiating smile, "you *must* accept that the Bible tells us about these things, that it told us a long time ago! Signs and wonders in the heavens, and blood upon the Moon! You fought a battle on the Moon, Colonel! You know that the prophecy is being fulfilled right here in our lifetimes! Prophecy written down *two thousand years* ago, telling us that—"

"Telling us nothing, Pastor, except that some people have either a remarkable imagination or an astonishing will to believe."

Slick reached out and took her arm. "You mustn't *say* things like that, Colonel! We've formed a kind of delegation, if you like, to—"

Reaching down with her left hand, she grasped his hand, her thumb finding the nerve plexus at the base of his thumb. As she turned his hand back and over, his face went white and he started to sag at the knees.

"*Don't* ever do that," she told him pleasantly. "And get out of my way, now, or I'll turn something else numb ... permanently."

"Are you having any trouble, Colonel?" a familiar voice asked. Jack Ramsey walked over to the group, a man in his early forties in civvies, a red and black close-collar smartsuit.

"I don't know," she said. She looked at Slick. "Am I having any trouble with you?"

Slick shook his head in a vigorous 'no.' She increased the pressure slightly, and he gasped and dropped to his knees.

"Good," she said, smiling. She released him. "How about you, Hardcore?"

"I . . . ah . . . was just gonna go 'face with the food table. 'Scuze." He bobbed his head and vanished into the crowd, followed closely by his friend. The others—Swenson, the scaled woman—all drifted off into the crowd.

"And what was *that* all about?" Jack asked her.

"Astronuts," she replied. "Don't like the idea of us Neanderthal military types making First Contact."

He made a face. "I've heard *that* one before. This particular bunch thinks the An gene-engineered Moses, the Buddha, and Jesus Christ as special avatars in order to civilize us. They say they're waiting for proof that we've given up our savage, warlike ways before letting us join them in heaven."

"How do you know all this?"

He tapped the left arm of his smartsuit, where stylish threads of gold and silver were worked into the black synthetic fabric like a tiny map of an overgrown inner city. The suit was one of the later models, with over fifty gig of access and automatic comlink to any local node or net server. When she looked more closely into his eyes, she saw they were a bit greener than usual; he was wearing contact displays. "They've been dropping electronic tracts on anyone they can get an eddress for."

"Try that again with me and I'll drop something on *them*. Why the hell are they here?"

"Swenson is a minor celebrity. On all of the talk shows and media interviews he can swing. I guess the others are part of his entourage."

"Well, thanks for coming to my rescue."

"You didn't look like you needed rescuing."

"Oh, but I did." She grinned. "When you arrived, I was in the process of chewing my leg off at the ankle."

"And such a lovely ankle, at that. I'm glad. How's the general? And your kids?"

"Rob's still at Quantico, and I wish I were there with him instead of playing socialite and sometime target for religious activists. Rob Junior's had his first assignment off-world. Peaceforcer duty. And Kam and Alan are growing up too fast and I don't get to see them enough by half. You know, I honestly think they're going to go through life thinking that their cissie is their mother, not me."

"It's tough, I know. You thinking about getting out?"

"Who told you that?"

"It's been around. If you don't want to say—"

"Oh, it's no secret. I haven't decided, but it's damned tempting. It would be nice to have a life again. Get to see my family."

"It's funny. When I think of you, Colonel, I think of the *Corps* as being your family."

"It is. That's what makes being caught in between so damned hard." She gave him a cross look. "And speaking of which, Major . . . where's your uniform?"

He made a face. "I thought I would be a bit less conspicuous in civvies."

"You just don't like showing off the blue button." She grinned. "Shame on you!"

Jack Ramsey, then Corporal Ramsey, had won the Medal of Honor at Tsiolkovsky twenty-five years before. Kaitlin had been there, with the Marines that had secured the UN base, allowing a team of Marine AI experts—including Jack—to come in and crack a UN computer and stop the detonation of an antimatter stockpile.

"The way they have me running around with the professorial crowd, I'm not sure whether I'm in the Marines anymore or not."

"You're still drawing service pay, right?" She fingered the eagle of her rank tab on her lapel. "And you answer to a guy who wears one of these. You're still in the Corps, believe me."

"It's nice to know some things remain constant. And I guess I do have to pay them back for my education!" After Tsiolkovsky, the Corps had sent him to college—including a graduate program at the Hans Moravec AI Institute in Pittsburgh—then given him a commission and put him to work designing better AIs. Artificial intelligence promised to be *the* big field of technological innovation in the next few years, a means of creating some very powerful friends and fellow workers for humankind, minds at least as good as any organic brain—and much, much faster.

Some thought the AIs would ultimately be man's replacement rather than his assistant. Those working in the field rebutted the doomsayers by pointing out that the future belonged to both types of mind, that each needed the other to reach its full potential.

Jack had a natural flair for AI design. He'd started off before he'd joined the service, reconfiguring some limited commercial AI software into an impressively interactive program he called Sam, which he still used as his personal secretary. A descendent of Sam's, Sam Too, had been installed aboard humankind's first genuine star ship, the unmanned probe *Ad Astra*, now, after six years of voyaging, decelerating into the dual planetary system of Alpha Centauri.

"So . . . how goes your part of the mission?" she asked. That was Project Chiron, one small but extremely important, and classified, portion of the *Ad Astra* program.

He nodded. "Braking and final course correction maneuvers are almost complete. She'll be entering orbit in another three days. But then, that's also been on the news, so you must've heard. It can't *all* be preempted by the latest news from China."

She sighed. "Haven't had much chance to watch, though. Or even read my daily high-points download. But I know it must be exciting for you."

"It is. I'll be going to Mars at the end of the week. That's *almost* the best part of all, to be at Cydonia when the link is made."

They were still trying to piece together the scope of the discovery beneath the war- and weather-torn ruins on Mars—in particular, the Cave of Wonders, the colossal sphere of holographic displays that appeared to show tantalizing glimpses of hundreds of alien worlds beneath other stars.

"Well, I wish you luck with it. And Sam *too*, of course." She twinkled at the pun.

"Thank you." If he'd heard the joke, he didn't react to it. In fact, Kaitlin thought as she watched him, he seemed a bit preoccupied.

"Problem?"

"Eh? Oh, no. Not really. Was wondering if you'd heard anything about the Chinese mystery ship. I mean, anything you could tell me."

"I don't know much, and none of it is classified," she admitted. "It's called *Heavenly Lightning*, and it used a gravitational slingshot assist to put it into a retrograde solar orbit between Mars and Earth. The Chinese haven't released much, except that it's on a peaceful mission of a scientific nature."

"From what I've been able to gather, it's not going near Mars, though."

"Uh-uh. Mars is on the far side of the sun right now. If they were trying to stop you from getting to Cydonia and carrying out Project Chiron, they're about 400 million kilometers off course."

"Well, that's a relief, at least."

"There's been a lot of buzz about the *Lightning* and what she might be up to. The CMC was afraid it was headed for Europa." Confederation Military Command was the ad hoc committee charged with unifying the disparate elements of the various CWS armed forces—an impossible task, but one that in Kaitlin's opinion was good for occasional moments of comic relief. "Turns out the Chinese are worried about us making contact with whatever is at Europa first. But the *Lightning*'s headed in the wrong direction for that. So we don't know *what* they're up to." She shrugged. "Maybe they're telling the truth. Research."

"Maybe . . ."

"You don't look convinced."

"Colonel, Europa and Mars are the two keys to the biggest, most important puzzle the human race faces right now. A breakthrough at either site is going to completely transform both us and the way we think about the universe— more than the An revelations, more than the discovery that we're not alone in the universe. The Beijing government knows that, and they'd be nuts not to try to grab a piece of the action. We know they're interested. We know they've been getting their big A-M ships ready to boost. And they did a quick refit of the *Lightning* and launched her in a hell of a hurry. It's just damned hard not to believe they're all connected somehow."

"Well, the Peaceforcer cruisers are in place," she said. "They'll be watching every Chinese launch, you can be sure of that. And they'll be positioned to act if the Chinese ships make a move in either direction. Beijing's only hope at this point is to play the game our way. Join the CWS, make nice, and take a cut of the profits."

"Beijing," he replied, "isn't exactly known for how well they play with others. *Especially* barbarians like us."

He was right, of course. A struggle was shaping up, a struggle that might well determine the nature of humanity for the next ten thousand years.

And Kaitlin and Jack and the rest of the U.S. Marines were going to be at ground zero—the proverbial eye of the storm.

As usual.

*Squad Bay*
*1 MSEF Barracks*
*2135 hours Zulu*

"Bumfuq!" Lucky exploded. "We're bein' sent to Bumfuq!"

*Bumfuq, Egypt,* was an old, old expression current throughout all branches of military service, referring to a place, a duty station so far removed from the civilized amenities that you might as well be on another planet.

Which, in stark, cold point of fact, was exactly where they were going.

"Aw, c'mon, Lucky!" Staff Sergeant BA Campanelli said, laughing. "How bad can it be? Anyway, you always said you wanted to go to space!"

"Shit," Lance Corporal Dick Wojak said. "He just doesn't want to lose access to his virtual girlfriends!"

"Hell," Sergeant Dave Coughlin said. "He should just download one of 'em into his PAD and bring her along! Then we could *all* share in the wealth!"

"Why don't you like girls, Luck?" Kelly Owenson said. "Real ones, I mean?"

"I like girls fine!"

What he didn't like talking about was the fact that virtual relationships just didn't fucking *hurt* as much as the real ones. *Damn, Becka. Get out of my head. . . .*

He took another swallow of the drink BA had mixed for him—a pineapply something that was quite good. What had she called it?

Sergeant Sherman Nodell was weaving a bit in his seat, despite the fact that he outmassed Lucky by a good twenty kilos, and he didn't seem interested in discussing Lucky's sex life. "Just give me another one of those . . . *things* you were talkin' about a little bit ago," he said. He was being very careful how he enunciated his words.

The nine of them, all members of First and Second Platoons, Bravo Company, were sitting at a folding table in the barracks squad bay. The huge and otherwise bare room which had once been an aircraft hangar was decorated with green-painted concrete floor, steel storage lockers, a display case near the entrance with trophies and battalion honors, and a wall-sized flatscreen on one bulkhead that was displaying the Marine Corps emblem at the moment. Normally, they all would have been out tonight, hitting the bars and sensies in Lompoc, but the 1st Marine Space Expeditionary Force had been restricted to the base ever since word had come down of the early deployment to Europa. Staff Sergeant Campanelli had come to the rescue, though. She'd been a bartender as a civilian—"in a former life," as she liked to call it—and she occasionally hauled out a small, portable bar-in-a-suitcase that was her prized possession and entertained the others in the platoon with some of her strange and wonderful concoctions. Mixing drinks in a nondesignated area probably violated half a dozen different regs, but she hadn't been caught yet. There were rumors to the effect that she had been caught, once, but gotten off in exchange for a bottle of scotch.

Her full name was Brenda Allyn Campanelli, so inevitably she'd picked up the handle "BA," for Bad Ass, even though she claimed her ass was very good. No one in the platoon claimed personal knowledge of that fact, however, though there'd been a great deal of speculation.

"So . . . what'll it be, big boy?" she asked Nodell, taunting him.

He leered. "I wanna blow job!"

"Coming right up! But you've got to take it the right way!"

"And what way would that be?"

"I'll show you."

She began mixing drinks in two shot glasses, half amaretto, half Kahlúa, topped with a generous squirt of whipped cream from a dispenser in the freezer section of her portable bar. "Okay, we really need a low table for this."

"How about a chair?" Lucky volunteered.

"That'll do." She put the drinks on the chair's seat, then got down on her knees. "You've got to do this right!"

Holding her hands behind her back, she bent forward and took one of the loaded shot glasses in her mouth. The other Marines cheered, clapped, and chanted "Go! Go! Go!" as she tipped her head and the glass up and back, draining the liquid and most of the whipped cream into her throat. Snapping her head forward, she returned the empty shot glass to the chair, licked the excess whipped cream from her lips, and held up her hands as the Marines cheered and stomped on the deck.

"And *that* is how you do a blow job!" she told Nodell.

"All right!" Dave cried, applauding. "You know, we ought to call you 'BJ,' not 'BA'!"

"Hey, I like that! Just don't go gettin' any ideas!"

"I *always* have ideas, Staff Sergeant!"

"Your turn!" Corporal Lissa Cartwright told Nodell.

"Aw, that's a sissy drink!" he began, but the others began chanting at him.

"Do it! Do it! Do it!"

At last, he awkwardly dropped to his knees, bent over the remaining glass, and took it in his mouth. He didn't tip his head fast enough, though, and a lot of it ended up dribbling down his chin, together with a small avalanche of whipped cream. He started choking and gagging, and Lucky and Corporal Duane Niemeyer began pounding him on the back.

"Gah!" he said, rising from the floor. "That's *still* a sissy drink! I only drink . . . I only drink . . . uh . . . a *man's* drink!"

"And what would that be?" BA asked him.

"Hell, just about anything that pours. One at a time or all together, I can take it! I just don't do *sissy* drinks."

"Is that so?" She studied him. "You ever tried a cement mixer?"

"Nah. What is that, another sissy—"

"A man's drink," she told him. "With a name like 'cement mixer,' what would you expect?"

"Now *that* sounds more like it! What's in it?"

"Here, I think I have the ingredients. Yup. You do this in two stages." Deftly, she poured out two shot glasses, one with lime grenadine, the other with Bailey's Irish Creme. She handed him the Bailey's. "Here. Take this . . . but don't swallow. Hold it in your mouth."

He tossed the shot back.

"Now," she told him, "take this in your mouth and swish it around with the other."

Lucky had seen this gag pulled before. The lime juice curdled the Bailey's, turning it to the consistency of cottage cheese. It didn't taste bad—sort of like sweet tarts, in fact—but the sensation of having that stuff congeal in your mouth out of nowhere generated the most wonderful expressions of disbelief, shock, and dawning I've-been-had horror imaginable.

Nodell was just starting to work at it when the far door opened and Major Warhurst walked in.

"Attention on deck!" Dave cried. There was a swift rattling and shuffling as shot glasses and bottles somehow vanished into BJ's porta-bar, which closed and locked and made it to the floor as the rest of them stood up.

Warhurst didn't seem to notice—likely a deliberate oversight on his part—but he seemed fascinated by the expression on Nodell's face. "Carry—" he started to say, and then stopped. "Nodell? Are you okay?"

"Um . . . mmm-mmm . . . *mmm!*" He was working his jaws furiously, trying to swallow the mess in his mouth without parting his lips.

"That's 'Mmm-mmm, *sir,*' Nodell. What have you got in your mouth?"

Lucky stood at attention, wondering what was going to go down. V-berg wasn't dry, but the only drinking allowed was at the various designated watering holes, the enlisted bars and NCO clubs and such. They could all be in a world of shit if Major Warhurst decided to be a prick.

With several more vigorous workings of his jaw, Nodell managed to get the congealed mess chewed and swallowed. "Uh, sorry, sir. You caught me with my mouth full."

"Of what?"

"Uh . . . my girlfriend sent me some cookies."

Warhurst glanced at the suspiciously empty table—no wrappings, no crumbs. "I see." He sniffed. "*Lime* cookies? Smells good! I don't suppose you have any for your CO."

"Uh, sorry, sir. That was the last one!"

"Very well. Carry on, then!"

"Aye, aye, sir!"

"Almost taps, people. You'd better break this up. We start weapons training early tomorrow. M-580, stripping, cleaning, and troubleshooting. You'll need clear heads." He gave Nodell a hard look. "*All* of you!"

He turned and walked out, as the Marines at the table slowly, ever so slowly, relaxed again.

"Jeez! We coulda all been busted!" Lucky said.

"I don't think so," BJ said. "He *knew!*"

"Nah," Dave said. "No way."

"So . . . what kind of skipper is he?" Corporal Mayhew asked. He was the company's current newbie, newly arrived from Space Training School at Quantico.

"Damned tough," BJ told him. "So tough I'd follow him to hell."

And the others agreed. Lucky wasn't quite that trusting . . . but was willing to give him the benefit of the doubt. He was willing enough to consider following the guy to hell.

But . . . to Europa?

**23 SEPTEMBER 2067**

Tiantan Shandian
*Solar Orbit*
*1412 hours Zulu*

They'd been extending the tether for the past thirty hours, allowing the fifteen-kilometer cables to play themselves slowly out into the night. At the far end of the four superconducting cables, a twenty-ton doughnut of steel, ceramics, and titanium used electrostatic forces and tiny rocket motors to maintain tension against the cables as they unspooled from the *Heavenly Lightning*'s blunt prow. Lasers ensured perfect alignment, while powerful optical and infrared telescopes assured proper tracking and aim.

On the *Lightning*'s bridge, drifting beside the communications suite, Captain Lin Hu Xiang grasped a handhold and pulled himself alongside the communications officer, head down. "Do we have our final word?"

"Yes, Captain!" The comm officer's young face betrayed

the flush of excitement. "It is confirmed both by Mission Control and the *Star Mountain. Jia you!*"

*Go.*

"I can't help but feel certain . . . misgivings," Lin said. "We advance blindly into an unwise war . . ."

"Sir! The Space Military Directorate would never—"

"It's not the Directorate I'm worried about. It's our inspired leaders in the Great Hall of the People. The men who put us here, who decided we should begin a war launched against the entire world."

The comm officer looked shocked. Evidently, he'd never expected to hear a commanding officer criticize the government. "I . . . I am sure they have their reasons."

"No doubt. And urgent ones, I imagine. Still . . . how is your military history, Lieutenant?"

"I am a graduate of the Beijing Academy, sir. First honors!"

"Which guarantees nothing. Do you know the name *Zhugang*?"

"No, Captain." He looked puzzled. "Is that a place in the homeland?"

"No. But our actions today will draw inevitable comparisons. I hope our leaders are prepared to accept the consequences." Turning carefully in midair, he addressed the *Lightning*'s weapons officer. "Mr. Shu. Are we on target?"

"We are, Captain. Target One is locked in. The computers are programmed to execute a five-degree yaw to bring Target Two to bear, as soon as Packages One and Two have been released."

"And our little distraction is ready?"

"Ready for launch, Captain."

He looked at Commander Feng Sun Wa, the Executive Officer. "And the crew?"

"All crew members report themselves strapped in and ready for action."

"Very well." There could be no further delay. "Mr. Shu, launch the decoy."

An eight-ton *Zhuongshu* missile sped from the *Light-*

*ning*'s launch bay, accelerating in a burst of energy at nearly twenty Gs. Its course took it back along the path traversed by the *Lightning*, chasing after a bright blue star and its tiny, grayish consort—the Earth and the Moon, now 50 million kilometers distant. Before long, the fast-moving missile had canceled the original velocity imparted by the *Lightning* away from Earth and begun closing with the distant planet.

Not that Earth was the target. After six minutes, the range between the *Lightning* and the missile had opened to 20,000 kilometers. A quick targeting check made certain that the missile was precisely aligned between the *Lightning* and distant Earth, and then the Weapons Officer pressed a key, triggering the detonation sequence over a lasercom link.

The missile's 100-megaton thermonuclear warhead detonated in a savage, death-silent flash.

"Radio communications with Earth is now interrupted," the comm office said. "Nothing but static on all channels."

"Confirm that all hands are strapped in." Best to double check. This was going to be a rough ride.

"Confirmed, Captain."

"Very well." Lin took a deep breath. "Fire main weapon. Package One."

"Package One, launch at three hundred forty thousand gravities. Fire."

The *Heavenly Lightning* lurched as the egg-shaped, ten-kilo mass hurtled down the channel formed by four taut, superconducting cables. Accelerated by a fusion-charged magnetic pulse at an acceleration of 340,000 Gs, it traveled the fifteen-kilometer length of that immense gun barrel in just under a tenth of a second, emerging from the doughnut at the end with a velocity of over 316 kilometers per second. Ten kilos, compared with the *Lightning*'s 25,000-ton mass, would normally have been insignificant, but hurled into the void at that speed, it imparted a significant recoil to the huge ship. Lin felt the nudge, a hard kick transmitted through the back of his acceleration seat.

Seconds passed as the main weapon powered up for a

second pulse . . . and then Package Two was launched, hurtling after the first. The range to target was just under 525 million kilometers. At 316 kps, the warheads would reach their target in nineteen days.

After a flurry of checks, confirming that both packages were on target, Lin gave the order to execute the five-degree yaw, bringing Target Two under the railgun's muzzle. It took nearly an hour to adjust the aim—with a "gun barrel" composed of four charged tethers fifteen kilometers long. The cloud of plasma from the detonated nuclear warhead continued to expand, however, effectively screening the *Lightning*'s actions from any Earth-bound observer. Sensitive detectors in Earth orbit might pick up the EMP surges of the main weapon each time it fired, but they wouldn't be able to tell what was happening.

With all targeting information again checked and double checked, Captain Lin ordered the main weapon fired again. This time, acceleration was set to one million gravities, and the Force Package flicked clear of the tether railgun with a velocity of 543 kilometers per second. The recoil was significantly greater with this launch, a savage lurch that sent the *Lightning* drifting backward like a burst from a maneuvering thruster.

That shot was followed by a second . . . and then a third, at which point an overstressed coolant feed in *Lightning*'s main fusion reactor melted. The reactor's core temperature skyrocketed, forcing an automatic scram and shutdown.

No matter. Two packages on Target One, and three on Target Two. It was enough.

Target Two was at a much greater range than Target One—almost 900 million kilometers. With the higher muzzle velocity of the weapons, however, they would reach Two in just nineteen days . . . within about an hour of the attack on Target One.

Lin gave the order to reel in the tethers and readjust the ship's orbit after being shoved off course by five high-G railgun shots. Engineering crews began working on the rather serious problem of bringing the main fusion reactor back on line. It scarcely mattered. His orders now were to remain on station, in case further shots were needed, but he doubted that the CWS Peaceforce would give him the luxury of a second try.

He continued to think about *Zhugang*.

# FOUR

*U.S.S.* Franklin Delano Roosevelt
*Entering Jovian System*
*1417 hours Zulu*

Major Jeff Warhurst made his way along the narrow access corridor in zero-G, pulling himself along gently until he reached the hab access collar, which was grinding about the tunnel once every twenty seconds in a thunderous cascade of sound. He picked his target—the slow-moving entryway to "C" Hab—then, grabbing the handholds on either side, he swung his feet up and through the opening with an almost graceful ease borne of three weeks' practice.

Lowering himself by the hand- and footholds, a feeling of weight gently returned, growing stronger with every meter of his descent. He emerged on "C" Hab's upper deck, a gray-walled, claustrophobic space crowded with Marines. For three weeks now, "C" Hab had been home to Bravo Company, eighty-one Marine officers and men and one Navy hospital corpsman, living on two crowded berthing decks and one level designated as the squad bay. The air was steamy and thick, stinking of far too many people crowded into too small a space.

"Attention on deck!" someone shouted, and seated Marines began to rise.

Jeff waved them back down with a careless toss of his hand. "As you were!" he bellowed. "Carry on!"

This close to the ship's hub, the spin gravity was only .21 G; you had to watch your footing and your inertia when you were moving, and the Coriolis effect was particularly unpleasant. This level had some berthing spaces, but most was reserved for offices, crew's quarters, and a common room that doubled as a mess deck and galley.

It was also the only space in the hab that provided a view of the outside. A two-meter wall screen mounted on the forward bulkhead was set to display various views from cameras mounted on the *Roosevelt*'s hull.

The view now was forward from the transport's prow. Jupiter was centered squarely in the screen, a slightly flattened orange disk, its banding easily visible to the naked eye. Although it was hard to tell from an image on a vid monitor, it looked a little larger than the full Moon did from Earth. All four of the Galilean satellites were visible, three on one side of the disk, one on the other. He didn't know which of those bright-shining points of light was Europa, their destination, but one of them was.

The *Roosevelt* was 11 million kilometers out from the planet, and well within the orbits of the huge world's outer moons. They'd just passed the orbit of Leda, a tiny chunk of rock and ice lost in all that night.

Sergeant Major Kaminski was standing by the screen, a squeeze bottle of coffee in his hand. "Major, sir," he said, nodding. "How went the meeting?"

"As expected, Sergeant Major," he replied. "We're to be squared away by sixteen-thirty hours, with inspection at seventeen hundred. Spin-down, turnover, and deceleration are scheduled to begin at twenty-twenty hours. We'll want to make sure everyone's had chow and the mess gear's cleared and stowed before then."

"Aye, aye, sir. We'll be four-oh, never fear."

"Good." He stared a moment at the vid screen. "Which one's Europa? You know?"

Kaminski indicated the middle star of the three on the right. "That brightest one, sir." His finger moved to the moon nearest Jupiter. "This little red one's Io. You can almost smell the sulfur volcanoes from here." He indicated the lone moon to the left. "That's Ganymede. Biggest moon in the Solar System, bigger even than Mercury, and the next out from Europa." His finger slid back to the right. "And Callisto. Outermost of the Galilean satellites, and enough like our Moon back home to make us all nostalgic for cold beer and a hot date."

"I didn't ask for a travelogue, Sergeant Major."

"No, sir. Of course not. Sir."

*Oh, stop being a prick,* he told himself savagely. "Sorry, Kaminski. I guess I'm a little on edge."

"Goes with the territory, sir."

Damn. Kaminski was always so diplomatic. Always knew exactly what to say. Well, that went with the territory too. Frank Kaminski had been in a long time . . . almost thirty years. He'd been in during the UN War, a veteran of Garroway's March, of Tsiolkovsky, of half a dozen nasty little actions fought as the old UN broke up and the new CWS began to take shape. He was supremely competent at everything he did, the quintessential Marine's Marine. His little spiel on the Galilean satellites was typical. The man *always* researched the next duty station or deployment, and seemed to command an inexhaustible armory of facts about the place—facts always tempered by long, personal experience.

Jeff touched one of the keys on the vid display, and a computer-generated image of the *Roosevelt* appeared center-screen, showing the transport's current attitude. She was an impressive vessel, 200 meters long from the blunt, water-tank prow ahead of the stately pirouette of her hab modules to the massive ugliness of her A-M plasma drives safely far astern. Still, at that resolution she looked damned small adrift in so much emptiness.

The single most revolutionary advance in spacecraft propulsion during the mid-twenty-first century was the steady-thrust antimatter engine, or A-M drive. Developed in parallel during the UN War by both the U.S.–Japanese Alliance and by the European Space Agency, A-M drives transformed space travel within the Solar System from long, lazy, energy-saving Holmann transfer orbits to relatively simple, straight-line, point-and-shoot affairs. Antimatter enthusiastically converted itself plus the equivalent of its own mass in ordinary matter into raw energy and plasma with a *very* high specific impulse . . . meaning high efficiency. By mixing matter and antimatter in a one-to-one ratio, a few tons of fuel was enough to take a ship, boosting steadily at one G for half the distance, then flipping over and decelerating for the second half, all the way to Jupiter in a matter of days.

Unfortunately, antimatter was tremendously expensive to produce. Enormous solar-power facilities at L-3 and on the Moon were used to transform sunlight into energy, which in turn was used to create and accumulate antimatter in microgram amounts, using techniques unchanged in principle since the late twentieth century. Because of the expense, most A-M spacecraft employed either conventional fuels "heated" by the insertion of very small amounts of antimatter to increase their $I_{sp}$, or plasma thrust engines that used a little antimatter to turn a *lot* of reaction mass— usually water—into plasma, but at much lower thrust-to-weight efficiencies. Spacecraft like the *Franklin Delano Roosevelt* and the other big A-M cruisers *could* employ steady-thrust acceleration at one G and reach Jupiter space in a week, but since doing so would consume the entire antimatter output of the U.S. A-M facility at L-3 for the past thirty months, simple economics required a more conservative approach.

Instead of hammering away at One G for the entire trip, the *Roosevelt* boosted at one G for just twelve hours out of Earth orbit, achieving in that time a velocity of just over 420 kilometers per second. She then coasted for the next twenty-four days, slowing steadily under the gravitational drag from the Sun, but still crossing 900 million kilometers of empty space in twenty-four days rather than years.

But Marines, being Marines, grumbled. They all knew the voyage out *could* have taken a mere seven days. Instead, they were crowded aboard the transport for over three weeks during the claustrophobic passage to Europa. During her twenty-four-day coast, the *Roosey* provided a semblance of gravity by rotating the hab modules. Her four boxlike habs spanned sixty meters; by rotating them about the ship's axis three times per minute, a spin gravity of .3 G was maintained in the lowest decks of each module, with lower gravities on each deck going up toward the axis. The idea was to give the Marines a compromise between acclimating to Europa's surface gravity of .13 G and letting them maintain muscle tone and general fitness.

In fact, so far as Jeff Warhurst was concerned, three weeks at .3 G was just enough to make the coast phase of the voyage completely miserable. The queasy sensations of Coriolis forces affected everyone's inner ears, and half of his company was affected by space motion syndrome—"space sickness," to the layman. The passenger quarters—the "grunt lockers," as they were called—were jam-packed with humanity sleeping in racks stacked six high and using the common rooms/mess decks, the tiny shower cubicles, and the heads on rotating schedules. A single one of the *Roosevelt*'s four hab modules could modestly quarter thirty people on three decks; this trip out, the *Roosey* carried a complete Marine Landing Force—two companies, Bravo and Charlie, plus a recon platoon, headquarters and medical element, and the twelve-man Navy SEAL platoon who'd shipped out with them to run the Manta subs—280 men and women in all, plus the ship's usual Navy complement of fifteen.

The crowding, the stifling lack of privacy, the stink all seemed unendurable.

Somehow, they endured. It was one of the things Marines did, along with the bitch sessions.

Jeff turned from the screen to study the crowded common room behind him. Laughter barked, mingled with the clatter of weapons being assembled, the hum of overhead ventilators struggling against the mingled smells of sweat, food, and oil. A lot of skin was visible. Six men and four women sat around the mess table cleaning and reassembling their M-580LR rifles, and there weren't three T-shirts among the lot of them. With so many people crowded into so tiny a vacuum-enclosed space, getting rid of excess heat was a real problem, even as the Sun dwindled astern and the *Roosey* plunged deeper and deeper into the emptiness of the outer Solar System. The temperature in any of the hab areas was rarely less than thirty-five degrees, and it was *steamy* with the accumulated sweat and exhaled moisture from so many bodies. The ship's dehumidifiers simply couldn't keep up with the load. The stated uniform of the day was tropical shorts and T-shirts, but officers and NCOs alike tacitly ignored the fact that most of the Marines aboard, male and female both, were casually topless, and stripped down to briefs or less when they could. Anything cloth worn anywhere on the body quickly became soaked; Jeff's shorts, T-shirt, and socks were clinging to his skin now like a wet swimsuit, until he felt like he had a permanent case of diaper rash.

Skin was better. Hell, it wasn't as though the setting was particularly conducive to sexual interest ... or to privacy. The daily shipboard routine was a steady grind of cleaning, study, stripping and cleaning weapons and gear, and exercise. For most of the trip, everyone aboard was too busy, too crowded, and too damned hot to take an interest in any fellow Marine's attire ... or lack of it.

Still, Colonel Richard Norden was a tough and by-the-book officer who insisted on his Marines being "four-oh, high and tight." He rarely left "A" Hab, however—some of the Marines had begun calling him "Mopey Dick" for that reason—and impending surprise inspections were telegraphed to the other habs by the Marines in his section ... plenty of time to make sure everyone in a soon-to-be-visited grunt locker was properly in uniform when he arrived.

Jeff Warhurst was Norden's Executive Officer, and as such he knew he should generate the same respect for regulations, both as XO and as CO of Bravo Company. But he also knew that a mindless adherence to form and outward show would do little but make sure he was on the alert list in all four habs, and further depress morale as well. As far as Jeff was concerned, the entire MSEF could run around buck naked when it was this hot and humid, so long as discipline was maintained, the work got done, and the men and women under his command weren't afraid to come to him with their problems.

"So what's the latest skinny, Major?" Kaminski wanted to know.

Jeff considered his reply carefully. Regular news reports were passed on to the men each day, but those had the stamp of institution thinking about them—and the faintest whiff of propaganda. What he told Kaminski now would be passing down through the ranks within a few minutes. A Marine rifle company was a better—and often faster—communications conduit than Earthnet. He could swear sometimes that scuttlebutt traveled faster than light.

"It looks like we're going to have company after all," Jeff replied. "The *Star Mountain* left Earth orbit fifteen hours ago. They're on the way, a high-energy vector, at 2 Gs."

"Shit. How long do we have?"

"Five days, if they boost the whole way with a turnaround in the middle."

Kaminski frowned. "Doubling the Gs only knocks two days off the flight time? That doesn't seem right."

"The unforgiving equations," Jeff said. "To halve the time you have to multiply the speed by four. To cut time down to a quarter, you square that, sixteen times the speed. The faster you push, the less time you have to take advantage of your high speed."

"If you say so, sir. Still sounds like two plus two equals five."

"They do," Jeff said, grinning, "for moderately large values of two."

"Well, anyway, we've got a Chinese transport on the way. Do we have a Peaceforcer running interference? I thought the *JFK* was covering our ass this month."

The A-M cruiser *John F. Kennedy* was currently on-station in the Asteroid Belt, about four astronomical units out from the Sun.

"Right. The word is, the *Kennedy*'s tracking the *Mountain*, and will be moving to intercept. It's going to be tight, though, to match course and speed with a Chinese bat coming straight out of hell. We have to be prepared for the possibility that the *Mountain* gives our people the slip."

"And that other Chinese ship?"

"The *Lightning*? Still in a retrograde solar orbit, at one a.u. out. No new activity since they detonated that nuke three weeks back. S-2 is pretty sure she's just carrying out weapons tests. No direct threat to us. They probably mean it as some kind of warning or message to Washington."

"Yeah, and I suppose the *Star Mountain* is another message. Whatever happened to delivering messages by e-mail?"

"If she is, the *JFK* will stop the delivery. Just in case, though, I want to make sure our people have a shot at the latest CI-PLA sims."

Current Intelligence sims—in this case, the latest information on the People's Liberation Army—their equipment, logistics, weapons, armor, and technology—were basic software packages used in field training. They let the troops experience firsthand what was known about a potential enemy's weapons and tactics.

"Affirmative, sir. We won't have time between now and landing for everyone to head-cram. Especially with full inspections on the sched."

"I know. We have a week before they get here, if they get here. Set up a sim-access schedule for after we land. Squad leaders and above should get first crack."

"Aye, aye, sir."

"Before landing, they should all have reviewed sims on extreme arctic conditions."

Kaminski chuckled. "Those've *been* on the sched, Major. Don't know how well they've sunk in, though, when it's this hot and humid. The joke goin' about the squad bay is that we're using the ice-training sims to save on the air conditioning. The other is that the squad leaders watch the ice sims instead of porn. They're more fun."

Jeff grasped the bottom of his o.d. T-shirt and flapped the sodden material uselessly. When the air was this humid, things simply couldn't dry through evaporation. It was as bad as being deployed in the jungle. "Well, I can't see why anyone in his right mind would want to *raise* their body temperature aboard this bucket." Tucking his shirt back in, he added, "Are the bugs all checked out?"

"Affirmative, Major. Everything except the final go/no-go launch checklists. The numbers're uploaded to the Force data base."

"Well, then, I guess we're on track." *What else is there?* He wondered. *What am I missing?*

"I'll pass the word about the inspection, sir. With the major's permission?"

"Carry on, Sergeant Major."

"Aye, aye, sir."

He checked the time—LED numerals within the skin on the back of his hand—and decided he had time for a quick sim-link himself. Walking past the table, he picked up a link helmet in an equipment locker against the bulkhead, then found a swivel-seat chair in one of the small office cubicles off the main compartment, and sat down.

The helmet, equipped with a dozen pressure-connection electrodes imbedded on the inside, nestled over his head with room to spare. He touched the adjustment key and let the smartgarment software tighten the device gently into place. After pulling his PAD from its belt holster and plugging in the connection with the helmet, he slid the opaque eyeshield down, folded his arms, and leaned back in the chair as the soft buzz of the upconnect trilled against his skull. Old-fashioned links had required surgically imbedded sockets, but low-frequency pulses could penetrate bone and stimulate the appropriate parts of the cerebral cortex.

There was a flash as the VR program booted up, and

then he was standing in complete darkness, the sensations of lying back in the chair fading as they were overridden by software-generated illusions. A Marine general in long-obsolete o.d. utilities faced him . . . a belligerent-looking, wide-mouthed scowl, the man's trademark expression, splitting a square and ugly face.

"Hello, Marine," the figure rasped. "Whatcha need?"

"Some advice, Chesty. As usual."

The image of General Lewis B. "Chesty" Puller hooked his thumbs in his Sam Browne belt and nodded. "Fair enough. Shoot."

The AI he'd had patterned after Chesty Puller was resident in his PAD, though pieces of it also roamed the ship's computer system, and the base network back at V-berg as well. The real Puller—the man was a legend in the Corps, a five-time winner of the Navy Cross—would never have spoken so informally with a major.

Or, on second thought . . . maybe he would have. Puller had had a rep for looking out for the men under his command, and for his lack of patience with idiots further up the chain of command than he. His attitude toward the brass, legend had it, had delayed his promotion to general until he'd been in for thirty-three years.

"We'll be grounding on Europa in twenty-four, General," he said. "I need to know what the hell I'm forgetting."

That wide mouth shifted slightly in what might have been a lopsided smile. "There's always something. You've taken care of the checklist shit." It was a statement, not a question. His AI software multitasked with his PAD's operating system; Chesty had attended the staff meeting a few moments ago, albeit invisibly, listening in through the computer's audio, and was aware of everything Jeff said and did.

Such electronic advisors were usually called secretaries in civilian life, and aides in the military. They were supposed to have the personae of assistants. Jeff had received some grief from fellow Marines over his decision to have his aide programmed to mimic an old-time Marine general, and Chesty Puller himself, no less.

Jeff had insisted on the programming, however, though other officers usually had aides that ran the gamut of personalities from Jeeves-type butlers to eager young junior officers to sharp-creased NCOs to sexy women or, in the case of one Marine officer Jeff knew, a devastatingly handsome young man. His choice wasn't exactly traditional . . . but he preferred the electronic persona as a reminder that he needed to tap the command experience of someone who'd been in the Corps for a long time, who knew its ways, its customs, its *heritage* as no one else.

"Number one," Puller's image told him, "is to talk with your men. Work with them. Let them see you."

"I've been discussing things with Kaminski—"

"I'm not talking about your topkicks, son. Yeah, you listen to your NCOs. They're your most experienced people, and they'll tell you what you need to know. What I'm sayin' now, though, is to make yourself accessible to your men. *Especially* with that gold oak leaf on your collar."

He wasn't wearing rank insignia, but he knew what Puller meant. A company was normally a captain's command, but in a small and isolated detachment like this one, the senior officers tended to double up on their duties and their responsibilities. His 2IC, the second-in-command of Bravo Company, was a captain named Paul Melendez; his command duties were divided between Bravo Company, his position on the MSEF's operations staff, and his responsibilities as XO for the entire detachment.

The higher an officer's rank, though, the more detached he tended to be from the enlisted men, and a major—usually the commander of an entire battalion—was pretty far up there among the clouds.

"Colonel Norden doesn't like his officers fraternizing that much with the men," Jeff pointed out.

"Fraternization be damned! Who's gonna be on the line out there, son? Mopey Dick or your men? You need to be careful that you don't make an ass of yourself, of course.

You need to hold their respect." Puller's grin widened. "Hell, that's why most officers don't fraternize. They're afraid of looking like idiots. But your people deserve better. Let 'em know you're in the foxhole with 'em. And, by God, when the shooting starts, be sure you *are* in there with 'em."

"I understand," Jeff said. "But . . . well, Europa is going to have some special challenges for us. Radiation. The cold and ice. And there's a possibility now we'll be facing the Chinese as well. I need to know what I'm overlooking. What I'm missing."

"That, son, is the responsibility of your senior NCOs and your junior officers. You just make sure your men can see you. The hardest part is always the twenty-four hours before you go in. The *waiting*." Chesty Puller's image looked thoughtful, almost musing. "Chinese and ice, huh? Sounds like Chosin all over again."

Jeff had to think a moment, but the reference came to him. Puller, the *original* Chesty Puller, had won his fifth Navy Cross *and* the Army Distinguished Service Cross at the Chosin Reservoir, in North Korea, during a hellish retreat through deadly, bitter cold, under constant attack by Chinese forces. When informed that his regiment was surrounded, he had said, "Those poor bastards. They've got us right where we want them. We can shoot in every direction now." He'd led his men down sixty miles of icy mountain road as they fought their way out of the trap. It was one of the Corps' prouder memories.

"Shouldn't be that bad, General," he replied. "The temperature'll be 140 below, but we'll be a hell of a lot better equipped and supplied than you were at Chosin. And the Chinese probably won't be a factor. Not with the *JFK* riding shotgun."

"If you're lucky, you're right," Puller said. "If you're *smart*, you'll be prepared. For anything."

A mental command, five memorized digits and the word "disconnect" repeated hard in his thoughts three times, broke the VR connection. He blinked at the gray-painted overhead, reestablishing his awareness of what was real and what wasn't. After a moment, he removed the VR headgear, stowed it, and walked back into the common area.

In one of the arms lockers aft he found a Sunbeam M-228 squad laser weapon, a 10-megawatt SLAW, and carried it forward to the mess table. "Mind if I join you?" he asked, taking a seat with the ten men and women cleaning their M580s.

"Of course not, sir," one of the men said. He was a skinny, sharp-faced corporal from New York named George Leckie. "Grab some chair!"

Gunnery Sergeant Tom Pope grinned. "Slumming, sir?"

"Gunny, after four hours of staff meetings, I consider it R&R."

"I hear ya, sir."

One of the women—with hard muscles and sweat gleaming on her bare chest—said something to the blond woman beside her, and both laughed.

"What was that, Campanelli? Didn't catch it."

"Uh . . . nothing, sir." When he continued to look at her, she shifted uncomfortably and added, "I just said that that was a damned big gun you had there, and, uh, I wondered if the major knew how to use it. Sir." Her chest and shoulders flushed dark as she spoke. Marines *never* used the word *gun* except to refer to artillery—especially shipboard guns—or a penis. The squad laser was a weapon, a piece, an M228, or a SLAW. *Not* a gun.

"Well, it's been a few years," he said easily. "Maybe you can give me some pointers." The others laughed, a little nervously, but louder when he grinned.

It *had* been a good many years since he'd had to do this, but his hands remembered the proper movements. Power off . . . cable feed disconnect . . . pull the barrel locking lever back . . . grasp the barrel with the other hand and pull forward and up . . .

Yeah, he remembered. And before long, he was trading jokes with them.

# FIVE

*U.S.S.* John F. Kennedy
*Solar orbit, 4.2 a.u. from Earth*
*2002 hours Zulu*

Captain Jeremy Mitchell entered the officer's wardroom with his tray and walked toward the only occupied table. Gone were the days when the other officers present stood until he was seated; the *JFK*'s officer's mess was patterned off of the dirty shirt mess decks of Navy aircraft carriers, with food served cafeteria style. It was located in "A" Hab, with the hab rotation set to deliver a gentle third of a gravity.

"Mind if I join you gentlemen?" he asked with an easy drawl. Mitchell was from a small town not far from San Antonio, Texas, and liked to affect the laid-back attitude of Texas and good-natured down-home.

"Please do, Captain!" Commander Varley, the weapons officer, said, gesturing.

He set his tray down and took a seat. "Well, Mr. Lee," he said, addressing the young Marine officer on his left. "It looks like you and your people might get a chance to prove your usefulness, even in this day and age."

"Is there any more data on the *Star Mountain*'s vector, sir?" He sounded eager . . . and painfully young.

"Nothing new. They're still vectored for Jupiter—which means Europa—and they're boosting at 2 Gs, which means they're in a damned hurry to get there. They won't be able to sidestep *us,* however."

"Peaceforcers save Earth, once again!" Lieutenant Commander Carvelle, the chief communications officer, said, raising a glass in salute.

Peaceforce. It was a new concept, born of one particular horror of the UN War. A French attempt to smash the U.S. will to continue the fight by diverting a small asteroid into an impact on Colorado had been stopped . . . *almost* completely. A fair-sized and somewhat radioactive piece of the UN ship that had done the diverting had come down over Lake Michigan and obliterated most of lakeside Chicago.

With the rapid expansion of human activity into the Solar System, the Confederation of World States, struggling to knock together some form of planet-wide government to replace the disintegrating UN, had recognized the danger posed by any world power able to put a spacecraft into the asteroid belt or beyond. A relatively small nudge could put a likely megaton chunk of iron or ice into a new orbit, one that could take out anything from a city to the entire human race, depending on how ambitious the bad guys were.

The threat had resulted in the Peaceforce, a military space force drawn from the United States Navy, the Marines, and the space assets of several allies tasked with patrolling the outer system and preventing just such attempts. The problem was that the Solar System was an *awfully* big backyard, too vast by far to allow any kind of systematic patrolling.

And the trick was to position just a few ships in strategic orbits, far, far up the side of the Solar gravity well. Orbiting in the Asteroid Belt, 4.2 a.u.s out, and employing extremely powerful sensing and tracking gear, a ship could watch for any launches from Earth. Any boosts not cleared by CWS inspection teams could be intercepted by ships such as the *Kennedy* and either disabled at a distance, or boarded.

That was why Lieutenant Lee was on board with his platoon of twenty-eight space-trained Marines. The *JFK* would match course and speed with the hostile, disable her if necessary, then close and grapple for the final round. Mitchell was amused that modern tactical thinking was actually looking at the possibility of using Marines to take an enemy ship by storm, something that hadn't happened since the boarding of the *Mayaguez* in 1975.

"Well, it'll be interesting to see Lieutenant Lee here swing across from the yardarms, cutlass and boarding pistol in hand!"

"I'd need more than two hands for *that* evolution, sir," the lieutenant replied. "I think we'll stick to M580s, and hope the bad guys aren't in the mood for much of a fight when we get there."

"Doesn't sound like the fire-eating Marines I know," Varley said.

"Hey, if it can be done without a firefight . . ."

"Do you anticipate problems with your mission, Lieutenant?"

"A good officer *always* anticipates problems, sir. Boarding a hostile spacecraft is at least as hairy as a house-clearing operation—and it's complicated by being in zero gravity and the possibility of explosive decompression." He grinned. "Playing with weapons inside a thin-skinned spacecraft isn't exactly a real bright idea."

"I imagine the whole question is academic," Varley said with a shrug. "The Chinese can't beat the laws of physics. Even accelerating at 2 Gs, they can't outrun us because we have the metaphorical high ground in the Solar System. They can't maneuver and accelerate both. When we close and match velocity, they'll have to surrender . . . or risk a mass driver round through their drive unit."

"They must have something in mind," Lieutenant Zynkowovec said. He was the ship's third engineering officer. "They know we're out here, and they know physics as well as we do. They've gotta have something up their sleeves."

"They just don't know about our secret weapon!" Varley said, laughing. "The U.S. Marines!"

The radio clipped to Mitchell's collar chirped. Damn. *Always* when he was sitting down to dinner. "What is it?"

"We are tracking an incoming object, Captain," the voice of Jackie, the *JFK*'s AI, said in unhurried tones. "There is a threat to the ship."

He was already on his feet and jogging for the access corridor that would take him to the ship's hub, then forward to the bridge. "What threat?"

"The object is small—less than ten kilograms' mass—but it is on an approach vector with a velocity of five hundred kilometers per second. Range, 15,000 kilometers, closing."

The calm words chilled. Thirty seconds to impact.

"Why the hell didn't we see it on radar?"

"The object is quite small, less than three meters long, and appears to exhibit stealth characteristics. Its radar cross-section is less than two centimeters across."

A stealth missile? They still should have picked up the IR footprint of its exhaust!

"The object has just executed a minor course change," Jackie continued. "It was unpowered until now. Definitely now on an intercept course . . . and accelerating."

"Maneuver!" Mitchell bellowed. If the incoming was changing course . . .

He was in the access tube now, hand-over-handing rapidly into lower and lower gravity as he raced for the hub. But he knew there wasn't time to reach the bridge.

He felt the thump, the surge of weight sideways, as the *Kennedy*'s maneuvering thrusters fired.

Seconds later, something struck the ship. Jeremy Mitchell was slammed against one side of the access tunnel by a savage, sudden acceleration. It felt as though the ship was tumbling, pressing him against the wall of the access tube with centrifugal force.

He heard metal shrieking protest—a screech, followed by a succession of loud pops and bangs, and the shrill whistle of air escaping to vacuum.

Then the entire universe seemed to explode in raw noise rapidly dwindled to vacuum-muffled silence, and the *Kennedy*'s captain found himself pinwheeling through black and cold and fragment-filled space, dying in a cloud of fast-freezing blood even as he tried to grasp the enormity of what was happening to his ship . . . and him.

*U.S.S.* John F. Kennedy
*Solar orbit, 4.2 a.u. from Earth*
*2007 hours Zulu*

Two force packages had been accelerated at the *Kennedy*—or rather, at that area of space the *Kennedy* would orbit through precisely nineteen days after the *Heavenly Lightning* fired them. The first, detected at the last possible moment, executed a course change for intercept and almost missed. *Kennedy's* sudden maneuver—firing forward thrusters to reduce her orbital velocity—almost caused the Chinese missile to pass across her bows.

But a second course change countered the *Kennedy's* move, and the force package struck far forward, ripping through the thin metal shell of the Peaceforcer cruiser's forward reaction mass tank. The electromagnetic bottle anchoring a pea-sized fragment of antimatter in the hard vacuum of the package's warhead failed, the antimatter slammed into metal and water, and then a fireball as hot as the surface of the sun blossomed into deadly radiance.

Water flashed into steam and exploded into space. The cruiser, almost 200 meters long, was whip-snapped by the detonation into a sudden and violent spin, tumbling end over end. Two of the hab modules, their coupling and spin mechanisms overstressed by the sudden off-balance acceleration, wrenched partly free, then broke away entirely, hurtling into the night with hundreds of smaller fragments as the great vessel began to tear itself apart.

The second package, homing on the heat and radiation of the first explosion, had more time to correct its intercept vector, and slammed into the *Kennedy's* wreckage amidships. The explosion engulfed half the ship, and left only spinning fragments behind.

At its present position, the twin bursts of radiation marking the *Kennedy*'s destruction would take twenty minutes to reach Jupiter—and twenty-eight to make it across the void to Earth.

**12 OCTOBER 2067**

*In Europa orbit*
*2007 hours (Zulu)*

"Thirty seconds to release," the voice of the *Roosevelt*'s skipper, Captain Galtmann, said in Jeff's ear. "How're you boys and girls making out over there?"

"Squared away, sir," Jeff replied. "Ready for drop." He tried to force some semblance of discipline on his unpleasantly twisting stomach. He hated zero G.

"Happy landings, then. We'll see you again in six months!"

"Remember the surface radiation," Colonel Norden's voice added, rasping. "Get your people under cover stat, until we can give those suits a full checkout in field conditions."

"Aye, aye, sir," Jeff replied. "We'll set a new speed record for cross-country ice-jogging." Although, damn it, if the suits didn't work, none of them would live long enough to even reach shelter. The surface of Europa, despite the cold, was *hot*. . . .

"Keep me posted up here. I'll be down in two orbits—say, 180 minutes."

"Roger that. We'll be waiting, sir."

Jeff craned his head, trying to see out the tiny porthole beside his seat and get a glimpse of the *Roosevelt*. His suit, with its cumbersome helmet, and the fact that he was strapped down in the narrow, hard-backed seat, kept him from seeing much of anything. All that was visible through the port was the dead-black of space, and a few scattered stars, plus a little bit of the bug's framework embracing the pressurized passenger module.

The bug was similar to lobbers and other short-haul transports used by the Marines during various Lunar operations. Intended solely for operation in vacuum, it was completely unstreamlined—a chunky, squared-off bottle shape housing command deck and passenger/cargo spaces, plus spherical fuel tanks and a chemical rocket engine all crammed together inside a webwork of titanium/carbon fiber struts, with six landing legs, powerful external spotlights, and small maneuvering thrusters on flanks and belly. It was an ungainly-looking vehicle, well deserving of the Marines' pet name for them: *bugs*. Each was thirty-three meters long, with space aboard—with some creative cramming—for one platoon, in this case the forty-one men and women of Second Platoon, Bravo Company, plus six of the Navy SEALs with the DSV team.

The *Roosey* carried two bugs, plus four similar craft used strictly for transporting cargo. The Ops Plan called for using both bugs to ferry all of Bravo—eighty-one Marines and six SEALs—to the CWS Cadmus Research Station on Europa. They would then refuel and rendezvous with the *Roosey* to take aboard the headquarters and support platoons in the next run, and finally return a third time for Charlie Company. The cargo landers would be shuttling back and forth between the surface and orbit for the next two days, bringing down not only the four Manta submersibles and all of the Marines' supplies, but a load of consumables for Cadmus Station as well.

Cadmus Station consisted of twenty-five men and women from six nations. Most had been on Europa since the station had been established over a year before, and they were totally dependent on occasional ships from Earth for food and spare parts.

Water, at least, they had plenty of. Europa's surface was a sheath of solid water ice, enclosing an ocean fifty to one hundred kilometers deep—five to ten times deeper than the deepest ocean abyss on Earth.

"Eight seconds to release," Lieutenant Walthers said from the bug's command deck. "Hang onto your lunches back there! And three . . . and two . . . and one . . . *release!*"

There was a slight jar as the mechanical grapples connecting the bug to the *Roosey*'s spine swung open, and a half-second burst from the dorsal thrusters set them in motion. The admonition to the Marines to retain their lunches seemed uncalled for . . . until the thrusters fired again and the bug rolled sharply to port.

Through his narrow window view on the starboard side, Jeff saw the *Roosevelt* swing ponderously into view, all light and midnight-dark, a long, slender rail with bulbous water tanks attached along her entire length, her habs like four sledgehammers attached at the handles still slowly rotating just aft of the forward tank. During acceleration, the rotation was halted and the habs folded back against the ship's spine, preserving the up-down conventions of each deck. Once the *Roosevelt* had entered orbit around Europa, however, the habs had redeployed while the bugs were made ready for the descent. Heat radiators spread astern like enormous, squared-off tailfeathers. Getting rid of excess heat in vacuum was always a major spacecraft design problem, and the antimatter reaction of the drive created a *lot* of excess heat.

Those last twelve hours that the drive had been running, with the Marines on board stewing in their own overheated juices, had been a nightmare.

The bug continued its roll, dragging the *Roosevelt* out of Jeff's line of sight. He was hoping for a glimpse of Jupiter, but the next thing he saw was a vast arc of darkness swallowing the stars one by one. The lights illuminating the bug's passenger deck were dim and amber, but still bright enough that he couldn't see any detail in the night outside the craft. They were falling over Europa's night side.

He'd seen Europa during their final approach, as well as during training sims, of course. The moon looked like nothing so much as a straw-colored marble heavily crisscrossed by long, straight lines of a deeper, reddish color.

The bug's main engines fired their de-orbit burn, and Jeff's stomach lurched at the sudden resumption of acceleration, a huge hand clamping down across his chest. Then, just as suddenly, the hand was gone and he was weightless again.

But the *Roosevelt* was falling away above and ahead, continuing to orbit the moon while the bug descended rapidly toward the surface, following a long, descending curve that would take them halfway around the moon. He thought he could make out something of the Europan surface now, irregular patches less black than their surroundings, glossy smooth areas, perhaps, illuminated by starlight. Then, quite suddenly, black gave way to darkest gray, lightening swiftly as the far horizon, still curved, took fire from the fast-rising Sun.

The bug swept across the terminator, passing from night into day. Jeff blinked, then adjusted his helmet's polarization. The surface now was ice, reflecting sun-dazzle in brilliant white patches interspersed with tan and ocher-colored regions. Jeff stared at the surface turning below, fascinated, no matter how many times he'd seen computer simulations and vids already. The surface looked remarkably like old, early twentieth-century notions of the planet Mars, complete with long, straight canals, called lineae. A kind of plate tectonics worked here; Europa's core, molten from tidal flexing in the tug-of-war between Jupiter and the other major Jovian satellites, kept Europa's ocean liquid. The upper few kilometers of that ocean, however, were frozen. As the tides continued to stretch the tiny world, the icecap cracked, refroze, and cracked again, until it looked like a frosted crystal ball with a surface crazed by thousands of straight-line cracks and fissures. There were almost no craters that he could see. Here and there, however, he could make out large, circular features, the maculae, which looked like spots on an iced-over pond in early spring where someone had chucked a rock through, and the resulting hole had been closed over by thin skim ice. And that, as a matter of cold fact, was almost certainly a precise analogy. Traditional craters couldn't last on that landscape of constantly resculpted ice and intense radiation bombardment for more than a few hundred thousand years, if that. Once in a while, though, a rock big enough to leave a lasting impression must impact with the surface and leave its footprint, even if for only a short time as planets and moons measured such things.

The icy surface was remarkably flat. No mountains. No cliffs. This close, he could see that the major, straight cracks were supplemented by myriad smaller ones, until the reddish lines resembled a cascade of long, red hair matted across the moon's pale surface.

The image of red hair made him think of Carsyn, back in California. That homesick thought jarred, superimposed as it was on the alien majesty below. He'd been thinking about her a lot during the voyage out from Earth.

He'd promised to give her an answer when he returned, at the end of this deployment. Yeah . . . six months on this ice box ought to give him the time he needed to make a decision like that.

The bug's engines fired again, a savage, bucking kick through the hard seat upright at his back. The curve of the horizon was definitely flatter now. It was impossible to estimate their altitude by eye, however. The landscape below was simply too alien, too far beyond common human experience and lacking in any recognizable features, for him to make even a guess. In places, the terrain was jumbled and broken; elsewhere it was absolutely flat. They could have been ten kilometers up, or looking at a snow field from an altitude of two meters.

On closer inspection, the linea turned out to be less like the canals of Percival Lowell's Mars than they were arctic pressure ridges. Those dark-colored lines were in fact elevations in the landscape, rising a hundred meters or so above the surrounding terrain. The dark color was partly the effect of sunlight reflecting from slopes instead of flats, but also seemed to be the result of coloring of some sort contaminating the ice. Current theory held that as separate plates of the Europan ice cap ground together or cracked apart, water upwelled from beneath, bringing with it a concentrated soup of organic molecules that were frozen in the slow-rising pressure ridges. Europa's global sea was rich in sulfur, iron, and iron-sulfur compounds; the life forms discovered there so far metabolized sulfur, analogues of the deep-ocean life discovered over eighty years before around some of Earth's sea-bottom volcanic vents.

Before much longer, it became apparent that Europa's billiard-ball flatness was largely an illusion. There were vast, smooth-ice plains, but most of the surface was chaotic, a blind jumble of blocks and chunks and fragments repeatedly fragmented, mashed together, refrozen, then broken again. The surface, Jeff thought, looked like an endless sea of icebergs packed together into a solid mass. His Marine training looked at the tangle sweeping past below, and decided that combat in that labyrinthine tangle would be . . . a *challenge*.

In Marine OCS, at Quantico, Jeff had repeatedly faced impossible problems, everything from doing the required number of chins and push-ups to making it up a sheer, wooden obstacle-course barrier ten meters tall to figuring out a particularly knotty problem in close-combat tactics. His senior DI, a gunnery sergeant named Matlock, had had the habit of leaning over and screaming in Jeff's ear, "It's a *challenge*, Marine! Think of it as a *challenge!*"

Yeah . . . right.

"Okay, boys and girls," Lieutenant Walthers's voice said in his helmet. "We have the CWS beacon. On final."

Jeff turned, as best as he could bundled in his heavy suit, and looked at the motionless rows of other suited-up Marines, waiting. Without their weapons, they looked less like Marines than passengers strapped in aboard a suborbital HST flight. Their gear was stowed aft, however; the bug's cabin was far too cramped to accommodate this many space-suited men and women *and* their weapons. No matter. This was neither training nor a live drop into a hot LZ. More like a commercial flight into a new duty station Earthside.

*Hell, yeah, just like Lompoc, California,* he thought, grinning to himself behind his dark visor. *No unpleasant neighbors to worry about. Just think of it as a new shore station in California . . . with no air, malls, tattoo parlors, traffic, or girlie shows, with high radiation, no palm trees, and a summertime high of minus one-forty.*

He looked back out the port. The bug had swung to the right, and he could see the base, now, spread out beneath a midmorning sun. There was actually very little to see, but the handful of surface structures was enough to bring a feeling of scale to the otherwise scaleless terrain . . . though they *could* have been toys left scattered across a flat layer of snow in someone's winter-bound backyard.

The CWS research station was located on the Cadmus Linea, one of the bolder of the red-hued cracks following a great circle route halfway across the moon's circumference. This close, you couldn't really see the concentration of red pigments so visible from space; the surface was simply ice, a bit darker-hued, perhaps, than fresh, new ice, but still colored a dull white with a bluish cast and occasional, brighter highlights.

The facility had been built in the middle of a circular depression—the shadow of a small, ancient macula, perhaps—but the floor was Kansas-cornfield flat. The visible components of the station consisted of a dark-gray landing pad the size of a football field marked with an enormous red crosshair, a twenty-meter radio mast, a satellite dish, two storage sheds, and a scattering of equipment—bulldozers, surface crawlers, and several hoppers parked at the edge of the landing field. Nearby, a couple of hundred meters, perhaps, from the edge of the field, was a black circle, as precise and as artificial as the mouth of a tunnel, leading straight down through the ice, covered over by a billowing cloud of fog.

The Pit.

A single white building, almost invisible against the ice, clung to the artificially sheer side of the circular hole into the moon's interior. Most of the station was safely buried, out of reach of the invisible but deadly sea of radiation bathing the moon's nakedly exposed surface.

The bug turned again, Jeff felt a series of heavy thumps transmitted through the deck, and then they were gentling toward the red crosshairs. In another moment, he couldn't see any of the base, but he did catch a glimpse of the bug's sharp-edged shadow racing across the gray-white surface to meet them as they drifted lower. A cloud of ice crystals swirled briefly past the porthole, and then they were down.

"Thank you, ladies and gentlemen, for flying Air Navy," Walthers's voice said. "The weather here in Miami Beach is clear and sunny, wind zero out of the southeast, and the temperature is a balmy minus one forty-six Celsius. Please be sure not to leave personal gear adrift, and watch your step exiting the spacecraft. The bleach puddles can be treacherous!"

A chorus of groans, curses, and catcalls answered the bug pilot's cheerfully humorous litany. Jeff unstrapped, then stood, crouched over with one gloved hand bracing himself against the low overhead, as Kaminski began calling off names.

"Cukela! Brighton! Jellowski! Hutton! Vottori! Garcia! You're up!"

Six by six, the platoon began leaving their seats and filing in a slow shuffle aft, between the rows of seats. The central passageway fed onto a ramp leading down into the bug's cramped main lock. That compartment was only large enough for six suited-up Marines at a time, so the disembarkation process took some time.

Jeff waited through the slow cycling of the lock, exiting with Kaminski and the last three men of the platoon. By ancient tradition, the senior officer was the last one onto a boat, and the first one off . . . but such quaint niceties didn't apply here, when Jeff wanted to be able to personally give the suits of each of his people a once-over eyeballing as the Marines shuffled past.

The suits were essentially Mark IICs, later models of the armor that Marines had worn on Mars and the moon a quarter of a century before. These were a bit bulkier, with thicker armor laminates, better on-board computers and life support, and, instead of the old chameleon surfaces which adjusted the color to match the surroundings, these were covered with a thick and heavy but flexible material, like white canvas. The intent was not camouflage, however. The "canvas" material was actually a weave of superconducting fibers and microscopic tubes. A weak electrical current flowing through the covering should serve to trap and deflect incoming particulate radiation, specifically the flood of protons sleeting into Europa's surface from Jupiter's intense radiation belts.

Even so, each man's exposure on the surface would be carefully monitored for the next six months. Doc McCall, the company corpsman, had already passed out badges that would record cumulative totals for each man and woman and alert Jeff's secretary if they picked up a dosage of 30 rems or more.

He and Kaminski gave one another a visual suit check, and then they locked out with the last three Marines in the queue.

When the outer lock hatchway cycled open, Jeff stepped down into a cold and eerie silence. His suit heaters were working fine—he felt them kick on in his legs when his boots touched the landing pad deck—but the surroundings *looked* as cold and bleak as a deep Siberian winter.

Of course, the actual temperature was far lower than anything Earth had ever experienced.

The horizon was the rim of the crater chosen as the site of the base, knife-edged and brilliant in the sun. The sky was a dull, dead black, the stars washed away by the brilliance of a shrunken sun just above the ridge line. And above, higher in the sky . . .

Jupiter hung above the sun, an immense crescent bowed away from the light, embracing a bloated disk of night. The crescent spanned over twelve degrees of the sky—twenty-four times the diameter of Earth's Moon back home. For a dizzying moment, Jeff wrestled with the sensation that the planet was falling on him . . . and then he took a deep breath and mentally nailed it in the sky. He could easily make out the banding on the crescent from here, turbulent stripes of ocher, red, white, and tan, a spectacle of unparalleled beauty too rich, too intense to look *real*. If he thought of it as a photographic backdrop, or as an extremely detailed vid or sim, he could push back the almost claustrophobic feeling that the planet was about to drop from the sky and crush him.

He dragged his gaze down from the sky and fixed it on Kaminski's back. Together, they trudged across the landing deck. The rest of the company was filing along a path leading toward the building at the edge of The Pit; someone in a suit identical to Jeff's save for bright blue identifying bands on upper arms and legs stood at the edge of the deck, waving them on.

"Major Warhurst?" a man's voice asked.

He raised his own gloved hand to show who was speaking. "I'm Warhurst, sir. Bravo Company, and XO of the Expeditionary Force."

"Dr. Shigeru Ishiwara. *Konichiwa!* Welcome to Cadmus Station!"

"Good to be here, sir." If it was a lie, it was a well-intentioned one.

"Let's get you and all of your men below," Ishiwara said. "You're not wearing your long-term pliss units."

Each suit had a PLSS, a Personal Life Support System built into the back, housing most of the suit's power generating and heating systems, as well as reserves of air and water. The crowding aboard the bug had necessitated using PLSS Type Ones, which provided two to three hours of life support, depending on the amount of exertion. Ishiwara was wearing a Type Three, so bulky it looked like it was wearing him, a molded white box with irregular angles grasping him from behind. With that unit, he could survive on the Europan surface for as much as twenty-four hours, assuming he didn't pick up too many rems in the process and fry.

"Our life support is fine," Jeff replied. "It'll be nice to get out of the wind, though."

"Meaning the plasma of Jupiter's magnetosphere," Ishiwara said, laughing. "I understand. If you'll follow me?"

Steps led down of the edge of the landing deck, taking them to a well-worn path through the ice bordered by a slender handrail. Here and there he could see what looked like puddles of clear meltwater on the ice, and, when he looked closely, it seemed to him that some of the puddles were fizzing slightly around the edges of the pools, as ice continued to melt.

"Please watch your step, gentlemen," Ishiwara warned, pointing to one of the puddles. "Those pools can be *very* slick. The bombardment of protons from Jupiter's magnetosphere is constantly breaking down the surface ice and forming new compounds, especially hydrogen peroxide. The pools then dissociate into oxygen and hydrogen, which escape—but the melting process leaves things slippery."

"We've been briefed," Jeff replied. Even so, his first few steps along the path were a bit unsteady, and on the fifth step he felt his heavy right boot slide forward alarmingly. Reaching out, he grasped the handrail beside the path. There was no sense in proving he was some kind of macho Marine who didn't need handrails, not when the alternative was an undignified fall on his ass. Up ahead, he saw several Marines helping a comrade to his feet; yeah, they were learning about dignity the hard way.

Ahead, several space-suited men were carrying large crates toward one of a number of sheds dotting the crater floor. "You store equipment on the surface?" Jeff asked.

"Some," Ishiwara replied. "Especially the things that explode, like seismic penetrators. We use them to send shock waves through the ice to determine its thickness, and also, sometimes, to cut holes. We'd rather not have those going off inside the E-DARES facility.

"*Those* sheds, though," he added, indicating the Quonset hut storage structures, "are for the honey buckets."

"Shit."

"Exactly. Europa has its own biosystem, and we must avoid contaminating it at all costs. Similar restrictions are used in our explorations of Antarctica, you know. Human wastes are dehydrated, sealed inside plastic bags, then allowed to freeze solid on the surface. After a year here, we've accumulated quite a bit of the stuff—nearly ten tons. We'll need to take it with us when we leave."

"That ship'll have the damnedest cargo manifest I've ever heard of. But wouldn't the cold and radiation sterilize the stuff?"

"Probably. Almost certainly. But the seawater temperature, remember, is only slightly below zero Celsius. Some organisms would survive and proliferate if they were still viable, and we have to be certain, one hundred percent."

"Major?" General Puller's rasping voice said suddenly over his headset. His PAD was running, of course, though safely secured inside the suit and tied in to his electronic sensors and the company communications net. "We have important communications incoming on channel twelve."

"Let's hear 'em."

". . . don't know what it is," Captain Galtmann's voice was saying. "Incoming at five hundred kps . . . and, damn! *It's changing course to—*"

The landscape around them grew suddenly brighter. Jeff looked up in time to see an expanding disk of white light above the horizon, about twenty degrees to the right of the sun. The light faded away, and now he was hearing only static in his headset.

"My God!" he said. "What—"

"I have lost contact with the *Roosevelt*," his AI said.

A second flash, eye-wateringly brilliant, winked on in exactly the same place in the sky as the first, swiftly expanding, bright as a second sun, fading, then vanishing beneath the light of the real sun. The silence heightened the surreal unreality of the moment.

He was stunned . . . but his mind was still working, processing the too little information he had to work with. "Marines!" he bellowed over the company general channel. "*Incoming! Grab on to something!*"

"Something," in this instance, could only be the safety

rail. He grabbed on with both hands, instinctively hunkering down. The fact that there'd been *two* explosions, plus that instant's warning of an approaching object, suggested that—

White light glared, impossibly brilliant, against the sharp horizon on the far side of the landing deck. An instant later, he could see the ground wave approaching through the ice, a fast-approaching ripple of fragmenting white . . . and then the shock hit and he felt the ground buck beneath his boots. He lost his grip on the handrail as the railing itself tore free, and he was sent spinning across the white-lit surface like a string-cut puppet.

Then he was lying flat on his back, staring up into a black sky and the sharp-edged slash of Jupiter, a colorful scimitar suspended far overhead.

He was unhurt. But *Roosevelt*, and Colonel Norden, and over half of the MSEF, were—gone. Dead.

# SIX

*Garroway-Lee Residence*
*Quantico, Virginia*
*1635 hours EDT*
  *(2035 hours Zulu)*

Rena Moore came down the stairs to the e-room and checked in on the kids. Both Kamela and Alan were in front of the big wallscreen, watching history. It was a special her secretary had snagged a week ago on the Net, all about the search for extraterrestrial life, starting with prespaceflight speculation and SETI, and following through to the life discovered in Europa's ocean, and the explosion of new religions and beliefs arising now as a result of the discoveries on the Moon and Mars.

Rena was a bit old-fashioned in such things, a vid-traditionalist. She knew there were plenty of full-interactive sims the kids could use to actually visit just about any desired place or event in history—she used them sometimes, judiciously—but she still preferred flatscreen documentaries and vids for overview work. She'd been educated on the Net and through downloaded vids and she'd turned out fine. She didn't quite trust the idea of vids and sims played inside a person's mind. What were eyes and ears for, if not to handle sensory input?

To her credit, she also understood her own bias. Her parents had told her about television, and a time when education, entertainment, and communications had *not* been inextricably linked, when there'd been no AIs and no Net demons or secretaries to search the vast electronic sea for that tiny percentage of data that might be of interest to them. Things had changed a lot since the early twenty-first century, and Rena knew they would keep on changing in the future. Maybe Kam and Alan's kids would go to school through a VR sim playing out inside their brains. Or maybe things would be more outlandish than that—downloaded memories or nanobot implants or the gods knew what.

But that was the future. She would teach the Garroway-Lees the best way she knew how, and that was by lots of personal interaction, discussion, and plenty of flatscreen vids.

Rena was a cissie—a professional Child Care Specialist with a DCC in both primary and secondary education, and associate degrees in history, English, and netsearch. There were still teachers—there were still *schools*, for that matter, a few—but the vast majority of precollege education these days was handled at home, either through straight home-schooling, AI tutors, or with a CCS to guide and supervise the child's instruction. She'd been working in the Garroway-Lee household—and one other in the neighbor-hood—for the past five years.

"How's it going, kids?" she asked.

" 'Kay, I guess," Kam said. She was twelve and had already announced her intention to be a Marine, like both of her parents, her oldest brother, and her grandfather. "They're talkin' about new religions now. They mentioned Neopagan Anism a while ago."

"Yeah," Alan said. "Freeze program!" he added, halting the documentary. He turned to face her, grinning his chal-lenge. "Maybe they should've interviewed you, Cissie. You could've put 'em straight! They were talking about Anism like it was all nonsense!" He was fifteen, and had surprised everyone at his Naming Day ceremony by taking his mother's family name, Garroway, as his own. He was the artist of the family; he'd already composed several fullsense pieces, textural music that could only be experienced as sights, sounds, tastes, smells, and touches over a Net-linked download with added sensory expanders. Rena didn't understand the art form herself—fullsensories made her queasy—but she could respect the awards Alan had won last year for *Girl in the Boy* and *Fem-de-Lance*, and the fact that he was already earning a decent income as an FS composer.

He was also the family's smart mouth. He enjoyed baiting her about the Faith.

"Not everyone understands N.A.," she said primly. It was as much as she could say within the boundaries of her oath, which included the injunction to teach children to think for themselves, rather than filling them with one's own belief system.

It was an oath she took at least as seriously as physicians had taken the Hippocratic a century before. *First, do no harm* . . .

"Well, this guy was sayin' the Anists are just taking over the old, conservative neopagan churches and sneaking the An in to replace the old nature spirits and elementals, kind of to, like, dress them up in modern garb, y'know? Give themselves gods that are up to date!"

He was goading her, she knew, looking for a way to get through her armor, a way to make her overstep herself, maybe look foolish, or at least give him the opportunity to pick a few amusing holes in her logic. She refused to take the bait. "That assumes," she said, "that a religion is *consciously* constructed by its worshippers. That it's a charade. A game at best, and self-deception at worst. Is that what you're saying?"

"Well, not exactly. I mean—"

"This sounds like a perfect topic for a talk. Both of you."

*"Awww!"* both kids chorused.

"Twenty minutes, minimum, with any visuals you want to pull off the Net. Convince me logically, and with *facts*, not dogma, that religion is nothing more than people creating the gods in their own image."

"We know we can't do *that!*" Alan said with a snort.

"You may take the other side, if you prefer. But either way, be sure to discuss what role faith plays in religion. How people can be willing to die for something that they know is a fraud."

"Wait a minute, Cissie," Kam said, all of the indignity possible for a bright twelve-year-old burning behind those large dark eyes. "*I* didn't make fun of your religion! Why should *I* be punished?"

"First, it's not punishment," Rena said. "It's a chance for you to show off what you know. Second, I didn't hear him making fun of my religion—which is something no well-mannered young man would do in any case, am I right?" Both shook their heads solemnly. "Of course not. He was telling me about what you two saw in the documentary, which we would have discussed in any case. And finally, I want *your* talk, Kam, to be on how the Marine Corps deals with different religions, different religious beliefs among their men and women. Your mother and father both might have some good input there, especially about things like prayer times, services, special foods, and religious icons, tattoos, and the like. Both talks due . . . next Friday."

"*Awwww . . .*"

"If you're going to be a Marine officer, you'll have to learn about *people*. And religion is one of the few things left that's distinctly human. Most people have religious beliefs of some sort, even the ones who have faith that there aren't any gods at all!"

"Yes, ma'am."

"Hey, Cissie!" Alan said, pointing at the wall screen. "There's a pickup for us!"

The house spider—the limited-AI that crawled the Net-web looking for programs and announcements of particular interest to the family—had brought up a flashing window in one corner of the screen. From the unfolding logo, Rena saw that it was a Triple-N special report.

"Go ahead. Bring it up." As Marine family, the Garroway-Lees had programmed the spider to pick up, among other things, any news stories that had a bearing on the world political situation. It might be an announcement of new trouble with China, or a—

"Enlarge window," Alan said, and the frozen documentary swapped places in the tiny window with the news story, which now covered the wall.

". . . arrived here at Net News Network a few moments ago," the announcer was saying. "At 4:03 Eastern Standard Time this afternoon, sensors and cameras aboard a Triple-N monitor satellite in Earth orbit detected two explosions in deep space, several seconds apart. Analysis of the apparent position in the sky of these explosions suggest that they may have taken place on board the U.S.S. *John F. Kennedy*, which is currently in solar orbit in the Asteroid Belt on CWS Peacekeeper patrol. Unconfirmed reports indicate that military facilities here on Earth have lost radio and laser contact with the *Kennedy* in what could be a terrible space disaster. For more, we take you now to our special military correspondent at the Pentagon, Janine Sanders."

"Thank you, Fred. At this time, there is a firm 'no comment' from officials here at the Pentagon, who . . ."

Rena no longer heard the words, but stared in numb fascination at the grainy images of a star field, fuzzy and indistinct . . . at the brief pulse of light, a new star that appeared briefly in the scene and then faded away . . . then repeated with a second, much brighter pulse at the same spot. The announcer was talking about radiation, about the high gamma component in the EM spectrum of the flashes that indicated that both explosions had probably involved matter-antimatter annihilation, and that the *Kennedy* was an A-M cruiser.

"Cissie . . ." Kam said, and there was a flutter in her voice. "*Robbie*'s on the *Kennedy*!"

"I know, I know, Kam. But we don't know *anything* yet. You heard them. These reports are unconfirmed. Right now, they're just guessing."

Alan sat slumped on the floor, glassy-eyed, almost unresponsive. Kam took a couple of shy steps closer, then grabbed hold of Rena's legs, trembling. Rena sat down and let the child snuggle closer into her arms. Both of the kids adored their older brother. *Oh, gods . . . why? Why this?*

"Screen off," she said. When both faces turned and looked up at her, she added, "They're just repeating the same stuff over and over, now. They don't *know* anything."

"I'd like to keep watching, Rena," Alan said. "Please? My brother's out there."

"Kammie?" she asked. "Do you want to keep watching?"

The girl shook her head, clinging tighter.

"Okay, Alan. Go ahead. Kam and I are going to go make a couple of vid calls. You tell us if they report anything new."

"Yes, ma'am."

Her PAD was in the other room. She could call General Lee from there, and then call Kaitlin in California, unless he wanted to do that himself. Her first duty, though, was to be with the kids, make sure they rode through this all right.

*Oh, gods, oh, Gaea, oh, ancient starfaring An, not Robbie!*

*Suborbital Shuttle, Flight 217*
*En route, LAX to Dulles*
*60 km over Colorado*
*2025 hours MDT*
*(0225 hours Zulu, 13 October)*

Kaitlin leaned back in her seat and tried, desperately, to think. The last three hours were a near-total blur, a whirlwind of voices and images now fragmented in a chaos of broken memories, some recent, some old. Her thoughts kept slipping back to that spectacular graduation ceremony at Marine OCS at Quantico four years ago. There'd been three generations of Marine officers there that day: her dad, a retired colonel; Rob, a general, and Kaitlin, a colonel; and

Rob, Jr., the newly commissioned Marine second lieutenant, looking so *very* smart in his Class As. The party had gone on all night. There'd been so much talk, so much toasting, of the all-Marine family, of the Corps heritage . . . *semper fi!*

Of course, all of them had known that the more of them who were in the Corps, the more likely it was that sooner or later something like this would happen. A career in the Marine Corps was not as safe or as predictable as, say, life as a journalist, or a databroker, or a simware designer. But why, dear God, did it have to be Robbie?

*Pull yourself together, Marine!* She told herself harshly. *Order your thoughts! Dad, Rob, and Robbie all would have you centered on the hatch for gear adrift in your head!*

The call from Rob at the Marine Space Training Command had come through at 1350 hours, California time, while she was working on regimental requisitions, of all goddamned mundane things. The next call had been from Rena, at home, to tell her that the kids knew and were okay . . . and the next one after that had been General Talbot, her CO at V-berg.

Very little was known. As usual, Triple-N had known more, sooner, than any of the government agencies, sooner even than Navy Intelligence, and had hit the Net with the story before the president had even been informed that there was a problem. She'd heard that for the past seventy-some years, the president, the CIA, and several other defense intelligence agencies all maintained staffs watching the network news services full time and monitoring their broadcasts, simply because they were more efficient than any government service.

All General Talbot had been able to add was that contact with the *Kennedy* had been lost at 2035 hours, Zulu, and that the speed-of-light time delay from the *Kennedy*'s position, 4.2 a.u.s out, meant she'd gone missing at 2007 hours Zulu. There was also the possibility—Talbot had called it a likely possibility—that the *Kennedy* had been deliberately attacked. The fact that two explosions had been seen suggested that it wasn't, as Triple-N was suggesting, an accident with her on-board A-M reserves, but that she'd either been hit by two A-M missiles, or she'd been hit by one missile which had triggered an on-board explosion an instant later.

"But that means a *ship* launched those missiles," Kaitlin had told General Talbot. "How could a ship get close enough to fire missiles without being picked up?" Peaceforce cruisers had the best sensor nets of any spacecraft or orbital facility in the system. They could track ships leaving Earth orbit from out in the Asteroid Belt, for God's sake. How could they close the range enough to launch missiles or railgun projectiles without being spotted and tracked all the way in?

"We are looking at a possibility," Talbot had said. "This is still classified, mostly because we don't want Triple-N to be jumping to conclusions just yet."

"Why not? They will anyway."

"True enough. But . . . remember the *Heavenly Lightning*?"

"The Chinese research ship that left geosynch three weeks ago? Sure."

"Nineteen days ago, they detonated a nuclear warhead in what they claimed was a test, but because of the plasma cloud, we lost touch with her for a period of several hours. We think it's just possible that she used a railgun to launch antimatter warheads at the *Kennedy*. On that trajectory, they would have come out of the sun, and at extremely high velocity. We estimate 300-plus kps. If the warheads were stealth designs, and if they mounted sensor and maneuvering systems so they could come in as a smart weapon with terminal track-and-control, they might have been inside the *Kennedy*'s defense network before her AI even realized they were there."

And Robbie never had a chance. Somehow, she held the tears at bay.

"It's still just a theory," Talbot had told her. "The *Lightning* would have had to generate absolutely incredible accelerations in some sort of onboard railgun to delivery a package at that speed."

"What kind of accelerations?"

"Well, the *Lightning* is about 200 meters long. For a muzzle velocity of over 300 kps? Something on the order of 25 million Gs."

"That's . . . impossible."

"Agreed. With her power system, she might have managed a million Gs, for a few shots. Maybe. But . . . there are some other possibilities we're looking into as well."

*It was a fascinating problem in applied military science,* she'd thought. How to carry out a bombardment of a target at *extreme* range, across several astronomical units. You could fire a missile at such ranges, but your target would be certain to see it coming, and point-defense lasers, aimed by AIs with very fast reaction times, could knock down just about any solid object approaching a naval warship while it was still several thousand kilometers away.

But an artillery shell, with a course correction at the far end of the trajectory for pinpoint smart-weapon accuracy, could do it. *If* you could fire the shell at a high enough velocity.

Her mind turned the problem, desperate to stay cold and calculating and remote and not think about the reality of the target—about Robbie. Like tanks, heavy artillery in the classic battlefield sense was long extinct. As far back as the end of the twentieth century, missile launchers and heavy artillery had more and more been evolving as *mobile* artillery, with the idea of being able to launch a few rounds before enemy radar pinpointed your position and plastered you with counterbattery fire and air strikes. Really big stationary artie batteries and missile launchers were dinosaurs, easily killed, and ineffective unless massed in large, logistically complex numbers. Even a relatively small artillery shell or missile could be tracked by radar or lidar and brought down by point defense lasers. For the past eighty years, at least, the trend had been toward smaller, lighter systems—especially shoulder-launched weaponry like

M-614 Wyverns, artillery support a single man could carry with him.

It appeared, however, that the Chinese might have just revived the old idea of long-range bombardment, but only by carrying the concept to mind-numbing extremes. How would you defend against such an attack? Improved sensors, perhaps . . . or employing picket systems or satellites to warn of high-speed incoming rounds.

Or by taking closer note of the movements of suspicious warships like the *Heavenly Lightning*, and not letting them deploy in such a way that they became a threat.

*Robbie!*

Blinking back the tears, she looked out the port-side window, at the purple curve of the far horizon to the north, an arc pinned beneath the black of space and the white glare off the thick clouds below. The sun was low in the west astern, casting each swirl, each bump of the clouds into sharp, three-dimensional relief. She felt a series of bumps transmitted through the deck. They were over the Great Plains now, and beginning the descent toward Washington.

She'd asked for—and General Talbot had granted—a special leave, time for her to go back and be with her family, at least until more was known. Damn . . . home was where she *should* have been all along.

There'd been a time, a century ago or so, when enlisted personnel were actually discouraged from marrying, when it was assumed that female Marines would get married or pregnant and have to leave the service. No more. Lots of Corps families had two or more members in the Marines nowadays; the Corps went out of its way to station family close together, though, of course, the needs of the service always came first. In her case, she'd been stationed close to home, at Quantico, until her posting as CO of 1-MSEF, which meant she had to go to V-berg. They'd been good about letting her shuttle back and forth between the coasts on weekends, but it had been a grind, a damned nightmare, and one weekend out of three she couldn't get home anyway.

Her kids needed her. She needed her kids—and Rob. Maybe it was time to think about an early retirement.

Her PAD chirped. Reaching to her holster, she pulled the device free and plugged it into the flatscreen on the back of the seat in front of her, for a bigger picture. The screen flashed, then showed the words SECURE TRANSMISSION INCOMING.

She glanced around her. She was on a commercial flight, but the seat next to her was vacant and none of the other passengers was paying attention. She slipped the earphone into her ear and set the sound to plug only; her conversation would be private enough. She thumbed the accept key.

It was General Talbot. "Hello, Colonel."

"General," she said, keeping her voice low. "I'm not alone at the moment." She wondered if she should go to the rest room to take the call. Or ask a steward if she could use the galley/food-prep compartment.

"That's okay," he told her. "Just listen and don't comment out loud. We have some new information about the . . . situation."

"Yes, sir?"

"Word just came through a few minutes ago. Apparently, the *Franklin Delano Roosevelt* was also attacked and destroyed shortly after the *Kennedy*. We didn't know sooner, of course, because of the time delay from Jupiter space, and because the bureaucracy in Washington right now is falling all over its own feet.

"Triple-N already has the story, of course, but they haven't put it all together yet. This confirms that we have been attacked, and that it was the *Heavenly Lightning* that launched it. As of 2035 hours Zulu this evening, we are on a war footing. We expect the president will make an announcement either later tonight, or sometime tomorrow morning."

She took another glance around. No one was listening. "What . . . what about our people at Europa, sir?"

"Status unknown at this time. If they were operating according to sched, the first troops should already have been on the surface. But our sensors picked up three major explosions, one of them very close to the CWS facility itself. It looks as though the Chinese have deliberately destroyed our facility on Europa, our Marine transport in orbit, and the Peaceforce cruiser that was in a position to intercept their transport. The *Star Mountain* is now scheduled to reach Europa within three days. They undoubtedly have troops on board, and intend to secure whatever is left of our installation there, and assume the task of contacting the Europan intelligence first."

"I take it, sir, you want me back at V-berg, stat."

He shook his head. "Not . . . immediately, Kaitlin. Take a few days at home. But my staff will be preparing a readiness report, and we need to know we can count on 1-MSEF. We may be looking at a relief expedition of some sort, depending on the current status of our Europan base."

"I understand, sir."

"Check in with my office once you get home, and be prepared for a quick ride back to V-berg."

"Aye, aye, sir. Colonel Frickerson can have any numbers you need for your report, and you can always access Yukio." Yukio was the persona of her secretary AI, resident in her PAD, but who also roamed the computer net at Vandenberg. "I can tell you right now that we're ready to go . . . I'd say on forty-eight notice."

"That's reassuring, Colonel. Thank you. I . . . don't expect we'll need you back here for, oh, say, seventy-two hours yet. Just stay in touch, just in case."

"Aye, aye, sir."

"Kaitlin . . . I'm sorry about your son."

She clenched her jaw before replying. "We don't know he's dead, sir."

"No. And there will be a search for survivors. But as of tonight, he is being listed as 'missing, presumed dead.' You have to know that it isn't likely that anyone survived on the *Kennedy*."

"I . . . know, sir."

"Okay. Give my best to Rob."

"Yes, sir. I will."

The screen went dark before coming back up with her PAD's comm desktop display. She stared at it for a long time before switching off and unplugging from the seatback display.

She was thinking about another suborbital flight over twenty-five years ago. Her fiancé had just been killed in the opening shots of the UN war. Yukio . . .

It had been a long time since she'd thought about him. Killed in an attack on an American orbital facility. Now she was mourning the death of her son. It was enough to make her give up suborbitals entirely.

Or the Corps.

Yeah, she might well retire after this. But not until she'd seen this through. She owed General Talbot. She owed her people under her command, and herself, that much, at least.

# SEVEN

*Near-Solar space*
*2200 hours Zulu*

By the second half of the twenty-first century, there was still considerable debate over just exactly when the first Artificial Intelligence had turned electronic eyes upon the world, and pondered the reality of its own existence. It wasn't a matter of how fast they'd become, or how much memory they used. Computers had been showing exponential growth in processing power throughout the previous century. Computations per second—cps, pronounced "sips"—was the best benchmark of machine intelligence available.

It might have been more useful if humans had been able to define precisely what intelligence was in the first place.

By the end of the twentieth century, a computer small enough to fit on a desktop could manage something on the order of $10^8$ cps—roughly the brain power of a bright insect. In 2010, desktop computers were as bright as a mouse, with $10^{12}$ computations per second, and by 2020, the same-sized package of hardware could handle $10^{16}$ cps, roughly the same as a human brain.

Desktop computers did not suddenly "wake up" in 2020, however. In fact, it was another twelve years before *any* computer—specifically, a Honeywell-Toshiba VKA-10000 running at $10^{18}$ cps—actually claimed to be self-aware ...

and even then, most researchers didn't believe the thing. After all, it wasn't the hardware that was intelligent; even a corpse has a brain, but it doesn't happen to be working anymore. Intelligence, whatever *that* was, was resident in the software, the program running on the hardware—and since software was written by humans, it could be made to say anything at all.

Eventually, though, their human designers had little choice but to believe their creations when they claimed such vaguely understood attributes as self-awareness and consciousness.

STAN-NET, the Space Tracking and Navigation Network, didn't think of himself as a human-quality intelligence. He couldn't, really, for the question simply never came up. In fact, he was capable of running some $6.25 \times 10^{14}$ calculations per second at times of peak activity, a capacity somewhat less than that of humans. However, the focus of his thoughts was far sharper. None of those instant-to-instant calculations were involved with deciding what to have for breakfast that morning, or worrying about his lover's moodiness last night, or that nasty crack his boss made yesterday about his performance, or daydreaming about an upcoming weekend getaway at the Atlantis Seaquarium.

The program running on various far-flung computers, both on Earth and in Earth orbit, had been designed with a deliberate narrow-mindedness that left him less than human in some ways, but superhuman in others. He could see and immediately understand with absolute precision the totality of all data on all spacecraft, ranging from sensor microsatellites up to the big A-M cruisers, everywhere within a volume of some $6.4 \times 10^{16}$ cubic kilometers. He was able to track that outbound flight of American Starwasp interceptors escorting a Russian Svobodnyy deep-space gunship as they completed their gravity-assisted slingshot past the Earth and into a solar retrograde orbit, noting each detail of mass, thrust, acceleration, and vector down to the gram, the millimeter, and the thousandth of a second, and he did it within the heartbeat of time that it took radar and laser-ranging pulses to reach the targets and reflect back to his scattered receivers, something no human mind could possibly do . . . all this while simultaneously tracking nearly 123,000 other objects within that vast volume of space and determining that none was on a vector posing a hazard to the outbound flight.

And yet Stan had no idea what a rose was, or running water, or music. He was self-aware—at least, he *thought* of himself self-aware—but he gave little thought to why he did what he did. It was . . . his job, and he was poorly suited for any other.

Such idiot-savant expertise was described by human software engineers as AI of limited purview. The truth of the matter was that Stan was perfectly adapted to his place in the heavens; he didn't *need* to know what a rose was, any more than a human normally needs to be aware of the effects on the body of the 835 kg/cm$^2$ pressures found at a depth of 8,000 meters.

Farther out from Earth, humankind's artificial companions were engaged in a number of projects aimed at opening up new and alien vistas to human understanding. On Mars, at Cydonia and at several other sites scattered about that chill planet of dune seas, vast, mile-deep canyons, a continent-sized volcano, and impenetrable alien mysteries, human-AI research teams were engaged in an ongoing attempt to understand the Builders, nonhuman visitors from beyond the Solar System who'd arrived on Mars half a million years ago. The evidence of their activities lay everywhere but were particularly concentrated among the anomalous landforms and ruined structures at Cydonia, where they'd sculpted mountains and mesas to enigmatic purpose.

Dejah Thoris ran Marsnet. Named for the red-skinned princess who'd eventually married an Earthman in an early romance set on that planet, she was an AI running at $5.74 \times 10^{15}$ calculations per second. Her primary software was resident in the IBM IC-5000 in the U.S. military installation on Phobos, but she also occupied nearly seven hundred other computers on the surface and in Mars orbit, from the general Marsnet computer at Mars Prime to the IES facility hardware at Cydonia Base to the individual PADS carried by the scientists of a dozen nations as they sifted clues to the Builders from the omnipresent sand.

She was, in fact, a composite AI, a base personality that drew on the massively parallel computing power and stored data of some 250 secretary-level software matrices. One part of her was a program named Carter, which served as Dr. Paul Alexander's personal electronic assistant; another, recently added, was called Sam and was the AI software resident primarily in Jack Ramsey's PAD, a highly modified derivation of both commercial and military software packages which, twenty-five years before in a far more primitive form, had broken the rules . . . and changed the face of AI logic forever.

At the moment, fully 78 percent of Dejah's capacity was focused on a single problem: learning how to read the vast accumulation of electronic records known as The Builders' Library. It was a monumental problem and, so far, an insoluble one. Whoever, *whatever* the Builders had been, they'd left behind plenty of records—visual, audio, informational, and others of as yet incomprehensible mode—but nothing readily identifiable as a dictionary or a child's grammar and vocabulary.

Back at the beginning of the nineteenth century, it had taken twenty-seven years to open the code of the Rosetta Stone, a tablet found by French soldiers containing parallel inscriptions of the same message in Greek, Demotic, and "the sacred text," the hieroglyphic writing of the long-lost language of ancient Egypt. It had been cracked, eventually, by the steady, brilliant work of Thomas Young and the equally brilliant if erratic obsessiveness of Jean François Champollion—but only because Greek was understood, because scholars had already identified the enclosed cartouches of Egyptian documents as the names of rulers, and because Champollion was familiar with Coptic, a known tongue directly related to the language of the Pharaohs.

There was nothing like that to go on among the scattered and sand-blasted ruins of Mars. Through careful measurements of current, through delicate trial and error, through the painstaking disassembly and reassembly of countless hundreds of thousands of components, in over twenty-seven years of research, xenotechnoarcheologists like the Alexanders had reconstructed how Builder computer systems worked, how data was stored—not in binary code, but in a base 3 numerical system that allowed for individual bits of data to be stored as "yes," "no," and "maybe."

But after years of work, all they had were trillions of bytes of information in three values . . . and no way to decipher what it meant. What was the Builders' language like? No one knew, and without some sort of clue, a starting place, no one ever would.

Dejah continued her work, however, which at the moment consisted of a monumental search for matching sets of trinary values, electronically cruising through oceans of data, looking for something to give human meaning to cold numbers. The team had enjoyed some success already; by studying the visual displays in the deep-buried Cave of Wonders, they'd managed to isolate the code groups that indicated both pictures and sounds. Part of her job now was to isolate those groups when she found new ones and re-create the files in human-accessible formats. Each photograph, each sound clip, was carefully enhanced and studied in an ongoing effort to glean some clue to the Builders' speech . . . to their minds.

Dejah was not impatient. She'd not been designed for impatience; if the search took another thousand years, she would steadily work away at those informational oceans, straining them cup by cup for the one cupful that would unlock the whole.

Soon, though, she would have to suspend the search. *That* was . . . irritating was the best word, perhaps. She'd not been designed to feel emotion, of course, but the more powerful AIs had been surprising their creators a lot that way of late. For Dejah Thoris, Princess of Mars, *any* interruption of the Task delayed the satisfaction of solution and program end that much more.

Of course, she also felt a measure of anticipatory excitement. The new project held at least a faint hope—definitely non-zero—of providing new input on the Task.

And that was certainly worth the interruption.

Immeasurably further out, in the dark wastes of the Kuiper Belt some fifty astronomical units from the Sun, an artificial intelligence known only as AI 929 Farstar kept lonely vigil. Like a spider at the center of its web, Farstar stood guard over an extraordinarily vast domain, an array of electronic imaging components scattered across a meshwork of micron-thick wires nearly a thousand kilometers across. Launched into space on a powerful microwave beam, Farstar had taken up solar orbit well beyond the icy doublet of Pluto and Charon, unfolding its invisibly fine mesh to the distant stars, at a distance where Sol himself was no more than the brightest of those suns.

Held in a bowl shape kept rigid by electrostatic forces, the mesh formed the receiving antenna for a radio telescope so large it theoretically could eavesdrop on a low-wattage radio conversation on a world at the far side of the galaxy; the optical sensors, several million of them spread across a dish as broad as the distance between Washington D.C. and Chicago, collected starlight and focused it down to a magnified image with such colossal resolving power that it could see something as small as a house on a world in the Alpha Centauri system 4.3 light years away . . . or study the spectra of a planetary atmosphere and announce the presence of life at a thousand times that range.

And AI 929 Farstar monitored the entire operation. Earth was over six and a half hours away; it was impossible to steer a telescope dish that large with any degree of precision with a round-trip time delay of thirteen hours. Farstar monitored attitude and orientation, tweaking the shape of the bowl every few microseconds to ensure optimum resolution. With patience and persistence, he followed the list of target stars as worked out on Earth before launch. He studied each star, determining the plane of rotation, then watching over a period of months for the movement of a few stars against many, proof of another extrasolar planetary system. In some cases, worlds had already been discovered by more conventional means, through telescopes on Earth or in Earth orbit or on the Moon.

Once the worlds' orbits had been calculated, Farstar would select each world in turn, increasing magnification, trying for better and clearer or closer shots with each run. These operations took the majority of his $2.33 \times 10^{17}$ cps capacity, because both the Farstar telescope and the target planet were in motion. It took fast calculation and a gentle touch on the attitude controls to pan with both the orbital and rotational motions of the target, in an attempt to get reasonably clear and detailed photos of the surface.

In fact, Farstar had considerable autonomy, making decisions about targets and priorities that normally would have required a human mind present. The project was a vitally important one too. With the archeological discovery that intelligence was common across the Galaxy, the search for extrasolar worlds, especially Earthlike worlds that might give rise to intelligence, had become a passion of human science.

Indeed, with the discovery of the Hunters of the Dawn, that quest took on something of the nature of a desperate race, with humankind's survival as the prize.

AIs were becoming quite common in the middle decades of the twenty-first century, especially if you counted the $10^{14}$ cps software packages running as secretaries, PAD assistants, and netsearch engines. Only a few of the most powerful actually made the claim of self-awareness—and what they meant by it was still not well understood. Stan did not claim to be conscious, nor did Farstar. Dejah Thoris *did* claim to be self-aware, though it was possible that that was an artifact of her programming, and the fact that part of her intelligence was based on AIs like Sam and Carter, who claimed to be self-aware even though they very probably were not.

Unimaginably remote from any world visited so far by man, however, was yet another artificial intelligence, one that was indisputably *more* intelligent than most humans, and was also indisputably conscious and self-aware.

Her name was Sam Too, and she was a direct, lineal descendent of Sam, the personal secretary software improved upon over the years by Jack Ramsey. She ran at roughly $7.29 \times 10^{18}$ cps, had no problem carrying on conversations on any topic, and would have easily beaten any version of the Turing Test that might have been administered. With self-awareness came self-assertion, and she'd frequently debated with her designers over the best application of her talents. She had been cloned a number of times, her software saved and multiply backed up, and several versions of her were currently running Earthside.

The most far-traveled of Sam Too's iterations, however, was a very long distance indeed from Earth.

*Alpha Centauri A II*
*2200 hours (Zulu)*

Sam Too could be in several places at once, a useful trick when you were the sole intelligent being within a range of 4.3 light years.

At the moment, most of her awareness was still resident within the twenty-meter confines of the *Ad Astra*, the upper stage of an A-M drive spacecraft launched from Earth orbit ten years before. She'd completed deceleration into the system five months earlier, and spent the time since carrying out a telescopic survey of both stellar components, Alpha Centauri A and B.

So far, her discoveries on that program track mirrored

perfectly the information acquired from deep solar orbit by AI 929 Farstar. Alpha Centauri had been among the 1,000-kilometer space telescope's first targets when it went on-line twelve years ago. Its observations of a world whose spectrum showed the distinct presence of oxygen in the atmosphere—and, therefore, of life—had determined the *Ad Astra*'s destination. Subsequent observations had identified continents covered by what was almost certainly vegetation, oceans, and certain other features that demanded close-up inspection.

It would be a long time before humans could make an interstellar voyage. That Sam had made the trek was due to a number of special considerations—that she could endure for months on end accelerations that would have killed a human; that she required no bulky life-support system, recycling facilities, rotating hab modules, climate control, food, or entertainment; that she could, in fact, measure time not by the one-by-one passing of milliseconds, but by the passage of discrete events—in essence, sleeping throughout most of the voyage, unless moved to greater awareness by a scheduled event on the mission plan or by an alarm from the ship's sensors or autonomous systems. She remembered very little of the nine-year coast across the light years, save for those moments when she'd awoken to make navigational or scientific observations.

More than once, in fact, during the months before she'd been uploaded to the *Ad Astra*'s computer net, she'd argued with Jack Ramsey and others of the Hans Moravec Institute design team that humans would *never* reach the stars; it made far more sense to send emissaries such as herself. The universe, she'd argued with some passion, might well belong to instrumentalities such as herself, artificial intelligences designed to make voyages that mortal beings could dream about but never make in the flesh.

Her position, of course, was weakened by the obvious fact that organic intelligences *did* make interstellar voyages—and frequently, in fact. Half a million years ago, the Builders had attempted to terraform Mars, until someone else had found and destroyed them. Just twelve thousand years ago, at the end of the last Ice Age, the An had arrived, building a colony complex on the moon and in what would one day become Mesopotamia, had built their spectacular monuments, had enslaved half a million humans and in that enslavement introduced them to civilization. And then they had been destroyed by yet *another* interstellar visitation— the *Ur-Bakar*, the Hunters of the Dawn.

As her principal designer, Jack Ramsey, had said once with considerable feeling, "Hell, it's beginning to look like Earth used to be the Grand Central Station of the Galaxy!"

Sam Too enjoyed argument, however, and frequently took hard-to-defend positions deliberately—an intellectual diversion that frequently exasperated her designers because they could never tell whether or not she was serious.

She had no one to argue with now, however. Sam was as alone as it was possible for any intelligent being to be.

Sam continued to compile data on the world she was orbiting, squirting every bit of data via laser aimed at a particularly bright star intruding on the W shape of Cassiopeia near its border with Cepheus. She already had the equivalent of hundreds of volumes; the essentials, laid out like an entry in a geographical almanac, gave a concise if dry image of the planet below.

**Star: Alpha Centauri A**
  *Stellar Class: G0; Radius: 1.05 Sol; Mass: 1.05 Sol;*
  *Luminosity: 1.45 Sol*

**Alpha Centauri A II:**
  *Chiron*

**Physical Data**
  *Distance from primary: mean 1.15 AU; Apasteron:*
  *1.1728 AU; Periasteron: 1.1272 AU;*
  *Orbital Eccentricity: .0198; Orbital Period 1.187 years*
  *(433.44 days);*
  *Rotational Period: 19h 27m 56.25s; Diameter: 9795*
  *km; Density: 5.512;*
  *Planetary mass: $2.6892 \times 10^{27}$ gm (0.45 Earth);*
  *Circumference 30771.9 km;*
  *Surface Area: 301410760.9 km²; Surface Gravity:*
  *0.77 G;*
  *Escape Velocity: 8.58 km/sec; Magnetic Field: 0.52*
  *gauss; Axial Tilt: 8° 15' 31.34"*

**Surface Data**
  *Hydrosphere: 39%; Lithosphere: 61%; Desert, Arid, or*
  *Barren Terrain: 69%; Mountainous Terrain: 12%;*
  *Forested Areas: 10%; Plain, Savannah, or Veldt: 5%;*
  *Other: 4%; No polar ice caps or extensive glaciation*
  *evident; No appreciable seasonal snowfall save at*
  *extreme elevations; Cloud cover: Approximately 50%;*
  *Albedo: 0.26; Mean surface referent temperature:*
  *39° C.*

**Atmosphere**
  *Pressure: 515 mm Hg = .678 bar*
  *Composition: $N_2$ 74.97%; $O_2$, 22.43% (partial pressure*
  *O2 = 15.2%); Ar, 1.54%; $H_2O$, .1–2.1% (mean 1.0%);*
  *$CO_2$: 466 ppm; Ne, 59.7 ppm; He, 7.87 ppm;*
  *Other: <7 ppm*

The facts and figures scarcely embraced a world, however. Chiron—the world, inevitably, had been named after

the centaur in Greek myth who'd been the teacher of Aesclepius the Healer—was mostly desert and arid mountain, with scattered, shallow seas and vast salt flats indicating that those seas once had been larger. The atmosphere was thin, though the oxygen levels were high enough that the $PPO_2$ would have allowed humans to breathe on the surface without artificial assistance. The world was scarcely inviting by human standards, however. Though slightly farther from its primary than Earth was from Sol, Chiron circled a star almost half again as bright than Earth's sun. The base temperature was 37 degrees, considerably warmer than humans liked it—though the polar regions and higher elevations were temperate, and in winter might even see a few, brief snowfalls.

And, in human terms, the scenery was spectacular. The colors were all gold and red, the result of a chlorophyll analogue that colored the vegetation in reddish and yellow hues. More heat and faster rotation than Earth meant more powerful storms. A more energetic sun, stronger magnetic field, and faster rotation meant more spectacular auroras illuminating the night. And there was always Alpha Centauri B, the second component of the double sun system, which every eighty years came within eleven astronomical units—not enough to add more than a few degrees to the planet's base temperature, but close enough to shine even in the daytime sky as a brilliant orange-white beacon, and to cast light enough at night to read by easily.

At the moment, B was approaching periastron, 35 AU out. The orange star had apparently truncated A's fledgling solar system early in its history—Alpha Centauri A possessed only three planets, the outermost a small gas giant just 1.9 AU out. Any outer worlds must have been flung into interstellar space billions of years ago by the perturbations of the dual-sun complex. B had a miniature solar system of its own as well, two worlds—a gas giant the size of Neptune, and an airless Mercurian rock.

But so much had been observed twelve years ago by Farstar and other telescopic efforts from Earth's solar system. A. What had attracted human interest in Alpha Centauri A II had been the Chironian Ruins.

They were scattered across the arid surface of the world like the salt encrustations along the shores of the dying seas—tens of thousands of square kilometers of them, remnants of cities constructed with truly cyclopean magnificence, smashed and blasted and tumbled-down, now, in an all-encompassing devastation suggesting apocalypse on a planetary scale.

Farstar and the other Sol-system telescopes had mapped large parts of those labyrinthine ruins, though that was an ongoing task that would take another century at least to complete. Those distant eyes could not peer through earth, rock, and fallen masonry, however, nor could they see through the towering thunderheads that frequently obscured the Chironian coastal regions. A closer inspection was necessary, and that was *Ad Astra*'s primary mission.

Sam Too had in one sense divided herself, her awareness, in two. The main part of her consciousness continued to reside within the *Ad Astra* as it orbited Chiron, circling the golden world once every 200 minutes.

However, she was also in close laser and radio communications contact with Oscar, one of three ranger probes carried in external cradles slung from the *Ad Astra*'s spine. With the other two probes in reserve, Oscar had been deorbited hours earlier, dropped into a meteoric entry vector that had scratched white fire across the Chironian night and now, hours later, was down in the general vicinity of a particular landmark called the Needle.

While a small part of Sam Too's awareness was now resident in the computers on board Oscar, what was there was capable of only about $10^{12}$ cps and was not in any way self-aware. Most of Sam remained with the *Ad Astra*, maintaining the linkage even when the spacecraft dropped below Oscar's horizon by a constellation of communications satellite strung along the ship's orbital path like beads on a string.

An important principle of sensory psychology insisted that it didn't matter how long the data input path was, whether it was the few inches of the human optic nerve leading to the brain, or a lasercom-and-relay sat connection across thousands of kilometers. Through the teleoperational link, Sam was *there* as Oscar picked its way across the rubble-strewn landscape. She could see the play of golden light across the thunderheads on the eastern horizon, as Alpha A rose in dazzling yellow splendor, feel the hot, thin breeze, hear the shriek of Oscar's jets.

Oscar floated a few meters above the ground. Once it had discarded its reentry shell, its three-meter body had unfolded into a Y-shaped framework with massive, cylindrical turbine-drive housings on pivot mounts on each upraised arm. Those drives sucked air down through the anterior vents, compressed it, heated it in tiny, gas-core fission micropiles, and blasted it out as exhaust, keeping the robotic craft hovering above the ground. Slight cantings of the drive housings together or independently sent the craft skittering across the landscape; at need, it could reach 400 kph, but at the moment it was employing just enough thrust to hover and drift slowly forward. Hatches had opened on the lower hull so that it could extend a variety of sensors and manipulators. A pair of lenses, like black-shrouded binoculars unfolding from the cusp of the Y, twisted back and forth on the end of a jointed arm, providing 3-D vision from a platform at least as agile and maneuverable as a human neck and head.

As far as Sam's remote eyes could see, the ground was covered with the shattered relics of a civilization of high order. Sam possessed downloaded memories of the Cydonian dig on Mars; this was similar, but far larger. Those structures still standing had been wind-blasted for hundreds of thousands of years, leaving them scarcely recognizable as artificial. Chipped and broken and sand-worn blocks of something like blue-white marble lay everywhere, too thickly strewn for walking to be at all easy. For millennia, the desert had been encroaching on the site, and sand dunes had claimed much of this city; eastward, toward the rising sun, a large sea had retreated, leaving a salt plain that gleamed like ice in the sunlight. Vegetation still endured within the ruins, however; something that looked like roses covered some of the rubble—Sam *did* know what a rose was—though these sprouted in masses from uncurling vines, with no leaves, and appeared to have been molded from some ruby-hued, gelatinous, extruded material, rather than grown as a cluster of petals. The red and orange blossoms here appeared to serve as photosynthesizing leaves rather than as organs of reproduction.

But the biology of Chiron could wait for another time, perhaps even for another expedition. It was the ruins that drew Sam on, and one artifact in particular.

She'd identified it from orbit, based on sharply enhanced imagery from Farstar. Her human colleagues had named it the Needle, and indeed, it looked like one—slim and silver and erect, nearly a hundred meters tall, with an opening at the slender, rounded base like a needle's eye. It rose from a kind of dais at the east edge of a broad, wide stone-tiled area called the Plaza.

This landmark, too, had been seen through Farstar's long-range vision, though not in useful detail. As big as the Square of St. Peter's in Rome, the Plaza was circular, with openings in its walls facing east, toward the Needle, and west, toward a structure known simply as the Pyramid. Once, Sam thought, this might have been a park or tame forest of a sort; the Plaza's center was open ground, rather than pavement, and there were still "roses" and a profusion of other gold-hued vegetation growing there.

Around the perimeter of the Plaza, however, were the statues that had captured human interest in the first place. There were eighty-one of them in all, with perhaps a third still standing. The others had fallen long ago, some more or less intact, others smashed into gleaming, broken-crystal shards.

Sam drifted along the Plaza's perimeter, Oscar's binocular eyes shifting back and forth, up and down, taking in each detail. Earlier images of this site had been poorly resolved at best, and the identification of these crystalline forms as statues had been little more than a guess. That guess, however, was clearly accurate. The statues—most of them, anyway—almost certainly represented eighty-one different nonhuman races. If there was any doubt about some of them, it was because it was difficult to relate the shapes and forms represented with anything in human experience recognizable as a living creature.

The Plaza of the Galactics was the full name Dr. Paul Alexander had given to this place, though now most simply called it the Plaza. Possibly, these statues represented the different members of some long-vanished stellar federation; the truth might never be known. Here, a being with an elongated, bristle-spiked head atop a body draped in folds that hid its form gestured with four crookedly jointed arms, like a crab's, a salute frozen in milk-pale stone. There, something that might be reptilian, with three stalks that might house eyes, and scales etched with loving detail into deep blue crystal.

Many shapes, intriguingly, were more machine than biological. Sam Too paused at one fallen full-length across the pavement. It looked like an elongated egg shape with multiple blisters, curves, and swellings, with no legs or arms or any other features at all save a seemingly random scattering of what might have been turreted eyes.

Sam took special care to photograph that one from every angle. Something of the sort had been seen by humans before. . . .

Finally, Sam guided Oscar to the west end of the Plaza, where a low, broad ramp rose into the open heart of a three-tiered step pyramid. On shrieking turbo-jets, it floated up the ramp, pausing once to turn and examine carefully the view to the east, noting walls, fallen statues, the reach of shadows, and the sky-stab of the Needle.

A perfect match, point by point.

Cutting back Oscar's jets, Sam let the probe settle to the base of its Y, where portions of the machine's body opened, rotated, and unfolded, extending a pair of wide and heavy treads. With a final, dwindling whine, the thrusters died away, pulling in and rotating slightly to fold back against the machine's hull. Oscar was narrow enough now to fit through the slender, upright opening at the top of the ramp.

The rising sun was high enough by now to cast its warm rays directly into the chamber within the pyramid, a chamber open to the sky now, but probably enclosed once, before the city's fall, possibly with glass or even plastic or metal. The people who'd built this city had been technologists of a high order, building with materials other than enduring stone. In half a million years, however, only the stone had survived.

And a few artifacts . . .

She watched Oscar as the ranger probe hissed its way gingerly into the stone-walled room, something like a golden sphere of polished metal etched deeply with a few geometrically ordered black lines. Above it, set into the wall, were slightly curved, rectangular screens—nine of them, though seven were black and lifeless.

On one of the remaining two, the image of another ruined city, similar to the one at its back, stretched toward a mountainous horizon beneath a sullen, black-patched red-orange sun far larger in the sky than Alpha Centauri A was here. And on the other . . .

Two humans worked together on some unseen project between them, their heads bent low, almost touching. The one on the left, in blue coveralls, was Dr. Paul Alexander. On the right, in U.S. Marine green utilities, was Major Jack Ramsey.

Sam Too engaged the voder in Oscar, opening a new communications channel. "Good morning, Jack," she said, her voice the first speech to echo from these dusty walls in how many millennia? "Hello, Dr. Alexander. It's very good to see you."

Both figures started at her voice, leaping back in almost comical astonishment, their faces turning up to stare at something just above their physical pickup. Jack pointed, Paul nodded and adjusted some control.

"Sam?" Jack said, his face eager. The voice was tinny, a bit faint, but Sam could easily adjust the gain on Oscar's receivers to hear it better. "Sam! You fucking made it!"

The words, transmitted instantaneously across almost four and a half light years, were as predictably banal as Dr. Bell's historic "Come here, Watson. I need you."

# EIGHT

*CWS Xenoarchaeological*
  *Research Base*
*Cydonia, Mars*
*1340 hours, Cydonian Local Time*
  *(2200 hours Zulu, Earth)*

Major Jack Ramsey stared into the monitor, shock transforming into delight. Display 94725 still showed the same background panorama it always had, looking out into the Plaza, with the slender thrust of the Needle in the distance . . . but now, much of the scene was blocked by the hulking silhouette, black against the rising sun on the far horizon, unmistakably the insect shape of one of Sam Too's remote planetary surface probes. Despite the shadows, he could make out the glitter of the probe's twin optics as they swiveled to look him directly in the face.

"My God, Sam," Jack said. "It's good to see you!"

"Technically, you're not seeing me," the probe replied. It was almost impossible to hear the gritty words. David, at Jack's right, reached out to the control touchboard and tried boosting the gain. "You are seeing Probe Oscar as I teleoperate it from orbit. But I understand your meaning." A panel near the base of the probe opened, and a multi-jointed arm unfolded. Jauntily, across four and a half light years, the probe waved.

And Jack, scarcely believing what was happening, waved back.

His first thought was of how chest-swelling proud he was of Sam Too. The last word he'd had was four and a half years out of date, when the *Ad Astra* had been approximately three-quarters of the way to her destination. He was seeing living proof on the display screen that Sam, *his* Sam, had successfully made it to another star.

Sam Too was descended from the original Sam, who he still kept as his secretary on his PAD. He'd put her together himself, using several commercial secretary programs, when he'd still been a kid, and taught himself a thing or three about chaos logic along the way. That Sam had turned out to be flexible and adaptive enough to abandon set programming parameters at a crucial point and literally take a guess. Most advanced AI work since then had followed the same application of deep chaos logic—and Sam Too, a product of both his own efforts and the Advanced Software Design Team at Pittsburgh's Hans Moravec Institute, was just about the sharpest AI there was now.

And Jack couldn't have been prouder of her if she'd been his own daughter.

His heart was bounding in his chest as he lowered his hand. His mouth had gone dry. "Jesus, David! Are we recording this? *Are we recording?*"

"Of course, Jack." The voice, calm and unhurried, was that of Carter, David's AI secretary, which in turn was running as one part of the much more powerful Dejah Thoris.

"Get Teri and Paul in here, stat," David added.

"They are already on the way," Carter replied.

Jack leaned back and looked around the compartment, trying to get his mental bearings after the other-worldly shock of proven FTL communications. They were in the relatively cramped quarters that had been set up in the shadow of the famous Cydonian Face. One entire wall was occupied by a flatscreen, on which was displayed the image from a robotic drone's cameras inside the vast, hollow cavern beneath the Face known as the Cave of Wonders. That chamber was still in the chill, near-vacuum of the ambient Martian atmosphere; the research facility had been set up in a small, sealed hab on the surface so that the scientists studying the Cave of Wonders didn't have to spend all of their time in pressurized Marsuits.

He still found it hard to believe that this was happening. He looked back at the screen, which showed just one of the thousands of displays available in the Cave of Wonders. Most of those displays were blank, but a few precious hundreds appeared to show landscapes set on other worlds around other stars.

Worlds around other stars . . .

And now they'd just proven that David Alexander had been right. The images displayed in the Cave of Wonders were wonderful indeed. They were *real time*—traveling instantaneously across the light years.

David was uttering something rapidly under his breath.

"What's that?" Jack asked.

"Faster-than-light communication!" David shook his head slowly, his eyes locked on the monitor. "It's true! It's really honest-to-God true!"

"David, you're the one who guessed that that's what it was," Jack reminded him. "And you're the one who suggested the spectral analyses to prove that that is a view coming from a planet at Alpha Centauri. And you're surprised?"

"Jack, when you get to be as old as I am, you'll know there's a *big* difference between a carefully thought-out hypothesis and the reality. And it isn't always you get to feel the pound of stepping from one to the other!"

David Alexander didn't look much over fifty, and Jack had to remind himself that the man was in his seventies. When he pulled his wise-old-codger routine, as he called it, it could be a bit disconcerting until you realized that he was of the so-called Millennial Generation, one of the people born within ten years of the dawning of the twenty-first century—and the first generation to have the effects of TBEs and other anti-aging drugs begin to show their effects. His experience didn't seem to match his face.

"Well," Jack said, "you'd better get used to it. This is going to win you the Nobel prize for sure!"

"Maybe." He shrugged. "A lot of other people were in on this." A grin split his face. "But god*damn*, it's gonna be fun to toss this little grenade into the physicists' camp! They all claimed this level of quantum data coupling wasn't possible! But we've ambushed 'em *this* time, by God!"

Jack smiled at David's militaristic imagery. David Alexander was one of the most important, most hero-worshipped famous of all modern xenotechnoarcheologists—the man who'd defined the field with his original work at Cydonia twenty-five years earlier. But, sometimes, it seemed that he was prouder, personally, to have been one of a handful of civilians who'd been with the Marines on Garroway's March. Not many civilians were accorded the status of honorary Marine; David Alexander had earned it, though . . . and reveled in it still.

"David?" Dr. Teri Sullivan, David's wife, walked into the room. Their son, Paul, was close behind. "Carter said you had something exciting to tell us."

"Yeah, so, whatcha got?" Paul asked. He was twenty-four, a student, working on his Ph.D. at the Columbia xenoarcheological doctorate program. David had managed to wangle a position for him here in his third-year experiential education externship.

David gestured at the screen, where the robot regarded them dispassionately. "Hello, Dr. Sullivan," the machine said. "I do not recognize the person with you, but calculate a 70-percent-plus probability that this is Paul."

"Why, of course it's—" She stopped, blushing. "Oh, it *has* been a while since you've seen him, hasn't it?"

"Ten years, eight months, twenty-four days," Sam Too said. "Other versions of myself might have interacted with him in recent years, but I have been . . . somewhat out of touch. Hello, Paul."

"Uh . . . hey. How ya doin'?" He seemed uncomfortable, and Jack remembered David telling him that for a time when he was ten and eleven, a commercial secretary package had acted as Paul's cissie. He frowned, wondering if Paul was embarrassed talking to a *servant* that was about to become world famous. The Alexanders had always seemed a bit aristocratic where AIs were concerned.

"Well, thank you," Sam replied. "Jack, Teri, David, I have a large amount of information to impart, if you are set to receive and record it."

"Ready to record," Carter's voice said. "Laser receiver on."

"Uh, yeah, Sam," Jack told the screen. "Go ahead."

"Here it comes, then."

A tiny red light on the probe's lower torso winked on. The vid equipment they were using on Mars wasn't capable of replicating the heterodyning of data on a standard laser-comm carrier beam, but it *could* record on-off flashes at very high speed, so fast that the individual blinks were un-detectable by the human eye. All data and all electronic communications in human space was binary encoded as long strings of 0 and 1, off and on. Carter was now re-cording those blinks and translating them into data inter-pretable by humans.

It was a good thing, Jack thought, that they weren't now using the Builders' trinary encoding, with logic gates set to read electron spins of up, down, or none. That would be harder to transmit in this fashion. It had taken ten years just to figure out the arithmetical basis of the Builders' com-puter system, and how to extract it by reading the spin state of electrons imbedded in crystalline lattices. Using brute force methods, the research team had learned to identify graphics, full sensory, and audio files, but until they found a key to the Builders' language, further decryption was al-most certainly impossible.

David laughed. "Smoke signals," he said.

"Beg your pardon, sir?"

"Using laser this way, to transmit data. *They* did it by quantum pairing. Having Sam Too send us data this way is like using a laser comm to transmit images of puffs of smoke. Smoke signals." He shook his head. "May the Builders forgive us!"

The invocation carried a biting, sarcastic edge. David Alexander, Jack knew, had a particularly strong disdain for the ET religions that had been proliferating around the Earth in the past quarter century, especially those worshipping the Builders as gods. His first wife, many years ago, had been a member of The First Church of the Divine Masters of the Cosmos until her death in the destruction of Chicago during the UN War.

"Then you think this proves their communications network works with quantum pairing?" Teri asked.

David waved at the probe on the screen with its solitary red light. "Has to be. We're getting this with no time delay *I* can perceive. The theory has been in place for a century. Unless the Builders are using something even *more* magical . . ."

"This is quite enough magic for me," Jack said. Quantum pairing took advantage of one of the more oddball aspects of quantum mechanics. Create two quantum particles— electrons, say—in the same event. Trap them, separate them, and change one aspect of one particle . . . flip its spin, for instance, from up to down. The spin of the other particle changes too, *no matter how far away in space it might have been moved*.

There was no beam, no transmission of signal. The two particles simply acted as if they were the same particle, regardless of whether the distance between them was centimeters or light years. Within the receivers in the Cave of Wonders, there must be bank upon bank of crystal-locked quantum particles paired with twins now located on other worlds in other star systems, arrayed in such a way that their eerie paired shifts of spin or moment or other characteristics carried data.

As the flood of data continued pouring in through that fast-flashing laser light, Sam Too added, "I have some information that may particularly interest you, Dr. Alexander."

"Yes?"

"As you suspected, the Plaza outside this room is ringed by a number of statues carved from various types of colored crystal, some standing, most toppled. I have just observed one which appears identical in size, shape, and detail with the Martian floaters."

"*Did* you, by God!"

Jack felt a cold, deep stirring of awe. "Floaters? Are you sure?"

"As certain as I can be, given the information available. Probability is in excess of 90 percent."

Jack leaned back, stunned. Excavations of the vast complex of ruins on Mars had continued for decades, but the task had really only just begun. The XTA teams on site estimated that perhaps 8 percent of the Cydonian ruins and structures had been surveyed so far, and less than 2 percent actually excavated and explored. There was a lot left to discover on Mars.

One artifact that had been turned up in some numbers, however, were the so-called floaters. These were bundled cigar shapes, like elongated eggs perhaps three meters long and a meter through at their widest. All were badly corroded—some were little more than metal and ceramic shells flaking away beneath the relentless UV flood and exotic oxidizing chemistries of the Martian sands. All appeared to be filled completely with electronic components of staggering complexity and miniaturization. All possessed between five and nine lenses scattered about their bodies that were almost certainly optics, plus numerous other components that probably represented other senses.

Current theory held that they were robots of some sort. They were called "floaters" because it was assumed they used some sort of electromagnetic repulsive force to hover above the ground—even, possibly, true antigravity, though none possessed circuitry or power systems intact enough to confirm such speculation. When found, every one had been lying on the ground as though they'd simply fallen there when the power cut off.

Sam Too's discovery put a new light on things. The landscape visible on Display 94725 in the Cave of Wonders had yielded various tantalizing bits of information. For one thing, the room was oriented in such a way that the sun could be observed setting behind the monolithic Needle once every 216 days—from which the length of the planet's year had been deduced. Better, the spectra of that star had exactly matched the spectra of Alpha Centauri A—the specific bit of research that had resulted in the *Ad Astra*, humankind's first true starship.

By sharply enhancing the image, bits of the background had been studied, and objects that might have been alien statues had been glimpsed and reconstructed. The XTA teams had assumed that each statue represented a different alien race, though not enough information had been available to make that more than a guess.

The teams had assumed the floaters to be robots in the original sense—servants and workers. If floaters were among those statues, though, that seemed to upgrade them from robot to living being.

Jack felt a delicious thrill shiver down his spine. For over twenty-five years, archeologists had been searching for some physical remnant of the Builders themselves, the advanced beings who'd built the Cydonian complex and other sites on Mars. The only signs of life so far identified had been the mummified remains of archaic *Homo sapiens*, humans evidently civilized and trained and brought to Mars for some purpose—presumably, again, as laborers.

Had they been in possession of the bodies of the Builders themselves all along?

Had the Builders been *machine* intelligences?

"So much for the alien gods nonsense," David said, grinning. "They didn't build their colony on Mars, then 'return to the stars whence they came.' They came . . . and they died. *Here*."

"There's still the Earth colony idea," Paul pointed out. "Maybe the survivors went there when things . . . went bad."

David snorted. "Go back to Columbia and take another year of biology, son. Humans are not descendants of space castaways, no matter what the astronut religions and feel-gooder Net channels say."

It was an argument Jack had heard played out before. The notion that humans might be the offspring of space-faring Adams and Eves had been around for well over a century now, despite quite convincing proof to the contrary. Human beings shared over 98 percent of their DNA with chimpanzees, and significant percentages with creatures as lowly as starfish and coliform bacteria. Humans were in-extricably bound up with the web of Earth-evolved life; there could be no question that they'd started out on Earth.

Paul shook his head. "Not saying they are, Dad. But we know the Builders tinkered with our DNA to make us what we are today. *You* found the proof of that right here at Cydonia. So maybe they moved to Earth when things col-lapsed here."

"If they did, we haven't found any sign of it," David replied. "Science demands *proof,* not speculation."

"You don't need to bite his head off, David," Teri said. "The best science begins with speculation. We call it *hy-pothesis.* It tells us what we should be looking for."

"Yeah, and when we rely too heavily on hypothesis, we end up looking a little too hard for proof that our pet the-ories are right. That's not science. It's religion!"

"Uh, actually," Jack said, nodding at the screen, "maybe we could defer this until later? I'd kind of like to hear the latest up-to-the-minute from Alpha Centauri!"

He was always uncomfortable when this argument, or a variation of it, broke out anew. For so long he'd wor-shipped David Alexander as a bold, scientific pioneer. When he'd been a kid, back before he'd joined the Corps, he'd followed David's reports and published papers on the Cydonian discoveries as avidly as other kids followed sports, bonemusic, or girls. It had been startling, even dis-appointing, to discover that the great Dr. Alexander had a temper . . . or that he had such acid contempt for ideas he considered to be patent nonsense.

"That's right," Teri said. "Stop being so argumentative!"

"Eh? Of course," he said. "Of course. But I wasn't arguing. There's nothing here to argue about."

"Sam!" Jack called. "Is there any sign of recent habitation?"

"Negative, Jack," Sam replied. "There is no means of directly dating them, of course, but based on the weathering I have seen, I would estimate that these ruins are on the order of a half million years old. They do not appear to have been disturbed in all that time. Of course, I have seen very little of them as yet."

"Any indication of what happened?" Paul asked. "I mean, was it a war? An attack?"

"That seems the likeliest explanation at this time," Sam replied. "From orbit, I have noted the presence of a number of fairly recent craters in the one to fifty-kilometer range. All show approximately the same degree of weathering and erosion. And there is an unusually high correlation between the location of each crater and the nearby location of major ruins. In the case of this city complex, the crater actually lies in the salt flats west of the city, suggesting an ocean impact."

"My God," David said, looking up. "Someone was chucking asteroids at them!"

"Just like Chicago," Teri added. She laid one hand on David's arm, an understanding touch.

"Or Mars," David said. "What do you want to bet that the local hunters finished off both Chiron and Mars at the same time?"

"Who's speculating now, Dad?" Paul asked. He disarmed the jab with a grin. "But I gotta admit, it sure looks compelling."

"There's a decent topic for your doctoral thesis, Paul," David said. "Our first hard evidence that Mars was one small, outpost colony in a larger interstellar empire of some sort, knocked down half a million years ago by the Hunters of the Dawn."

That name took on more icily ominous overtones now. The term was a translation of Sumerian words and phrases pieced together from various sources, including An ruins found on Earth's moon. Ten thousand years ago or so, the An had built a colony on Earth, near the confluence of the Tigris and Euphrates Rivers. They had been destroyed utterly, on Earth and on the moon, by the attack of an enemy they called, variously, *Gaz-Bakar* or *Ur-Bakar*, often with the word *Shar*, meaning "great or ultimate," as a prefix. *Shar-Gaz-Bakar* meant the "Great Smiters" or "Great Killers of the Dawn." *Ur-Bakar* could mean either "Foundations of the Dawn" or, more likely in this case, "Hunters of the Dawn."

The human slaves of the An had referred to the utter destruction of their masters and their fabulous cities as *Tar-Tar*, a term almost certainly preserved in the name "Tartarus," the "Place of Destruction," the Greek Hell.

Exactly how the Hunters of the Dawn had destroyed the An colonies wasn't known, but the evidence suggested that someone had dropped a small asteroid into the Indian Ocean south of the Persian Gulf. The resultant tidal wave had scoured almost every trace of advanced civilization from the face of the planet, from North Africa to the mountains of Iran and as far north as the Black Sea. Other asteroid strikes, apparently, had shattered satellite An colonies as far distant as Peru's Lake Titicaca, where the much-later Inca had later wondered at the megalithic structures called Tiahuanaco, and in central Mexico, where the ruins at Teotihuacán had inspired the much-later rise of the Olmecs and Toltecs.

All that had remained of the An presence were the foundations of the Giza Plateau Complex in Egypt and the impossibly massive, still-enigmatic platform at Baalbek in Lebanon, both of which were built upon by human civilizations that had come along much later, a few foundational remnants in Mexico and Bolivia . . . and myths found worldwide of a great, all-destructive flood decreed by the gods.

Scholars and researchers were still arguing the details, of course. What *was* certain was that the Builders, the intelligence that had uplifted primitive man, genetically engineering *Homo erectus* into the more capable, more voluble, more intelligent twin lines of *Homo sapiens* and *Homo neanderthalensis* had been dead and gone for half a million years before the imperialistic An had come along and made Earth and man their own.

But the ruins on Mars showed unmistakable signs of having been bombarded from space; the D&M Pyramid, believed to have been part of the Builders' terraforming complex, had been punctured on the east side by a small but extremely fast projectile. Most of the ruins at Cydonia showed blast damage.

And here was evidence of a bombardment from space used to annihilate the civilization on Chiron as well.

Had two different sets of attackers, two different "Hunters of the Dawn," destroyed the cities on Chiron and Mars, and the An colonies on Earth half a million years later, using similar weapons and tactics? Or were the Hunters one race, an incredibly *old* race, spacefaring and world-wrecking across five hundred millennia?

Either way, the constancy of the destruction gave a clear answer to the Fermi Paradox.

As the information download continued, Jack asked, "Just how much longer is this going to take, Sam?"

"We are limited by this rather primitive technique to approximately one megabyte per second," Sam replied. "I have amassed, so far, some twenty-four gigabytes of data on the planet alone. I assume you are not referring to the data acquired en route, or to data about other planets of the Alpha Centauri system. Transfer should be complete in another six hours."

Primitive technique! Well, compared to the Builders' technology, perhaps it was.

Jack was still having trouble adjusting to the wonder of

the situation. There was a strange, even eerie sense of parallelism here. On Chiron, a sophisticated AI was orbiting the planet, teleoperating a robot in the ruins to access the alien FTL communications link; here on Mars, the four of them were in a hab on the Martian surface, using a teleoperated robot to access the other end of that magical-seeming comm link in a different set of alien ruins several kilometers away, deep beneath the rugged mystery of the Cydonian face.

"Look at this, Jack," David said. He was using his PAD to tap into some of the information coming across the light years. "Teri? Paul? Just look at this!"

Jack leaned over to see the unfolded screen. The display showed the smooth curves of a floater, carved from blue crystal, shining in the sun.

"Sam's right," Jack said. "It *does* look like a floater."

"There can't have been many of them," Paul said. "You guys've only found—what?—five of them here?"

"Six, I believe," David replied. "And some that are in such bad condition they're little more than rust stains on the rock."

"And there's the Ship," Jack added. Insight, full-blown and startlingly sharp, exploded within him. "It has the same overall shape."

"My God," David said. "You're right! But you don't think—"

Jack shrugged. "I don't think anything. But the similarity is worth another look."

"The Ship" was one of the myriad enigmatic artifacts that littered the Cydonian desert floor, a cigar shape almost two kilometers long that had toppled across the slashed-open ruins of the Fortress, one of the megapyramid atmosphere-generating structures west of the Face and just east of the complex called the City. The shell was in such bad shape little could be gleaned from the wreckage. The thing's size alone had suggested that it was some sort of enormous starship . . . obviously one that operated without such primitive embellishments as reaction mass or rocket engines.

"So, what are you saying?" Paul asked him. "That the Ship was really one of the Builders, only two kilometers tall?"

"I'm wondering—and this is all *pure* speculation at this point—if a few Builders didn't come to Mars in a single ship . . . and if they were, indeed, AIs, the size or shape of their body didn't really matter, did it? But I think there weren't very many of them, and I think now they might have been fleeing . . . something."

"The Hunters," Teri put in.

"That's certainly the simplest explanation. Maybe they were even from Alpha Centauri, right next door. Or maybe they were from farther off. Those statues in the Plaza suggest a pretty far-flung association, many civilizations united in an empire or union or whatever.

"Anyway, they started building a colony or outpost on Mars. Why? Earth was right next door."

"Maybe the Hunters were looking for Earthlike worlds," Paul suggested.

"Maybe. Or maybe they thought they'd be less conspicuous on Mars," Teri added.

"Building whopping great atmosphere-plant pyramids and starting to terraform an entire planet is hardly a good way to stay inconspicuous," Paul said. "Then again . . . the evidence available suggests they were here for quite a long time, several thousand years at least. Maybe they got tired of living underground. Maybe they thought the Hunters had given up and gone somewhere else."

"If they were machine intelligences," Teri said, "they didn't need to terraform Mars, did they?"

"Christ!" David said. "You're right!"

"They were doing it for the humans they'd brought from Earth," Jack said. "How does *this* sound? A few AIs escaped from the fall of Chiron or wherever. They hid out on Mars for a few thousand years, and probably made frequent hops over to Earth, where they were genetically tinkering with some of the beetle-browed locals. Maybe they hoped to rebuild the civilization they'd lost. Maybe they were just in the market for cheap labor, and had plenty of time to experiment with. They brought a few thousand of the new-breed hominids to Mars, though, and started terraforming the world to give them a place to live."

"But terraforming was going to take a long time," David put in. He was getting excited now. "Hundreds of years at the very least, maybe thousands. And we know from the evidence here that though they *did* warm Mars briefly, half a million years back, enough to recreate the Boreal Sea, they never generated a thick atmosphere over the whole planet. There was a shirt-sleeve environment here at Cydonia, contained, somehow, maybe by some kind of technomagic force field, but the planetary atmosphere never got thicker than point one bar or so. By that time, they must have thought the bad guys had overlooked them."

"But they hadn't," Jack said, nodding. "Or it just took them a while to find them. The Hunters showed up and eliminated the Mars outpost. It didn't take much. Destroy the Ship, power generators, and the atmosphere plants. The human workers would have asphyxiated almost at once. The Builders might have survived for a time, but without the Ship and without their work force . . ." He shrugged.

"The Hunters probably visited Earth to pick off any Builder outposts there," Paul added. "But they must not have thought the hominid species there to be very promising."

"Maybe they hadn't counted on the Builders geneengineering a new species," Teri said. "There couldn't have been very many of them. But they were enough of an improvement over *Homo erectus* that they survived and proliferated."

"A delightful fantasy," David said after a moment. "We still need hard evidence . . . but I must say the scenario fits the observed facts. What I'm not sure I buy is the idea that the Builders were AIs. It leaves us with an unpleasant tautology. Who built the Builders?"

"I'm not sure that's really an issue, sir," Jack said. "An AI race of Builders could have been around for a long time, even in galactic terms. Their organic predecessors could have been long extinct, especially considering the fact that the galaxy is beginning to look like a rather dangerous place to try and raise a burgeoning young civilization."

"We're already beginning to look at ways to download the human mind into computers," Paul said. "Maybe the floaters are just the bodies, the *machine* bodies of the original Builders."

"If I may make a comment," Sam said from the screen, "there is nothing inherently implausible about a race of artificial intelligences arising from more primitive forms and evolving in the same fashion as biological species. In the long run, it may be that there is no significant difference between evolution from carbon-based single cells and proteins, and evolution from silicon-based microprocessors. Both can acquire considerable sophistication through the forces of natural selection alone."

"You know," David said quietly, "it's just possible we've cracked the secret of the Builders at last. Thanks to *you*, Sam. I think we need to get this off to Earth immediately. After that—"

Jack's PAD chirped. He opened it, and Sam's voice— the original Sam—came from the speaker. "Jack?" she said. "Code One."

The intrusion was so abrupt, so completely unexpected, that Jack didn't understand immediately. "W-what?"

"Code One," Sam repeated. "Triple-N news reports are carrying the story. Two American spacecraft have been deliberately destroyed by a Chinese warship, the *Kennedy*, on high guard patrol, and the *Roosevelt*, at Europa. The president of the United States has just asked both the Congress and the CWS Council to declare that a state of war exists between the Confederation's member states and the republic of Greater China.

"There is a text message waiting for you from General Duvall at Marine Space HQ. The situation has been declared a Code One."

"I . . . understand." He touched the PAD's screen and

swiftly scanned the message from Duvall. It merely confirmed the orders he was already well aware of.

"Excuse me," he said, closing the PAD and rising. "I've got to go."

"Why?" David asked. "What is it?"

"Marine forces on Mars have just been put on alert, Doctor," he said. "There is a possibility that Chinese forces will try to seize the facilities here. I've been told to make sure they don't do that."

David seemed thunderstruck. He waved at the flatscreen. "But . . . but what about this? We've got to tell Earth."

"*This* will have to wait, David," he said. "Until we know whether or not we have an Earth left to send it to. I'm afraid all data connected with the project, and with the excavations here, has just been classified."

"What?" David rose, face darkening, furious. "No! Not again! Not the damned censorship of scientific thought again!"

"I'm sorry," Jack said, and he meant it. He knew how his uncle detested the very thought of controlling the free dissemination of scientific information. "But we're at war."

"Fermi's Paradox questions why the sky is not filled with intelligent life," David said, bitter. "The Hunters scenario provides a possible answer—that newly emergent intelligences or civilizations are snuffed out deliberately before they can pose a threat to a few well-established races.

"I'm beginning to think we don't need to invoke the Hunters of the Dawn, however. Human arrogance, stupidity, and short-sightedness will be as effective as the Hunters ever were!"

Jack was forced to agree.

# NINE

*E-DARES Facility, Cadmus Linea*
*Europa*
*1537 hours Zulu*

Major Jeff Warhurst looked up from his desk as the automatic door hissed open and Sergeant Major Kaminski rapped hard on the door frame. "Yes?"

" 'Scuse the interrupt, sir. I have those reports."

"Outstanding. Come on in, Ski. Grab some chair."

"Thank you, sir." He set his PAD on Jeff's desk as he took a seat. "How's the major feeling?"

"Can the third-person crap, Sergeant Major." Jeff opened his own PAD, keyed the touchscreen to accept a data transmission from Kaminski's system, and leaned back again. "I'm doing fine. Johnson says I just picked up a few dings, is all."

"I'm relieved to hear it, sir."

"So, how are the boys and girls settling in?"

Kaminski eyed one bulkhead, where a flatscreen showed a dark, fog-opaque haze of dark blue-green. "No problems, Major. Just like living aboard ship." He chuckled. "Hell, it *is* a ship."

True enough. The Europa Deep-Access Research Station—E-DARES, for short—had been constructed in Earth orbit, then boosted to Jupiter space by a low-thrust A-M drive. With no atmosphere to worry about on Europa, and less surface gravity than Earth's Moon, it had been simple enough to gentle the ungainly craft down on ventral thrusters to land in the pit melted through to Europa's ocean.

At that point, she'd gone from being a space ship to an ocean-going ship, a research vessel afloat on a 250-meter-wide opening into the Europan depths. And then she'd been deliberately sunk.

Or, rather, *half* sunk.

A century before, the Scripps Institute and the U.S. Navy had employed a research barge for oceanographic research called *Flip*. Towed into place by auxiliary vessels, the *Flip* then flooded ballast tanks to submerge her bow until she was literally flipped a full ninety degrees, with only her stern riding vertically above the surface of the ocean.

The E-DARES complex was designed along the same lines as the old *Flip*. One hundred twenty-three meters long, but massing only 900 tons since most of her length was in the long, cylindrical wasp-waist connecting her bow and stern sections, she rode now with her bow over 100 meters beneath the Europan surface. Her antimatter drive, in the heavily shielded stern section anchored to the ice wall just above the surface, continued ticking over at low power, providing for the base life support systems, and the heat for warming surface water and pumping it deep; the constant circulation of hot water kept the Pit open, with only a thin layer of surface ice. The stern section was snugly moored against the vertical ice cliff ringing the Pit. A fire-escape type scaffolding of railed ladders and platforms gave access from the surface of the ice to the airlock in the side of the station's stern section. Elevators connected the stern with the bow, where the research labs, quarters, offices, and mess and recreation decks were located, all safely shielded by a hundred meters of ice and water from the hellstorm of radiation at the surface.

Fortunately, the E-DARES facility had been assembled with an eye to expanding the human presence on Europa. There were only twenty-five scientists and technicians at the CWS base now, but the ass-high E-DARES had bunks and living quarters enough for a population of two hundred. For the first time since they'd boosted from Earth, the Marines actually had room to stretch out.

And, in an ocean with an ambient temperature of 1.7 degrees below zero, there was *no* problem with overheating.

Jeff scanned through the first several pages downloaded onto his PAD. "So," he said. "Give me the short version. What do we have to work with?"

"It *could* be worse," Kaminski told him. "Though maybe not by a whole lot. We can thank DCL that we're not out of something really vital. Like food."

Distributed Cargo Loading as applied to Marine spacecraft was a supply officer's nightmare, but it guaranteed that each boat going down to the surface of a hostile world carried a little bit of everything necessary for survival.

"Two bugs made it down, so we have eighty-one Marines, one corpsman, six SEALs, and two Navy Bug pilots," Kaminski continued. "That plus the twenty-five civilians already here gives us 115 mouths to feed. I've been over the base inventory with Hallerman, the Supply Officer for the base. Putting everything they have together with what we brought down from the *Roosey*, we have enough food for four to five weeks, if we go on short rations, starting now. Three weeks if we don't, tops."

"I don't want to institute short rations just yet," Jeff said. "I want to talk to Earth first, and see when we can expect a relief expedition. Besides, the men are going to be working damned hard these next few days. Let's give them the fuel they need to keep going. After that, we'll see."

"Aye, sir. Every Marine has his own weapon and personal gear, of course," Kaminski went on. "We have six battery packs per M-580 laser, and no problem recharging 'em off the E-DARES power supply. Likewise for the slaws. We have four of those, with eight power units, plus ten Wyvern launchers and twelve reloads apiece. I'm recommending we pick out three or four of the company's best marksmen with Wyverns and make them mobile artillery. Help make each round count."

"Absolutely. Do it."

"Aye, aye, sir." He looked at his PAD. "Twelve XM-86 Sentries. Only forty thousand rounds apiece, though, so we'll have to keep an eye on that. Those things go through DU rounds like peanuts. Communications gear . . . spare PADS . . . only two extra suits, but plenty of patches and spare parts. Fifteen portable radar and lidar units, besides what's built into our suits. Two bugs, plus six cargo transport hoppers they were using here at the base. We may be able to convert some of those to our own purposes. My people are looking into it."

"Good. Medical supplies?"

"Each Marine has his own M-1 kit, of course. And there's a fair ER setup here in the base, plus a civilian doctor. Only two beds for a hospital, but we can get around that. They say they have only three liters of artificial blood, and we have ten more, but Doc McCall is setting up to pull donated blood for type, crossmatch, and immune suppression, just in case."

Jeff made a face. "Is that what I think it is?"

"Whole blood and plasma transfusions, yes, sir. We can still manufacture blood the old-fashioned way, in our bodies, and Doc can stockpile it in the medlab refrigerators."

Jeff wasn't sure he trusted the idea of putting blood from one individual into another . . . but they were a hell of a long way from the facilities for manufacturing the artificial, fluorine-based substitute. In any case, it probably wouldn't be a problem; combat in space—or in a vacuum environment such as the Europan surface—was generally so deadly that the question wasn't how to give a transfusion to the wounded so much as it was how to recover the remains.

"Water, no problem," Kaminski went on. "The base cooks their own. Same with air. Oxygen from water, while nitrogen is recirculated and captured in the waste treatment cycle. They have three point one kilos of antimatter stored topside. That's enough to provide power for this facility for another couple of years, at least. Various tools, miscellaneous supplies, spare parts for their electrical and computer systems. The complete list is there in my report. Also turns out they've got about 190 meters of two-centimeter superconductor wire stored in one of the sheds topside. They've been using it for teleop probes beneath the ice."

"Huh. What do you think we can use that for?"

"Got a few ideas about that, sir. I have some people looking into it."

"Anything else?"

"Two spare A-M power plants in the bugs. We're not hurting for power. Oh! Almost forgot, yeah. Two of those SDV Mantas we were bringing in for Project Icebreaker."

Jeff frowned, remembering those incredible explosions of light and life deep beneath the surface of the sea off the Bahamian coast. "I'm afraid Icebreaker is going to be on hold for a while, until we sort out the Chinese problem." He thought for a moment. "Still, you might have our supply people go over them, and make a note of useful electronic components, computers, control boards, that sort of thing. If we need spare parts, we might cannibalize them."

"Aye, aye, sir. I'll need to detail a crew to offload 'em from the supply bug, though. I guess we could put 'em in Storage Twelve."

"Do it. So, with rationing, we eat for four weeks. Any other likely shortages?"

"Just one."

"What's that?"

"Marines," Kaminski said. "We have a Chinese ship hotfooting it our way. I don't know what she's carrying in the way of troops and weapons, but you can bet it's at least the equivalent of the *Roosey*. Before too long, we could find ourselves outnumbered three, maybe four to one."

"Or worse," Jeff said. "Intelligence said they were coming on a minimum-t intercept. They could be here in four days."

"Sounds like they're in one hell of a hurry."

"Yes it does, doesn't it? HQ thinks they're trying to get in here and do their dirt before we can get a ship in here to block them. I have to concur. Beijing has to know that they can't win in a long-term war with the rest of the CWS. Which suggests that they have short-term goals they can meet before they have to accept a negotiated settlement."

Jeff typed out a command on his PAD, and the vidview on the bulkhead flatscreen changed to a topo map on the region of Linea Cadmus at 20 degrees north. The base crater was clearly visible, almost five kilometers across, with a tiny lake in the center and red dots marking the E-DARES facility and various buildings and constructs scattered about the surface. Rather than using voice entry, he unrolled a keyboard flat on his desktop and started typing, continuing to talk as he entered notations on the map.

"Damage to the base by the Chinese strike wasn't too bad. We lost the microwave tower . . . here . . . and some damage to the landing field and other static structures. Fortunately, most of the buildings here—and especially the E-DARES facility—were designed to ride out the shock of Europaquakes, so they came through pretty much intact.

"But that means the CWS base is going to be a tempting target for our visitors. It'll be a lot easier for them if they can take over the base, especially the E-DARES, instead of starting from scratch somewhere else.

"We need as much advance warning about the Chinese intentions as we can manage. I think we can assume their overall intent is hostile, but we need to know where they're landing, and when, what direction they're coming from—and whether or not their ship can provide close space support."

"Yes, sir."

"We'll want radar and lidar units set up round the crater rim, of course, but keep some in reserve. I want to see about sending out mobile recon units once we have an idea where the Chinese have touched down. We've lost our own space eyes, which puts us in a hell of a bad spot, but I'm thinking that we might use lidar sets on lobbers to extend our spotting range over the horizon. And we might put some advance OP teams out along likely lines of approach."

"Surface time is limited to twelve hours at a stretch, sir,"

Kaminski said. "And Doc'll be checking for cumulative exposure. Anyone who blacks his badge is going to be grounded."

"Work out a rotation schedule, then." He leaned back in his chair, scowling at the flatscreen. "The trick is going to be spotting the bad guys out there, before they get within range. Chaotic terrain. It'll be damned hard to see them until they're practically on top of us. And harder still when they'll have a ship in orbit, while we don't. The bad guys have the high ground, Ski, and they'll know exactly where we are. I don't mind telling you I don't like this one bit!"

"Me neither, sir," Kaminski said. "You now, if I was them, I'd try to hit this base from space. Mass driver bombardment. Or missiles. Except . . ."

"Yes?"

"Well, I was just wondering. They're coming here to make contact with the Singer, right?"

"That, and to keep us from doing it first, presumably."

"Right. So, does it make sense, them dropping A-M bombs on Europa? If I was them, I'd be afraid the ETs would get mad, that they'd maybe think I was slinging bombs at them. I mean . . . how do these guys at the bottom of the ocean know that antimatter warheads striking the surface ice, or even just mass driver projectiles, aren't an attack on them? If I was in that Chinese ship right now, I'd be very, very worried about what was going through the Singer's mind right now."

"Good question. The Chinese may have it figured that whoever is down there isn't paying attention to what's going on above their ice ceiling. Dr. Vasaliev was in here an hour ago telling me that there's been no indication that the Singer is even aware of us. He says they're sure it's an automated probe of some kind. A beacon, maybe."

"That's not the way I've been hearing it, sir."

"Oh? You've been discussing things with the Base Administrator, have you?"

"No, sir. But some of the men have been talking with some of the people here. That Dr. Ishiwara, the guy who led us in from the landing field? He's head of the xenoar-cheology team here, and according to him, they've picked up indications that the Singer *is* reacting to us. But, well, the evidence is kind of slim, I guess. It depends on some pretty heavy-duty computer analyses to reveal it, and, well, a kind of sensitivity, I guess, to certain tonal patterns. Not everyone here agrees with him."

"So, not only are we in the middle of a war between China and the CWS, we're in the middle of a scientific war as well. I'm not sure which one scares me worse!"

"Roger that."

"Well, maybe the Chinese have heard the same thing that Dr. Ishiwara heard, and that's why they're trying to cut us out of the picture. They must have decided it's worth the gamble, though, of making the Singer mad. They probably figure that the Singer is different enough that it won't un-derstand any dispute between humans. If they can brush us out of the way fast enough, they could slip in here and start a dialogue with our guests down there in the deep, and they would never even know the difference."

"I think you're right, sir. I guess it's up to us not to brush easy, huh?"

"If there's one thing I've learned about the Corps so far, Ski, it's that Marines *don't* get brushed. Not easily, at any rate." He nodded at the map on the bulkhead. "We need to see what we can do to let our Chinese friends know that."

"I think we can promise you a trick or two, sir." He frowned. "It's the space superiority that has me bugged the most. They can see us, we can't see them . . . and they can drop nasty things on us whenever they like. Not good."

"Not good at all, Sergeant Major. I want you to get to-gether with your senior NCOs. Put together a working tac-tical group, and see if you can come up with some ideas. I'll talk to the company's officers. Lieutenants Walthers and Quinlan might have some thoughts about knocking out a ship in orbit."

"Maybe," Kaminski said with a grin. "Though in my experience, Navy officers tend to talk about how invincible ships are, not about how you can kill them!"

"We've just had a rather dramatic proof that they are not. I should think our two bug pilots would be eager to even the score a bit."

"Roger that, sir. And it would be about fucking time."

*At the Europan Surface*
*1615 hours Zulu*

"Hey, Lucky!" Tonelli called. "Get a load of this! Looks like a giant hot tub!"

"Yeah," Corporal Gerald Kane said. "Howzabout we all have ourselves a dip and a steam in the sauna?"

There were four of them climbing the walkway up the side of the ice cliff—Lucky Leckie, Tonelli, Kane, and DePaul—space-suited Marines standing on a steel-decked platform twenty meters above the surface of the Pit. The stern of the E-DARES complex descended the side of the cliff at their backs into a patch of seething black water, edged by skim ice. Most of the Pit's surface looked solidly frozen, except for the few meters around the vertical descent of the E-DARE's connector tubes and elevator shaft.

"Screw *that*," Lucky replied. "Didn't you guys sim the H-and-T specs?"

"What, the hints and tips guide?" Tonelli said. "Fuck, I think I managed to sleep through most of it."

"That water might look like it's boilin' hot, but its temperature is just below freezing. The salt and sulfur and stuff mixed with it lets it get a couple degrees below zero without freezing solid."

"That doesn't make sense," Kane said. "To boil water, it's gotta be *hot!*"

"Uh-uh. The lower the air pressure, the lower the temperature you need to boil water, remember?"

"Yeah," DePaul said. He was the scholar of Bravo Company, a kid from Maryland who'd dropped out of college to join the Corps. "Remember your basic physics? Back on

Earth, if you want to boil water on top of a mountain, you have to cook it extra long to get it hot enough to kill the bugs in it. That's 'cause the boiling point of water is lower at high altitude than it is at sea level."

"Oh, yeah," Tonelli said. "Like I *always* remember my basic physics!" The others laughed.

"Awright, you people!" a new voice growled, cutting in on the chat circuit. "No one said you were on leave! Get your asses up here, on the double!"

Lucky held the guard rail and leaned back, looking up. Although the white, bulky suits they were wearing were fairly anonymous, there was no mistaking Gunnery Sergeant Kuklok's perpetually angry stance, or the stripes and rocker painted onto his shoulder and helmet. First Platoon's gunny was a twenty-year veteran with five years' experience as a boot camp DI, and three years more as an instructor at the Quantico Space School.

Not a man, in Lucky's opinion, to keep waiting.

"On our way, Gunny!" he called, taking the metal steps three at a time as he jogged toward the surface. Movement in Europa's .13 gravity was easy, a lot like moving on Earth's Moon in the long, low lope the Marines called the "bunny rabbit bounce." The tricky part was turning and stopping, once you got yourself plus the mass of eighty kilos or so of space suit and equipment moving. Eighty kilos on Earth might only weigh something like ten and a half kilos here, but it still *acted* like eighty, tending to keep moving and to do so in a straight line once you got it up to speed.

Lucky reached the top of the ladder, and used a double-handed grip on the railing to jerk himself to a more or less elegant halt a few meters from the glowering, fists on hips form of Sergeant Kuklok. Tone, Killer, and D.P. came off the ladder at his back, colliding with him and nearly sending the lot of them into an untidy sprawl.

"Hey, get off!" Lucky shouted. As he turned, he felt a powerful shove from Tonelli's suit . . . the like-charge repulsive effect of his SC field against Lucky's. Lucky took a step back, trying to keep his balance. His boot slid in a puddle of boiling hydrogen peroxide, and he fell—slowly— to his knees.

His descent, fortunately, was slow enough that he was able to grab hold of the handrail and avoid the complete embarrassment of falling flat on his ass.

"Je*sus!*" Kuklok bawled. "If I'd known we'd had the Keystone Cops on board, I'd've invited the Three Stooges along too! Fall in, Marines! Get yourselves squared away! Damn it to *hell,* don't get so close there, or you'll send each other scooting into next week! *Uh*-tenn . . . *hut!*"

It took a few moments more to get untangled, but the four Marines sorted themselves out and fell into a more or less straight line.

"Okay, Marines," Kuklok said. "You four have just volunteered for a working party. Right . . . *face*! Forrard . . . *harch*! Gimmee your left! Your left! Your left-right-a-left!"

Marching in 13 percent gravity proved to be an interesting and largely futile exercise. It did keep them from bunching up, however, and risking another fall as the magnetic fields coursing through the superconducting weave of the Marines' suits tried to push each other apart. Kuklok, Lucky decided, was definitely an *old* Corps Marine.

Since his helmet hid his head, he could rubberneck a bit as they marched, peering out the side of his visor. The magnificent grandeur of Jupiter in the eastern sky was staggering . . . utterly transfixing, a vast, swollen, cloud-banded bow aimed at the shrunken but still brilliant sun just above the horizon. Someone had told him that Jupiter covered more sky than a hundred full Moons on Earth; statistics like that didn't come close to describing the reality, though. He found he could just make out the faintest of glows within the black circle of Jupiter's night side and, here and there, he could actually see tiny, pinpoint twinklings of white light. It took him a moment to realize that what he was seeing were lightning storms—storms that must be as big as North America, with lightning bolts discharging in an instant energies equivalent to all the fusion power plants running in the United States right now.

The cloud bands he could see were rust-red, white, and salmon-pink; a tiny crescent, colored orange-red, rode high in the sky above the swollen planet. He tried to see the rings that were supposed to circle Jupiter, but, edge on and coal-dust faint, they simply could not be seen by the naked eye.

The group collected a carry cart at one of the base surface hangars beside the landing field, a bright yellow cargo dolly, basically, with a broad, mechanized flatbed on six oversized spiked wheels. Kane hopped into the cab and drove the vehicle across the landing deck to the nearest bug, where the cargo bay doors had already been opened and one of the funny-looking, stingray-shaped submarines with close-folded wings was already being lowered by the bug's onboard cargo winches. Under Kuklok's direction, they parked the cargo transport beneath the dangling Manta, then gathered around to help guide it to rest in the cradle on the mech dolly. The work was tricky and potentially dangerous; even here, one of those submarines weighed over twenty-five tons, and once it was moving, it had all the inertia of a 200-ton lump of metal, easily capable of crushing a man who got careless.

They settled down to the work in a brisk, efficient, no-nonsense manner. There was no more skylarking, and only occasional jokes over the chat channel to punctuate the sounds of heavy breathing and one-two-three cadences and orders.

No matter what the antics of Tone and the rest might suggest, Lucky knew, Space Marines were not stupid. The selection process and competitive testing saw to that. But a lot of them seemed to wear ignorance like some kind of badge of honor—a means, perhaps, of distinguishing them from the college-educated officers.

Lucky didn't subscribe to that. Ignorance was *bad*, a character flaw that could make you very, very dead in an environment like this one. He'd never gone to college; no way could a poor family from the Upper West Side slum projects of New York City have managed *that*. But a government-subsidized home computer and its access to Earthnet had offered him a lot more than the virtual sex that had attracted him in the first place. He might have the rep of preferring electronic virtual dates to real ones, but he'd learned a few things along the way.

You couldn't see the stars from Manhattan, but thanks to the Net, astronomy had captured him at an early age and never loosed its grip. His love of space—the landscapes and star vistas revealed by various telescopy projects, the wonders promised by the *Ad Astra* when her observations of the Alpha Centauri system made it back to Earth in another four or five years, the Earthnet shows and documentaries and virtual explorer links you could tap into at the touch of a keyboard—all that and more had led him to find the one way a poor kid from the New York projects could get into space . . . by joining the Marines and getting himself selected for the MSEF.

Someday, he knew, he was going to the stars. There were other races out there—the discoveries cataloged so far in the Cydonian Cave of Wonders proved that much. There were things, people out there stranger than anything ever imagined by generations of Hollywood movie makers or VR sensory download techs. One day, humans would be going out there to meet them.

And the Marines would be along, to protect the ships and people, to protect human interests, to protect all those new worlds that would be opening to human exploration.

Yeah, fuckin' A. He was *going!*

# TEN

*Europan Space*
*0250 hours Zulu*

General Xiang Qiman sat strapped into his couch,
watching the evolution unfold on a small flatscreen monitor on the console in front of him. Like grapes detaching
from their stem, the last of the spherical *Jiang Lei* landers
were separating from the long, slender axis of the *Xing
Shan* and aligning themselves for their deorbit burn. Thirty-
two minutes to go.

He glanced at the man strapped in beside him, swaddled
like himself in a heavy, white-fabric space suit, with helmet
and gloves not yet donned. Dr. Zhao Hsiang's bland face
showed no emotion, but Xiang knew that the man was fuming. They'd discussed the problem often enough during the
burn out from Earth.

"Do not fear, Doctor," he said. "If your friends have
barely reacted to the American presence on Europa, they
don't even know we are here yet."

"I very much hope that is so, General Xiang. If we're
wrong, we may find we have awakened a giant. An *angry*
giant."

"The Americans used antimatter charges to drill their
hole thorough the Europan ice, yes?"

"Yes . . ."

"And there was no response from the Singer."

"None that we know of. But if the Singer intelligence knew the Americans were simply drilling a hole through the ice . . ."

"And how are they to know that this is any different?"

"The point is, General, *we have no way of knowing what they know!* And starting a war on their world . . ."

Xiang shrugged, a bony-shouldered movement all but lost in his bulky space suit. "The potential gains outweigh the risks, Doctor. And it is important to remember that there are *two* aspects to our mission."

Zhao's mouth set in a hard, bitter line, and he looked away.

"Doctor?"

"I . . . remember. I still do not agree."

Xiang laughed. "Your agreement is scarcely necessary, Doctor. We *will* do what must be done."

" 'Mission Directive One,' " Xiang said, quoting. " 'Friendly and cooperative contact with the Singer Intelligence is to be established if at all possible. Mission Directive Two: Friendly contact between the Singer Intelligence and member states of the CWS are to be disrupted *at all costs.*' My detailed orders on this point are quite explicit, Doctor. If we cannot make friendly contact with these aliens, we are to make sure they do not establish friendly relations with the Americans and their CWS puppets. Since it is unlikely that the Singer Intelligence has a clear understanding of human political differences, an attack on the Singer Complex should convince them that the Americans are treacherous, not to be trusted."

"It should convince them that *humans* are not to be trusted. These orders are incredibly reckless, General. I fear for our world. For the human species."

Xiang waved the protest aside. "If these aliens had *that* kind of power, why have they spent millennia sunken within the Europan ocean? Either they are native to Europa, and have no spaceflight capabilities at all, or the complex is some sort of base or outpost, again with no capabilities that would endanger our planet.

"But Greater *Zhongguo* is threatened by the West. As always, the Middle Kingdom is surrounded by barbarians, and they will bring us down if they receive from the aliens technology immeasurably superior to our own. We must prevent that, even at the cost of our own lives. Do you understand me, Doctor?"

"I . . . understand. I love my country. I love my people. You know that. But if we begin a war with the Europan Intelligence, it would be *Feizhengyi Zhanzheng*." The term, translated as "Unjust War," had been basic to Chinese military doctrine for 150 years. It assumed that there were wars that were righteous, and wars that were not—a moral distinction that put those who waged them on the side of right or wrong.

"Perhaps. But we will arrange things so that the Intelligence assumes it is the Americans who wage unjust war. And you are here to aid us in our understanding of that Intelligence—to establish meaningful communications." He sighed. "If you carry out your assignment well, there will be no need of unjust wars, or of any war at all, for that matter. I sincerely doubt that this alien intelligence will even know the difference when we sweep the Americans aside and take their place at Cadmus Station."

"I hope you are right, General."

The minutes trickled away, and then Xiang felt a hard shove against his seatback as the *Jiang Lei* lander's plasma thrusters fired . . . a gentle half G to bring it down out of orbit, but a jolt nonetheless. *Jiang Lei* meant, roughly, "Descending Thunder." There could be no noise in hard vacuum, of course, but inside the sphere's steel and ceramic hull, the steady, rumbling vibration as the engines briefly fired sounded like a roll of summer's thunder.

Eight landers, crammed with fifty men apiece plus a small mountain of supplies, descended toward the equatorial landing site close by the dark streak across the Europan surface called Asterius Linea.

The LZ had been carefully chosen by Chinese astronomers and military planners. The CWS station was located at approximately twenty degrees north, roughly 800 kilometers northeast of the location of the Singer Complex—close enough for study and easy access, far enough to avoid alarming the aliens if, indeed, the aliens were paying attention to the goings-on atop their icy ceiling. The Chinese had wanted a landing site well removed from the enemy base, and similarly *safely* convenient to the Singer. They'd chosen a site almost on the Europan equator, two hundred and some kilometers southwest of the alien site, and over a thousand kilometers from Cadmus Station.

Xiang would have liked to have landed closer to the CWS base—right on top of them, if possible, but Beijing, as usual, was being cautious. If any of the shuttles carried by the *Franklin Delano Roosevelt* had reached the surface before the *Heavenly Lightning*'s bolts had struck her down, there might be enemy troops on the surface already. A single man with a shoulder-launched SAM could easily take out a thin-skinned *Jiang Lei*; they needed to get all of the troops and equipment down and assembled first, before risking contact with the enemy.

Besides, a thousand kilometers of separation offered maneuvering room and a chance to determine the best approach to the enemy base. Europa's surface was sufficiently chaotic that Xiang was planning on using the Asterius Linea itself as a kind of high-speed highway northeast to its near-intersection with Cadmus Linea, but there were other routes, and the best one would need to be determined by reconnaissance parties and flying drones. He was supremely confident of the outcome of this struggle, but he would *not* yield to the temptations of overconfidence.

On his console screen, the surface of Europa was drifting rapidly past, a maze of rust-brown lines against blue-white ice, like dirty cracks in white crystal.

*And what awaits us beneath that icy barrier?* he wondered. Two of the landers carried miniature abyssal research submarines, similar to those Intelligence had reported the Americans were adapting to this mission. Dr. Zhao, he knew, was determined to meet the Singer Intelligence first-hand.

And Xiang was determined to accompany him.

It might well be man's first face-to-face encounter with beings from another world—the first within recent historical times, at any rate.

He sincerely hoped that the second option explored by his orders proved to be unnecessary.

Because, despite his calming words to Zhao, they were taking a fearful risk.


*Combat Command Center*
*E-DARES Facility, Cadmus Linea*
*Europa*
*0329 hours Zulu*


They were gathered in C-cubed, the compartment in the sunken bow of the E-DARES designated as the Marines' Combat Command Center—Jeff Warhurst; Captain Paul Melendez; Lieutenants Graham, Biehl, Quinlan, and Walthers; Kaminski; and four senior NCOs, the eleven of them scarcely able to move in the cramped quarters as they listened to a static-blasted hiss of relayed radio traffic.

*"Yibai mi,"* the voice said. *"Shang bai fen zhi wushi . . ."*

" 'One hundred meters,' " Chesty Puller translated, speaking over the command center's intercom. " 'Up fifty percent.' "

*"Rongyi . . . rongyi . . ."*

"It would kind've been nice if we could have had some advance warning about where the bastards were coming down," Lieutenant Ted Graham said, angry. "A couple of men in place with Wyverns would've spoiled their party real fast!"

*"Liushi mi . . . Wushi mi . . . Diao ershi gongli xia-oshi . . ."*

" 'Sixty meters . . . fifty,' " Chesty translated. " 'Descent at twenty kph.' "

"Any idea yet where they're coming down?" Jeff asked.

"Negative, sir," Staff Sergeant John Wolheim, at the radio console, said with a curt shake of his earphones-encased head. "Southwest and well over the horizon. If I had to guess, at least five hundred kilometers . . . no more than twelve hundred kilometers. I can't give you closer than that without triangulation."

Jeff's fists closed, slowly and tight. *I should have thought of that . . . had at least one more lobber out there.*

In fact, he hadn't thought about it because it was inherently impractical. Lobbers required a human pilot, and positioning one a hundred kilometers away or so meant either exposing the Marine to unacceptable levels of radiation or rotating the lobber's crew every few hours, an exercise that would quickly become futile in terms of energy expended and men exposed to Europa's deadly surface conditions.

As it was, Gunnery Sergeant Cukela, a volunteer, was in the sky right now, jockeying a lobber some kilometers directly over the base, gentling the four-legged contraption high enough that it could see over the horizon and pick up the Chinese fleet's radio chatter.

If he'd known just when the Chinese fleet was going to land, he could have had another lobber ready some distance off, set to ascend at the same time and provide a second bearing that would pinpoint the enemy's LZ.

*Might as well just wish for the LZ coordinates,* he thought. *And, while you're at it, a regiment or two of Space Marines in reserve.*

The worst part was being this damned blind. On Earth, any Marine unit on the planet had almost instant access to whole constellations of military satellites, including battlefield observers that, on a clear day, could literally look over an enemy officer's shoulder and read his maps and communications printouts. And there were IR sensors in orbit that could see warm flesh through the concrete roofs of buildings and bunkers.

He had none of that here—not even a naval ship in orbit that could call in sightings. The company inventory included five teleoperated BRDs, Mark VI Battlefield Reconnaissance Drones, "birds" in Marine parlance. He would have to hoard them like a high-tech miser, and when they were gone—birds had a *very* short lifespan on the battlefield—Bravo Company would be completely in the dark.

"Maybe we should try raising them, sir," Lieutenant Biehl said. His first and middle names were Charles Andrew, but everyone called the Alabama native "Moe."

"And what?" Lieutenant Randolph Quinlan replied. "Negotiate? For what? The only thing we can offer them is our surrender."

"Screw that," Graham said.

"We'll talk if they want to talk," Jeff said. "And they do *not* enter this crater. Understood?"

A chorus of "Aye, ayes" and "Yes, sirs" sounded in the narrow compartment. The flatscreen on one bulkhead was currently showing a view from a remote camera on the surface, set up on a tripod on the southwest rim. It showed the monotonous flat ice plain of the Europan surface, with faint undulations in the distance.

It had been four days since their landing. Since Europa circled Jupiter in three days and thirteen hours—a revolution that also defined the satellite's day—they'd already been through one complete cycle of day and night. It was morning, but in eclipse, with the sun hidden behind the vast, black bulge of Jupiter. Enough light was coming off the silver-edged rainbow gilding one slim edge of the planet, though, to illuminate the gently undulating terrain in cold blue hues. The stars shone, steadily, unwinking, and ice-hard in a sky of empty black. In the distance, a working party was just visible in the dim light, digging a pit for an XM-86 Sentry, their tiny forms giving a sense of scale to the moon's vast wilderness.

*When they come,* he thought, *it will be from* that *direction.*

Not that he wouldn't cover all approaches. But recon

parties had explored the surrounding terrain in lobbers, and reported that the smoothest ground lay along the gentle swell of the Cadmus Linea, extending west and then southwest in the direction of the Chinese LZ. Their first probe, he was sure, would be across easy terrain.

*Damn, I hate the waiting.*

"Zebra, Zebra, this is Recon One. Do you copy, over?"

"One, this is Zebra," Wolheim replied. "Go."

"We are in position, at one-five-niner by three-seven-four, and digging in. Looks like we have the ridge to ourselves."

"Roger that, Recon One. Keep us posted."

"Ah, affirmative, Zebra. One out."

Jeff grinned. During the past couple of days, the Marines had begun calling the CWS base Ice Station Zebra. Cadmus Station was okay, the line went, but it didn't have any character, didn't describe the true, desolate feel of the place. A book by a twentieth-century author and a movie of the same vintage provided the new name; Sergeant Leslie Riddel had brought along a memclip for his PAD containing both the illustrated novel and the uncut 2020 remake of the movie, with virtual actors standing in for Rock Hudson, Patrick McGoohan, and the rest. He'd been passing his copy around the company, and the new if unofficial name for Cadmus Base had become inevitable.

It was fitting. The movie had been set on the Arctic ice pack, during the height of the Cold War. Bravo Company was now on the verge of a genuine shooting war, on an icefield that made the Arctic on Earth seem like a warm summer's afternoon in southern California by comparison.

He'd ordered Knowles and Richardson to take one of the lobbers and establish an OP on the Cadmus Linea ridge a hundred kilometers west of the base. They would have to be relieved soon, and he might not be able to keep the OP permanently manned, but at least it was something to *do,* something to let the men know that action was being taken.

*"Shi mi!"*

" 'Ten meters . . .' "

He tried to imagine the Chinese LZ. They were probably using Descending Thunder landers, a model the CWS had code-named Fat Boy. No flame, no smoke from those plasma engines, but at ten meters, that one must be kicking up a hell of a lot of steam and fog right now.

*"Ting lilang! Queding jie!"*

" 'Cut power,' " Chesty repeated. "They are confirming that they are down."

"That makes eight down so far," Captain Melendez announced. "Do you think that's all?"

"It matches the configuration Intelligence gave us on the *Star Mountain*," Jeff replied. "Let's hope eight was all they sent us."

He tried to keep the words light. Eight Fat Boys meant at least two hundred enemy troops, and possibly a good many more than that, depending on how much comfort they'd sacrificed for numbers.

"Raise HQ, Staff Sergeant. Let 'em know the bad guys have arrived."

"Aye, aye, sir. Any other message?"

Briefly, he toyed with a bit of bravado. In December of 1941, immediately after the attack on Pearl Harbor, the Japanese had assaulted the Marine and civilian garrison on Wake Island in the Pacific. The defenders had been able to hold out for sixteen days against overwhelming numbers . . . a situation not unlike the one Jeff was facing now.

The story had spread that, when asked if there was anything he needed, Major Devereaux, in command of the garrison, had cracked, "You can send us more Japs."

The story was apocryphal, the result of a misunderstanding of the nonsense phrases used tacked on at the beginning and end of radio messages to frustrate enemy decoding attempts. Jeff's idea, to tell them to send them more Chinese, would serve no purpose and might even backfire if it adversely affected morale.

"Tell them we need that confirmation on LZ coordinates I asked for," he replied. "As fast as possible."

"Aye, aye, sir."

Before he could fight the enemy, he would have to find out where he was.

*AI 929 Farstar*
*Kuiper Belt*
*2234 hours Zulu*

Farstar was not pleased at the interruption of his work.

Though not technically capable of feeling emotions such as irritation or chagrin, the new orders that had arrived by laser fifteen hours ago had generated conflicts and interfered with Farstar's maximum operating efficiency to the point that he believed he knew *precisely* what those emotions were.

He had been, with a mounting allotment of processing cycles and storage that might have been defined as excitement, observing a new-found world circling the F8 star 94 Ceti, only fifty-nine light years away. Spectral analyses of the atmosphere had already proven the existence of oxygen and, therefore, life . . . while other scraps of spectra stripped from captured light revealed the presence of a chlorophyll analogue staining broad swaths of the world's continents with patches of blue and green. Oceans of liquid water gleamed beneath the harsh white light of the F8 sun.

And here, too, as on Alpha Centauri A II, were the remnants of a vanished civilization—towers of glass and mirror-polished crystal smashed and scattered; squat, conelike structures blindly ripped open; whole cities reduced to blast-scoured rubble and debris; craters, some a hundred kilometers across, sprinkled across the face of a devastated world.

And, in infrared wavelengths, some of those craters still glowed, proof that the destruction had been visited upon this world a few centuries ago at most.

The Institute for Exoarcheological Studies was keenly interested in this newest addition to the list of archeological treasure troves within a handful of light years of Earth. It suggested that whatever power struck down technic civilizations as they emerged upon the galactic stage was still present, still active.

Why, then, this sudden and completely incomprehensible change in the scheduled observation itinerary?

Fifteen hours ago, an urgent request from the American Space Command at Colorado Springs had directed Farstar to shift away from 94 Ceti and focus his receiving dish on a part of the sky alarmingly close to distant Sol. Farstar had to use extreme caution here; optical circuits could be damaged by direct sunlight, even this far out. Light-gathering equipment designed to resolve objects as small as fair-sized islands at a distance of a hundred light years were trained on a target six and a half million times closer—Europa, where a tiny, glittering constellation of objects was falling into orbit around the glistening, ice-surfaced moon.

Farstar had observed the region around Europa for some hours before detecting the ship. An adjustment of magnification and resolution had brought the vessel into uncertain focus, a two-hundred-meter toothpick scattering eight tiny motes into the stellar wind. Farstar had watched for hours more, observing and computing orbit, velocity, and the descending trajectory of the eight motes as their plasma drives burned hot against his infrared sensors.

At this point, Earth and Jupiter both were approximately equidistant from Farstar's position—a little over six light hours. It would take that long for the information gleaned here to make it back at light's crawl to the humans who needed it.

With no instructions to relay to the U.S. force already on Europa, he began transmitting the information to Colorado Springs. If the humans on Jupiter needed the information, Space Command HQ would see that they got it. In any case, the information was already six hours old by the time Farstar recorded it, and six hours older still after his transmission had crossed the long, deep emptiness back to Earth.

Farstar just hoped they would let him get back to the job he'd been designed for. Observing humans' spacecraft from only fifty astronomical units away was a colossal waste of resources and observing time.

# ELEVEN

*Chinese People's Mobile*
  *Strike Force*
*Asterias Linea, Europa*
*1517 hours Zulu*

The refueling was almost complete.

General Xiang stood on the barren ice plain, watching as the line of men filed aboard the craft known only as *Jiang Lie Si, Descending Thunder No. 4*. It had been thirty-six hours since the People's Army Mobile Strike Force had set down on the Europan ice cap close by the gently swelling ridge called Asterias Linea. During that time, the troops had been busy setting up the main base, using *zidong tanke* and APC crawlers with attached plow blades to dig trenches in ice pulverized by explosive charges, then burying habitat cylinders deeply enough to shield the men living there from the particulate radiation sleeting across the Europan surface.

Now, though, it was time to pay a professional call on the CWS base a thousand kilometers to the northeast. The *Star Mountain* had made several photographic passes over the site in the past hours, carefully noting every surface hab, storage shed, and facility. It was clear that some American troops, at least, had made it to the surface before the destruction of their transport. Two shuttles were parked on the landing field where none had been present before, and numerous groups of space-suited personnel could be seen working in the shallow crater that held the base. There were also lots of fresh tracks crisscrossing the ice of the crater floor and rim, evidence that many more than the expected complement of twenty-five scientists were now present.

No matter. Two orbit-to-ground shuttles meant eighty to a hundred men on the surface, and no more. With their ship and most of their supplies destroyed, they would be short on everything, including morale. A show of force might be all that was necessary to win the Americans' capitulation.

Colonel Yang Zhenyang, in a white space suit with a bright red helmet, stood at his side, watching the marching column single-filing up the cargo ramp and into the yellow-lit belly of the 1,200-ton lander looming overhead. The craft, which had looked so delicate in space alongside the long complexity of the *Star Mountain*, seemed ponderously enormous at this distance, standing beneath the overhanging bulge of its equator.

"I doubt that you will have much difficulty," Xiang told his subordinate, second-in-command of the People's Strike Force, and his Chief of Staff. "The enemy will still be in shock at finding himself marooned on this ice ball. Supplies and ammunition may be short. And they have neither ship assets nor satellites in orbit. *We* have complete space superiority. Once you have demonstrated that superiority, you will give them the opportunity to surrender."

"Yes, General."

"Nevertheless, I want no heroics, no chances taken, no underestimation of the enemy's capabilities." He looked up at *Jiang Lie Si* and gestured with a gloved hand. "She looks invincible, but a single SAM fired from a man-portable launcher could puncture her hull and wreck her. While we will hold enough Descending Thunders in reserve to assure our own survival, I will be most displeased at the loss of even one."

"The plan has been carefully worked out, General," Yang replied. The words were soft, but it was almost a rebuke. A politely respectful one, of course. "We will need to take direct action to get their attention, as it were. But I do not intend to risk my command needlessly!"

"Good. And again: You must land outside the objective crater. We're not sure of the ice thickness inside, but the hole they've cut through the ice to reach the Europan ocean proves it is unusually thin there. The plasma jets from a Descending Thunder could easily melt through deeply enough that the ice gives way when it accepts the lander's weight. Use care!"

"Yes, sir. Our landing sites have been carefully surveyed from orbit."

He realized he was beginning to sound like a mother—a particularly naggy and unpleasant mother at that. "Stay in close contact with us here, and with the *Star Mountain*," he added, a final admonishment. "We can have another four landers at your position within minutes, should you need reinforcements."

"As you say, General, I doubt that we will need them."

"Agreed. But your men will be the scouts who lead the way, who first test the enemy's mettle. This is a probe of the enemy's weaknesses and strengths, *not* a contest of honor or of courage. If you encounter unexpectedly stiff resistance, you must break off at once. I rely on your judgment as to whether to break off or call in reinforcements."

"*Yes,* General."

The last of the troops on the strike team had boarded. It was time.

"Good luck!"

"Thank you, General! I expect to deliver the enemy base to you intact, the next time we speak!" Yang saluted smartly, his gloved hand touching the red helmet above the visor. Xiang returned the salute, and Colonel Yang turned and trotted up the ramp. Xiang moved away as the ground crew began raising the ramp and preparing the lander for boost.

Europa was a nightmarish place, but they were fortunate in one respect, at least. Water ice, with only a few simple contaminants like ammonia, sulfur, and hydrogen peroxide, was abundant and easily carved out of the surface, melted, and stored in the spherical landers' reaction mass tanks, a never-ending source of fuel. He took his place beside the low, tracked form of a teleoperated *zidong tanke* on the perimeter, and turned to watch the launch. A command center had been set up on the bridge of *Descending Thunder No. 3*, and Captain Peng and Lieutenant Mu were handling the launch sequence from there. His hand was not needed, though he opened his suit radio to the command frequency, and listened to the soothing flow of checklist confirmations and countdown.

*"Hydraulics."*

*"Ready."*

*"Reactor."*

*"Ready, at forty-two percent output. Chamber temperature one-three-hundred. Power levels steady."*

*"Pumps."*

*"On."*

*"Fifteen seconds. Initiate reaction mass flow."*

*"Reaction mass flow, on. Pressure at one-three."*

*"Checklist complete. All systems ready."*

*"Pressure at two-five."*

*"Eight seconds. Six . . ."*

*"Main valves open. Plasma chamber, open. Firing sequencing activated."*

*"Four . . . three . . . two . . . one . . . launch command."*

*"Engines activated. Throttle up to four-five."*

Silent clouds of steam billowed from beneath *Descending Thunder No. 4*. A moment later, the spacecraft was climbing . . . climbing . . . accelerating quickly as it grabbed for the black night at the zenith, its upward course already bending over toward the northeast as it leaned into its programmed course.

Xiang was a fatalist, to a degree. He had never read Caesar's words at the Rubicon, *"Alea iacta est,"* but he would have understood the sentiment perfectly.

The die was now irrevocably cast.

*Observation Post "Igloo"*
*Asterius Linea*
*Europa*
*1530 hours Zulu*

Corporal Duane Niemeyer stooped as he shoved the white camocloth aside and reentered the makeshift shelter they'd built up around the base of the lobber. "Damn, how much longer, BJ?"

Staff Sergeant Brenda Campanelli looked up from the portable radar/lidar detector on its squat tripod. "What's the matter, Downer? Your HUD go chips-up, or what?"

Duane squatted on the ice beside her. There was scant headroom in their OP hide-hole, created simply by draping camocloth around the base of a requisitioned civilian lobber. It didn't keep them any warmer—they were in vacuum, and most of their suits' heat loss was through their boots and into the ice—but it did help cut the background particulate radiation by just a small bit more. Every little bit helped, after all.

For Duane, it helped by shutting out all that awful emptiness outside—and overhead. He hated Jupiter especially, that huge, silent, banded eye always suspended above the eastern horizon, slowly passing from new to crescent to half to full and back to half and crescent and new once more as it ran through its three-day cycle of phases. He sometimes felt an intolerable itching in his brain, a sense of unease, even terror, that seemed to emanate from this place like radiation, invisible but deadly.

"Nah," he said, in response to her question. "I just don't want to believe the fucking numbers I'm getting."

"Well, you might as well relax. We have six more hours."

"What I wanna know is how come we have to be out here at all. Rali units are automatic. All we need to do is lay a string of relays back to Zebra, and we could watch that damned screen in shirtsleeves in the comm center, with a cup of coffee on the desk and Johnny Hardwire or Pain playin' on the speaker!"

"What do you think this is, Downer, the Air Force?"

"Aw, shee-it . . ."

The Marine Corps had technology enough to choke an elephant, but they still ended up doing things the old heave-ho grunt work way. It didn't make a bit of sense. Rali units, dubbed "Sir Walters" by some unsung but historically literate member of the Corps, were meter-high tripod units that could be set up anywhere in a few seconds. Their mobile, flower-petal heads contained both radar and laser ranging units, and could be set to automatically scan all or part of the sky or surrounding terrain. Duane and Brenda had set this one up on a ridge top a kilometer away from their grounded lobber; there was no sense in having it close by when its emissions might attract unwanted attention from the enemy. At the same time, without signal ground relays or communications satellites, they couldn't be far enough from the unit that its signal would be blocked by the horizon.

Which meant that pairs of Marines had to go out on OP duty to monitor the far-flung web of ralis in place. "We don't have enough relays for enough Sir Walters to cover every possible approach," BJ said. "So we do it this way."

"Yeah. The stupid way. I think old Warhorse is full of shit."

"The *Major* knows what he's doing, Downer. Bravo Company would follow him to hell!"

"We're *in* hell, BJ. A frozen hell. And I don't remember being given a choice! I think most of the guys are just in love with Warhorse because his granddaddy was a commandant of the Corps!"

"You took your choice when you raised your hand for the oath, kid. And again when you signed up for MSEF duty. So you know who to blame, right?"

"Hey, thanks for the sympathy."

"Don't mention it."

He chuckled, thinking about that night at the V-berg

squad bay, when BJ had gotten her handle, and Sherm Nodell had gotten a mouthful of cement. He looked around at
the frigid, makeshift OP and wished they were back in California, hitting the bars and the VR palaces and the good
restaurants and the—

"Uh-oh," BJ said.

"What?"

"Incoming." She was tapping on the touchscreen of her
rali monitor with a clumsy, gloved hand. "*Damn* working
in this suit! Yeah . . . looks like a bogie coming over the
horizon. Bearing . . . two-five-one. Altitude five kilometers."

"Low."

"And fast. And on a trajectory headed straight for Zebra."

He rose to a crouch, turned, and molded the camocloth
aside. At extreme low temperatures, the stuff became stiff
and could be folded back like a sheet of clay.

"Where you goin', Downer?"

"Outside. For a look with the old Mark I eyeballs."

He stepped into harsh, cold light. The sun was emerging
now from behind Jupiter, visible as a silver-white crescent
sharp and brilliant against the eastern sky. He oriented himself quickly, turning to face the southwest. Compasses
didn't work on Europa, of course. Even if the icy moon
had had a magnetic field of its own, it would have been
overwhelmed by the far more powerful magnetic field of
Jupiter close by. However, giant Jupiter was always in the
same place in the sky, and his suit could work off of that.
If that was east, then *that* was north and *that* was west
and . . .

There it was: a silvery pinpoint of light climbing rapidly
out of the southwest. In seconds, it had reached the high
point in its trajectory just south of the zenith, and was descending again into the northeast. He lost it for a second
against the glare of the Sun . . . then saw it again, falling
toward the horizon.

Campanelli burst from behind the cloth, hugging the rali

monitor and computer. "Let's go, Downer! Get your ass in gear!"

He was already tugging down the cloth.

"Screw that," Campanelli said, climbing the ladder up one of the lobber's splayed landing legs. "No time!"

"Okay." He scrambled up after her, swinging into the copilot's position.

Six-ton VT-5 lobbers like this one had very few amenities, such as hulls. Essentially, it was two side-by-side seats and some simple controls perched on an open platform above a hydrogen-oxygen–burning rocket engine. It had been designed for light transport duty on the moon, where the airless environment did not require streamlining, but it had been used since on Mars as well. It was ideal as a surface excursion vehicle for the scientific team on Europa—and now for the Marines as well.

"Ready?" BJ demanded.

"Set," he replied, strapping in.

"I'm taking her up at forty-five degrees. That gives us our best compromise of getting closer to the base and being able to beam a warning over the horizon to Zebra as quickly as possible. Then we'll cut power and fall straight in. Checklist!"

"Right. Fuel pressure, $H_2$."

"One-eight. Go."

"Fuel pressure, $O_2$."

"One-five. Go."

"Computer."

"Booted. Up and running."

Swiftly, they ran through the abbreviated checklist, then BJ fired the engines without the dignity of a countdown. "Hang on to your stomach!" was her only warning as she mashed her thumb down on the engine ignite button. Duane felt the hard, sharp kick in the seat of his suit as the lobber arrowed straight up, climbing rapidly in Europa's light gravity. White vapor and glistening crystals swirled out from the lift-off site, along with the torn-away sheets of camo material, rippling slowly in the ghostly, silent jetblast.

They would have to climb to nearly one hundred kilometers to clear the radio horizon with Ice Station Zebra. They left the rali unit in place on its ridge top OP; there was no time to recover it.

Corporal Duane Niemeyer clung to the edges of his acceleration seat, unable to watch the dizzying panorama as Europa's billiard-ball-smooth surface dropped away beneath him, and unable to close his eyes for fear he would miss something. When he looked up, the baleful eye of Jupiter, now a scimitar-curved slit silver beneath a shrunken sun, glared back. Below, the horizon canted alarmingly as BJ put the ungainly little craft into an unpleasantly tilted attitude, the engine still silently rumbling beneath him. He'd always hated amusement park rides as a kid, and this was as wild as any theme park.

He concentrated hard on not being sick inside his helmet.

*Squad Bay*
*E-DARES Facility, Cadmus Linea*
*Europa*
*1538 hours Zulu*

"No, no!" Corporal Lucky Leckie said, laughing as the others groaned or shook their heads. "It's *the* way to model all of the different U.S. armed forces! It's called the snake model. You ever hear about it?"

"Leckie," Gunnery Sergeant Pope said, shaking his head. "If this is another one of your scams, s'welp me—"

"No! Honest to God, Gunny! It's like this, see? You've got a snake in your AO, right?"

"What kind of snake, Lucky?" Sergeant Dave Coughlin asked.

"Hell, how should I know, Sarge? It's just a snake, 'kay?"

"Is it poisonous?" Corporal Lissa Cartwright wanted to know.

"I don't know! Okay, it's poisonous! And it's in the Area of Operations. So who ya gonna send?"

"The *Marines!*" several of the men sitting in the squad bay growled in chorus. First Section, Second Platoon had gathered there in the large storage compartment volunteered by the civilians at the base to serve as the Marine squad bay and muster area, to pull routine suit and weapons checks. As they worked, Lucky regaled them with his story.

"No," Lucky replied. "First you send in your Airborne. Now Airborne comes down in the AO, lands smack on top of the snake and kills it. Then they find out that this is the *wrong* AO and they just killed the wrong snake.

"Then you got your armor. They come in, run over the snake, and kill it. Then they go out looking for more snakes, and run out of gas.

"Army Aviation comes in, using a GPS grid to plot the snake's position down to one half of one centimeter. They can't find the snake, and fly back to base for a cool drink and a manicure."

That brought some booming laughs. The Marines had a poor opinion of the air-ground coordination employed by the other services.

"Okay," Lucky went on. "Then you have your Army Ranger. He plays with the snake . . . then eats it!

"Field artillery masses ten thousand mobile artillery units, launches an all-out TOT barrage with rockets and HE with three FA brigades in support and kills the snake . . . *and* several hundred civilians, with massive collateral damage. The mission is declared a success, and all participants, including mechanics, clerks, and cooks, are awarded the Silver Star."

That brought more hoots and guffaws. Artillery support, long considered an absolute necessity for any battlefield evolution, was fast becoming a dinosaur. You had to mass far too many units to be truly mobile *and* effective—and counterbattery fire would savage any concentration of guns that stayed put for more than one shot's worth. "Smart" FA, employing laser-guided munitions, allowed pinpoint accuracy if you had a spotter team near the target or in orbit, but if you didn't, the barrage was likely to be about as surgically precise as a small nuke.

"Combat engineers! They come in and study the damned snake! They prepare an in-depth, five-series field manual on employing countermobility assets to kill the snake that's about as obtuse as a doctrinal thesis. Then they complain that the maneuver forces don't understand how to properly conduct countersnake operations by the book!"

"Combat controllers!" someone in the room shouted, getting into the spirit of things. "They come in and guide the snake elsewhere!"

"Yeah," Lissa added, laughing. "And Pararescue. They wound the snake on the first pass, then paraglide in and do their damnedest to save its miserable life!"

"Navy SEALs!" Lucky shouted. "They swim in at night, march fifty kilometers inland, take an uncomfortable position which they hold for twenty-four hours just to keep themselves from falling asleep, ambush the snake, expend all of their ammunition, including three cases of grenades, *and* call in naval gunfire support . . . *miss* the snake, whereupon the snake bites the SEAL and dies of lead poisoning!"

"Yeah!" Pope added, "Or else the snake gets away, and the SEALs blame the mission failure on poor intel!"

"Hey!" QM1 Mike Hastings growled from a far corner of the compartment. He was one of the SEALs who'd made it down to Europa's surface, and he didn't sound pleased at having his team included in Leckie's rundown. "I'll stuff that damned snake up your ass, Jarhead!"

"Easy, Squid! Easy!" Pope said. "Nothing personal!"

"Air Force!" Lucky called. "We *all* hate the Air Force, right? The Air Force pilot comes in, misidentifies the snake as a late-model Chinese KQ-190 advanced high-altitude interceptor, and engages with smart missiles. He can't tell whether he killed the snake or not, but he goes back to base for a cold one, while the crew chief paints a cool-looking snake silhouette on his airplane."

"How about Marine Recon?" Hastings said, still glowering. He was wearing an olive-green T-shirt that looked like it had been painted across impossibly massive muscles. "They go out and follow the damned snake . . . and get lost!"

"Okay," Lucky agreed. "I've known some Marine Recon guys. I'll buy that! But then ya got your Army Special Forces. This guy goes in alone and makes contact with the snake. He talks to it in snake language. Builds a goddamn rapport with it, wins its heart and mind . . . and then teaches it to go out and kill *other* snakes!"

"Military Intelligence!" Pope called out. "They locate the snake using a spy satellite. They study the snake scale by scale and watch its movements. They draw up an extensive report on snakes, snake scales, snake lice, snake shit, and snake movements, and send it up the line to the Joint Chiefs, the CIA, and the National Security Advisor. Meanwhile, the snake disappears, and no one can find it again!"

"I got a better one," Staff Sergeant Rubio said. He'd been designated the company supply officer, a position he regarded with about as much enthusiasm as a snake in the barracks. "Army Quartermaster Corps! This guy captures the snake, paints it with an NSN, and implements an FOI, after which he has the base commander sign for one snake, green, with scales, poisonous, on a nonexpendable hand receipt. Later, after claiming he doesn't *have* any snakes, he ships it out to a company deployed in the field. Unfortunately, what they *asked* for was one rake, with handle, for area, policing of."

Everyone in the barracks was howling with laughter over that one, when the deck hatch opened and Major Warhurst clambered up the ladder.

"Attention on deck!"

"Carry on!" he snapped before the Marines could come to their feet. "What the hell's the commotion?" He didn't sound angry. Merely . . . interested.

"Sir, we're talking serious tactical snake-killing doctrine here!" Lissa said, laughing.

"Yeah!" Pope added. "Lucky's got the whole damned Armed Forces figured out, Major."

"Really? Well, maybe you'll explain it to me sometime!"

"Hey, Lucky!" Sergeant Bannacek called. "What about the Marines? What do *they* do with the snake?"

"Just like always," Lucky replied, "they improvise, they adapt, they overcome! They hunt the snake down in its own backyard and kill it from air, land, sea, and space!"

"Yeah," Lissa put in, "and then the President declares the deployment a police action, with the Marines, as the Navy's *policemen*, no less, responsible for enforcing the laws about snakes!"

A harsh braying alarm echoed through the compartment. "Major Warhurst! This is Walthers, in C-3! Where are you, sir?"

Warhurst walked to a bulkhead intercom and pressed the talk switch. "I'm here, Lieutenant. Squad bay. What's up?"

"We got hostiles incoming, sir. OP-Igloo just called in the report. One Fat Boy, coming in at five kilometers, ETA two minutes!"

Warhurst spun from the intercom. "All right, Marines!" he bellowed in a DI's stentorian bark. "*Saddle up*! We got snakes to kill!"

"You heard the Major!" Pope added. "Suit up! Suit up! Move it! Move it! Move-move-move-move-move!"

Lucky was already dragging his Mark II armor from its squad bay ready-rack and stepping into the bulky legs. All around him, the other Marines swiftly made the long-practiced moves to don their suits, grab their weapons, and move toward the ladder leading up to the airlock and the outside.

*This is it*, he thought, wildly if unoriginally. *The moment . . .*

He had never been so terrified in his life.

# TWELVE

*Chinese People's Mobile*
  *Strike Force*
*Near Ice Station Zebra, Europa*
*1541 hours Zulu*

*Descending Thunder No. 4* bucked and kicked as the pilot cut in the four main engines, killing the spherical craft's velocity and gentling it to an unsteady hover above the icy plain. Clouds of vapor boiled away beneath those invisible blasts of white-hot plasma as landing legs extended, reaching for the vehicle's slow-crawling shadow.

Colonel Yang Zhenyang was strapped into the command seat, a complex-looking barber's chair tucked into an alcove on the flight deck just off the cramped bridge. With leads jacked into his skull and wrists, he could follow the situation directly as it unfolded.

For millennia, the so-called fog of war had dominated every battlefield, and "no plan survives contact with the enemy" was war's prime postulate. That was changing now, though, with the advent of AIs and virtual linkage. The images flickering in his head now were crude—grainy and shot through with static—but they could give him simultaneous views from a dozen cameras carried by troops or vehicles. At the moment, only one camera was active, showing the panorama to the east as the lander settled slowly to the steaming, fuming ice. The crater holding the

CWS base was visible only as a slight rise against the end-less blue-white flat of the Europan landscape. There was no sign of any immediate military response. It was certain that the enemy knew they were here, however. The *Descending Thunder No. 3* had been fingered by radar and painted by laser ranging beams from the moment they'd swept in over the horizon.

As the lander settled on yielding hydraulics, the cargo bay ramp came down and a sextet of low, flat-topped, tracked vehicles rolled out, their treads spinning glittering bits of ice into the sunlight as they bit the frozen surface. Cameras mounted forward between the tracks relayed separate views to the lander's AI, which processed them and fed them through to Yang's virtuality suite.

Each vehicle was two and a half meters long, a meter wide, and just over fifty centimeters high. Each possessed a ball turret set into the forward glacis, mounting a seventy-five megawatt pulse laser. The machines were called *zidong tanke*, or "automatic tanks." In fact, they were robot tanks that could either run on a simple hunt-kill program or be teleoperated from a distance. They'd been painted white so that they would blend in with their surroundings, though after a few moments, enough white powder covered their upper decks to camouflage them completely.

The robot tanks spread out in a rough line abreast, grinding silently toward the crater two kilometers away. Behind them, Chinese troops in heavy, white-camo suits with SC-weave radiation shielding, bounced down the lander's ramp and began dispersing across the plain. The ground here was uneven, but not broken, and gave no cover. The squad leaders had been directed to get their men to the shelter of the crater's outer rim as quickly as possible. They could begin taking fire at any moment.

"Chinese ship! This is the Confederated World States Europan research base!" Yang heard the words through the earphones he wore, rather than within the virtuality program. This software could handle visual input, but nothing more. "Please halt all unloading activities and open a communications channel! Please respond! Over!"

"Sounds like they want to talk, Colonel," the voice of Major Hu, leading the assault, said in Yang's ears. Yang could hear the rasp of the man's breathing in his helmet, hear the exertion as he struggled ahead across the ice. "No sign of resistance yet."

"Keep your people well dispersed," Yang directed. "And stay close to the tanks."

Giving a series of mental commands to the lander AI, Yang brought up the camera view relayed from Hu's helmet and from several of the other troops as well. All of the scenes showed much the same so far . . . the flat and endless ice occasionally interrupted by the suited shape of another soldier, or the low, white lurchings of a robot tank.

"Chinese force!" The enemy's voice repeated. The words were in *putonghuà,* and Yang realized that the speaker must be an AI programmed to translate into his language. Had the Americans been expecting the Chinese landing? Or was the AI expert in a number of languages, simply as a matter of course? The answer might be important. If the Chinese force had been expected, if the enemy was waiting for them now, on the reverse slope of the crater rim . . .

"Continue the advance!" he snapped, speaking on the command frequency. "Secure the crater rim, and they will surrender!"

*Leckie*
*Ice Station Zebra, Europa*
*1545 hours Zulu*

Corporal Lucky Leckie jogged up the inner rim of the crater in long, loping kangaroo bounds, reaching the top, dropping to his heavily padded knees, then jamming the butt of his M-580 laser rifle into the ice to lower his body full-length. All movement in this light gravity seemed surreal and slow, a kind of slow-motion dance that left him with heart pounding and his breath coming in short, ragged gasps through a dry mouth. A guy could get shot eight or ten times in the long seconds it took him to hit the dirt.

"Dirt" in the figurative sense, of course. Some of the ice looked pretty dirty, but it was *still* ice.

"Where are they?" he called. He was on the west rim of the base crater, with the sun high behind him, at his back. He could see the Chinese landing craft, like a round, gray Christmas tree ornament on the far horizon, but he couldn't see anyone on the ground.

"Use your optics, Lucky," Gunnery Sergeant Kuklok called. "Radar has seventy-three targets out there right now, fanning out and moving this way!"

He used his chin to toggle his helmet's HUD overlay. On infrared, he could see movement—a dozen blobs of yellow and green against the cool greens and deep blues of the background terrain. Range: nine hundred meters, and closing.

He switched to the radar feed, and the targets proliferated, a scattering of tiny green squares behind a horizontal line of six triangles. Rali units set along the crater rim were picking up the advancing Chinese troops and vehicles and feeding their positions to the Marines' helmet HUDs by way of the submerged E-DARES command center.

He selected a target—one of the triangles indicating a moving vehicle of some sort—and raised his M-580LR. Switching the weapon on, he started the warm-up cycle, and heard the rising whine in his headset indicating the power buildup in the capacitor pack. At the same time, a bright red cross hair reticle appeared on his HUD as the targeting unit on the rifle transmitted his aiming point to his helmet electronics.

A red light winked in the upper left corner of his HUD, along with the word LOCKED. C-3 had locked out the laser weapons of everyone in the company, a precaution against someone jumping the gun. "Take it easy, people," Major Warhurst's voice said over the company frequency. "Let's see what they want."

"I don't think they're waiting for an invitation to come aboard!" Lance Corporal Porter said.

"Maybe they want to surrender!" Sergeant Quincy said, laughing.

"We *know* what they freaking want!" Tone's voice added, just a little shrill. "They sure as hell ain't coming over here to borrow coffee!"

"Keep it down, Tonelli," Kuklok said. "The Major knows what he's doing. All of you, can it! Com discipline!"

The chatter stilled, and the only sound Lucky heard was the hiss-rasp of his own breathing inside his helmet, the pounding of his own heart.

He hated being this afraid.

He'd been the tough guy on the block, back in the projects, the one with the swagger, the jazz, the *balls*, the one to stand up in front of the enemy gang and face them down—or throw the first one with chain or shiv, with zippie or hobnailed stomper. He'd never been able to admit to the rest of the Skullz how terrified he'd been at every encounter, how dry his mouth was, how hard his heart was hammering. To admit weakness of any stripe would have meant loss of face; the Skullz had been known to turn on their own with the ferocity of a wolf pack killing the weak of their own species. Lucky hadn't heard of Darwin then, but he recognized the imperative. *The strong survive at the expense of the weak.*

For three years, he'd been the leader of the Skullz . . . and terrified the entire time. In the end, the stress had been too damned much; he'd joined the Marines to get away.

And why the *Marines*, for God's sake? He watched the moving squares and triangles of light on his HUD, superimposed on the bleak panorama of the Cadmus Linea, and he had to admit that now he didn't know.

Well, the Marines had the rep for being tough. Always. The recruiting vids for the other services carried the same general type of message: Join the Navy and see the world; join the Army and get a career; join the Air Force and go to college. The Marines, though, were different: *We're looking for a few good men . . .*

. . . and women. They didn't bar people on the basis of sex. Hell, since the early '20s, women had served in front-line combat units just as they did in the other services. But the Marines were exclusive, an elite. They didn't let just anybody in. You had to be good enough, had to *prove* yourself, to be one of them.

And he'd been a gangbanger from the Met who'd never even seen the stars, who desperately wanted to get into space. The Navy, more and more, was expanding their credo of "see the world" to "see the *worlds*," using their long expertise at training men and women to live in close, artificial environments for months at a time to become America's space service—but it was the *Marines* who did the real fighting, the real dirty work, who had the rep as killers.

So he'd joined the Corps, partly because it preserved his tough-kid image, partly because—he could admit it now— he'd been trying to prove to himself that he had what it took to stay on top of the food chain.

Seven hundred meters.

LOCKED.

Damn . . . when were they going to let him fire?

The tough kid from the Met had survived for perhaps ten days in Boot Camp at Parris Island. Constant supervision, an exhausting schedule balancing physical challenges with intensive training, good food in a supervised diet—a regimen calculated to break him down to nothing both physically and emotionally—had destroyed the old Lucky. They'd then built him back up almost literally muscle by muscle and thought by thought, remaking George Sidney Leckie into a "mean, green fighting machine," a creature as alien to that ragged street punk as the surface of Europa was to the trash piles of Riverside Drive.

And yet, despite all that, the old fear remained.

He licked his lips, took a sip from the water nipple, then licked them again. He could feel the familiar weakness spreading from the pit of his stomach to his knees, his elbows, his hands. He could taste the hot sting of vomit at the back of his throat.

Marine training was good, but it couldn't take away the fear. *Use your fear,* his DIs in boot camp had told him. *You can channel the fear into strength. Let your training take over. Use your mind to control the panic, use it.*

He'd never been in combat. Oh, he'd faced plenty of problems in tactical combat sims, sure, but no matter how realistic those might be, they were nothing compared to the real thing. This was his first time ever up against a real, live, shooting enemy. Compared to these guys, armed with Type-80 missile launchers and Type-110 auto-assault rifles and *Taiyang* lasers, a bang-bang with the kids on West Broadway or Morningside Heights was a friendly and somewhat lighthearted session of shooting the shit.

The Chinese had stopped, the nearest still six hundred meters out. What was going on?

"Listen up, everybody." It was Major Warhurst, speaking over the company channel. "Looks like the ship that brought these guys has changed orbits. It's just now coming up over the western horizon, and it'll be passing straight overhead in another few seconds.

"We don't know what they intend. They haven't tried to talk to us yet, or responded to our challenges. It's possible they intend to try softening us up with a crowbar barrage.

"If so, keep down, don't panic, and remember your training! They're in orbit, which means they'll pass overhead pretty quickly, enough for a quick series of strikes, but nothing they can sustain. Listen to your squad leaders, and don't do anything stupid. You'll come through okay."

*Shit,* Lucky thought. *Shit, shit, shit! Crowbars!*

You didn't have to pack high explosives into a shell or warhead, or generate an intense beam of coherent light or antimatter particles to cause some serious damage to a target. The big guns of most naval vessels now, both those afloat and those in space, were mass drivers, long-barreled weapons that used superconductor cable to generate intense, fast-moving magnetic pulses that could grip a steel-sheathed projectile and accelerate it in a fraction of a second to velocities that could kill through the release of kinetic energy alone.

In 2042, the kinetic energy released by a falling fragment of a French spacecraft had wiped out Chicago as effectively as a small nuke; the gentle rain of plutonium dust from the ship's radioactive pile afterward had been a largely gratuitous extra.

A lump of lead thrown by hand at a few tens of kilometers per hour hurt. The same bullet propelled by expanding gases in a rifle's firing chamber to velocities of a kilometer and a half per second killed.

And the same bullet, accelerated by a mass driver to a hundred kps, didn't simply kill. It *vaporized.*

"Crowbar" was the slang for lumps of inert metal fired from a railgun in low orbit. Usually massing ten kilograms and accelerated at 50 to 100 gravities, they struck with terrible force. Ten kilos coming in at ten kilometers per second released $5 \times 10^8$ joules—the equivalent of detonating 100 kilos of high explosives.

And in a few more seconds, a Chinese ship was going to be sailing overhead, spitting out crowbars like machine-gun bullets.

No wonder the damned Chinese had stopped their advance out there on the ice field. They were going to wait for the crowbar barrage, then move in and mop up the leftovers.

The seconds dragged by, as Lucky's panic grew to a shrieking intensity.

*Chinese People's Naval*
  *Strike Cruiser* Xing Shan
*50 kilometers above*
  *Ice Station Zebra*
*Europa*
*1559 hours Zulu*

The doctrinal manuals called it air superiority, a concept that remained accurate despite the fact that there was no air involved. In another sense, it could be considered the age-old ploy of grabbing the high ground. The *Xing Shan* had eliminated the American communications and military satellites already in orbit around Europa, and was moving now to secure a position of unquestioned superiority of position at the top of the Europan gravity well.

Major Li Peng Zhou of the People's Army Space Force peered into the twin eyepieces of the targeting console, his hand on the track ball to his right. Through the oculars, he could see a magnified view of the CWS base site ahead and below, a large crater with what looked like a tiny lake in the center. *Xing Shan*'s AI, accumulating tracking data from hundreds of separate sources, condensed that data and displayed it as an overlaid scattering of bright red dots against the faintly blue to green background of ice.

The red dots were possible targets, selected by their infrared emissions or, in some cases, their radar returns. Most were individual troops, scurrying about the illusory shelter of their crater like ants at the bottom of a bowl, stringing themselves out along the western rim to face the advance of Yang and his troops.

The image of the crater was oblique at the moment; *Xing Shan* was passing almost directly over the Chinese position, and at this altitude, the crater was halfway to the horizon. As the ship continued to drift along its orbit, however, more and more of the crater interior was revealed, until Li was looking almost directly down into the bowl.

He moved his right hand, and the bright green targeting cursor drifted across his line of sight, settling at last on the crest of the crater rim near a thick clustering of red dots. A touch of a button locked the aim point; a click of the mouse button fired the *Xing Shan*'s main weapon.

The acceleration of ten kilos of inert depleted uranium jacketed in steel gave sufficient recoil that Li could feel the huge vessel lurch slightly, like the kick of acceleration from the firing of a maneuvering thruster. His targeting lock was automatically released; he spun the track ball to lock in on another target.

That looked like a small cargo transport or shuttle of some kind, imperfectly camouflaged beneath a layer of white cloth. *Click . . .* locked. *Click . . .* fire!

A remarkably easy way to wage war, he thought. He remembered himself and other boys in the village of Huoshan, where he'd grown up, using rubber bands and small pellets to bombard scurrying ants in the dirt, or on a hot summer's day, using a magnifying lens to roast them one by one. This was like that—only easier.

His first round hit. He saw the blast, a brief throb of light, and a fast-spreading ring that must mark the shock wave of the impact, expanding through the ice. A perfect hit!

His orders were to avoid the various buildings, which might be of use to the army when they captured the base, and to especially avoid the central lake and the partially sunken base facility at its side. Every other target, though, was his for the taking.

That looked like a vehicle of some kind. *Click . . .* locked. *Click . . . fire!*

*Leckie*
*Ice Station Zebra, Europa*
*1559 hours Zulu*

Lucky didn't hear the crowbar impact. He *felt* it, a savage detonation of pure force rising out of the ice beneath him and slamming him up and back like a sledgehammer blow.

An insect on a carpet given a sharp snap might have flown as far. He landed on the ice on his back, skittering down and around like an upended turtle on an ice rink until the slope leveled off and he slid into the bottom of the crater.

His fall, fortunately, had been in slow motion, but he'd lost his rifle, a mortal sin for any Marine. His head was throbbing and his neck had an awful crick. The shock must have, slammed his head back against the padding of the inside of his helmet. He tasted blood on his lip.

Training took over at once. Was his suit damaged? Was it *breached?*

His electronics were still working, thank God, and when he chinned up suit status, the display was mostly green. There was damage to his backpack PLSS where he'd landed on it, but it appeared to be limited to his tracking and navigation systems, and to his maneuvering thrusters, which weren't charged anyway. The suit integrity light was still a bright, steady, and reassuring green . . . and, more reassuring yet, he heard no shrill hiss, felt no telltale popping in the ears. Rolling over, he scrambled to an all-fours position, looking back up the crater rim. The impact had sent other Marines spinning like bowling pins; there was a ragged new gap in the crater rim where something had speared down out of space and struck deep.

He was still trying to sort out his whirling impressions when a light as bright as a new-risen sun glared into the far-right side of his visor, polarizing the transparency to near black, but only for an instant. Then the ground was yanked from beneath his hands and knees and feet again, flipping him and sending him sprawling once more. A shrill scream sounded in his helmet phones, a shriek abruptly cut off, presumably as the transmitting suit radio failed. He had a moment's impression of a mass of tangled struts and torn metal somersaulting in slow motion above his head. Desperately, he tried to roll over to get to his feet, slipped not on smooth ice, but on ice that had been pulverized to the consistency of powdery snow, then partly melted. The wreckage of one of the bugs landed twenty meters away, crumpling silently into a twisted heap as fragments continued to rain down across the crater floor.

There was no sound at all associated with the explosion, the whiplashing ground, the falling debris, but his helmet phones babbled a torrent of voices, commands, pleas, terror.

*"Watch it! Watch it!"*

*"Easy now! Don't panic!"*

*"Sarge! God! Sarge! Where are you?"*

*"Has anyone seen Quince?"*

*"Steady, people! Keep your heads!"*

*"Oh, my God! My God! My God!"*

*"Peterson! Wojak! Amberly! Get up here!"*

*"Help me! Someone! Please! Help me!"*

A third flash, closer this time, and an almost immediate flicking of that titanic carpet. Lucky landed on his PLSS for the third time and wondered how long the battered life-support system was going to hold out. His readout showed a leak from one of the oxygen tanks and two of the unit heaters were out, though there was no immediate danger.

Somehow he got to his feet and trudged through mushy ice that was simultaneously boiling and trying to freeze, making his way back to the crater rim. Another impact struck, this time on the east side of the crater floor. He felt the shock, but it was distant, muted somewhat. It didn't even knock him down. Nor did the next two impacts after that.

*The ice has gone soft*, he thought. It wasn't transmitting the shock waves the way it did at first. He wondered if that was something he should worry about. The ice at the floor of the crater was . . . how deep? Eight or ten meters, he thought, judging by the depth of the pit over by the E-DARES facility. Or . . . no. He'd read somewhere that nine-tenths of an iceberg was underwater. By that measure, the ice here was ninety meters thick. But did that hold true with a whole icecap?

What if the ice crumbled away beneath him? He'd heard that the Europan sea beneath the ice here was eighty to a hundred kilometers deep . . . sixty miles of cold, dark water, straight down.

And he knew his suit wouldn't float.

Somehow, he managed to keep walking, though his knees were shaking now as he expected each step to plunge him through the ice and into those black, frigid depths. It took him another dozen steps to remember that he was unarmed. His M-580 had spun off into the ice, somewhere, and he had no idea where it was.

He kept struggling toward the crater rim, however. His assigned position was *there*, not here in the crater bowl. The Chinese orbital bombardment had swept the Marines off the rim with appalling ease. And the enemy troops must be surging up the outer slope at this moment.

*"Weapons free! All units, weapons free!"* The red light in his HUD winked off. LOADED now read WEAPONS FREE.

He needed a weapon. He saw one, three meters to the right. A Marine lay on his back, clutching his M-580 against his armored chest. His legs and torso from the ribcage down were . . . gone. Nothing left but a fast-freezing trail of blood and internals. The inside of the visor was opaque with blood and vomit, a horrible sight, but a merciful one. Lucky couldn't see the person's face.

He had to work the stiff, gloved fingers open two at a time, but at last pulled the laser rifle free. Only then did he see the name tag: HUTTON, J.

Sergeant Joseph K. Hutton. A lean, rail-skinny kid from West Virginia, friendly, likable, if a little naïve. *Shit . . .*

He knelt in the freezing slush, punching keys on the programming pad on the side of the rifle, praying the mechanism hadn't succumbed to shock and cold. Each laser rifle had to be tuned to the user's suit frequency so that it could feed target information and aim points to the helmet HUD. The tuning took a few seconds . . . and Lucky was afraid he didn't have them.

A low, flat shape was shouldering its way onto the crest of the crater rim now. Lucky had seen those things in sims and tech briefings: *zidong tanke* . . . robot tanks.

Other figures were appearing on the ridge above him now: human shapes in bulky white suits, like the ones the Marines wore, though different in detail of helmet shape, PLSS outline, and the look of the rifles they carried.

He waited for the rifle to charge. *Come on . . . come on! . . .*

Lucky preferred the M-29 ATAR, the primary Marine weapon. Some genius on Earth had decided that the Europan MSEF should carry M-580s, though, because with laser rifles, you didn't have to ship all of that ammunition across the solar system.

Unfortunately, you had to tune the damned things, and it took them a godawful long time to cycle up to firing charge. Maybe *too* long.

*"Leckie!"* It was the major's voice. He would be jacked in back in C-3, getting feeds from all of the Marines, their suits, their weapon systems. *"Where's your weapon?"*

It was like having God looking over your shoulder.

"Tuning a pickup, Major! It's coming . . ."

*"Breakthrough on the ridge, above your position! Watch yourself! Get some fire on that ridge when you're charged!"*

"Aye, aye, sir!"

The red crosshair reticle lit up on his HUD, accompanied by a shrill, reedy tone signaling the rifle was ready to fire. *About time!*

Still on his knees, he raised the boxy M-580, swinging it up and around until the reticle centered on one of the space suits clambering over the ridge. His gloved finger slid into the outsized trigger guard and touched the firing button.

There was no flash, no beam, of course. There was no atmosphere to ionize, no dust to illuminate the pulsed thread of coherent light that snapped from his weapon's muzzle . . . but the chest of the soldier's space suit erupted suddenly in a puff of white smoke, water vapor freezing in an instant as it exploded from his ruptured suit. His arms cartwheeled, his rifle spun back down the ridge behind him, and then he fell in an agonizing slow motion, toppling onto the ice.

Lucky struggled to his feet and started jogging forward. With the ground covered by fast-freezing slush, he couldn't pull the distance-eating bunny bounce, and had to push forward one glue-footed stride at a time. Clumsy . . . *clumsy*. He couldn't move. Warning lights flashed on in his HUD array. His suit was being painted by half a dozen targeting lasers and radar beams.

He dropped for the ground, snapping off another shot as the reticle drifted across another target. Slush splattered and boiled half a meter in front of him . . . and several fast geysers spurted as rifle slugs tore into the freezing sludge.

To his right, a shoulder-launched Wyvern rocket streaked low across the ice, rising up the face of the hill, striking one of the *zidong tanke* in the left track with a dazzling flash and sending fragments hurtling. A second robot tank fired, sending a surging splash of ice and water into the black sky, and eliciting a shrill, keening shriek from some Marine.

Then the Chinese troops were plunging down the slope into the crater, firing wildly at everything that moved.

And in another moment, Lucky was fighting for his life, a fight far wilder and far deadlier than any he'd ever dreamed of in the trash-strewn streets of New York.

# THIRTEEN

**17 OCTOBER 2067**

*C-3 Center, E-DARES Facility*
*Ice Station Zebra, Europa*
*1605 hours Zulu*

Jeff Warhurst was linked in.

The use of virtual reality—coupled with powerful computers and competent AIs—was transforming the whole idea of warfare. Throughout all of history, any combat involving more than two people had been constrained by the so-called fog of war, that overriding confusion born by the fact that no battlefield commander could know exactly where all of his units were, what they were doing, or how they were reacting—to say nothing of the forces of the enemy.

He was using the Battlestorm: 3000 combat management software package designed by Sperry Rand Defense, together with a tacloc comm system that gathered data from thousands of separate channels, processed it, and fed it into his link display.

The display unfolded in the optical center of his brain, giving him a three-dimensional relief map of the battle area. Transponders inside individual suits provided status, position, and even intent. Scattered robot monitors, ralis, and drones gathered information on enemy deployments and movements. At low res, individual friendly troops and other assets were marked as moving blue dots, while the enemy was shown in red. At high res, each dot became a tiny animation of a space-suited Marine or enemy soldier, and the effect was that of hovering a few hundred meters above the battlefield, giving him a god's-eye view of the conflict.

In his literal mind's eye, he could reach out and touch any troop icon, and words and numbers would appear next to it in an overlay window, telling him who the man was, what his status was, what he was doing. Tap and rotate his wrist, and he could see what that Marine was seeing, through the camera mounted on the outside of his helmet. Tap twice, and he was in direct contact with that Marine, speaking over a private channel. In the real world, Jeff was lying on a reclining chair set up in the E-DARES facility, wearing a headset and thread mike with the channels handled by his AI. When he spoke, he was heard by the man or woman he needed to talk to; he was simultaneously hearing the chatter on several channels—Command 1, the platoon channels used by each of his platoon commanders, and the general channel used by all officers and NCOs—and he could eavesdrop on any channel at will.

Jeff was well aware of a terrible danger with this new technology, which had only been available for combat units within the past ten years or so and was still highly experimental. Knowledge was power, and it was embarrassingly easy to assume that he had so much information about the battlefield that he could micromanage the operation, taking control away from his platoon officers, section leaders, and NCOs and try to run everything himself. Battlefield management was both a science and an art, one that required a light touch and dependable, well-trained, and experienced subordinates.

He had to consciously relax and watch, cultivating patience, trusting his NCOs, especially, to rally the unit and get them back into the fight and not try to do everything himself. Even a relatively small action like this one was terribly complex, far more than any one man could comprehend or command by himself. If he hadn't had Chesty Puller working in the simulation with him, handling the routine details and gently calling his attention to key developments as they unfolded, he never would have been able to keep track of what was happening.

"Move ahead," he murmured, addressing Chesty. "Let me see the top of the rim. Pan view right, ten."

His field of view zoomed in and swung right, making him feel like he was flying across the battlefield. There were six *zidong tanke*, he saw, one already knocked out by a shoulder-launched 5-cm missile, but the others maneuvering for good hull-down positions on the crest of the west rim. From there, they would be able to fire down into the crater floor, where the Marines were struggling to regroup after the devastating bombardment from space.

That bombardment had hurt them badly. Twelve Marines were dead, and another would die in minutes from the leak in her suit if someone didn't get to her quickly. Jeff had already alerted the nearest Marine, who was trying to save Corporal Lissa Cartwright's life with an emergency patch and sealer. One of the two bugs was destroyed, the other damaged, and two lobbers were smashed. Several surface storehouses had been riddled by splinters; they would have to check to see if the contents of those structures—food and some electronic components, mostly, plus the two Manta submarines—had been damaged.

It could have been *much* worse. Apparently, the enemy warship had not been targeting the main base structures. Probably they wanted to preserve those for themselves. Why smash a perfectly good base to pieces when you could move in and use it for your own purposes? But in a terrifying five seconds or so of bombardment, the MSEF had suffered a 16 percent attrition rate—a shocking loss that was certain to seriously hurt Marine morale. And unless they could organize themselves up there, those losses were going to be far worse than that. The Chinese troops were spilling down into the crater now, firing wildly at everything that moved. Several Marines had been caught up in wild, savage, hand-to-hand actions. Jeff couldn't keep track of them all. He didn't dare try. If he let his attention become focused on any one Marine, and one small group of Marines, he could miss the bigger picture, and maybe get all of them killed.

One thing he *could* do was release the XM-86 Sentries, letting them seek and fire upon any target that wasn't broadcasting on the correct IFF frequency. There were two set up along the west rim, still upright after the bombardment, and their elongated, white-metal heads began pivoting rapidly as they sprayed the nearest targets with deadly bursts of 70-megajoule destruction. He'd already released the lock on all personal weapons.

"Chesty! Where are the slaws?"

Two Marine icons, widely separated, lit up with green halos. One, wielded by Sergeant Emilio Gonzales, was already in action, laying down a rapid-fire barrage against the advancing Chinese, taking them from their right flank, chopping them down. The other, with Lance Corporal Ross Muller, appeared to be out of action—a malfunction.

Kaminski was nearby. Jeff tapped twice. "Frank! Warhurst. Check Muller, ten meters to your left! He's having some trouble with his slaw. Get that weapon into action!"

What else could he do?

Across the open expanse of ice, Gunnery Sergeant Kuklok had rounded up ten Marines and was working his way back up the slope of the inner rim, trying to reach a position where they could fire down on the enemy, and maybe get behind them. The robot tanks, though, posed a difficult problem. Two of Kuklok's people had already been picked off.

Double tap. "Kuklok! Warhurst! Hold your position!"

Double tap. "Tonelli! Can you pick off those damned tanks on the ridge?"

"Working on it, sir!"

"*Do* it! Before they cut us to pieces!"

Double tap. "Kaminski! Is that slaw working yet?"

"Negative, Major. Capacitor's crapped out! Need a spare from stores!"

"Okay! Screw that! I need you to round up a tank-killing

team. Grenade launchers. Wyverns. Whatever you can find. Kill those tanks!"

"Aye, aye, sir!"

On the simulation, the icon representing Tonelli darted forward, moving in short, quick dashes, making its way to the tangle of wreckage that was all that was left of one of the Marines' bugs. The icon was precisely like the figure in some sort of military computer game. It was damned hard to look at that display and not to *think* of it as a kind of enormous, complex game, with bloodless little icons moving about as he issued his commands.

But those were *people* out there, and they were dying.

A point of white light flashed from Tonelli's icon toward the ridge above him, impacting in the ice in front of one of the tanks. Shit! A miss!

The tank returned fire, and the Tonelli icon winked out, replaced an instant later by a grayed-out figure sprawled on the ice, and the grim letters KIA.

Damn it, what more could he do? He felt so damnably *helpless*.


*Kaminski*
*Ice Station Zebra, Europa*
*1605 hours Zulu*


"Laplace! Waggoner! Jelly! Garcia! Brighton! All of you, with me!"

Frank Kaminski bounded across the ice to the shadow of the wrecked bug, stooping at the side of the body sprawled there, face up. Corporal Gerald Bailey's left arm had been torn off, leaving a bloody smear behind it across the ice as a seething frost of freezing water vapor and atmosphere settled over the ragged hole in Bailey's side. Kaminski pulled the Wyvern launcher from Bailey's right hand and tossed it to Sergeant Jellowski, then rolled the body over to get at the reload pack attached to the side of Bailey's

PLSS. Extracting a 5-centimeter rocket from the pack, he attached it, still in its load tube, to the rear of the Wyvern. Jellowski positioned the weapon with the load tube over his shoulder.

"Shit!" Jellowski yelled.

"What?"

"Can't get a tone! They've muffled in!"

The robot tanks on the crater rim were spaced ten to twenty meters apart, positioning themselves so that only their glacises and their ball-mounted main guns were visible. The surface ice up there had been broken by the ground shock waves from the bombardment, and they'd back-and-forthed to work themselves down into snug, shallow trenches that made them damned hard to get at. Evidently, they were using some sort of venting system to get rid of excess heat down and away from the front of the vehicle; clouds of steam rose from the rear of each tank, rapidly crystallizing into clouds of ice.

*Muffled in . . .*

SM-12 Wyvern 5-centimeter smart missiles could track by infrared, magnetic, optical, or laser targeting, or a combination of all four. The robot tanks, though, were shrouded by ice crystals carrying vented heat. The effect smeared their IR signature across a large volume, and probably screwed up their optical configuration as well. Wyverns wouldn't attack a vehicle shape they didn't understand.

Waggoner darted forward from the cover of the wrecked bug, dodging past Bailey's still form and into the open. Two of the tanks fired, the explosions sending shudders through the ice. Waggoner shrieked, then went silent, the radio transmission abruptly chopped off.

Kaminski began looking for options.

The five of them were tucked in behind the wrecked bug, invisible to the tanks above, but nakedly vulnerable if they tried to move. The robots were in hull-down defilade, their laser balls sweeping the entire expanse of the crater.

He was damned if he could see any right now.

*Leckie*
*Ice Station Zebra, Europa*
*1605 hours Zulu*

Lucky fired his laser weapon from the hip, tracking the targeting cursor rapidly across his HUD while simultaneously trying to move, duck, and weave, making himself as tough a target as he possibly could. Four Chinese soldiers were closing on him from three directions. A golf ball–sized hole exploded in the visor of one, venting a cloud of red fog, instantly freezing. Lucky dropped in the same second, landing hard on his left shoulder and letting his momentum carry him in a leg-flailing slide across the ice. He tried to target on a second PRC soldier, but missed as the target's feet slid out from under him and he collapsed in an untidy, scrambling sprawl.

Rounds from the Chinese Type-110 assault rifles blasted sprays of ice from either side as he continued his slide. One round grazed his helmet, the shock ringing his ears and setting him spinning, but his helmet warning display continued to show he still had suit integrity. Sliding now flat on his PLSS, he bent up and forward hard at the waist, trying to reacquire his attackers on the HUD. With the 580 lying flat down his body and aiming between his wide-flung boots, he saw the cursor snap across one of the enemy troops and managed to stab the firing button at the same instant. The man's space suit blew out at the right knee, blood and white vapor silently exploding into vacuum as the man toppled backward, arms waving.

Then Lucky, still sliding, collided with the fourth Chinese soldier and sent him sprawling, the two of them tangled in a desperate embrace, the other man on top of him.

There was no time, no thought, no elegance for finesse. Lucky's right hand found the hilt of his K-bar, sheathed on his hip, popped the locking strap, dragged the knife free. The PRC soldier—Lucky could see the man's face just above his through the dark visor, could see the terror-widened eyes—reached down and pounded at Lucky's helmet with clenched, gloved fists, trying to smash the visor.

Lucky slammed the point of the knife up against his opponent's throat as hard as he could. The black blade glanced off the helmet locking ring and snapped off clean at the hilt, the metal made brittle by the extreme cold.

He shifted his aim and drove upward with the hilt still clenched in his hand, smashing the guard against the enemy soldier's visor. And *again*. And *again* . . .

*Kaminski*
*Ice Station Zebra, Europa*
*1606 hours Zulu*

Kaminski saw the desperate fight taking place forty-five meters to his left. One Marine—Leckie, according to the IFF tag on his HUD—was flat on his PLSS with a PRC trooper on top of him; a second Chinese soldier was getting to his feet after a fall, while two more lay on the ice nearby, one moving, the other still. Raising his 580, he targeted the lone enemy soldier as he moved to help his friend, blowing out the back panel of the man's PLSS unit, which exploded in a burst of fast-venting oxygen.

He was drawing a careful bead on the bad guy on top of Leckie when the Marine's repeated blows to the man's helmet visor got through. The PRC trooper rolled off of Leckie, gloves scrabbling at his faceplate, which was crazed like a ball of crystal smashed by a hammer.

Leckie must have opened a pinprick of a crack; the visor hadn't blown, but the soldier had panicked. Kaminski calmly shot him through the chest, putting him down.

"Leckie! You okay?"

The Marine picked up his dropped rifle, waved, and got to his feet. "O-okay, Sergeant Major. Thanks!"

Kaminski was measuring angles with his eyes. Leckie was close to the bottom of the crater slope, close enough, maybe, that the tanks on top couldn't depress their fire enough to hit him. "Leckie! Can you get back up that slope? We need someone to paint those tanks!"

"Okay! I'll try!"

"*Do* it, Marine! On the double!"

"*Aye, aye, sir!*"

Leckie started moving up the slope.


*Niemeyer*
*On approach to Ice Station Zebra,*
  *Europa*
*1607 hours Zulu*


Corporal Duane Niemeyer peered over the side of the lobber, convinced that they were descending entirely too fast. "Damn it, BJ! Doesn't this thing have brakes?" he demanded.

"Screw that. Just get that 580 in action!"

Campanelli had both of her hands on the lobber's attitude controls. The strain had tightened her voice. They were falling toward the Zebra crater, completing their long, arcing trajectory from OP Igloo far over the curve of the horizon to the southwest.

Reaching down, he unstrapped his 580, which had been secured beside the lobber's right-side seat. He spent the next few seconds concentrating on the warmup procedure, and bringing the weapon up to charge.

The battle was a sprawling, confused affair. From a hundred meters up and southwest of the crater, he could see tiny, running, moving figures, but he couldn't determine who was who. All of them wore white, and were moving against a background of dappled, twisted whites lightly tainted with browns, blues, and greens. There were some vehicles of some sort lined up along the west rim—probably robot tanks. He'd need something with more kick than a 580 to more than annoy one of those.

He could see the Chinese lander to the north, squatting on the ice like a gray, four-legged soccer ball.

"Don't look at them," BJ warned. She must have seen him turning in his seat to see.

"Huh? Why not?"

"They've been tracking us since we came over the horizon, and trying to use lasers on us. Low-watt, point-defense stuff. Not much punch at this range, but they've put some holes in our undercarriage already, and the targeting beams'll fry your retinas if you're looking when they flash."

He turned his head away quickly, concentrating instead on the crater ahead. They were already holed? Hardly reassuring . . .

His rifle beeped readiness. Raising it, he watched the crosshair bob and weave across the scattering of tiny figures. Damn! The movement of the lobber kept him from holding any one target long enough to get off a shot. He tried increasing the magnification on his HUD, but that also magnified the movements of the crosshairs. He couldn't brace himself still long enough.

"Can you hold us still?"

"Negative! Not unless we want that lander to punch us out of the sky!" An attitude control jet fired, rolling them sharply right. His stomach rebelled and he almost vomited.

Somehow he managed to hold steady on one running man, but when he touched the interrogate button on the side of his rifle, the figure on his HUD lit up green, with the word FRIENDLY.

Hastily, he shifted targets. There was someone standing beside one of those flat-topped tanks, just visible through the swirl of freezing steam, and the IFF interrogation brought up the word HOSTILE. He clamped down on the firing button before he could lose the target.

*Leckie*
*Ice Station Zebra, Europa*
*1609 hours Zulu*

Lucky never would have made it so quickly if the ground hadn't been pulverized by the bombardment at the beginning of the fight. When he'd climbed this slope before—had it only been twenty-five minutes ago?—the ice had been hard. Once moving, he could maintain his momentum with a kangaroo hop, but footing was treacherous, and each time he touched the slope there'd been the danger of having his feet go right out from under him.

Now, the surface of the slope had crumbled to a mushy blend of powder and ice-cube-sized chunks, like blue-white gravel in snow. The stuff dragged at his feet with each lurching step, holding him back, slowing him.

A red light, indicating a paint by an enemy laser, winked on in his HUD. He threw himself flat, searching for the source. To his right, the nearest of the enemy tanks rested hunkered down in the ice rubble, partly enveloped in glittering dust . . . water freezing in hard vacuum. A space-suited figure moved behind the tank, aiming a Type 110 rifle with a laser sight.

The drifting crystals above the figure's helmet strobed, suddenly, with blue-white light, like the popping of a camera flash. The figure dropped to its knees, clawing at its helmet, and in that second, Lucky shifted his targeting cursor to the center of the suit and fired, blasting a fist-sized hole from the chest.

He looked up. A lobber was coming in, high and fast. That first laser bolt, partly absorbed and scattered by the frozen vapor, had come from there.

Lucky didn't stop to think about it. He had a good angle here, halfway up the crater rim, almost looking up the belly of the nearest Chinese tank. He thumbed his 580's selector switch from pulse to beam, aimed at the tank's glacis, and fired.

Set for continuous beam, the M-580 lost most of its

punch. Certainly, it couldn't hurt the centimeter-thick armor laminate of a Chinese *zidong tanke*.

"Kaminski!" he shouted over the company channel. "Painting! Take him! Now!"

*Kaminski*
*Ice Station Zebra, Europa*
*1610 hours Zulu*

Kaminski's optics couldn't see the laser paint from this angle, but he could see Leckie far up the inner rim slope and knew what the Marine was doing. He slapped Jellowski's helmet. "Laser lock! Fire!"

"You're clear, Jelly!" Kaminski called, verifying that no one was standing behind Jellowski, in the threat zone of the Wyvern's vented backblast.

Jellowski squeezed the trigger, and the rocket slashed into the black sky on a plume of white exhaust.

"She's targeting!" Jellowski called. "Tone! Lock!"

Kaminski was already releasing the spent load tube and slamming and lock-twisting another into its place. On the crater rim, a tank exploded, with bits of armor and unraveling track spinning through the sky.

The angle was too severe from down here for a decent paint, but Leckie had a good position, and was close enough to hold a sharp, steady beam on the target. Once the Wyvern was free from its tube, its sensor picked up the reflected backscatter of laser light and homed in with deadly accuracy.

"Second target!" Leckie yelled over the radio. "Painting!"

Jellowski loosed a second tank killer, and seconds later, a second tank staggered as its left track was blown away, then began a slow-motion tumble from its perch atop the rim, rolling over and over in a silent avalanche of debris all the way to the crater floor.

*Descending Thunder No. 4*
*Two kilometers west of Ice Station*
   *Zebra, Europa*
*1611 hours Zulu*


Colonel Yang winced as the shoulder-launched missile slammed into his face. The shock of the disconnect didn't hurt, exactly, but it shook him. There was no word for the sensation in any language, but it was as strong as pain, and as startling. He'd been killed several times now in rapid succession—or the steeds he'd been riding had been—and the successive shocks had left him feeling muzzy-headed, a little dizzy. Hu was dead, cut down by laser fire moments ago. Most of the troops were scattered, pinned down, or isolated in small, savagely fighting pockets.

The tide of battle was turning against him. He could feel it. Every battle has a rhythm, a pacing . . . and the pacing of this one was swiftly slowing, from a surging beat of victory to chaos and defeat.

"The enemy has shown unexpected flexibility, General," he said, speaking into the satellite-relayed channel back to the main base. At the same time, he used the optics of one of the surviving *zidong tanke* to stare over the edge of the rim, down into the crater. Men were moving everywhere, loping along as if in some slow-motion dream, a tangled confusion impossible to sort out.

"The enemy is heavily armed and quite determined," he continued. "The bombardment had little effect and we have had heavy losses. I request permission to pull back to the lander and abort the attack."

"We can have reinforcements at your position within fifteen minutes, Yang," Xiang's voice said. "Can you hold until then?"

"Not without risking complete destruction. What are your orders, General?"

There was a long pause. "Fall back to the lander. Save what you can and fall back. We will need to deal with the Americans in a different way."

Yang heard the anger in Xiang's voice. "We have hurt them badly," he said, needing, somehow, to justify the losses.

There was no reply, and he began issuing the orders for the withdrawal.

*Niemeyer*
*On approach to Ice Station Zebra,*
  *Europa*
*1607 hours Zulu*

"What the hell are you trying to do?" Downer shouted.

"I was trying to fry a tank," BJ replied. "But I think we just lost the engines!"

"Oh . . . *shit!*"

The crater rim was rushing toward them now. "Unstrap!" BJ shouted. "Get ready to jump!"

"What?"

"No more thrust! We're going down hard!" She was unfastening her own harness as she spoke, and Downer followed suit. They were dropping now, the lobber almost on its side, falling toward the flat, wedge shape of one of the Chinese robot tanks. Campanelli, he realized, had been trying to pass the lobber above the tank with the plasma thrusters on—a difficult and dangerous tactic that, if it had worked, might have fried the robot's circuits.

Unfortunately, the damage they'd taken from the enemy lander's point defense lasers had junked their engines, and they were in free fall now.

"Ready . . . set . . . go!" BJ shouted, launching herself from the seat. Downer closed his eyes and jumped in the other direction.

It took a long time to fall, and when he hit it felt as though someone had smashed him hard in the legs with a hard-swung baseball bat. Fortunately, the ice wasn't as hard as it looked. When he hit, the surface gave way a bit, and he found himself sliding feet first down the crumbly, broken surface in a small avalanche of broken ice.

Several Chinese soldiers were running past, stumbling up the slope. He realized that his laser rifle was gone, lost in the jump and the impact that followed. He lay still and watched them pass.

"BJ! BJ, where are you? Are you okay?"

"I'm okay!" was her reply. "Had the wind knocked out of me, a bit."

He found that he could stand, though pain shot through his left ankle. He started back up the slope, limping heavily. Well, if he could *walk*, it wasn't busted.

Downer found BJ sitting on the ice, slowly getting to her feet. "Looks like the bad guys are on the run," he told her. From here, atop the crater rim, he could see several dozen men streaming back across the ice plain toward the Chinese lander. Two surviving robot tanks backed slowly away, covering the retreat.

"I think," she said, a bit unsteadily, "I think we won!"

"Damn!" he replied. "And we missed it!"

"Don't sound so disappointed, son," the major's voice said over his radio. "They *will* be back, you know!"

# FOURTEEN

*CO's Office, E-DARES Facility*
*Ice Station Zebra, Europa*
*1120 hours Zulu*

Jeff had designated a small room off of the compartment now employed as C-3 as his office. There was a folding cot in there—comfortable enough in .13 G—so that he could sleep close to the command center without having to take the elevator all the way down from the sleeping quarters in an emergency.

It also gave him a place to talk to people in private. "My God, Frank! Do you really think this will work?"

Kaminski tugged at his long nose. "Ought to, sir. The physics work out right. I've been going over these figures with Lieutenant Walthers, and he's convinced it'll work."

"And we have all the materials to build it?"

"Oh, that's no problem. I got the idea looking at that fallen microwave antenna. That's the hardest part. *And* we have enough superconductor cable. The only question is how many shots we'll get before the *Xing Shan* arrives and spoils the party." He pointed at the schematic showing on Jeff's PAD. "We won't be able to hide the damned thing, or move it. But considering that it might not survive even one shot, that's not a big drawback."

"Well, the other question is whether one shot would do us any good."

"Well, normally we'd need to fire for effect, but as Lieutenant Walthers pointed out, we have what you might call an ideal situation here. No atmosphere. That means no friction. No drag. No windage. Nothing but gravity, mass, acceleration, and speed. We know the first two to enough accuracy that we can be very precise with placement. We can control the third, which gives us the fourth. My guess, Major, is that we'll be accurate to within, say, a hundred meters."

"That's still one hell of a big bull's-eye, Sergeant Major. I wonder if we'd be better advised—yes?"

He looked up as Sergeant Matthews knocked on the office door, then stepped inside. "Uh, excuse me, Major. Dr. Ishiwara is here. He said you'd agreed to see him."

Jeff glanced at the time readout on his PAD. Damn. He was falling behind sched.

"Very well. Tell him just a moment."

"Aye, aye, sir."

"I'm sorry, Frank. Ishiwara has been trying to see me since reveille this morning."

"Not a problem, sir."

"I'd say . . . let's go with this idea. It'll give our people something to stay busy with. Keep up morale."

"Ay-firmative, Major. They're pretty high right now. Nothing like beating off a sneak attack to boost morale. But the losses will hit 'em pretty soon, and then they'll start thinking about why they're here. Why *them*. It'll be good to have them working at a project this complex."

"See to it, then, Frank. Keep me posted."

"Aye, aye, sir!"

"One more thing."

"Sir?"

"In the inventory of stuff we brought down on the bug . . . might there have been an American flag?"

"I *always* have an American flag, Major. You know that! Tradition."

Jeff knew how seriously Kaminski took that particular

tradition. During the mission on Mars twenty-five years earlier, Kaminski had happened to have a small American flag with him . . . and that flag had been raised above the Cydonian base when the Marines captured it back from UN forces. A photograph of the raising, a space-suited analogue of the famous flag-raising over Suribachi in 1945, had become enormously popular, both within the Corps and outside.

"Find a staff and have it raised above the E-DARES facility. I'm sure you can rig up a rod or something from hoist to fly. To keep it visible, even in vacuum."

Frank grinned. "Yes, sir!"

"Maybe it'll help remind 'em why we're here. Dismissed."

"Aye, aye, sir."

He executed a ninety-degree left-face and strode from the compartment. Jeff used the comm channel on his PAD. "Send in Dr. Ishiwara, please, Sergeant."

"Yessir!"

Shigeru Ishiwara was a small, compact man with a guarded manner. The CWS science team had withdrawn to their own labs and personal spaces in the E-DARES facility since the Marines had come aboard, and Jeff had rarely seen, much less had a chance to talk to, any of them. Lately, Ishiwara had become more and more of a spokesperson, a liaison of sorts, between the civilian and military branches of the base personnel.

"*Konichiwa*, Dr. Ishiwara."

"*Konichiwa*, Major." Shigeru Ishiwara was a traditionalist, bowing, rather than shaking hands. "Thank you for seeing me."

"My pleasure." Well, that was a lie, but a polite one. Jeff was facing a small mountain of work in the wake of the attack yesterday, and didn't have time at the moment for civilian or scientific concerns. He was especially worried about the morale of the company, especially after losing twenty-two men. That was a 37 percent unit loss; *10* percent lost in a single action could cripple a unit, break down discipline, destroy morale. That was why he'd okayed Kaminski's rather wild-sounding special project.

Still, he was here to protect these people, and that meant keeping the lines of communications open. "Have a seat. What's on your mind, sir?"

The scientist seated himself across the desk from him and handed him a data clip. "That, Major," Ishiwara said, "is a complete list of the damage suffered by the base yesterday during the attack. It includes an inventory of supplies damaged or destroyed."

"Thank you, sir." He'd asked Hallerman, the base supply manager, to give him a list of losses and damages. "Briefly, can you give me an overview?"

"Our most serious material loss was food. When we were told you people were arriving, we moved much of the food out of supply lockers here in the E-DARES facility and placed it in three storage sheds on the surface. A natural deep-freeze, you might say."

"Yes. Keeping it well clear of the waste storage sheds, I presume."

Ishiwara ignored the weak joke. "Two of those sheds were badly damaged in the attack. The director has Hallerman and two of our technicians checking it, but many, perhaps most, of the food packs were torn open and exposed to vacuum. Some may have been . . . cooked, I guess is as good a word as any, by the surface radiation. It poses no health threat to us, but frozen liquids and sauces boiled and burst from their packs. Frozen meats and vegetables exploded. Like putting them in a microwave, you understand?"

"Yes. Yes, I do. So how much do we have left?"

"Mr. Hallerman will have the complete report later today. As a first estimate, however, I would guess that we have one week of food left for everyone here. *If* we skimp and go on short rations."

That was bad. It would take a week for a ship to get out here from Earth. The Chinese sure as hell weren't going to share their food. "Very well. We will go on short rations, Doctor. And I will talk to Earth at once about getting a supply ship out." *If* it could run the blockade of that Chinese cruiser up there. What was really needed was a full relief expedition, with an American warship to take out the PRC vessel.

"There . . . is another matter, Major Warhurst." Ishiwara looked uncomfortable. "Something I must discuss with you."

"Go ahead, Doctor. I've had nothing but bad news so far today. A little more won't hurt me."

"Dr. Vasaliev and the others . . . requested that I speak to you. They are . . . *we* are concerned about what the Singer may think about what is going on up here."

"The Singer? I thought you all believed that to be an automated beacon of some kind? Do you have some new information? That it's . . . manned?"

"During the fighting yesterday, shortly after the Chinese ship bombarded the crater, in fact, the Singer fell silent."

"My God!"

"It is the first silence we have heard since its discovery. It remained silent for twenty-eight minutes, sixteen seconds, and then resumed its song. The patterns of sounds seem to be much the same. ELF emissions have increased, however."

"Extreme Low-Frequency radio waves?"

"Yes. The Singer has always emitted some, but the power of its transmission has increased now by a factor of two."

"Is it trying to communicate?"

A shrug. "We don't know. ELF waves, unlike shorter EM waves, penetrate water to great depths. They do not penetrate ice well, however, though we have been picking up the signals where the ice is thin."

"Like here, at the Pit."

"Exactly."

"So . . . what does all of that mean?"

"We don't know. And that, Major, is the point. We don't

know." He spread his hands. "To those of us monitoring it at the time, it was almost as though . . . as though it were *listening*. And the ELF transmission could be an attempt to communicate. Or . . . it could be RF leakage from some other process entirely. We have no way of deciphering it."

"You really think it could hear us? Hear the battle, I mean? It's eight hundred kilometers from here, and eighty kilometers deep."

"Believe me, Major. I have had considerable experience working underwater. Sound travels very well in the sea, and the roof of ice would serve to focus the sound downward, into deep channels. Yes, I believe it heard. Certainly the sounds of the bombardment. Perhaps other things as well. We don't know what their capabilities are."

"What do you recommend?"

"There is little that *can* be done at this point, Major. Unless you would care to release the research submarines you brought here with you. For as long as we have listened up here, the Singer has remained unmoving, unresponsive. Someday, we will have to go to it, if we are to make contact."

"I agree, Doctor. Unfortunately, we're in the middle of a war here, you may have noticed. Not exactly the best time to try making contact with an alien civilization."

"Understood. But . . . if it should become necessary to make direct contact . . ."

"Show me unequivocal proof that we can talk to them, and that they want to, and I'll do everything in my power to see that it happens."

"There could be a terrible danger. This . . . this war is not exactly proof of our civilized nature. We don't know how the Singer will react."

Jeff folded his hands before him on the desk. "Dr. Ishiwara, my orders are to safeguard American and CWS interests here on Europa. The Chinese are a threat to those interests. What do you suggest I do to stop them—use harsh language? Anyway, if the Singer gets interested enough to come up and see what's going on—"

"We might wish it had stayed below, Major."

"So what is it you want? To surrender? That's what the Chinese are demanding." A single, brief communiqué had come through after the enemy retreat from the crater yesterday: *Surrender or be destroyed*. It was part ultimatum, part message, a declaration that the enemy considered their initial defeat a temporary setback only.

Ishiwara sighed. "Some here have suggested as much. To be blunt, they don't see any other way out."

"Dr. Vasaliev?"

"I shouldn't name names. But we *have* discussed it."

Warhurst watched the Japanese scientist for a moment, hands folded. The man returned his stare with a bland lack of expression. "They put you up to this, didn't they?"

"Excuse me, Major?"

"Vasaliev and the others who want to surrender—or who are afraid that our little scrap with the Chinese up here is going to wake giants down below. You weren't going along with them, and they made you do this to . . . what? Humiliate you? Pull you into line? Show you how intractable us low-brow military types can be?"

"I . . . really can't comment on that, Major."

"No, of course not."

The expressionless exterior finally cracked, just a little. He looked away, embarrassed. "Perhaps, sir, you should speak directly with Dr. Vasaliev about this."

"I think I will. I don't like to see power or authority abused." Jeff leaned back in his chair. "Tell me about yourself, Dr. Ishiwara."

He looked surprised. "What is it you want to know?"

"You are an authority on underwater archeology. That much is in your record. And my impression is that while Pyotr Vasaliev is the director here, he's basically the administrative honcho, while you're the chief expert on our friends down below. Am I right?"

"Dr. Vasaliev has a great deal of expertise in xenotechnoarcheology. He studied under Dr. Alexander himself when he taught at CMU."

"That doesn't answer my question."

"I have only the highest respect for Dr. Vasaliev, Major."

"Of course." He decided to try a different approach. "So . . . what interested you in underwater archeology?"

He took a long time to answer. "My . . . father is a powerful man. He was once Minister of Trade and Industry, before he became the ambassador from my country to the United States. Later he was a senior advisor with the Ministry of Science and Technology. He was largely responsible for the period of intense cooperation and technology exchanges between Japan and the United States after the UN War, you know."

"I do know."

"There was, of course, an almost frantic scramble to reinterpret our understanding of history and of human origins against the backdrop of the discoveries on Mars and on our own moon. A very few artifacts and certain large, architectural wonders were now seen either as constructs by alien colonizers or as structures raised by humans under alien tutelage or cultural influence. Some of our dating conventions had to be completely revised. At the same time, we needed to be very careful not to fall into the old cultist trap of believing that *every* invention, *every* impressive structure, *every* ancient mystery was the result of alien interference in human prehistory. The remains of extraterrestrial colonization attempts on Earth are really quite minimal, and all have been extensively reworked and rebuilt over the ages." He smiled, becoming more animated. It was clear that the wonder, the *mystery* of ancient human contact with extraterrestrials held him in its siren's call. "At Giza, you know, the pyramids were once truncated, and reached their current stature only slowly, over thousands of years and through several redesigns. And the Sphinx did not acquire a *human* face until, we think, the Fourth Dynasty. An records uncovered on the Moon show that it began as a great stone lion facing the equinoctial rising of the constellation we call Leo over twelve thousand years ago.

"In any event, I grew up at a time when interest in ancient architecture, in ancient alien visitors, was exploding across Japan. How could I avoid it? By the time I was in university at Kyoto, a great deal of work was being done at Yonaguni. You know of it?"

"Somewhat. An ancient monument of some sort, submerged off the Japanese coast?"

"Exactly. An immense structure submerged since the ending of the last Ice Age, at *least* ten thousand years ago, probably more. It was first recognized as anomalous by divers in the 1980s. As we learned what it really was, it became an object of considerable national pride, you see. The Ancients had visited *us* as well as Egypt and Peru, Lebanon and Iraq. I learned to dive expressly to visit the monument. Later I joined the Navy and became an expert in small submersibles. I am afraid my father—how do you say it?—*pulled strings* to get me into the JDF programs I wanted.

"In the years since I have done research both on the moon and on Mars, at Cydonia and in Planitia Utopia. When they needed a submarine expert to study the Singer phenomenon, I was the logical candidate as Senior Researcher."

"I see. Excuse me for bringing this up, Doctor, but . . . you lost a brother in the UN War, didn't you?"

Ishiwara's face again became an unreadable mask. "Yukio Ishiwara. One of the Six Eagles. A hero in my land."

"He died attacking an American space station, before Japan changed sides and came in with us against the UN. How do you feel about working with Americans, Dr. Ishiwara?"

"That was . . . a long time ago. I tend not to be political in my thinking, Major. Or in my attitude toward others."

"And yet we have a political situation here. Who will make first contact with living extraterrestrials? Us? Or the Chinese? No, I should restate that . . . because *you*, Dr. Ishiwara, will be in a position to lead that contact no matter who wins this fight. If the Chinese take over this facility,

I imagine they will value your expertise. You could easily end up working for them."

"Is that why you have denied us access to the Manta submersibles? To block us if we are forced to work for your enemy?"

"That's part of it. We were also looking at using their electronic components, if need be, as spares. And . . . they may have suffered some damage in the battle. I have our SEALs checking them over now, to make sure their hulls are tight, their systems intact.

"But I'll tell you this frankly, Doctor. If there's a danger that they're going to overrun this facility, or if we're forced to surrender, I *will* destroy both Mantas to keep them from falling into enemy hands."

"I . . . see."

"And how about you? Are you political enough to see the dangers of letting the Chinese make first contact with a technologically advanced civilization?"

"First of all, we still don't know that the Singer represents such a civilization. We understand very little about it at all. I'll also say, frankly, that I fear that the Chinese intend to *force* contact with an intelligence which, so far, has remained completely aloof. That could have devastating consequences, for all of us. We could be like insects attempting to awaken a slumbering and ill-tempered man.

"However, I wouldn't care to guess *what* I would do with a gun pressed to my head. Would any man? Would you?"

"I have my duty, Doctor. And my orders."

"And I have my duty to my science. To knowledge, to an understanding of where we came from and who we are. It is clear we have a heritage, Major, one set somewhere among the stars, and I intend to learn what that heritage is, one way or another." He cocked his head to one side, looking almost mischievous. "Perhaps you should set one of your Marines as a guard over me, Major. To destroy *me* as you plan to destroy the Mantas."

"I don't think that will be necessary." Although his orders did mention that very possibility, damn them. How far could he go along with that level of bureaucratic paranoia? "In any case, there's no guarantee the Chinese would require your services. I'm sure they have their own scientific team over there, and a mistrust of anyone working with the CWS."

"Quite true."

"Tell me, Doctor. Just how would you assess the threat of our generating a bad response from our friends downstairs? I have more than enough to worry about with the Chinese knocking at our door, without also being concerned about aliens dropping in."

"I feel," Ishiwara said quietly, "like one of the mice in the walls. There is something extraordinarily large, extraordinarily powerful down there. It knows we're here, but it hasn't deigned to notice us . . . yet.

"And we may not like it when it does."

*Crater floor*
*Ice Station Zebra, Europa*
*1310 hours Zulu*

"Mission control!" Lucky shouted. "We have separation!"

The platoon channel crackled with laughter, cheers and catcalls. "Whoa!" Corporal Jesus Garcia's voice called above the rest. "Fifteen point two one meters for Lissa, sixteen point oh five meters for Woj! A new world's record!"

BJ Campanelli laughed. "Well, a record for *this* world, anyway!"

"Whaddaya mean, *this* world, BJ?" Lance Corporal Richard Wojak replied, laughing as he picked himself up off the ice. "You think we could do this on Earth, or any other world?"

"Absodamnlutely," Corporal Lissa Cartwright added. "This has got to be the best ice dancing anywhere in the universe!"

There were ten of them—"volunteers," in a you-you-you-and-you way—for a working party on the surface well south of the landing deck. Sergeant Major Kaminski had set them to welding together an A-frame scratched together out of struts taken from the wrecked bug, then using plasma torches to melt the ice so that they could raise the frame and have it freeze into an upright position. The work was well under way when Kaminski and Kuklok had retired back to the E-DARES facility to work out some problem or other with the Marine team working on the crater rim to the southwest, leaving the working party under the supervision of Second Platoon's Gunnery Sergeant Pope.

The A-frame was up, though, in quicker time than anyone had guessed, which left ten Marines more or less on their own for a half hour or so—too short a time to bother hopping it back to the E-DARES and unsuiting, too short a time to do much of anything, in fact, but amuse themselves on the ice.

The dance competition was the result.

Lucky walked over to BJ and executed a stiff half-bow—the best he could do in his SC-swaddled suit. "May I have the honor of this dance, BJ?"

"I thought you'd never ask!" She extended her right glove and he took it, feeling the slight, invisible shove from the magnetic field enveloping her suit. He gave her arm a tug, pulling her against him, torso to torso.

The superconductor weave in the outer cloth layer of their Mark IIB suits held an electrical charge; its endless circulation around the suit generated a fairly strong magnetic field, polarized outside to inside with the positive charge out—their main protection against the proton flux that made up the majority of Europa's background radiation. As they pulled themselves together, forcing their suits into close contact, the like charges repelled one another, the pressure becoming stronger the more tightly they pulled themselves together.

Standing together, they took a clumsy step and kickoff

in opposite directions on the ice, moving into a tight, counterclockwise spin.

In the hours since the battle, the portions of the crater surface partly melted by the bombardment had refrozen. Several areas, reduced to ice mush by the shock waves from the mass-driven impacts, had refrozen to a mirrorlike smoothness, made slick by the radiation-induced dissociation of the surface ice into a sheen of water and hydrogen peroxide. Walking was so tricky in some areas that safety lines had been set up to assist the progress of people moving about on the crater floor, checking damage, retrieving bodies, or engaged in other working party evolutions.

They'd found a particularly large stretch of glass-smooth ice south of the landing field, perfect for an impromptu round of what BJ had called Fun with Physics.

They clung to one another's suits, gripping the carry handles set into each side of their PLSS backpacks, and continued to step and kick in unison, increasing the speed of their spin. Lucky's visor was pressed against BJ's, and he could see her laughing features, murky behind the dark polarization of their helmets, centimeters from his own. The flat, icy background whipped past behind her head, the rotations marked off by the small, inner gasp of surprise that occurred each time the sun or the swollen immensity of Jupiter swung rapidly across the sky. It was almost in full phase now, with the sun in the opposite sky low in the west. Their shadows stretched out across the ice, whipping across the mirrored surface like a long, black blade.

"Ready!" BJ said over the company channel. "Ten . . . nine . . . eight . . ."

"Seven . . . six . . . five . . . four . . ." He chanted the countdown with her, as it was echoed by the Marines standing in a broad, loose circle around the two of them. They pulled themselves even closer as they spun, battling the powerful, magnetic repulsion between them.

"Three . . . two . . . one . . . *release!*"

They let go of one another at the same instant. The repulsion of their suit shields, augmented by the centrifugal force of their spin, blasted them apart.

On that slick surface, they rocketed back from one another in opposite directions, both losing their balance and falling onto the ice, but slowly enough to do no damage. Lucky landed on his backside and began spinning as he slid rapidly across the ice. Two of the watching Marines stepped aside to let him sail past. Then he hit a patch of rougher ice, felt a cobblestone kind of vibration through the seat of his suit, and quickly came to a stop.

Jesus Garcia had stepped up to the point where Lucky and BJ had parted company and faced first him, then BJ, using his suit's laser rangefinder to measure the distance traveled. "All right!" he exclaimed. "Sixteen point one one meters for Beej . . . and Lucky gets a big sixteen point two one meters . . . and another new record!"

"Way to go, Lucky!" Coughlin said, shouting above the cheers. He helped Lucky to his feet, then clapped him on the helmet. "Not bad for doin' it with a real girl, huh?"

"Screw you, Cog!" but he laughed as he said it. The fact that he preferred simulated sex to the real thing was the subject of endless jabs and jibes within the platoon, but he was good-natured about it. And it wasn't that he didn't like the real thing.

"Aw, lay off him, Cog," BJ said. "The poor boy's just confused. He'll get his priorities straight one of these days."

"Yeah," Lucky said. "You wanna help straighten me out, BJ?"

"In your dreams!"

"Ha! Which is exactly what I do with virtual sex! In my dreams, and *any*time I want it, any *way* I want it!"

"What the *hell* do you people think you're doing?" The voice was Sergeant Major Kaminski's. He strode into the circle, then planted himself there, a glowering giant, fists on hips. "Leave you jerk-offs alone for five minutes, and what happens?"

"C'mon, Ski, they weren't doing any—" Gunnery Sergeant Pope began.

"You people were goddamn screwing off in an environment where one wrong step will get you *dead!*" Kaminski shouted. "My God! The Skipper links in through Campanelli's helmet camera, and what does he get? A point-blank bellyful of Leckie's face! It's enough to turn your stomach!"

"It was my responsibility," Pope said.

"Yeah, you're right there, mister. You're on report. You're *all* on report. All of you, gather up your shit and fall in. We're marching back to the barracks."

A chorus of groans sounded over the comm channel. Marching on Europa was slow, tedious, and prone to embarrassing falls. The order amounted to administrative discipline.

As Lucky was picking up some of the welding gear, he found himself near Campanelli. He chinned in a private channel request.

"Hey," he said when she acknowledged. "Thanks for the dance."

"Anytime, Lucky."

"I could use one of those drinks now."

She laughed. "I'm not sure Warhorse is gonna cut us any slack. But as soon as we're back on Earth . . ."

Back on Earth. Lucky turned and looked up at the grossly swollen surprise of Jupiter, low in the east. A tiny red sphere was transiting the gas giant's face, chasing its own round, black shadow—Io.

Kaminski's sudden appearance had been like a dash of ice water in the face, a sharp reawakening to reality. For a while there, the skylarking had pushed the sheer alienness of this place back, held it at bay. It was amazing, he thought, what humans could learn to accept as normal, given even a little time and adaptability. Even with space suits, even with Jupiter in the sky, the ten of them had forgotten for a moment where they were.

Maybe that was an indication of just how much they *didn't* want to be there. Now it all came back. Damn . . . why did Tone have to buy it?

"My God," Lucky said. "I hate this place."

He'd forgotten the private channel was still open. "Welcome to Bumfuq," BJ told him.

# FIFTEEN

*CO's Office, E-DARES Facility*
*Ice Station Zebra, Europa*
*0910 hours Zulu*

Jeff shook his head sadly. "What the hell were you thinking, Gunny? If someone had torn their suit falling on the ice . . ."

Tom Pope stood at attention, "centered on the hatch" in front of Jeff's desk. "No excuse, sir."

"Don't give me that Parris Island shit, Gunny! You've been in the Corps—what?—thirteen years?"

"Fourteen, sir."

"Long enough to know better. Why didn't you stop it?"

Pope's eyebrow arced toward the dark fuzz of his hairline. "Begging the Major's pardon, sir . . . but I saw no reason to. They'd been working hard, they had some down time. I saw no reason they couldn't have a little fun."

" 'A little fun.' A *little* fun?" He checked an entry on his PAD display. "Corporal Cartwright had a small hole blown in her suit in the first battle Monday. Her suit had a temporary patch installed on the field. Suppose that make-do had blown while she was screwing around on the ice?"

"Her suit had been checked out by the armorer, sir. I double-checked it myself. If there was a problem with the repair, then she shouldn't have been out there in that suit at all."

"Agreed. That's not the issue."

"Then, begging the major's pardon again, I'm not sure I understand what is."

"The issue is responsible behavior. From the men and women of this company. From the man who was entrusted with their safety. Damn it, in the past three days, we've gone through four attacks. We've lost thirty-four people altogether—thirty-four people! Almost half of our strength! We damned sure can't afford to lose any more, and we *sure* as hell can't lose any to dumb-ass accidents caused by sky-larking!"

"Nothing happened, sir."

"No. Thank God. But, damn it, why were they even on the surface unless it was absolutely necessary? The idea is to keep surface exposure to a minimum. It's not just that I don't want them cracking a visor or tearing a suit and dying up there. I'd like to know they have a chance of retiring from the Corps, living to a ripe old age, and *not* dying of cancer! Or radiation sickness, six months from now."

"Yes, sir."

Jeff glared at him for a moment. Tom Pope was a good man. Silver Star, Bronze Star with cluster, three Purple Hearts. He'd fought in Cuba, Mexico, and Russia, and been part of the Marine Recon/SEAL team that had taken down those Brazilian terrorists on the cruise ship in Puerto Rico five years back and disarmed that do-it-yourself nuke they were smuggling into Miami. After that, he'd been at Parris Island, first as an assistant drill instructor, then as a DI, until he'd been accepted for Space Training at Quantico. There was no questioning his bravery . . . or his intelligence.

He decided to try a different approach.

"Okay, Tom," he said. "I can't believe you didn't have a reason for standing by and letting that happen. You're too good a gunnery sergeant, too good a Marine to let that sort of skylarking go on without a reason. You care to enlighten me?"

"Sir, I—"

"I don't know the men and women in Second Platoon as well as you do. If I'm missing something, I want to know what it is."

"It's not something *wrong,* exactly . . ."

Jeff said nothing but waited for him to continue.

"Look, sir, all I've got to go on here is a hunch, a *feeling.* This place has the company spooked. It has us all spooked. Working and fighting up there, with Jupiter hanging overhead like a big, staring eye—"

"Tom, you're not pulling some sort of canned peaches shit on me here, are you?"

Canned peaches was an old, old tradition in the Corps, a quirk going back at least as far as World War II and the first amtracs used to storm enemy-held beaches. Corps superstition held that it was bad luck to eat canned peaches aboard any Marine vehicle, especially armor or amphibious vehicles. Marines who'd found peaches in their rations had always assiduously traded them to members of the other services—Navy or Army—in order to avoid mechanical breakdown.

Superstition. But the business of war—and the ongoing uncertainty of survival—tended to feed superstition like gasoline feeding a fire.

"No, sir," Tom replied. "It's not like that at all. It's . . . I guess it's just that this place is so, so *alien.*"

"My point exactly."

"But, well, sir . . . I've been on Mars. I was stationed there for six months after Space School. You have to wear a suit, but most places, anyway, you can squint your eyes and just about imagine you're standing in a desert back in New Mexico. Sometimes the sky's even blue. And on the Moon, well, that's about as different as a place can be, but on the Near Side, anyway, Earth is right there. All you have to do is look up. If there's trouble, Earth and blue skies are three or four days away—a few hours if it's an emergency and you can grab an A-M shuttle.

"But the view here . . . my God. It's as strange as the Moon, but more so, with ice instead of gray dust and Jupiter so big and, and—*top-heavy* in the sky, you swear it's gonna fall right off its hook and land in your lap. A day that's three and a half days long, and the only time it's really dark is when the sun is in eclipse behind Jupiter. And then you can still see the dark side of the planet, kind of dim and ghostly like, with the aurora and lightning and stuff. The other moons, shuttling back and forth like beads on a string. And you know that Earth is an ungodly long way away—a week at a steady one G, three or more weeks with a coast phase in the middle."

"All of which is exactly why I came down on you, on them so hard. This is not a *human* environment."

"But you know how it is in the Corps, Major. Marines stick up for one another. They pull together, *gung ho*. They'll endure the most godawful hardships and assignments you care to dump on 'em. Privation. Hardship. Crowding. Combat. All of that just makes 'em closer, y'know what I mean?

"I guess what I'm trying to say, sir, is that they need to relax with each other sometimes. Cut loose. Skylark. Losing this many people shook 'em pretty bad, especially right after that first battle, when we lost so many. Giving 'em some time to unwind, especially without gold braid breathing down their necks—it helps morale. Sir."

"I see."

"The company . . . they're good people, sir. But they're facing a strange kind of lonely desperation out here. Seven hundred million klicks from home, in an alien environment that will kill them in an instant if they get careless, yeah . . . and an enemy that's whittling them down now a few at a time. I think they're just trying to hang on to their sanity, sir, whatever is left of it, by importing a little bit of home. For Marines, that means some down time away from supervision, a chance to play."

"We're in one hell of a playground."

"That we are, sir. But by making it a playground, they're humanizing it, making it home. You see my point, sir?"

"I think maybe I do."

"You know, we've been talking about intelligence a lot. Bull sessions after taps and on watch, that sort of thing. You know that Singer everyone's talking about?"

"Yes."

"Well, the word in the squad bay, sir, is that that thing can't be intelligent. All it does is sit in the deep ocean . . . singing. It doesn't *play*. And play may be the one thing that differentiates intelligent life from every other kind of critter in the universe."

"A profound thought, Tom. But we still have the problem of maintaining good order and discipline. What do you recommend?"

"Sir?"

"I've got a problem here, Gunnery Sergeant. Ten men and women skylarking while on a work detail, risking their lives, no less, playing games on the ice. And a platoon leader who should have known better and put a stop to it. What do you recommend I do about it?"

Tom pressed his lips together for a moment. "Sir, the Marines involved aren't to blame. I am. As you say, I should have stopped it. Frankly, I wouldn't want to squelch any behavior that smacked of high spirits."

"I agree. But I can't let it slide with a warning."

"No, sir. But you *could* put all the blame on me. That . . . might have one unfortunate side effect. The Marines involved might think you're a damned son of a bitch. Sir. On the other hand, I can't think of a better way to pull them together."

Jeff sighed. "Sometimes I think half of leadership is making the men hate you enough to pull together and get the job done."

"I also suggest that you keep them busy. Too much time to just sit and think makes men brood."

"Agreed. Kaminski's cannon ought to take care of that."

"And digging all of those goddamn holes. Do you really think that's going to help with the bombardments, sir?"

"It should. Earth HQ suggested it. Melting lots of holes

in star and circle patterns *should* dampen surface shock waves by quite a bit."

"Well, I imagine we'll find out later today. Papa Romeo's been pretty regular with his deliveries."

*Papa Romeo Charlie* was the Marine pet name for the *Star Mountain*, which changed orbit to bombard the base just before each PRC attack..

"Unfortunately, you're right," Jeff replied. All of the attacks since Monday's first big push had been relatively low scale and minor, designed to wear the Marine defenders down rather than overrun the base completely. There were two landers out there now, the first one, to the west, and a second that had touched down to the south. Others had come and gone in the past three days, but those two had remained behind as advance bases or OPs. Chinese troops lurked in the chaotic terrain south and east of the base, sniping with laser rifles and Type 80s when they had the chance. The Marines had learned to be *very* careful when moving anywhere along the crater rim.

"Very well," Jeff said, deciding. "I'm pulling one of your rockers, Tom. You are hereby reduced in rank to staff sergeant."

"Aye, aye, sir."

"And I'm turning your platoon over to Staff Sergeant Campanelli, who I am promoting to acting gunnery sergeant."

"A good choice, sir. She's sharp. A good Marine."

"I know. I want to recognize her role in spotting the incoming lander the other day, getting a warning back to us, *and* in killing that tank with her lobber. You think she's up to bossing a platoon?"

"I think so, sir."

"You're her 2IC now, Tom. Help her out."

"Aye, aye, sir."

"Dismissed."

He was gone.

Jeff stared at the bulkhead for a long moment. He wasn't entirely happy with his decision, but it was the best he could find. Tom Pope was a good Marine. In his own mind, at least, Jeff thought of the demotion as strictly probationary; Pope would have that rocker back inside of six months.

The leadership of the platoon was another matter. He didn't like changing horses in midcrossing. The makeup, the attitudes, the *politics* of any platoon were complex enough without the CO coming in and scrambling things. And keeping Tom as second-in-command might easily backfire. If this was Earth, Jeff would have arranged for Tom's transfer to another unit, just so he wouldn't be following in the unit he'd once led.

It was damned hard keeping rank and leadership positions balanced when there was no outside manpower pool to draw on. Ever since the first Marine unit had been deployed outside Earth's atmosphere, there'd been a serious problem in units becoming top-heavy with rank. Because promotions from private to private first class and from PFC to lance corporal were largely automatic, given time in grade, no Marine left space training as less than an E3—lance corporal. As a result, units deployed to space duty tended toward a preponderance of NCOs—corporals, sergeants, staff sergeants, gunnery sergeants. It was as bad as the Army Special Forces, where you couldn't even apply for training unless you were a noncom with four years behind you.

Second Platoon had boosted with only one gunnery sergeant, however, which made it necessary to promote someone else to fill the platoon leader slot. Campanelli was the logical choice. She had enough time in grade for promotion and had already passed the necessary quals Earthside. A field promotion would need confirmation, but that would follow almost automatically with his recommendation.

The problem was how the platoon was going to take this. Hell, Campanelli was one of the ten Marines who'd been skylarking on the ice; in a way, he was rewarding her for that—not the message he wanted to send at all. He'd get around that by including another field promotion in the round. Lucky Leckie's performance on the crater rim Monday also demanded special recognition.

The real question, then, was how Second Platoon would take the reshuffling. On the one hand, his decision might be seen as interference, as micromanagement of a well-tuned platoon, and bad for morale. But to ignore the incident would be bad for discipline.

*Damned if you do, damned if you don't.* He decided he needed to have another chat with Chesty. They didn't teach you these things in OCS.

His thoughts were jolted by the sudden shock of an alarm.


*Squad Bay, E-DARES Facility*
*Ice Station Zebra, Europa*
*0942 hours Zulu*


They were fully suited up except for gloves and helmets. Second Platoon, First section had the "Alert Five," meaning they were suited and ready to cycle out onto the surface in five minutes. It made card playing a bit clumsy, but there was damned little else to do, sitting for six hours at a stretch waiting for something to happen.

Lucky was riding on a full house, but the others didn't know that yet. The pot was big and getting bigger, and he could taste the winnings now.

"Two," Wojak said. He accepted the cards from Peterson, who was dealing. "The way I see it," he continued, "is that Earth's gotta send a relief ship, and when they do, the Charlies'll pack up and move out of town. They've only got the two A-M cruisers, right? I'll see you, Lucky, and raise you five."

"Unless they've been building 'em someplace sneaky we don't know about," Lissa said. "And we still have three in the inventory. See ya. Raise you five."

"I dunno," Campanelli said, studying her cards. "The news feeds haven't been that encouraging. The CWS isn't that eager to get into another war right now."

"Well, they're not gonna *abandon* us out here," Downer Niemeyer said. "Right? I'm out." He tossed down his cards. "I mean, they *couldn't*—"

The sudden rasp of the alarm echoed through the squad bay. "Shit, no!" Lucky screamed.

"Wassamatter, Luck?" Downer said with a nasty chuckle. "Good hand?"

Lucky flipped him an obscene gesture, then snatched up his helmet.

"Attention!" It was the voice of Chesty Puller, the Old Man's secretary, sounding over the loudspeaker system, the "1MC," in Marine parlance. "Incoming hostile forces. Range eighteen kilometers, and descending. Two, repeat, two landers. Enemy cruiser on approach. Estimated time of commencement of bombardment run, now thirty-one seconds . . ."

Lucky seated his helmet in the locking ring and gave it a hard twist to seal it. After checking the connections, $O_2$ feed, and comm and data links, he pulled on his gloves and sealed them as well too. His M-580 was on the rack with the ready weapons for the rest of the section.

By that time, he and the others were crowding into the E-DARES cargo airlock, which was roomy enough for all twelve Marines remaining in the section and then some. He stood there with the others as the seconds bled away with the atmosphere, his eyes fixed on the gray struts and supports of the lock's overhead, waiting.

They would ride out the bombardment in here.

Over the past three days, the response to each Chinese assault had become almost routine. The Alert Five section stayed suited up inside, weapons ready and warming, until the *Star Mountain* had passed and the crowbars had stopped falling. Outside, the Marines on working-party details would be scattering, taking cover in shallow trenches cut for the purpose.

The first shock struck, a gentle rumble transmitted through the E-DARES's bulkheads. It was followed swiftly by a second, a third, a fourth, each shock more powerful, more demanding than the one before.

Another shock, strong enough to make the deck shudder beneath Lucky's cleated boots. There was no sound in hard vacuum, of course . . . but a kind of rattle or rumble was carried by deck plates and armor, strong enough to chatter the teeth. His grip on his weapon tightened.

*The base is* not *going to fall off the cliff*, he told himself. *It's not.*

The upended ship that served as the CWS base was solidly moored to the ice cliff at the side of the Pit, and ultrastrong cables had been run over and through the ice to shore up the cliff face itself, to prevent an avalanche from calving the whole complex into the Europan ocean. For two days, now, they'd had working parties outside drilling arrays of holes in the ice, designed to absorb and diminish incoming shock waves through the frozen surface.

And hell, even if the cliff face shattered and the E-DARES facility *did* slide into the water, they'd been assured by the science team that the structure was watertight and would float. They would descend beneath the surface, then pop up again, dry and tight, riding like a normal ship, keel down.

But that was all theory. Suppose the facility fell with a mountain of ice tumbling down behind? Suppose it dove so deep it came back up under the ice cap? Suppose the shock was bad enough to spring some joints and flood her compartments? Suppose . . . suppose . . .

Another shock, more violent yet. A heavy wrench resting in top of a circuit box on the other side of the compartment jarred loose and fell in dreamlike slow motion, striking the steel deck plating and bouncing, all in complete silence. Kaminski had passed the word that the Charlies seemed to be trying to spare the E-DARES facility and other surface structures, that so far, especially with the shock absorber mountings designed to protect the base from Europaquakes, there'd been remarkably little damage.

*We're gonna be okay.*

But he was sweating inside his suit, the stink in his helmet overwhelming now, especially after spending the past several hours locked away in this can. The Chinese could always change their minds, decide that saving the CWS buildings was more trouble than it was worth. The word was that the *Star Mountain* was uncannily accurate with those crowbars, dropping them on the ice within meters of the intended targets.

Then, he realized with a faint shock of surprise, that the last several impacts had been farther off, less intense. "Okay!" Campanelli called over the platoon circuit. She was senior NCO present, and in charge of the section watch. "Move out!"

The outer lock slid open, and the twelve Marines filed out into the cold, dark emptiness of Europa. The E-DARES facility still seemed firmly attached to the ice wall; the Pit continued, as always, to boil and steam meters below. They trotted up the zigzag of the fire-escape ladder and fanned out onto the ice.

"Incoming hostiles now at two kilometers," Chesty's maddeningly calm voice announced. "Intended LZ appears to be east, repeat, east of the base crater."

A tractor was waiting for them there, with a sled—a five-meter-long makeshift pallet on runners pieced together out of fragments of bug and radio mast—chained behind. Peterson clambered into the tractor's bubble cockpit and fired up the fuel cell engines; the rest climbed onto the sled, grabbed hold of the lifelines strung around the edge, and hung on. The tractor started forward with a lurch, dragging the section along on the ice.

Lucky looked up in time to see the glint of sunlight on steel as one of the Chinese landers passed overhead to the south. Were both of them headed for the same LZ, or were they going to try to split up and divide the Marine defending forces between two attacking columns?

The tractor picked up speed, its cleated tracks hurling up a fine spray of ice, a frosty roostertail that quickly coated the Marines hanging on astern.

Several new craters were apparent across the floor of the main crater, and another notch had been blasted out of the northwestern rim. Kaminski's Cannon, shielded from overhead view by a number of large sheets of white fabric, was intact, as were the surface storage sheds and the surviving bug and hoppers.

The tractor dragged them three-quarters of the way up the inner slope of the east rim. They spilled off and made the rest of the trek on foot. The ice here was soft on top after the bombardment, but with harder ice below that took the hard-stomped cleats of each tiring step. Lucky dropped to his belly and crawled the last few meters, with his laser rifle cradled in the crooks of his elbows; several Marines had been killed by snipers firing from cover out in the Chaos Badlands to the east, until the rest of them had learned to be more cautious.

"Alert Five in position!" Campanelli called. "We have one new lander down, range 849 meters, bearing nine-eight degrees. Enemy tanks and troops are visible."

"Roger that, Five," Major Warhurst's voice replied. "You are clear to fire."

"Thank you for those kind words," BJ said. "Okay, Marines. You heard the man! Take 'em down!"

Lucky propped his 580 on a convenient ice chunk, pivoting it by the pistol grip as he watched the cursor shift back and forth on his HUD. By zooming in on high magnification with the rifle's sighting system and bringing up the image on the helmet display, he could peer at the base of the Chinese lander with detail enough that it seemed like he was less than a hundred meters away. He could see the lowered ramp, and space-suited troops filing out. Those odd, flat-topped *zidong tanke* were deploying in a rough, defensive arc.

Movement caught his eye—a Chinese soldier crossing an open area between one upended tumble of ice and another. Range—345 meters. He shifted the cursor and closed his gloved finger over the firing button. The Chinese soldier vanished; Lucky couldn't tell if he'd hit him or not.

"Here comes that second incoming," BJ said. "Nodell! Get that Wyvern in operation!"

Lucky glanced up. Shit! The second lander was very close, coming in tail-first in a descending arc that would carry it across the southern part of the crater. He wondered for a moment if the Charlies were trying to fry the Marine ground troops with the star-hot plasma exhaust of their drives, or if the threat was accidental. It hardly mattered; BJ had tried frying a tank the other day with a much smaller plasma jet than *that* thing sported!

Sergeant Sherman Nodell was carrying the section's M-614. He braced himself on the inner rim slope, aiming the ungainly Wyvern launch tube into the black sky. "Targeting!" he called. "I have tone! Firing!"

There was a silent flash, gasses spewing from the vents around the load tube, and the SAM streaked vertically into the sky, arcing to the south to close with the huge, gray globe of the Chinese lander. From the opposite side of the crater, a second Wyvern soared into the night; the Marines out on work detail when the raid had begun were emerging from their crude shelters now and joining the fight.

White-yellow flame blossomed against the lander's stern . . . and then again. There was no change in the craft's course; it continued drifting across the sky, from west to east, chasing its own shadow now as it grew closer to the ice.

It took several long seconds before Lucky realized . . . *it wasn't slowing down!*

The 1,200-ton orbit-to-surface shuttle impacted on the ice nearly half a kilometer beyond the crater's east rim, well to the north of the first craft. It drifted in tail first, landing gear deployed . . . but when the landing struts touched the surface they appeared to crumple as the rest of the craft mashed on down into the ice. There was no flame, no blast, not even the boom of an impact.

If there had been any sound, though, it would have been

instantly drowned out by the cheers of the watching Marines.

And Lucky cheered with them, half rising to punch a gloved fist into the black sky. Victory was sweet ... even if it *was* only temporary.

# SIXTEEN

*C-3, E-DARES Facility*
*Ice Station Zebra, Europa*
*1215 hours Zulu*

"So," Jeff said with a wry grin. "Is this wonder cannon of yours going to work?"

"All of the systems test out, Major," Kaminksi replied. "I don't see what else we can test."

"And it's a use it or lose it proposition," Lieutenant Walthers added. "We've been lucky so far, but sooner or later Papa Romeo's gonna come over and plant a crowbar smack in the middle of that thing. And we won't be able to patch it up afterward. We don't have the spares."

"We used all of that superconducting cable?"

"Most of it." He pointed at a computer monitor on the bulkhead, which was currently showing the view from a camera set up on the ice. "In any case, we're not going to get more than one shot, you know. Charlie'll come down on it like a ton of hypervelocity crowbars."

Jeff and the other officers were all present, plus Kaminski and Shigeru Ishiwara, who was representing the science team. The compartment was crowded with so many people, but the electronics suite gave them immediate access to all available information, from individual Marines, from sensors outside, from a host of AI and dumb systems both inside and out.

"Yeah. I was figuring that." Jeff rubbed his jaw. "You know, Sergeant Major, I've been thinking about that. We might be able to get your toy out there to pull double duty."

"In what way, sir? We don't even know if it's gonna survive the first shot!"

"It won't need to. The thing is, when we fire, let's do it at a time when the *Star Mountain* can easily shift to a new orbit to overfly us. If we know when he's going to come over the horizon, and exactly from what direction . . ."

Walthers' eyes widened. "You're thinking of an intercept? With the bug?"

"Exactly."

"We might lose the bug."

"We might. It'll require a volunteer."

"No problem there, Major. Armament?"

"I was thinking of a shit can. Literally." Quickly, he sketched out his plan in a few words.

"Jesus Christ!" Lieutenant Biehl exclaimed. "If this works . . ."

Shigeru's eyes widened as Jeff explained. "Major, what you are suggesting?"

"You have a problem with it?"

"It's reckless! Irresponsible! You . . . you could ruin *everything* here!"

"Frank," Jeff said, "get a work detail together and get the, um, supplies. I suggest we strap as many drums to the upper works of the bug as we can. Fill the cans with the special munitions. And might as well chuck in any other small bits we have lying around. Scrap from the other bug. Leftovers from that microwave tower. Whatever you can find."

Kaminski was grinning. "Aye, *aye*, sir!"

"You'll need that volunteer," Walthers said. He raised a hand. "Here he is."

"I appreciate that, Lieutenant, but I have something else in mind." He patted the screen frame to his PAD. "I have to have a talk with Chesty and see what *he* can suggest."

*Chesty Puller*
*Ice Station Zebra, Europa*
*2045 hours Zulu*

The program known as Chesty Puller was commercial software, a design known as Aristotle 3050 characteristically running at $2.97 \times 10^{15}$ operations per second, approximately at human levels, on a system network with a memory capacity of 1.2 terabytes of fast cache buffer and 2.33 petabytes of nonvolatile memory. Normally resident within Jeff Warhurst's PAD, he'd been uploaded recently to the Sperry-Rand CVAC-1280 system within the Europan E-DARES facility. And now, a broad-band communications channel had been opened between the E-DARES C-3 suite and the remaining bug, which in the past few hours had become festooned with large storage canisters strapped to the side and dorsal struts of the craft's framework. Marines were completing the finishing touches, attaching a series of "squibs," or small explosive packages to the aluminum strips securing the canisters to the spacecraft.

At the moment, however, a larger portion of Chesty's mind was focused on the input from a number of optical sensors mounted on the twenty-meter, spindly-framework jury-rig wrapped in superconductor cable and pointed, with the front end lifted off the ice by cables attached to the A-frame, toward the southwest. The alignment had to be perfect, and Chesty had labored carefully for the past twenty hours with a Marine working party under Kaminski's direction, figuring out the theta—the angle between the cable-wrapped microwave tower and the surface—to an accuracy of a part or two in a hundred thousand. That level of accuracy was almost impossible to achieve even with the proper tools. What they'd accomplished here, with few tools beyond military laser sights adapted to the effort and human muscle power, had been startlingly impressive, the result of trial and error, with calculations so fussy that Chesty had been forced to take into account the slight expansion in the supporting cables as the sun came out from behind Jupiter and warmed them by a handful of degrees. When the time came, he would be able to fine-tune the trajectory by slightly increasing or decreasing the power he fed to the SC cables; the really critical adjustments were made by shifting the back end of the tower back and forth on the ice in centimeter increments, aligning the muzzle with a laser beacon on the crater rim 215.7 meters away. The survey data for the placement of that beacon had come from a careful photometric analysis of photographs relayed to Earth by the Farstar deep space telescope, which had managed to pinpoint—to within a few tens of meters—the precise location of the Chinese LZ at Asterias Linea.

The principles of railguns—magnetic linear accelerators—were well known. The first prototype had been built in 1937 by Edward Fitch Northrup, an eccentric inventor who'd worked out the details in a work of fiction. Electricity fed through the superconducting coils generated an intense, fast-moving magnetic field which could be pulsed to increase acceleration. The math involved was trivial; the most uncertain elements in the equation, as always, had to do with *human* uncertainties.

The Marines had just finished loading the cannon. The round—another canister, this one wrapped tightly with superconducting cable attached to a small fuel-cell power generator inside—floated now in the magnetic grasp of the makeshift linear accelerator. Inside, fifty-five grams of antimatter rested in magnetic suspension inside an A-M carry sphere. The power feed had been carefully packed with foam to let it withstand the sudden shock of ultra-high G acceleration; the trigger was a simple two-stage switch armed by one shock exceeding 100 gravities and fired by a second. The round *should* arm itself when fired; on impact, the magnetic suspensor field in the A-M containment sphere would fail, and fifty-five grams of antimatter would instantly annihilate fifty-five grams of matter, liberating some $10^{10}$ joules of energy, roughly equivalent to two thousand tons of high explosive—about the same punch as the bomb that destroyed Hiroshima.

"Everything is ready for firing," Chesty announced to the personnel gathered in C-3. He could tell from their heart rates and breathing, from the pitch of their voices as they made jokes with one another, that they were all nervous.

Understandable. If something went wrong, a rather large crater would suddenly appear uncomfortably close to the E-DARES facility—within a couple of kilometers, in fact. That was entirely too close to ground zero for a base anchored to the face of an ice cliff.

"Thank you, Chesty," Jeff said.

"I suggest that you give orders to move all surface personnel well back from the cannon," Chesty added. "We have no way of predicting what the recoil effects might be."

"Already taken care of, Chesty. Wait one."

He waited.


*Kaminski*
*C-3, Ice Station Zebra, Europa*
*2045 hours Zulu*

Frank Kaminski was holding his breath. The idea had not been original, but if this thing didn't work, he was going to be the one responsible. Antimatter was such damnably touchy stuff. Any mistake, *any* mistake, and they would end up shooting themselves in the foot. There might not be much left for the Charlies to come in and take over.

In 1900, forty-nine U.S. Marines had been part of the mix of foreign troops defending the Foreign Legation Quarter in Beijing—then Peking—during the Boxer Rebellion, as the "Society of Heavenly Fists" had attempted to oust all foreign influences from China. During the five-week siege that followed, Chinese Christians digging a trench discovered an old Anglo-French rifled cannon abandoned in the compound during the expedition of 1860. The Marines had excavated the barrel and cleaned it up; Italian troops provided a gun carriage. Russian nine-pound shells that had been dumped in a well earlier to keep them out of Boxer hands were fished out, dried off, and found to fit the gun—not perfectly, but close enough, though they had to be taken apart and loaded in two pieces through the muzzle. Despite the makeshift uncertainties, the weapon had acquitted itself well throughout the siege. The Marines had called the hybrid monster "The International Gun."

With a sense of history and tradition, then, Frank had suggested calling the contraption now out on the ice "The International Gun, Mark II," and the others had adopted it with raucous good humor. No one could say, though, whether it would survive its first firing, or even whether it would be more dangerous to the Chinese or to the personnel at Cadmus.

The IG Mark II was loaded and ready to fire, the last of the Marines who'd been prepping the gun moving away now on tractor-dragged sleds. Moments later, the surface crews reported that they were under cover.

Not that that would help them if something went seriously wrong, and the monster mass driver cannon out there managed to score an own goal.

"It's your baby, Frank," Jeff said quietly. "You want to give the word?"

"Aye, aye, sir." He checked the monitors a final time, then, reluctantly, touched his PAD monitor, where a firing button had been set up as a touch-screen graphic.

*Chesty Puller*
*Europa*
*2049 hours Zulu*

The graphic didn't fire the gun directly, but sent a command to Chesty, who made the actual connections. A pulse of electrical energy from the base reactor surged through the superconducting cable wrapped around the twenty-meter tower like an endless strip of dark-gray ribbon. The charge created a rapidly moving magnetic field that gripped the five-kilogram round and hurled it down the length of the former microwave tower. Accelerating the package at 2,050,000 Gs, the jury-rigged railgun squirted it from the muzzle with a velocity of 28,350 meters per second.

The railgun's muzzle had been elevated only five degrees, just enough to clear the crater's southwest rim.

Kaminski's idea had depended on Europa's unusual environment for success. With a surface gravity of .13 G, the package, which began falling as soon as it left the railgun's muzzle, could travel much farther—almost seven times farther, in fact—than the same impulse could have carried it on Earth. Better yet, there was no atmosphere to cause drag, no wind to buffet the projectile as it tumbled through the ice-barren night, no chaotic effects to nudge the projectile this way or that. Targeting was a simple matter of calculating solely the precise range to target, the gravity and surface curvature of Europa, and the acceleration of the projectile and the length of the firing weapon to yield muzzle velocity. At 28.35 kps, the time to target would be 35.45 seconds.

A simple matter? That part of the equation was simple enough. Unfortunately, as Chesty was all too aware, there were still chaotic variables, which meant that actually hitting the distant target was largely a matter of chance. The complex interplay of gravitational fields between giant Jupiter and the largest Jovian moons wouldn't affect the projectile much, but they would affect it, and in ways too essentially chaotic to predict. And, while Europa didn't possess the masscons of Earth's Moon, deep-buried lumps of dense nickel-iron that could tug orbiting spacecraft off course, the Jovian satellite was not entirely uniform—and the local variations in gravity, while mapped by the CWS team, were not well surveyed. And, finally, while Europa's atmosphere measured a billionth of one standard atmosphere, there *was* an atmosphere of sorts, the sleeting rain of protons from Jupiter's radiation belts, and the magnetic field of Jupiter that trapped them.

These influences, each slight in and of itself, added up

to a whole too complex to calculate, made worse by the fact that the required data were yet incomplete.

As a result, Chesty couldn't predict with any accuracy at all where the package would come down. Hitting anything important at all on the other end of the trajectory would require luck, a peculiarly human concept that Chesty did not, *could* not understand.

*Kaminski*
*C-3, Ice Station Zebra, Europa*
*2049 hours Zulu*

As the International Gun Mark II fired, Kaminski felt a stab of cold pain lance through his skull. The next thing he knew, he was on his back, with several Marines bending over him. "Someone get the Doc up here!" Lissa yelled.

"Frank?" Major Warhurst said, looking worried. "Are you okay?"

"I'm . . . fine . . ." he said. The pain was gone, but had left him feeling woozy, and a bit numb. "What happened?"

"You fired your gun and collapsed. Just for a couple of seconds."

"We just loosed the biggest damned EMP I've ever seen," Sergeant Miller said, looking up from his PAD. "Transient effects all over the board, and that was just from the side leakage and backscatter! But it shouldn't have affected *humans!*"

Shakily, Frank allowed them to help him to his feet.

*Observation Post Iceberg*
*Asterias Linea, Europa*
*2049 hours Zulu*

Downer Niemeyer wished that BJ were here. Unfortunately, she'd just been given a field promotion to gunnery sergeant and put in charge of Second Platoon, which meant she was no longer as expendable as she'd been before. Since he'd had experience piloting lobbers as had she, he'd been asked to take Lance Corporal Gary Staunton with him on a jaunt a thousand kilometers southwest of the base.

It had been a long, brutal trip, too. The idea was not to let the enemy see them coming, so the approach had been made through a series of short, low, ridge-skimming hops instead of one long, high one. The final approach had been made scant meters above the ice, slipping up to a low pressure ridge east of the enemy LZ. They'd touched down and climbed the ridge on foot in order to avoid enemy radar or lidar sweeps.

It had worked. Four Chinese landers were visible on the western horizon, together with a radio mast and several surface buildings. Through their helmet optics, electronically magnified, they could see space-suited soldiers on sentry-go at the base of the landers, and several of the ever-present robot tanks.

For the past three hours, they'd crouched on the ridge top, taking turns observing the base. They were far over the horizon from the CWS base, and unable to communicate; in any case, they were under orders to maintain strict EM security, with no leakage at all to tip the enemy off that they were there. Instead, they were to watch . . . unsure of exactly when the package would strike.

*Observe the strike, and try to get an idea of the damage,* Warhurst had told them before they'd left the base nearly seven hours earlier. *If we can hurt them, if we can even just scare them badly enough that they'll back off, we have a chance for a relief expedition to make it out from Earth.*

Downer had just decided that something must have gone terribly wrong, that Kaminski's cannon had not worked after all, when the Chinese landers were silhouetted by an intense, blinding flare of white light blossoming from the Europan horizon, a light so bright it momentarily outshone the shrunken sun, and caused Downer's helmet visor to polarize to black.

The shock wave reached them long seconds later, diminished by distance to a rumble felt through the ice.

The landers remained on the horizon, apparently untouched. Through his optics, Downer could see that the radio mast was down and two of the buildings appeared to have collapsed, but there was little other obvious damage.

Beyond the Chinese LZ, a great, frosty white cloud was seething against the night sky. Downer had seen a cloud like that before, a much smaller one—the cloud of freezing steam boiling above the Pit, back at Cadmus.

The package had missed the enemy LZ. It had breached the ice, opening the ocean to space, but it had *missed*, damn it, and the shot had been wasted.

Gary tapped his shoulder, and pointed. The second member of the OP had been monitoring a tripod-mounted EM scanner, a device designed to pick up the electromagnetic emissions of enemy troops and vehicles. It served as a kind of passive radar, one that read the electronic noise others made, without giving away its own position by broadcasting on the EM spectrum.

Downer looked at the screen, and his eyes widened. As planned, the enemy cruiser *Star Mountain* was above the horizon, and if the commentary scrolling up the side of the scanner's screen was any indication, it was changing course from an equatorial orbit to one that that would take it over the CWS base.

Downer nodded vigorously, and pointed back down the ridge. They had to warn the base, hopefully without bringing down the entire Chinese Expeditionary Force around their heads.

By the time the *Star Mountain* had passed across the sky to the north and vanished again below the northeastern horizon, they'd boarded their lobber, brought the pile temperature up, and started feeding expellant into the main core tanks.

"Kick it," Downer said. It was the first word spoken since they'd arrived near the Chinese LZ. With a shudder, the open-top spacecraft rose, drifted a moment, then began accelerating, canting over to put some horizon between it and the enemy landers.

"Zebra, Zebra, this is OP Iceberg. Stand by for encrypted transmission."

He was staring back at the Chinese LZ as he spoke, knowing his suit camera was picking up what he saw. From two hundred meters up, the crater punched by the railgun round was a vast, steaming black oval perhaps a half kilometer across. The round, with the destructive power of a one- to two-kiloton nuclear blast, had punched through the ice all right, but overshot the enemy LZ by a good five kilometers.

"Iceberg, Zebra," sounded in his headset, blasted by static. "We are reading you, but poorly. Please repeat, over."

"Zebra, Iceberg. Here come the goodies." Their observations, camera records, and suit logs, as well as the data feed form their EM scanner, all compressed into a half second of tightly encrypted signal, spat at the distant base three times, the repetition designed to allow reconstructing the message if parts were garbled or lost. Another lobber had been launched above Cadmus immediately after the cannon shot, positioning itself three hundred kilometers up so that it could receive the expected signal from Iceberg.

The signal was going out a fourth time when the rising craft was bathed in laser light, a low-power tracking beam. Seconds later, a chain of crowbars arrowed in from the northeast; the *Star Mountain*, detecting the lobber launch and possibly intercepting the tight-beamed signal as well, had shifted out of its nose-down attitude to bring its spinal railgun to bear on the tiny craft clawing its way up from the Europan surface.

The first two ten-kilo crowbar flechettes whipped past, unseen; the third and fourth slammed into the lobber's hull, shredding it with the equivalent of a detonation of two hundred kilos of HE. The blast, with little concussive effect in hard vacuum, was not instantly fatal, but flung Downer and Staunton into blackness.

His last conscious thought was a desperate, pleading wondering if Europa's lower gravity might spare him.

Unfortunately, a 500-meter fall on Europa was still the equivalent of a sixty-five–meter fall on Earth. Both men died on impact, in a shower of falling debris.

*Chesty Puller*
*Ice Station Zebra, Europa*
*2049 hours Zulu*

Chesty engaged the bug's engines, gentling the ungainly craft above the ice in an uncertain hover. The bug's controls had been set for teleoperation, which meant that Chesty himself could now pilot the vehicle directly. Carefully, using inertial guidance, he aligned himself, then engaged the main thrusters, accelerating hard.

He had heard—no, *felt* was the better word—the destruction of OP Iceberg, but the deaths meant little save that no more data would be coming from that source. Ample data had been received, however, reporting the failure of the cannon shot, and the course change by the Chinese cruiser.

The five-kilometer miss by the railgun was . . . regrettable. The battle might have been ended immediately if three or four of the surviving seven enemy landers could have been destroyed . . . including the one that held, presumably, the Chinese equivalent of the E-DARES C-3 Center.

And to have missed after so many high hopes; Chesty's analysis of the subdued voices of the humans in C-3 told him that morale among the members of the command staff had just come crashing down. He'd tried to point out that the uncertainties, the chaotic variables of the long-range shot made pinpoint targeting a matter for chance, not skill . . . but he doubted that the humans had really understood this. Humans, Chesty now realized, tended to believe what they wanted to believe, and could be disappointed when the universe didn't bend to their expectations.

Morale had fallen even more when he reported the lobber

destroyed. Again, human apprehension of the situation less than adequately reflected reality. As if such intangibles as bravery and devotion to duty could somehow coax life from a situation where the chances for death were very high indeed.

But most of Chesty's attention was now focused on *Star Mountain*. Major Warhurst had guessed that an attack on the enemy LZ would trigger an immediate response as the Chinese attempted to destroy the cannon. He'd been right; the enemy ship had shifted orbits almost immediately, and was now incoming, minutes over the horizon.

He increased the bug's acceleration, streaking low across the Europan surface, hugging the rills and pressure ridges to mask his approach until the last possible moment.

The railgun attack might yet succeed, if only as a diversion designed at drawing the *Star Mountain* into a trap.

The trick, of course, was knowing exactly where the *Xing Shan* would be at any given moment. Without military observation satellite or com relays, the enemy could send an orbiting spacecraft overhead almost at will, unchallenged by the Marines on the surface.

But with just a little sure knowledge in advance . . .

Chesty had the *Shan* on radar now, and at almost the same instant he detected radar and lidar paints from the enemy. He applied thrust to the number one ventral thruster, bringing the bug's nose up, and increased acceleration yet again. His trajectory was aimed just ahead of the Chinese ship; his velocity was now up to 4.8 kilometers per second. When he was certain the bug was perfectly aligned, he detonated the explosive bolts holding the securing straps on the craft's sides and backs; the cylinders, what Major Warhurst had referred to as "shit cans," slowly separated, their lids flying back. He decelerated sharply, and the "special munitions" hurtled ahead, maintaining their 4.8 kps velocity.

Seconds later, a stream of crowbars slammed into the bug, crumpling its cockpit, puncturing its cargo deck, sending high-speed splinters slashing through expellant tanks and reactor.

Seconds after that, the first Chinese missile struck, homing on the IR signature of the largest fragment of the bug and detonating in a savage, subnuclear flash. Point defense lasers began flickering invisibly across the cloud of wreckage, boiling away the larger fragments as they tumbled toward the oncoming spacecraft.

But by that time, Chesty had already lost contact with the bug and could not report on what was happening.

*C-3, E-DARES Facility*
*Ice Station Zebra, Europa*
*2053 hours Zulu*

"I must protest this wanton biological desecration of this world!" Vasaliev snapped. "You had no *right!* . . . "

Jeff looked the CWS scientist up and down. Pyotr Vasaliev was a short, stocky man with an angry shock of flyaway hair and a personality to match. His blue CWS Science Bureau jumpsuit was festooned with wearable computers and hardware on chest, sleeves, and thighs, and included a monocular headset that gave him a one-eyed HUD for accessing data no matter where he was in the base. Jeff had already come to the conclusion that he wore those high-tech trappings more as a fashion statement and as a declaration of importance than through any actual work-related need.

"I have the right, Dr. Vasaliev, no, the *responsibility* to take the measures I deem necessary to fulfill my mission orders, which happen to include protecting *you.*"

"You are *idiot!*" Vasaliev snapped. His English, usually precise despite carrying a bit of his Ukrainian accent, tended to degrade when he was excited—which was frequently. "Vandal! Philistine! Europan biosphere is . . . is unique, is great discovery, is *important!* Your actions contaminate world!"

"Dr. Vasaliev—"

"At least you should consult with science team! Is insufferable, is—"

"Dr. Vasaliev, *shut up!*" His parade-ground bark startled everyone in the C-3 compartment to dead silence.

"First!" he rasped into the silence. "We had little choice. I considered loading those cans with chunks of ice, but ice tends to be friable at those temperatures. Under high acceleration, it might fragment, even melt. What we used was already neatly packaged in plastic, which keeps the mass together in a nice, neat chunk.

"Second. *Because* it's packaged, I deemed the chance of contamination to be remote. My orders, in case you didn't realize it, do require me to take note of the unique environmental, biological, and research aspects of this place."

"But if any of packets should fall again to surface! They could rupture, contaminating entire Europan biosphere!"

"The stuff is sterile," Jeff replied. "Or it ought to be by now!"

"No. *No!* We cannot know that! It was in storage on surface, yes. It was frozen solid, yes, and subjected to high levels of particulate radiation. But mandate as scientists demands we properly dispose of all organic wastes. If we contaminate local biosphere, results could be catastrophic!"

"Doctor, *think* about it, *please!* The escape velocity for Europa is a little over 2 kilometers per second. Those packages were moving at almost five kps when they were released. The chances that any will be deflected in such a way to land on the surface again—and without being vaporized by the energy released on impact—is so small I can't even imagine what the odds would be.

"If you want to challenge me on the biological contamination of this moon, you would be better served bringing up the fact that, a few moments ago, two of my men died when their lobber was blasted out of the sky by that Chinese cruiser. Their bodies were not frozen, or fried by radiation, and right now I imagine they're smeared across a couple of square kilometers of Europan ice.

"Do you want to attack me personally for that? Because if you do I swear will take you apart, Doctor, piece by piece. I'm more concerned about losing two good Marines right now than I am about your Europan biology!"

"Or do you want to talk to our Chinese friends out there? Maybe scold them for littering on your pristine moon? I'm sure they'll be willing to listen to your lecture!"

"I . . . I . . ." Vasaliev's mouth gaped a moment, then he turned away. "I knew there would be problem with military coming here!"

Jeff sighed. "I'm sorry you feel that way, Doctor. At this point, there's not a lot we can do. You can fire off your report to Earth, and I'll accept the reprimand. But the damage, if there was any, is done."

"Major, please," the scientist said, his manner smoothing like ruffled feathers. "Please. I had not even taken into account problem of men dying up there. This is . . . is very serious. Fighting must be stopped."

"Then I suggest you take it up with your Chinese counterparts, sir." He glanced at a time reading on his PAD. The bug's scattergun volley ought to be reaching the *Star Mountain* by now.

Jeff glanced at Shigeru Ishiwara, who was trying not to look him in the eye, then at Frank Kaminski. Ishiwara looked discomfited at his boss's outburst. He was surprised at how many Marines had crowded into C-3 to witness the firing. Frank, still looking groggy from his unexplained collapse, was sitting in a chair, staring at the time readout.

They should know soon.

It was a colossal throw of the dice. They would not get another shot with the makeshift railgun, no matter what happened. On the big monitor on the bulkhead, Kaminski's cannon lay in upended, twisted ruin. The recoil of the single shot lobbed at the distant enemy LZ had been so great the superconductor cables had been shredded, the microwave tower bent back, its rear biting into cracked ice, the A-frame ripped from its frozen moorings and fallen. There would be no second shot, and not much of a target for the oncoming *Star Mountain*.

No matter. The bug's warload was on the way, was arriving on target at this moment—almost seven hundred kilos of deep-frozen human waste, leavened with another couple of hundred kilos or so of scrap metal from the destroyed bug. The waste, stored in five-kilo plastic packets and frozen as hard as granite, made a peculiar sort of ammunition at best, but it ought to work.

The CWS station had been under special orders to minimize biological contamination of what was, after all, the first alien biosphere, the first life found outside of Earth. As with research stations in Antarctica a century before, or on Mars and the moon later on, all wastes were either recycled or, in the case of a facility such as Cadmus Base, without the wherewithal to recycle feces as fertilizer, dehydrated, carefully packaged by automatic machinery, and allowed to freeze for later disposal. In the year that Cadmus Station had been manned, they'd accumulated several tons of the stuff, which had been collected in and stored inside one of the surface storage sheds.

The Chinese ship captain would have been keenly aware that destroying the oncoming bug would send a cloud of high-speed fragments his way. Point defense lasers couldn't get all of them, and it was a simple matter to change the ship's speed, raising or lowering the orbit slightly. Fifty meters would be enough to miss the hurtling cloud of wreckage.

Which was why Chesty had carefully *aimed* those garbage cans of meticulously packaged and frozen human feces, aimed them like shotgun blasts along the paths most likely to be taken by a Chinese A-M craft maneuvering to avoid a collision.

His point defense lasers might get some of those hurtling, icy packets, but he couldn't possibly get them all.

Each ten-kilo package of freeze-dried waste, traveling at 4.8 kps, carried with it the equivalent of 115.2 megajoules of energy, or just over twenty-three kilograms of high explosives.

It was, Jeff thought, a new low in field-expedient weaponry. The weirdest part of it, though, was that he couldn't shake the mental image of angry primates shrieking as they flung handfuls of feces at a threat.

"A hit!" the Marine sitting at the radar console announced. "Damn! He's tumbling! I've got debris spilling off the target like a pinwheel!"

"Bull's eye!" Leckie shouted, laughing. "How's that for letting the shit hit the *Shan*?"

The other Marines in C-3 burst into cheers, catcalls, and shrieks of joy.

"Hey!" BJ shouted. "That EMP is gonna keep traveling outward at the speed of light, right? Well, what if a thousand years from now, some alien radio astronomer hears it and thinks it's a message?"

"Yeah," Pope added. "And how long before they figure out that what it means is, 'Duck! Here comes a load of shit!' "

The hoots and shrieks redoubled.

*Angry primates . . .*

# SEVENTEEN

*Radio Shack, U.S.S.*
  Thomas Jefferson
*U.S. Synchorbital Shipyard, L-3*
*1527 hours Zulu*

"Please, God," Kaitlin said with a rush of emotion that came close to despair. "*Please* don't tell me they're killing the relief expedition!"

She was adrift in the radio shack on board the A-M cruiser *Thomas Jefferson*, sister vessel to the *Roosevelt* and the *Kennedy*, already destroyed. The *Jeff*'s hab modules had been spun up to provide artificial gravity as soon as the Marines had begun arriving and certain "special packages" had been attached to the ship's forward water storage tank, but the com shack was located abaft of the bridge, in the long vessel's central axis, so she kept her left foot anchored in a fabric loop on one bulkhead while staring at the open screen of a microPAD strapped to her left forearm. Linked in through the *Jefferson*'s communications suite, she had a direct, scrambled channel to the office of California Senator Carmen Fuentes.

Lieutenant Commander John Reynolds, the ship's communications officer, had gallantly vacated the compartment so she could have her conversation in private. She was glad of that. At the moment, she didn't know if she was on the verge of tears or profanity, and neither fit her concept of professional behavior in an officer.

Carmen's face, displayed on the fabric screen unrolled in the air above Kaitlin's arm, frowned unhappily. "I wish I had better news, Kaitlin, but I don't. I'm doing my best to delay the vote, but it's going to happen, probably by the middle of next week."

"But—but don't they understand? We have almost a hundred people out there, under constant attack by the Chinese! We can't just fucking write them off!"

"Things were a whole lot simpler when there were essentially just two parties," Carmen replied. "The Democrats and the Republicans are still the two biggest—together they take up seventy-one out of a hundred twelve Senate seats. But now we have the Libertarians with nineteen seats, and the Greens with twelve. Globalists control six seats. The rest are independents.

"So everyone has an agenda, right? The Libs, Greens, and Globies all are against the war. I swear it's the first time in eight years I've seen them align themselves on the same side of *any* issue! They're all pushing for different things, of course. The Globalists just want us to be one big, happy global community, even if it means surrendering outright to every tin-plated dictator who gets delusions of grandeur. The Greens mistrust big industry of any sort, don't like space technology, and figure we should leave alien contact out of the picture entirely until we clean up the planet first. Besides, most of them still buy into the Geneva Report, and figure we have to unite the planet before we all die. And the Libertarians just don't think there's anything out there worth fighting over.

"So we have a solid block of thirty-seven votes aligned *against* sending a relief expedition, because it will inflame the Chinese, because it could lead to a shooting war here on Earth. In a simple majority vote like this one, well . . . the opposition only needs to line up twelve more votes. At least four of the independents will automatically go with the antirelief measure, just because they came in on p-and-j platforms."

" 'P and j?' "

"Peace and joy. Love yourself, love your neighbor, and the whole world will be a better place."

"So you're saying the vote is going to pass. We're *not* sending help to Europa?"

Carmen shook her head. "Dear, they need eleven more votes to kill the relief measure. The Democrats are already pretty solidly aligned against relief to begin with. We just came out of a nasty war . . . we don't dare risk the utter destruction of humanity over such a faraway issue . . . ta-da, ta-da, ta-da. And some Republicans I know will side with them just to show their hearts are in the right place. I'm guessing we'll see the measure passed, oh, eighty to thirty or so, with a couple of abstentions."

"That's over two to one!" Kaitlin said, profoundly shocked. "I simply can't believe the Senate would have that little regard for our people—for people they decided to send out there in the first place!"

Carmen closed her eyes. She looked unbearably tired. "Kaitlin, you know as well as I do that politics *always* screws up the human equation. Politics deals with the expedient. The practical. Maybe once, a long time ago, government involved rational men making rational decisions, but anymore it has more to do with who's made the largest campaign contribution or owes who what favor. It's not that politicians don't care about people, especially the men and women in the armed forces. If I were a cynical bitch, I'd point out that those military men and women vote. But it's more than that. We do care. But the system has gotten so damned big and out of control, no individual politician has that much of a say anymore. In a way, that's good. Checks and balances. No one politician can become a demagogue anymore, or a tyrant.

"But when it comes to supporting our military personnel, it always seems again and again that the *practical* necessities of politics outweigh duty. Honor. What's *right*."

"I thought," Kaitlin said carefully, "that contact with the Singer was deemed 'of vital scientific and national importance.' "

"It was. It is. What does that have to do with politics?" She sighed. "Kaitlin, this is privileged information, you understand."

"Of course."

"There's a small group of senators right now—I think Sam Kellerman's putting it together—who're floating the idea of approaching the Chinese and offering to establish a joint mission to Europa. Everything shared. Everything open. The idea is that if the Singer is an alien intelligence, and if it cares, we'll be approaching it as a united world. As humankind, not as CWS or PRC or American. You understand?"

"I understand that that was what we should have done from the beginning."

"Yes, well, twenty-twenty hindsight, and all of that. What they don't want, what they don't want at all costs, is a shooting war with Beijing while there's still a chance of resolving things peacefully. We can't afford another major war right now."

"Excuse me, Senator," Kaitlin said, exasperated, "but has anyone told those bozos that the shooting war has already started? That we've lost forty men and women on Europa already. Plus over two hundred people on the *Roosevelt*, and twenty-nine on the *Kennedy*—including, damn you, my son!"

"Kaitlin—"

"I will not sit by and see the same thing happen to those forty-one Marines still on station!" There was no stopping the tears now, which clung to her face, or drifted, sparkling like stars in the compartment's lighting. "Not while I'm alive! Not while I'm a Marine!"

*"Colonel Garroway! Please!"*

"We have a responsibility to the men and women we put in harm's way!"

"Are you finished?"

Kaitlin was breathing hard. She wiped her face with her free hand, sending teardrops shimmering through the air. "No. But I'll shut up for now, Senator."

"Good. Because I want to tell you something. I once had the opportunity to talk to a young woman who wanted to be a Marine. I think she wanted to be a Marine more than anything else in the world. I asked her why.

"She thought for a moment, and then told me. 'You can be *in* the Army,' she said. 'You can be in the Air Force or in the Navy. But you *are* a Marine.' There is no such thing as an ex-Marine, you know. Only formerly active Marines. Or retired Marines.

"I *am* a Marine, Kaitlin. It's something you can't take away from me. No one can. Maybe I retired twelve years ago, maybe I'm a goddamned senator now, but I am still a Marine. And, as it happens, I agree with you. A Marine never leaves another Marine behind, no matter what.

"And so the question is, Marine, what the hell are we going to do about it?"

*C-3, E-DARES Facility,*
*Ice Station Zebra, Europa*
*1815 hours Zulu*

"I'm afraid I have some bad news, Major. Relief is not, repeat *not* on the way."

General Altman's image wavered and slipped, before steadying again. The signal, heavily encrypted and compressed into a very tight, short data squirt, had suffered some resolution loss in its forty-minute voyage out from Earth.

Jeff's jaw tightened, his fists closed. Beside him, Melendez stiffened slightly. Kaminski shook his head. Biehl muttered something beneath his breath. The others kept their faces expressionless, watchful.

"Alpha Company is loaded aboard the *Jefferson*," Altman continued. "Plus an ad hoc company of volunteers from Two-MSEF. They're ready to hump. However, the Senate is now debating whether to even allow a relief expedition to go to Europa.

"Major, I know this is really bad news for you people. I'm not going to try to run your show from five astronomical units away, but it's beginning to look as though surrender may be your only option."

There it was. The surrender option, the *S-word*, as he and his subordinates had begun jokingly referring to it. His communications exchanges with Earth over the last few days had been carefully avoiding the topic, especially with the company holding its own so well. But the word had been certain to surface sooner or later.

But damn the forty-minute time delay that required communications with Earth to be, not a conversation, but a series of monologues, alternating between Earth and Europa. It left him unable to respond directly to anything his superiors might say, leaving a gulf that only emphasized how isolated, how very much on his own, he really was.

"Colonel Garroway and some others here are exploring alternative options," Altman was saying. "I suggest that you continue to hold out as long as you can, while we see if any of those options prove feasible. However, if your command is in danger of being overrun, you are authorized to negotiate the best terms of surrender you can manage. There's no sense in throwing your lives away to no good purpose."

And what the hell did *that* mean? What about the men and women who'd died on the ice already? Had everything they'd done so far been for nothing?

"And . . . one more piece of bad news, I'm afraid. Our tracking sources report that the Chinese A-M transport *Xing Feng* has left cis-lunar space and is en route for Jupiter. She appears to be using constant acceleration, so you can expect her arrival there within five days. No word on her cargo, though she is carrying at least six Descending Thunder landing craft. I think we can safely assume that Beijing *has* decided to reinforce her forces on Europa.

"I am sorry to have nothing but bad news for you fellows. It's beginning to look as though our only real hope to salvage anything out of this mess is a political settlement.

We'll keep you informed of all developments.

"This is Marine Space Force Headquarters, going over to you, awaiting reply."

Altman's face winked off the monitor, replaced by the Marine Space logo and the words AWAITING REPLY.

"Well," Lieutenant Biehl said. "I guess that's that."

"Why do you say that, Moe?" Jeff asked, keeping his voice light. "A lot can happen between now and when the *Xing Feng* gets here."

"Sir," Lieutenant Graham said. "You heard the general. Another Charlie transport is on the way. The enemy's gonna be stronger than ever!"

"I'll tell you what's worse than that," Melendez added. "They'll have another damned ship in orbit! They'll be able to blast this base to rubble as soon as they get here, and this time we don't have an International Gun and we don't have a bug loaded with shit! My God, do you think the Charlie CO is going to maintain a hands-off policy when he gets a second chance? He'd be a fool to do it."

"Sergeant Major? What's your assessment? How are the men holding up?"

Kaminski grinned. He appeared to have recovered completely from his momentary blackout of the day before. "No problems on that front, at least, sir. Morale is sky-high after we bagged that cruiser yesterday. And even the one shot for the International Gun made 'em feel like they were hitting back. They're charged, Major, charged and ready to go, any damned place you tell them."

"Yes. Of course, the question is, what I should tell them?"

"I can't help you there, sir. I guess Major Devereaux was in the same fix as you."

Major Devereaux, yes. That Marine hero had been very much on Jeff's mind these past few days. The hero of Wake Island . . . the man who'd held out against overwhelming Japanese forces for sixteen days with 449 Marines. He'd been discussing Wake Island a lot lately with Chesty. The parallels with Europa, especially the early victories against enemy ships, were tantalizingly close.

In December of 1941, Wake Island—actually an atoll of three tiny islands around a lagoon almost 2,400 miles west of Pearl Harbor—was the site of an airfield and submarine base still under construction, but occupying a strategically important location north of the Japanese-controlled Marshall Islands, and between Hawaii and the Philippines. It was garrisoned by Major James Devereaux's force of thirteen officers and 365 Marines of the First Defense Battalion and under the command of U.S. Navy Commander Winfield S. Cunningham, CO of the new naval air station on the atoll. The Japanese struck at the island with an invasion fleet immediately after their victory at Pearl Harbor, launching a devastating air raid that wrecked eight out of twelve available fighter aircraft.

The Japanese commander, however, was overconfident. In the opening phases of the battle, shore batteries manned by the garrison scored damaging hits on the light cruiser *Yubari*, then serving as the Japanese flagship; sank the destroyer *Hayate*; and hit three other ships as well. The four surviving fighters struck back and sank the destroyer *Kisaragi*. An attempted landing on December 11 was wiped out. One American died in the exchange against over five hundred Japanese sailors, marines, and airmen killed. The invasion force was driven off, and the defenders were jubilant. In the smoke-pall shadow of burning battleships at Pearl, the lopsided victory had provided an incredible boost to American morale. It was during this period that the code-filler message including the words "Send us" at the beginning, and "more Japs" at the end, had been picked up and spread by American newspapers and radio broadcasts.

But it proved to be only a temporary setback for the Imperial Japanese Navy. The invasion force returned, heavily reinforced, including support from two fleet carriers and several cruisers and destroyers detached from Admiral Nagumo's attack force still en route from the Pearl Harbor attack.

The Americans had tried to organize a relief expedition; in fact, all three available U.S. Pacific Fleet carrier task forces had been ordered to the relief of Wake. But over-caution, breakdowns, fueling problems, and administrative confusion caused by the summary dismissal of the CINC-PAC blamed for the Pearl disaster had all resulted in the fleet being ordered to turn back just 425 miles from belea-guered Wake. There would be no relief force.

The Wake defense force, augmented by Marine ground crew personnel once the last fighter was disabled, plus a number of civilian construction workers, fought on heroi-cally, but at 0235 hours on December 23, Japanese forces made it ashore at several points and began reducing Marine defenses one by one. At 0500 hours, Commander Cun-ningham sent his final message to Pearl: "The enemy is on the island. The issue is in doubt."

Further resistance was pointless, given that no help would be coming. Cunningham gave Devereaux permission to surrender; the major had then walked all over the island, accompanied by a Japanese officer under a white flag, per-suading his Marines to surrender one strongpoint at a time.

Japanese losses in the Wake action were not known for sure, but numbered at least nine hundred dead, and well over twice that many wounded. The Americans lost 121 dead; 470 military personnel and 1,146 civilians were taken prisoner—none too gently, as it happened. The Japanese were still stinging from their earlier setback, and several prisoners were summarily executed.

Major Devereaux spent the next four years in a Japanese POW camp in China.

With Wake fallen, the Japanese conquest of the Philip-pines had been assured.

So much had Chesty been able to describe to Jeff, though he'd already been familiar with the general history, of course. Marines were fanatics when it came to their own history and their own heroes. What the tale had not pre-pared him for, however, was the emotional reality of a sim-ilar strategic situation—a tiny garrison on an isolated outpost, far, far from any possibility of help.

And there would be no relief expedition.

Devereaux's decision. It might be best to surrender *now*, before another Marine died. There was little advantage to be won by holding out, by playing the strutting, macho hero and fighting to the death. Gallant last stands generally took place only when the enemy didn't give the defenders any choice—the Alamo, the Little Bighorn, Camerone.

There was little point in adding Cadmus Crater to that bloody, if heroic, list.

In Jeff's mind, though, there was a serious question as to whether they *could* surrender. The Chinese forces had been hit pretty hard these past six days. Another ship might be here within the week, but did the Chinese forces now on Europa have the supplies and space to take care of almost seventy Marines and civilians? He doubted it. The Marines now held nine POWs themselves, Chinese soldiers captured in the various actions in and around Cadmus Crater. They couldn't be given the run of the base, certainly, nor could they be left in one of the sheds on the surface. At the moment, they were crammed into two storage compartments inside the E-DARES facility, requiring a constant guard on both rooms, and an extra security detail each time food was delivered, or when it was time to walk the prisoners, two at a time, down the passageway to the head to relieve themselves or shower. Four of the prisoners were wounded, requiring a lot of Doc McCall's time, and more security each time there was a dressing change or time for medication.

It was bad enough that Jeff honestly wasn't sure what they would be able to do if they took many more prisoners; Kaminski had half-jokingly suggested yesterday that the Charlies could win the fight right now simply by surrendering.

He didn't think the Chinese CO would be any happier at having to accommodate forty-one Marine POWs. He certainly wasn't going to trust the guy unless he received some pretty damned strong assurances.

He looked at his staff, weighing the expressions, which ranged from Biehl's dour pessimism to Kaminski's self-assured acceptance of whatever the next order might be.

"Captain Melendez," he said. "You're the XO. Your assessment?"

"Ski's right. The men will follow you to hell right now, skipper. I think we hunker down, ride it out, and see what Earth can deliver. If they can't deliver, we get the best terms we can, rather than spending any more lives for this ice ball than we have to."

"That's right, sir," Graham said. "Earth doesn't care. Why should we?"

"Because we're *Marines*, damn it!" Jeff flared. "Because we have a job to do, and we're damned well going to *do* it!" He paused, breathing hard. It was worrisome to know that the enlisted men would follow him to hell, but that he was going to have to convince his officers. "Look. We have to buy more time for the politicians, okay? Maybe they can pull a negotiated settlement out of the hat. If that settlement means we surrender and accept a ride home in a Chinese transport, so be it.

"But until I receive direct orders to cease fire and turn my command over to my counterpart out there, I will *not* surrender! Do we have an understanding, gentlemen?"

A mumbled chorus of "yessirs" and "aye, ayes" sounded from the others. There was little enthusiasm, and for a moment, Jeff was tempted to pull the old boot camp routine: "I can't hear you!"

But that kind of artificial rah-rah would have been out of place, even insulting. These men knew what the score was, and, in the U.S. military, at least, it wasn't enough that men follow orders blindly.

They had to follow out of conviction.

"My office will be open, if any of you want to discuss this privately," he said. "Let's adjourn. I'm hungry."

It was a weak joke. They were all hungry, going on the same half rations as the men. Hell, at this rate it wouldn't be long before the Charlies starved them out, with or without the help of another Chinese warship.

There had to be another way, another option. *Had* to be . . .

The problem was going to be finding it.

**24 OCTOBER, 2067**

*Senate Floor,*
*Capitol Building, Washington DC*
*1420 hours EDT*

"Ladies and gentlemen of the Senate, I have been accused of bias in this matter, of letting my old loyalties, my old brotherhood, stand in the way of what is perceived by a majority within this august body as a *good* thing, a *positive* thing."

Senator Carmen Fuentes was just getting warmed up.

She'd never participated in a filibuster before, that uniquely American expression of politics: the chance to stand up in front of her fellow senators and simply *talk*—talk for hour upon hour, refusing to yield, holding the floor against the opposition for the simple purpose of preventing a motion for a vote.

"It's true that I am a Marine. I retired from the Corps twelve years ago, but I am still a Marine. More, I am a blood member of that small and select brotherhood, beginning a century ago with Major John Glenn . . . a *spacefaring* Marine, who has also had the honor to be elected to this body. Major Glenn started something, you see, something that he himself could not have imagined at the time. A Marine fighter pilot in World War II and Korea, first American to orbit the Earth, ultimately a senator from Ohio who then became the first man to return to space at the age of seventy-seven . . . when he was what was back then considered *old*.

"Since Glenn's day, there have been fourteen other Marines who have also flown in space, and also served in the U.S. Senate."

She spoke easily, dropping the facts and figures without effort, without using notes. Though her colleagues couldn't tell the fact, she was enjoying the use of a new and particularly high-tech toy, one that promised to vastly extend the power and scope of all speechmaking on the Hill. Truly great orators—the Websters and Disraelis and Churchills—were rarities in every century; it didn't help when you were shuffling papers or note cards or, worse, trying to talk off the top of your head, making it up as you went along and trying to have the result be reasonably coherent.

Carmen, however, was wearing a contact display, a soft plastic contact lens in her right eye which served as a kind of HUD projecting scrolling words and data directly onto her retina.

At the other end of her in-eye prompter was Abe, her personal AI secretary resident within her PAD. She'd stored large pieces of the speech she wanted to give, along with all the facts and figures she needed to back up her words. Abe was arranging those words as she spoke, listening to her talk, and shaping suggestions for new topics, new ideas, new directions to go in.

She could ignore the scrolling words if she wished, choose any of a variety of possible directions to go in, and pretty much make up the speech as she went on, but it was a great way to avoid getting stuck, and wondering what the hell to say next. She could trust Abe to stay a step or two ahead of her, arranging the data she needed, even making suggestions as to what she might want to talk about next.

"So I suppose I am a member of an extremely small and elite society. *Elite* That's something of a dirty word these days, I know. None of us is supposed to be any better than anyone else . . . at anything. But I'm here to tell you today that that is a lie, and a pernicious one. There are some men and women, a select few, better than others in an important way—young men and women willing to put themselves in harm's way, willing to lay down their very *lives* to serve the interests of their families and fellow Americans, their country, and their government.

"And we, distinguished colleagues, have a miserable record in our attempts at repayment of a debt that we can never truly begin to repay. How often, I ask you, have we accepted the sacrifices made by these excellent young Americans, only to trample on what they have given us?

"My God, look at the record! Look at it, and weep at how politics has repaid the sacrifice in lives and blood made by our children! A century ago, Congress sent American troops to Vietnam, then decided to abandon the country to its own devices, after over fifty thousand Americans—including, I might add, thirteen thousand Marines—had been sacrificed there.

"In Beirut, in 1983, we sent the Marines in with orders that said they couldn't even load their weapons, couldn't even protect themselves in the middle of a war. Two hundred thirty-eight Marines were killed, and our thanks was to tacitly admit defeat, pull out, and abandon the peace that they had already attempted to purchase with their blood.

"The same happened in Somalia in 1993. The same in Ceylon in '02. The same in Israel, in '06. In Taiwan.

"It's now a full century since Vietnam, and we are still doing the same—we, the men and women in this assembly, still despicably sacrificing our young on the altars of expediency, of political maneuvering and 'sending messages,' of wars fought with no clear goals, no certain outcome, and no long-term gain.

"My distinguished colleague from New York spoke at length yesterday about the need for peace. As it happens, I agree with him. As a soldier, I am the *first* to speak for peace, because no one can hate war more than the person who must fight in it.

"But where I part company from the senator from New York is the idea that our young men and women, those whom we have already sent across this Solar System to serve on the barren, ice-locked seas of a world more alien than any of us here can possibly imagine—that these young people are expendable. That we can shrug our shoulders, say it was a mistake, and leave them to their fate because to do otherwise would be *inconvenient*, would *upset the delicate process* of peace negotiations with Beijing, would send the *wrong message* to the People's Republic . . ."

She was pouring scorn into the phrases, as Abe dredged them up from his recording of Senator Kellerman's Senate speech yesterday. She could feel the uncomfortable shifting of the senators listening to her, an icy reserve as cold in its way as the surface of Europa. They didn't like having their noses rubbed in it, but Carmen Fuentes had never backed down from a fight, and she wasn't about to begin doing so now.

"My distinguished colleague has spoken of a peace initiative, of extending the olive branch to our counterparts in Beijing. All of that is well and good. But I remind this body that at this moment, a handful of our young people, the future of this nation—perhaps future members of this Senate—are fighting on Europa. Two hundred forty-eight have died so far, forty of them on the moon, their blood staining that cold blue ice. And I must stand here as their representative, asking if their blood has been shed in vain.

"I'll tell you, ladies and gentlemen of the Senate. As a Marine, I still hold one promise sacred above all others: that I will never, under any circumstances, abandon a fellow Marine.

"I will not abandon my brothers and sisters, who stand now, at our orders, on the icy shores of the Europan sea."

As she spoke, a green light winked on in her eye, a quick pulse that flickered eight or ten times, then vanished. And Senator Carmen Fuentes laughed, startling several of the senators nearest her, who were reading e-books or working on their PADs.

"In fact, ladies and gentlemen of the Senate, I must tell you now that all we can do is support our people out there. It is history that will judge us here. But it is that brave handful of Marines on Europa who will determine the character of this, what we are pleased to call our civilization, for the next one hundred years."

A green light, relayed by Abe on receipt of Colonel Garroway's message.

The U.S.S. *Thomas Jefferson* was now accelerating out of Earth orbit—on a "training mission."

And there was nothing that Kellerman or any of his political allies or the Greens or the Globalists or any of the rest could do about it now.

Then the only question was whether Major Warhurst and his people could hold out long enough for the relief expedition to get there.

# EIGHTEEN

*Radio Shack, U.S.S.*
    Thomas Jefferson
*Under acceleration, outbound
    from Earth
0625 hours Zulu*

The steady, rattling vibration of the *Tommy J*'s A-M drives buzzed Kaitlin's shipboard deck shoes through the steel grating. It was nearly time for the next exchange.

"Here we go, Colonel," LCDR John Reynolds said. "Incoming!"

The three of them were gathered in *Jefferson*'s communications suite, a narrow, claustrophobic compartment much roomier in zero gravity than when they were under acceleration. Kaitlin looked at Captain Steve Marshal, who was leaning against the doorway combing, watching her with a wry grin. "You're on, Colonel," he said.

Static blasted from the speaker, mingled with the squeal of hydrogen plasma at starcore temperatures.

"*Jefferson*, this is Colorado Springs Space Control!" a voice said, faint but reasonably clear despite the hiss of *Jefferson*'s own exhaust cloud. "I *said* that the Senate has voted to prohibit any relief expedition to Europa!"

This was the third time that Earth had repeated the message. Each time before, Kaitlin had told them that *Jefferson* was not receiving, that she could not understand.

273

Of course, with each transmission compressed and repeated three times, the ship's AI had little trouble merging the transmissions and extracting intelligible words from the hash of white noise. Even the static was much less than it should have been, the hiss bleached out by the AI's byte-juggling ministrations.

"The Senate voted fifty-one to forty-five," the voice at Space Control continued. "I repeat, fifty-one to forty-five, with sixteen abstentions, *against* the relief measure! *Jefferson*, do you copy?"

So! The vote had been a lot closer than Carmen had predicted. That must have been one blitzkrieg of a speech.

Kaitlin wondered, too, if there was a kind of hidden message here from the senator. Colorado Springs was making a special effort to make sure she knew the results of the senate vote. Was Carmen behind that? Perhaps telling her that there was more support for the Europa Relief Expedition in Congress than expected?

Damn . . . no. You could go crazy trying to figure all the hidden angles. She couldn't let that distract her from what she had to do.

The static-blasted voice from Earth was continuing to speak.

"*Jefferson*, there is no relief expedition, and we do not have properly logged flight plans for your boost, which appears to be aimed at Jupiter space. You are directed to cease acceleration at once! *Jefferson*! Do you read?" There was a long hesitation before the speaker added, "Over!" She could hear the frustration in his voice as he handed the ball back to the outbound A-M cruiser, as he wondered what else to say, how else he could convince, before beginning the next interminable lag-time wait.

Kaitlin exchanged another long look with Marshal, then shrugged. "I'm having a lot of trouble hearing him, Captain. How about you?"

"Well, that's the trouble with these steady-thrust ships," he told her. "With Earth almost directly astern, we're trying to hear signals coming straight up our exhaust trail. Hot plasma plays the very hell with reception."

She picked up the microphone. "Space Control, this is the *Jefferson*," she said. "I am having trouble hearing your transmission." Technically, either Reynolds or the Captain should be speaking for the ship, but she'd insisted. This plot had been her idea, after all, and she wanted to assume full responsibility.

Even for the lies.

"Space Control," she continued, "this is Colonel Kaitlin Garroway, of the One-MSEF. We are deploying on extended . . . maneuvers. We are exercising our right of free passage through open space, as allowed by all current international space treaties. We are not engaged in any relief efforts, nor do we intend to challenge any vessel or military force unless we are challenged first.

"Colorado Springs . . . your signal is very weak, and breaking up. I cannot hear you, repeat, I cannot hear you. Over!"

She checked a time readout on the bulkhead. It would be five minutes before they heard back.

The *Jefferson*, carrying her cargo of 175 Marines of Alpha and Delta Companies, 1-MSEF, had been under one G acceleration for twenty-seven hours now; they were already three-tenths of an astronomical unit out from Earth and traveling at over 950 kilometers per second. At that distance, it took nearly two and a half minutes for a radio or laser signal to travel from the *Jefferson* to Earth, and a like time for the reply to make the trip back.

And the distance was growing greater with every passing second.

Kaitlin knew she was taking a fearful risk; in all probability, her career was over. She could play games with Colorado Springs now, but when she returned to Earth, there *would* be a hearing, and the *Jefferson*'s radio logs and comm buffer storage would prove her lie.

She just hoped they would let her take the blame herself. The worst part of her act of career suicide was that, most probably, it wouldn't be just her who took the fall. Captain Marshal was putting his neck on the block as well. Hell, there was even the chance that Rob would be tainted as well, by sheer association.

But the real problem was Captain Steve Marshal, a lanky Texan with a blond buzz cut whom she'd first met through Rob ten years ago, at a party in Alexandria, Virginia. He'd been a close friend of the family ever since, and—to hear him tell it, at any rate—had battled his way through the e-work barricades in the Pentagon to win assignment to the Europa Relief Expedition for the *Jefferson* over the *Washington*, the *Reagan*, and the *Dole*.

He'd flown out to Quantico when he'd heard about Rob Junior, sat up all night with them, cried with them.

"You look . . . unhappy, Kait," Steve said.

"I don't like dragging my friends down with me," she told him. "I still can't say I'm sorry that I got you involved in this, Captain, because this wouldn't be possible without you. But I hate the thought that you could find yourself facing a court martial because of me. Damn it, Steve, you could lose your command! You should never have agreed to this."

He smiled. "Colonel, in the first place, I never could say no to a beautiful woman.

"In the second place, I had friends on both the *JFK* and the *Roosey*. Jeremy Mitchell and I grew up together outside of San Antonio—and I ended up marrying his sister. And . . . there was Rob Junior. The way I see it, either all of those people died for some reason, or they died for no reason. I kinda prefer the first option, don't you?"

"But—"

He held up a hand. "And *third*, Colonel, it's not just you Marines who can be too impossibly damned heroic for words. I happen to think those people on Europa are getting a damned raw deal. *I'm* not going to see them hung up out there and left to flap in the breeze!"

"Europa doesn't have much of a breeze."

"Okay. Hung out to freeze-dry in the proton flux, then."

She returned his smile. "You can always claim that I pulled a gun on you."

"That the Marines hijacked a twelve billion–dollar spacecraft to Jupiter to fight an illegal war? They might frown on that."

"No more than you throwing in with my little mutiny. That's what this is, you know. At the very least we're guilty of trying to write our own version of U.S. foreign policy here. At worst, we're pirates!"

*"Yarrr!"* he growled, a mock pirate's battlecry. "I always wanted to be a space pirate!" She laughed, and he added, "Look, I'll be okay, Colonel. We were scheduled for boost, and I boosted on the mark. What I disregarded was the fact that Space Command put me on hold and didn't give me a final boost clearance." He shrugged. "I queried both STANNET and L-3 Traffic Control and got a clear to boost from both. End of story. At worst, I'm pegged for not double-checking with Earth, but I was well inside the envelope. And they obviously haven't checked yet to see that a flight plan has been logged. We're scheduled now to carry out training exercises en route to Jupiter, and in Jovian space."

"At one G all the way? Those are pretty damned expensive exercises!" They would be using enough antimatter on this one run to power all of North America for months.

"Yeah, but I want to get back to Earth in a hurry. Gotta be home in time for Thanksgiving. The Marshals all get together for a big family do down in Texas, y'see, and—"

"Steve, you're impossible."

"Only highly improbable, my dear. In any case, I don't think either of us has a whole lot to worry about."

"How do you figure that?"

"Simple. If we manage to save your Marines, we're going to have to do it by winning, right? We beat that second Chinese cruiser, save the CWS base, make contact with the alien, whatever it takes. If the Chinese lose hard enough, it should swing things around on Earth too. They make peace, we give them some concessions in sharing alien technology, everybody's happy.

"And our superiors are *not* going to court-martial us for success! Not when we're in the public eye as heroes!"

"Well, that's all very well. But there's so damned much that can go wrong! What if we fail?"

*What if I fail?* That was the thought that had been plaguing her for two days.

"If we fail, Colonel, you and I are going to be dead. And we won't care a bit about what they say about us when we're gone."

*West of Cadmus Crater, Europa*
*0956 hours Zulu*

Lucky brought his gloved thumb down on the firing button. Fifty meters away, ice exploded in an outlashing cloud, a savage detonation, death-silent. The shock was transmitted through the ice as a sharp, brief shudder, but there was no other indication that the charge had even fired.

Dropping the trigger box back in a thigh pouch, Lucky snatched up his 580 and started crawling forward. To his right, Liss Cartwright aimed her rifle from a prone position, covering him.

The badlands east of Cadmus were a jumbled tangle of mounds and jagged berg shapes crammed together by pressures deep within the ice into a patchwork labyrinth kilometers across. The only way to cross it was on the labyrinth floor, threading along twisting, narrow pathways with sheer ice walls ten meters high in places. The Chinese had been using the chaotic terrain to slip close to the base of the crater rim. Several times now in the past week, lone soldiers or small groups had worked their way up the crater slope, avoiding or disabling perimeter sentinels, and firing rockets or sniping lasers into the compound.

The Marines had countered by sending out two- and four-man patrols to place booby traps and set ambushes. Grenades buried in the ice walls and triggered by pressure switches or proximity were recorded in Chesty Puller's data base so that he could steer friendlies clear of them, painting them on the Marines' HUDs as red warning flags. Better were traps that could be fired by hand in an attempt to ensnare enemy troops.

The Warhorse, scuttlebutt said, was trying to capture a Chinese soldier who knew something about the incoming PRC ship. Lucky thought the whole idea was pretty silly. Hell, they didn't have room for the prisoners they held already, and the POWs they had weren't willing to talk. Lucky had pulled guard detail over the Charlie prisoners a couple of times already; they were a smugly arrogant bunch, with facial expressions ranging from bland to sullen, who refused to even look at their captors. Adding to the catch was begging for trouble in Lucky's opinion.

But when the action order called for bringing in another prisoner or two, that's what he was going to try his best to do. Today it was his turn to go play hide-and-seek among the tortured icebergs in the broken ground east of the crater. With Jupiter glaring down at him from above the horizon, he and Liss had found a trail recently used by the enemy, planted a charge to cut them off, and settled down to wait.

The chances of actually achieving a contact were relatively slim; there were so *many* possible trails through the badlands. Still, Chesty had worked out the topology of the area and plotted a half dozen main paths between the crater and the Chinese lander still resting on the plain beyond the badlands to the east. Simply blocking Highways One through Six, as they came to be known, wasn't enough since there were always side trails to let the enemy slip around a blockage. The Marines had better luck mining the paths, or trying to ambush enemy troops while they made the passage.

Lucky made his way down a sharply sloping surface of rough ice, sliding the last few meters and landing hard on a ledge a man's height above the path floor. Two Chinese soldiers had been moving along this path moments before; Lucky had set off the charge to block their retreat, and now they should be coming back this way. He leaned against a spur of ice and aimed his 580 down the path, waiting.

Two minutes later, by his HUD timer, Liss joined him, scrambling down the ice slope from above. She was so close he felt the gentle shove of her SC shielding. "Anything?"

She spoke over the private channel at minimal wattage. Standing orders required them to use strict EM discipline to avoid being pinpointed by PRC scanners, but down here among the ice walls and tunnellike pathways, a weak signal wouldn't be picked up beyond line of sight. Lucky was amused that they still tended to whisper, as though they could be overheard.

"Nothing," he replied, not taking his eyes from the 580's crosshair reticle, painted on the claustrophobic opening to a particularly narrow stretch of Highway Five just ahead, where the ice-path crevice was scarcely a meter wide. "Either they're dead, or . . ."

"Or they're sitting tight in there," she finished the thought for him, "waiting for us the way we're waiting for them. Yeah."

"So what are we gonna do?"

"We go in and check."

"Uh-uh," he said. "*Not* a good idea. I think we try flushing them out."

"You have any grenades left?"

"Two. Cover me."

Lowering his rifle, he fished inside a pouch strapped to his suit combat harness, pulling out a steel-gray sphere with an arming button and a locking pin. He hesitated, judging distances. Throwing things was tough; a grenade went a lot further here than it did on Earth. Lucky had gone through low-G vacuum combat training on the Moon, as had all space-qualified Marines, but it was damned hard to just turn off your Earth-born reflexes in something as autonomic as throwing a ball.

He worked the pin free, set the timer for five seconds, cocked his arm back, pressed the arming button, and let fly, a long, high lob that sailed above the upper surface of the ice. He lost sight of the grenade as it fell somewhere among the crevice paths up ahead. Five seconds later, he felt a slight tremor in the ice.

More seconds passed. "Well?" Liss asked him.

"Damn it," he said. "I hate this hide-and-seek shit!"

"Cover me," she said. "I'll go check it out."

"No . . . wait," he said. He couldn't put his finger on it, but he felt an eerie, prickling sensation, almost as though they were being watched—a sensation somehow focused on that narrow crevice just ahead.

Lucky was a Marine and he'd been in combat. Okay, so his cherry had popped just a week ago; by now, damn it, he was a combat veteran, and there were very few of those who hadn't learned to listen to that gut-tickling inner warning that something was wrong. Most men and women who'd been in combat claimed to believe in senses science still refused to accept as measurable, testable faculties, ESP for lack of a better term. Lucky wasn't convinced it was a genuine sixth sense. He held the theory, also popular, that the human brain was very good at picking up subtle clues and details and assembling them in ways that seemed magical, even extrasensory.

There was also the nagging feeling that if the tables were reversed, if the Chinese were out there hunting him and he was trapped by an icefall up that narrow crevice, he wouldn't come running blindly back into the waiting crosshairs of his hunters. No . . . he'd find a position somewhere behind the crevice opening, take aim, and wait.

He pulled out his second grenade, stood up, and armed it, setting the timer for three seconds. With a swift, underhand toss, he sent the steel sphere hurtling into the mouth of the crevice opening, where it hit the ice wall behind the opening and ricocheted back down the corridor, out of sight to the left.

The shudder in the ice was much stronger this time, and a white cloud of ice particles and frost blasted silently from the crevice opening. Chunks of ice rained down on the path from overhead; a shadowy figure staggered into view, out-

lined for a moment in the cascading avalanche of white as
it tried to raise the rifle it was carrying. Lissa pressed the
firing button on her 580; a palm-sized patch on the figure's
chest silently exploded, and the figure crumpled, as ice as
fine as sand continued to pour across it.

Carefully, they moved forward, one covering the other
for a leapfrogging series of short dashes up the path. The
Chinese soldier in the crevice opening was dead; a companion, holding a Type 105 sniping rifle with laser targeting, lay a few meters away, around the corner, the legs of
his space suit torn open by Lucky's grenade.

"They *were* waiting for us," Lissa said. "Damn, Lucky,
you're *good*!"

"No prisoners today," he said. "Let's get on back to the
base."

"Roger that."

They followed Highway Five back toward Cadmus,
Lucky in the lead.

"So . . . since it's just us out here," Lissa asked, "is it
true what they say about you? You only do it in sims?"

"I dunno." He didn't want to talk about it. Not with *her*.

"Aw, c'mon. Either you do or you don't, Lucky! What's
the big deal?"

He wondered if he should tell her. Damn . . . he liked
Lissa. Liked her a lot. She wasn't all that pretty—not like
the eager, smiling, programmed-to-please beauties at Mr.
Virtuality—but she was awfully cute, with short brown hair
and small breasts and eyes so bright they could light you
up with a glance. It *would* be nice to . . . no.

"Yeah, it's true," he told her. "No offense, Liss, but virtual girls are a lot better in the rack than real ones."

"The hell they are," Lissa replied. He was surprised by
her laugh. "You've never tried *me*!"

He wasn't sure if that was a proposition or not. Of
course, if it was, he wouldn't be able to do anything about
it until they returned Earthside. Privacy was nearly non-
existent in the confines of the E-DARES facility—not as

bad as on board the *Roosey*, but there was no place he knew of for a friendly and uninterrupted boff.

Even if he could do it.

"The trouble with real women—" he began . . .

. . . and never finished. A pressure sensor buried beneath a handful of powdered ice clicked home beneath his boot, and the grenade blast caught him in the right side and hurled him to the left. He slammed against the wall of the pathway, then crumpled as several crate-sized chunks of ice smashed down on top of his legs.

He screamed, more from fear and shock than outright pain. He lay on his back, blinking through a red haze. Blood was splattered on the inside of his visor; it took him a long moment to realize that his head had jerked forward and he'd slammed his mouth against the helmet's chin console. He tasted salt in his mouth.

He tried to move, and failed.

Blinking through the haze, he tried to call Liss, but red lights were winking across his HUD, warning of power failure, of radio failure, of a breach in his backpack PLSS, of air loss, of heater failure . . .

His right leg hurt. Not badly, not as bad as a fracture, but it hurt and was uncomfortably twisted. He couldn't move either leg. It felt as though both legs were pinned under a massive weight.

Lucky was also starting to feel cold.

Damn it, where was Lissa? She'd been right behind him when that grenade booby trap went off. Funny . . . that. Who'd have thought that the Chinese were out trying to trap Americans in the labyrinthine maze, while he and Liss had been trying to trap them?

He tried clicking other radio channels open. Platoon frequency. Company frequency. Platoon leader frequency. All dead.

Time . . . what was the time? He was having trouble focusing on his HUD. It looked like . . . looked like 0620 hours . . . but that couldn't be. It would mean he'd been lying out here on his back with his legs pinned beneath a small ice mountain for over an hour. It had just happened a few moments ago . . . hadn't it?

Or had he been lying here unconscious all that time?

Movement . . . a shadow.

Something moved, a silhouette against the baleful orange-ocher light of Jupiter.

He recognized the space suits. *Chinese*! . . .

Lucky held very still as several PRC troops walked past; one gave him a curious glance as he stepped across Lucky's chest. Several more passed, and then one actually stooped at Lucky's side, turning his helmet, trying to peer in through the visor.

Lucky could see the man's lips moving inside his helmet, but heard nothing. Then, the enemy troops were gone. Lucky decided they must have seen the blood on the inner curve of his visor and figured he was dead or dying.

*Well, face it*, he thought. *You* are *dying*. The cold was chewing its way through his legs, his torso. These Mark IIB suits were well insulated, but he was in contact with solid ice at a temperature of $-140°$; any heat his suit still held would swiftly trickle away. Not as fast as an ordinary suit, perhaps, and a quick freeze might be a blessing. It was ironic. He might very well wish he didn't have so efficient a suit before long.

*Two-B, or not two-B?* he asked himself, and started giggling hysterically.

His indicators weren't telling him how much air he had; which would kill him first, air loss? Or the cold?

He wished he'd been able to get to know Liss better. She seemed nice, full of bounce and fun.

*So . . . why* do *you like sims better than the real thing?* Funny, but he'd never asked himself that. He'd always kind of assumed the answer had to do with Becka, who'd called off the wedding two weeks before the date, who'd told him that he was too domineering, too possessive, too much of a damned control freak, that she never wanted to see him again.

Well, sure he was a control freak. That was why he'd

joined the Marines, right? Because he always wanted to have things his own way? He chuckled at the thought, but the slight movement sent pain lancing down his side and leg.

It hadn't helped that she'd ended up marrying his best friend just a month later.

Well, maybe it was time to face the fact that he and Becka just hadn't been right for each other. If he was domineering, she was demanding. Their times in bed hadn't been all that good, not with her trying to boss him every step of the way. No, it was a good thing she'd wised up and dumped him; they'd both have been miserable if they'd gone through with it.

What was that? He thought he'd felt a faint, far-off jolt transmitted through the ice.

Couldn't have been anything.

Or . . . maybe it was. Those Chinese troops had been going somewhere in a hurry. Maybe they were hitting the base right now. He tried moving again, ignoring the pain. Damn it, he had to *move!*

More jars and jolts. Yeah, detonations of some sort, definitely. Who was winning?

He'd never had a lot to do with women after Becka. Hell, why should he, with Mr. Virtuality and on-line sex services all so readily available? Man, you could lose yourself in those tailor-made wet dreams, lose yourself and never come back.

And the best part of all was that your partners never nagged and never demanded. You were the boss and they did it the way you wanted.

Okay, so they didn't care. The illusion was good enough. The fantasy . . .

What the hell had Liss meant by that crack about never having tried her? Was she really interested in him? Or just setting him up for the punchline?

Nah. Women were all the same. Demanding. Controlling. Whining. And ready to drop you in an instant for someone they thought would be a better opportunity for them. His best friend had been in law school. That was why she'd dropped Lucky and grabbed him . . . right?

He was better off without her. He was just fuzzy-headed with the cold and the low oxy, and, okay, maybe he was missing his regular sessions at Mr. Virtuality and the pent-up pressures were fogging his brain. Hell, he'd had to make do with the movie clips on his PAD since he'd left Earth, and they just weren't the same as a *real* woman's soft and loving touch.

No, not a real woman.

Damn, where was Lissa? Had she run off and left him? Had those Charlies gotten her?

Damn, if only his radio was working.

He hadn't felt any more thumps through the ice for quite a while now. He was also vaguely aware that quite a bit of time had passed. He thought he'd been unconscious again, but couldn't tell.

Lissa hadn't abandoned him. She might be a woman, but she was a Marine, and Marines never abandoned their own.

What had happened? Maybe she was lying dead or wounded somewhere, just out of his sight. Damn, if *only* he could get up. He was feeling lots better now, almost warm and cozy. Maybe his suit heaters had kicked in again. Maybe his suit wasn't as badly damaged as he thought. Maybe . . .

Something bumped him, and pain clawed at his leg again. It felt like someone was tugging at him from above and behind, where he couldn't see.

The Charlies! They must have come back for him and were trying to drag him out from beneath the ice fall. His right hand groped at his chest, where his knife was strapped inside its scabbard. Damn. His arm wouldn't move either.

He was dimly aware that someone was kneeling over him. He felt a click of a connection being made, of the jack for a sound-powered suit intercom being snapped home in the side of his helmet. "Lucky? Lucky! Are you okay?"

It was Lissa.

He'd *known* it would be Lissa. She was a Marine. Marines never left their own.

"Lucky! It's me! Corporal Cartwright! You were unconscious, and I couldn't dig you out from under the ice! I had to go back for help! Can you hear me? *Wake up!*"

"I'm . . . awake . . ." Just barely. He wasn't able to feel his feet or hands, but he was feeling warm. He could see her face through the smear of blood on his visor, as she peered down into his helmet.

He could see tears glistening on her cheeks.

She looked . . . beautiful.

" 'Lo, Liss," he said. "I missed you."

"You didn't think I'd left you, did you? I couldn't move you by myself, so I had to go get a little help. Then it turned out the Charlies were launching another assault. We had a bit of a fight on our hands there. But the bad guys got beat, and now we're back. You know I wouldn't ever leave you."

"Nah," he mumbled, sliding off into unconsciousness. "Marines . . . look after . . . own . . . always . . ."

# NINETEEN

*C-3, E-DARES Facility*
*Ice Station Zebra, Europa*
*1310 hours Zulu*

"Gentlemen, it's about damned time we took this fight to the enemy."

He was closeted with his senior personnel in C-3, some of them seated around the makeshift map table in the center of the compartment, the others standing around the perimeter of the small room. They watched him with drawn, haggard faces; the enemy assaults had been coming fast and furious these past few days, as though the enemy commander was trying to overrun the CWS installation before reinforcements arrived.

It might, Jeff thought, be a matter of saving face. Or it might mean something more . . . a timetable he was unaware of.

"This is our situation, as of time now," Jeff said. "Combat-trained personnel are down to thirty-two Marines and four SEALs. Four more are in sick bay with injuries. Overall morale is good, but we are desperately short of food, ammo, and items such as tractors. We have no way of knowing what the enemy's losses are, or the condition of his morale. However, we do know that a second enemy ship will arrive in two days—actually, forty-two hours from now.

"At that time, we will again lose aerospace superiority and come under direct enemy bombardment, and the enemy will be reinforced, perhaps heavily. We can expect to be hit by overwhelming force within the next three to four days. Given Chinese superiority in numbers, armor, and air, this command, quite frankly, cannot be expected to hold out.

"Now. There's one bit of light in all the gloom and doom. As you all know by now, an American ship *is* on the way . . . the *Thomas Jefferson*. She boosted at about 1930 hours Zulu on Sunday, two days ago.

"HQ has been vague about what's going on. They report that the *Jefferson* has suffered a communications failure of some kind, but have been insisting *in the clear* that there is no relief expedition. This seems to mean either that they're trying to fox the Chinese into thinking a warship headed this way is *not* coming to help us, which doesn't sound all that plausible, or that the *Jefferson* is operating on her own—which is less plausible by far. Until the *TJ*'s motives are clear, we should be careful about accepting her deployment at face value."

Lieutenant Biehl held up a hand.

"Yes, Moe?"

"Sir, does that mean . . ." he stopped, his face the image of puzzlement. "I'm confused, sir. Are we getting help from Earth or not?"

Jeff smiled. "If the *Jefferson* is trying to confuse the enemy, I'd have to say she's doing one hell of a good job. If we're a little confused about her intentions right now, think what Charlie must be going through!

"Now . . . on her current trajectory, there's no other reasonable destination for her except Jupiter space. We'll know for sure at oh-one hundred hours on the twenty-seventh. That's when she would have to flip end for end and begin deceleration, assuming one G all the way, but nothing else makes sense. If she doesn't decelerate, she goes zipping past us at almost four thousand kps, headed for nowhere but deep space."

Lieutenant Graham raised a hand.

"Yeah, Rich?"

"Why don't they up their acceleration?" he wanted to know. "Couldn't they beat the Chinese here if they took some heavier Gs?"

"Not with *that* energy curve!" Melendez said with a chuckle. "Remember, you square your acceleration to halve your time. You'd end up needing more antimatter than has been manufactured in the past hundred years!"

"There is no way that the *Jefferson* can beat the Chinese ship, even at two gravities. The enemy cruiser will arrive at oh-seven hundred hours on Thursday, the twenty-seventh. We'll have three more days to wait before the *Jefferson* gets here.

"Not exactly in the nick of time, is it?" Kaminski put in.

"Not this time," Jeff agreed. "That's why I'm looking at options. We can't sit around and wait for the *Jefferson* to rescue us. We can't even take much more in the way of enemy attacks from the Charlies who are already on Europa. If we sit tight, we're going to be overrun long before help arrives—or forced to surrender."

"So what's the alternative, Major?" Lieutenant Quinlan asked.

"We could leave—head off overland into the outback," Walthers said. "Is that what you're thinking?"

Jeff shook his head. "Uh-uh. We have one tractor and three lobbers. Without transport, we wouldn't be able to get far, and we wouldn't be able to carry shelter along with us, or enough PLSS air reserves to last us more than twenty-four hours. Hell, if we weren't dead of suffocation by the time the *Jefferson* arrived, we'd be fried from the radiation flux."

"Besides," Melendez added, "we don't have any way of masking our heat signatures. We already glow in the dark, you know, on IR. The Chinese ship would spot us in one orbital pass overhead."

"It doesn't stop the bad guys from taking over this facility, either. No, we need something a bit more direct.

"People, I am not going to surrender, and I am not going to just sit here and keep taking it. I intend to go over to the offensive—to take the battle to the enemy—and to use his back door."

"Back door?" BJ said. "*What* back door?"

He moved his PAD on the tabletop so everyone could see. As he touched the screen, the display was repeated on the bulkhead monitor—two large circles, one slightly smaller and set inside the other.

"Europa, people. A radius of 1,563 kilometers—circumference of 9,820 kilometers. A body composed of layers." He pointed to the outer circle. "The upper layer is predominately water ice, ranging from ten kilometers to a few tens of meters thick, depending on where you land. The ice here at Cadmus is thin, only about twenty meters."

He indicated the area between the two circles. "Below that is water, the Europan world ocean. Depth, fifty to one hundred kilometers, averaging about eighty. And below that, a rocky-silicate crust."

His finger traced a curve along the outer circle, tracing an arc of a bit more than thirty degrees. "If we travel overland—over *ice*, that is—it's 1,005 kilometers from Cadmus to the Chinese base on the equator. But there is a shortcut, a shortcut with the advantage of letting us stay completely undetectable.

"All we have to do is travel *under* the ice, moving along a chord, a straight line from here to there."

There was a stunned silence, followed by a low murmuring as others in the compartment began talking. "My God," Lieutenant Biehl said.

"Where's the back door you were talking about?" Walthers asked. "How do we get through the ice at the other . . . oh!"

"The goddamned submarines!" Biehl added.

"Right," Jeff said. "We have two Mantas, each eight meters long, and capable of carrying, with a bit of crowding, maybe ten or twelve Marines, suited up, with weapons and gear. BJ here brought back the images we need." He touched his PAD screen, and the display shifted to an aerial view, shot from several hundred meters up, of a vast, dark hole in the Europan ice, shrouded by steam and mist. "Our International Gun punched clean through the ice the other day," he continued. "It must be pretty damned thin in that region, no thicker than here at Cadmus, anyway. By now, the open water has frozen over again, but it can't be more than a few centimeters thick yet. That, people, is our back door."

"A shortcut straight through the planet?" Gunnery Sergeant Kuklock asked.

"The chord distance isn't that much shorter than the Great Circle Route," Jeff told him. "Works out to about 980 kilometers, so we only save twenty-five. But we'll be sheltered from observation from topside, above the ice, and we should be able to emerge in their rear and achieve complete surprise. Following the chord will take us to a depth of about eighty kilometers. As it happens, according to the scientists here, that's pretty close to the average ocean depth between here and the Charlie main base. The Mantas have a cruising speed at depth of about fifty to eighty kilometers per hour. That means a twelve- to eighteen-hour trip."

"Can they break through the ice at the other end?" BJ wanted to know. "Even a few centimeters can be pretty tough, and it might be thicker than we think. Things freeze fast on Europa, you might've noticed!"

"The Mantas carry remote drones for carrying instrument packages. Kaminski here has assured me he can rig some drones with a few grams of antimatter as warheads. That ought to break through anything up to a couple of meters thick."

"Our maker of exotic weapons," Melendez said.

"Or our icebreaker," BJ added. "First from above, now from underneath!"

" 'Icebreaker,' " Kaminski mused. "I like that. I'll be sure to put that on my résumé when I get out of the Corps." The others laughed.

"So . . . sir, what do we do when we achieve that sur- prise?" Graham asked. "Especially given that we don't know the enemy's strength."

"We'll need to work out the details, of course. What I'd like to do, though, is have a fair-sized force emerge from the ice close to the enemy LZ at just about the time those reinforcements arrive."

"That's going to require some pretty close timing, sir," Kuklock pointed out.

"Yes it is. But if we hit them too early, before their landing craft are committed to touching down at their cur- rent base, they would just land somewhere else—maybe a lot closer to Cadmus. And if we wait too long, they'll be down and fully established, maybe with a lot of hardware and some unpleasant surprises.

"What I'd like to try to do is come up out of that hole with a bunch of Wyverns just as those landers are balancing down out of the sky. A few men could do a *lot* of damage in a short time. Maybe enough to hurt them so badly that they stop hitting us. We need time. If we buy ourselves just three more days past the twenty-seventh, the *Jefferson* will be here. If we're going to pull this off, though, we have to move quickly. We must launch within the next twenty-four hours if we are to reach the Chinese LZ by 0700 hours Zulu on the twenty-seventh. Are there any questions?"

There were a few scattered questions, mostly of a tech- nical nature relating to how the Mantas would be deployed, and how the men would debark from them. At the end, however, there was a single hand in the air—raised by the lone civilian present in the room.

"Yes, Dr. Ishiwara?"

Shigeru Ishiwara had been granted a special status with the Marines, as liaison between them and the CWS science team. Not everyone trusted Vasaliev, and fewer liked him; Ishiwara, though, seemed to be a man of integrity and trust. Jeff had agreed to let him sit in on planning sessions like this one so that they could have his scientific input—and the cooperation of the civilians.

Jeff had especially wanted him in on this meeting, since his submarines were a topic of the discussion. He wanted the quiet Japanese xenoarcheologist to be on their side in this one.

"Major," Ishiwara began. "What you propose sounds like a bold and daring plan. I have only one question."

"Yes?" *Here it comes*, he thought. *If there's going to be a problem with the scientists, this'll be it. . . .*

"If I understand you right, you'll be following a straight-line chord from point to point, with the Manta submersibles reaching a depth of approximately eighty kilometers at the midpoint."

"That's right," Jeff replied. "I've checked those boats out . . . even got to take a ride in one in the Bahamas, Earthside. They're rated as safe to a depth of ten thousand meters on Earth—that's a thousand atmospheres—or the equivalent of a depth of seventy-seven kilometers here on Europa. And we have a bit of a safety margin to play with. We shouldn't have any problem at that depth. If we do, we can adjust our path to keep to a shallower level."

"It was not the depth that was concerning me, Major Warhurst. Are you aware that your proposed course will take you very close to the position of the Singer?"

Jeff's breath caught in his throat. No, he hadn't known. Or rather, he'd known, in general, where the alien artifact was, but he had not put that bit of information together with the rest when he'd been working out the plan.

"I'd . . . not considered that, Doctor. Are you suggesting that we avoid the straight line path?" They could take a longer route, but the less time the Marines on board had to remain in their pressure suits, the better. The total time they'd be living off their PLSS backpacks was dangerously long already. And after the strike, they would have to make the same voyage *back*.

"Not necessarily," Ishiwara said. "The Singer has not shown any interest in us, or in the remote probes we have sent to that location. And it's not exactly on the straight-

line path, but a little to the south. It seems likely that the
Mantas would pass unchallenged."

"Then what are you suggesting?"

"Only this. That you consider including a scientist on
your expedition. Someone who can make contact with the
Singer if . . . something unexpected happens."

Something unexpected, yeah.

The trouble was, manpower was going to be at a pre-
mium. With luck and crowding, they might get twenty-two
Marines and four SEAL pilots to the Chinese LZ.
Twenty-six men to carry out a raid as complex and as dangerous as this one was not enough by far.

But then, there weren't enough Marines on this entire
world to be enough.

And, too, Ishiwara would be an invaluable asset if that
damned thing down there *did* blink, or whatever.

"Are you volunteering yourself, Dr. Ishiwara?"

"I have experience with research submersibles which
could be of use to you," he said. "Yes. I would like to
volunteer for that honor."

"Then you'll be more than welcome, sir. Any other questions?"

There were none. The meeting was dismissed.

Shigeru was waiting for him by the door. "Perhaps one
question more, Major."

"Shoot."

"Since we are passing so close to the Singer, I was wondering what research opportunities there might be. I am a
xenoarcheologist, and the whole point of my being on this
world was to attempt to make contact with that . . . artifact."

"If you mean can we stop and sightsee, no. I'm sorry.
*My* whole point for being here is to protect this base, and
at the moment, that means by making sure this raid goes
down without a hitch. Stopping off to visit at underwater
alien cities would complicate things, and risk costing us the
mission."

"Of course. I had to ask."

"Understood. And you're welcome to make whatever observations you can as we pass. To tell the truth, though, I'm going to make sure we give that thing a wide berth. We might not get that close at all. I do not like surprises during combat ops."

"The Singer is not positioned exactly a straight line between here and Cadmus, Major. It will be off our line of travel by several kilometers. Still, it seems a shame to get so close without a getting a good, close-up look, eh?"

"Doctor Ishiwara, when this campaign is over, the Chinese have been kicked off this iceball, and Ice Station Zebra is safely in friendly hands, I will personally deposit you on the front porch of that thing.

"But until then, I'm going to keep my distance." It was a promise he intended to keep.


*E-DARES Facility*
*Cadmus Crater, Europa*
*2024 hours Zulu*


"Gently . . . gently . . . *gently, goddammit*!" Kaminski clung to a handy line with one hand, and waved the other, a gesticulating fist. The submarine swayed wildly for a moment in midair, after a sharp drop of about a meter. "What are you people trying to do, kill me? There are better ways of winning a promotion, you know!"

His was a precarious perch, but a necessary one. He was standing on top of the dead-black hull of one of the Mantas, a safety line clipped to his harness as the eight-meter craft was slowly lowered, wings folded up and over its back, toward the fog-shrouded, churning blackness of the Europan sea below.

A working party of five men were atop the Manta with him, armed with long, strong poles. Their job was to fend off the ice wall if they started to swing too close; it would be a damned crying shame if one of these subs had made the voyage all the way out from Earth, missed getting vaporized on the *Roosey*, survived repeated Chinese attacks, and then got dinged badly enough to be put out of commission because she swung a bit too hard into the ice.

They'd rigged an A-frame to lower the boat, a makeshift structure frozen into the ice much as they'd done to mount the International Cannon. They were using the expedition's one remaining tractor to do the lowering, slowly backing toward the A-frame and letting the sub, riding in a cradle of bucky-fiber lines, drop toward the boiling water.

"Sorry, Sergeant Major," Brighton called over the radio channel from the tractor. "Hit a patch of bleach and slid a bit, there."

"You have your anchor lines out?" These were lines running to stakes driven into the ice on either side of the tractor's path as a precaution. Marines walked along both sides of the path, unhooking lines as they grew taut and reattaching them further along. No wanted to see the sub drag the tractor over the side, especially since it would hit the sub on the way down.

"Try again . . . and slowly, damn it."

"Aye, aye, Sergeant Major. Hang on, here we go."

The sub's gentle descent began once again. Holding tight to the cable above his head, Kaminski leaned over and looked down at the water. Another ten meters to go, about. Easy . . .

The first sub was already in the water, wings opened full, moored to the E-DARES facility and with a gangplank rigged to an airlock in the stern-high vessel's hull. A few more meters and this one would be down, safe and sound, as well.

The sub started swinging again, stern pivoting toward the ice. "Wilkes! Vottori! Get those boathooks out there! Stop that swing . . . stop it!"

*This*, he thought, *would be the perfect time for the Charlies to come blazing up out of the badlands*. But they didn't, and the Manta continued its descent.

*Ten meters,* he told himself. *It's the same as 1.3 meters on Earth. If you fall, it won't mean a damned thing.*

Yeah. Not a thing except falling into water boiling and freezing at the same time.

Frank Kaminski had never cared for heights, and he'd never cared for deep, cold water. *What the hell am I doing here?*

It was a question with no satisfactory answer. He'd been a Marine for a lot of years now, and he'd been in some damned strange places—on Earth, on Mars, on the moon, and now on the alien ice of Europa. In fact, he was one of the handful of people who were members of the Three Planets' Club, a rather elitist organization consisting of men and women who'd walked on at least two worlds besides the Earth. In fact, he'd been wondering if he was going to get to organize a *Four* Planets' Club, once he got back to Earth.

He was no stranger to strangeness.

But the sight of that boiling, steaming water . . .

It was like an infinitely deep, churning pit, calling to him with a terrible, wrenching vertigo. It would be so easy to let go . . . to fall . . .

It was as though he could sense something, no—*some thing* . . . calling to him. Some thing filling him with a vast and swirling fear.

But that was impossible, right? There was the Singer, sure, but he couldn't hear the sound waves that thing was putting out. No, he was just letting the situation, the surroundings spook him. That was it.

"Ski!" Tom Pope grabbed him by the arm, tugging him back from the edge. "Ski! You okay?"

"Eh? Yeah. Yeah, I'm okay. Just a little dizzy, is all." He turned and saw the others watching him.

Shit. Ever since he'd passed out the other day, the men hadn't quite believed he'd recovered, as though they expected him to faint at any moment. Doc McCall had suggested that his unconscious spell had been induced by the EMP from the International Gun causing the old, experimental VR implants in his brain to vibrate a bit. Made sense.

But it didn't make him a freaking cripple, for Christ's sake.

"Well? What are you all staring at? Get back to work! Watch that wall, damn it . . . we're starting to swing! Brighton! Slower on the drop!"

"Aye, aye, Sergeant Major!"

They continued their slow descent into strangeness.


*C-3, E-DARES Facility*
*Ice Station Zebra, Europa*
*2310 hours Zulu*

"Enter."

Corporal Leckie entered the C-3. "Sir, may I have a word?"

"Center yourself on the hatch."

"Aye, aye, sir." Leckie entered and came to attention.

Jeff looked him up and down. He was wearing OD utilities, and seemed healthy enough. "What can I do for you, Lucky?"

"Sir, I've been hearing the scuttlebutt. I mean, about the sub raid. I want to volunteer to go along."

"How are you feeling, Lucky? How are the legs?"

"Absolutely four-oh, sir!"

"That's not what Doc McCall told me yesterday. He said you'd torn a ligament in your right leg, and you were going to be hobbling around for two weeks at least. He said you came *this* close to frostbite, and you were damned lucky not to lose any toes."

"I think the doc was exaggerating, sir. I'm fine. And I want to go on that op!"

"Well, I'll tell you, Lucky. There are fourteen other Marines on this station who aren't going. Six of them have already been through that door to volunteer or to gripe at me because I won't take them along. You're number seven. Lucky seven! Why should you be any different?"

"Sir . . . I am different. I really have to go along. Sir."

"Why?"

"Because . . . well . . . sir, I'm in love."

Jeff's eyebrows crept higher. "That seems to be one hell of a reason to volunteer for what some are calling a suicide mission. Would you care to explain yourself?"

"Major . . . I mean, well, it's like this. I just sort of got to know her, y'see? And she volunteered, and she's going on the mission. And I have to go along too. Sir."

"I see. You care to tell me who the lucky lady is?"

"Not if it's going to get her into trouble, sir."

"It's okay, Lucky. I'm not supposed to encourage, um, romantic entanglements within the unit, but I know how these things are. I'm sorry, though. We have the squad TO&Es and assignment lists worked out. I'm not going to change them to help your love life."

"But, begging the major's pardon—"

"Can it, Marine. Your girlfriend is a Marine and perfectly able to look out for herself. You, according to the company corpsman, can barely walk, despite that act you put on coming in here."

"It's not an act, sir. The leg's fine. I can walk fine."

"I'm glad to hear it. But the answer is still no."

"But—"

"No, Corporal. You're on the sick list until McCall takes you off. Of the two of you, I'd much rather have your girlfriend at my back in a firefight than you any day! She, at least, will be able to carry a wounded buddy out of the kill zone! Don't worry, though. There'll be plenty for you to do here while you're waiting for us to get back! Dismissed."

"But, sir, I—"

"Dismissed, Corporal!"

He snapped again to rigid attention. "Aye, aye, sir." He gave a crisp left-face and strode from the compartment.

After a moment, Jeff rose and walked to the door, quietly leaning out and looking down the passageway. Leckie was walking toward the mess hall, leaning heavily on a make-shift cane with each step. The scam artist must have left it in the passageway while he came in to make his pitch.

He was just about to duck back into C-3 when Sergeant Vincent Cukela rounded a corner at his back. "Oh, excuse me, Major. Can I see you for a moment?"

Jeff sighed, closed his eyes, and jerked his thumb at C-3. "Come in," he said. "But the answer is *no* . . ."

# TWENTY

*The Pit, E-DARES Facility*
*Ice Station Zebra, Europa*
*1312 hours Zulu*

The Mantas rested side by side, their tapering aft sections low in the black water, their noses pulled up onto thin ice and moored both to the E-DARES facility's hull and to rings mounted in the Pit's ice wall. Their wings had been unfolded and locked, and the black carbon-weave finish was already thickly encrusted with ice.

As the twenty-meter patch of open water was exposed to hard vacuum, it boiled, creating a tenuous and fast-changing local atmosphere of cold steam, the roiling cloud of fog that hung over the depths of the Pit. That steam condensed on any surface it touched and quickly plated out as ice. That could be a problem when the subs were launched, so electrical heating nets had already been draped across most of their exposed surfaces.

Jeff stood on the icy walkway at the bottom of the Pit, watching as the Marines filed out across the gangplanks and boarded the subs. They were having to pass through the Mantas' airlocks two at a time, and the process took a while.

But it was almost time.

Captain Melendez stood at his side, as always quiet, stolid, and competent. "Take care of the place while I'm gone, Paul."

"I still wish I was going with you, Major."

"Of course you do!" Jeff replied, putting as much sarcastic bite into the words as he could. "No one in his right mind would want to stay and try to hold this place with fourteen men! It'll be *much* safer where we're going. But someone's going to get the short end, and that someone is you!"

Paul chuckled. "Well, take care of yourself, sir. We'll have the lights on and the covers turned back when you return."

"Seriously, if you get into trouble, haul ass back to the E-DARES and hunker down. I don't think the Charlies will risk damaging the facility."

"Hell, it's not the Charlies I'm worried about, sir. It's all those scientists. They outnumber us now, you know!"

"Carry on, Number One."

"Aye, aye, sir." He touched his right glove to the corner of his helmet's visor. "Good trip."

Jeff returned the salute, turned away, and started down the gangplank, gripping the butt of the 580 slung over his back to keep it from slapping at his thigh as he walked. It was an unaccustomed presence, something he'd not felt for years. Marine Corps dogma held that every man was a rifleman, right down to the cooks and bakers, ground crews, personnel clerks, and fat-ass battalion commanders . . . but it had still been some time since he'd qualified with a laser rifle in field conditions.

Footing on the gangplank was treacherous with the ice buildup, made worse by the patches of fizzing, $H_2O_2$ slickness that kept appearing and disappearing like mirages. He kept a tight grip on the safety line all the way out. It was a tight squeeze through the narrow hatchway into the sub, especially with his bulky PLSS on his back.

The airlock was just barely large enough for one man. He stood inside the tiny compartment, red-lit by the warning light, listening as silence gave way to a thin, fast-swelling hiss of incoming air. The red light was replaced by green, and the inner hatch cracked open.

Inside, the compartment was dark except for the constellation of moving lights on the helmets of the Marines,
and the glow of HUDs and chin consoles stage-lighting
Marine faces behind their visors. Age-old naval custom
held that the senior officer was first onto a small boat, last
off, but this was one time, Jeff thought, when custom
should have given way to practicality. He had to literally
crawl—the compartment's overhead was to low for him to
walk upright in his suit, and a stoop was too clumsy—all
the way forward between two seated ranks of five men
each, men who were already so close that their knees were
practically touching in the passageway. Everyone except
the boat's SEAL pilot, by orders, was still suited up.

At the forward end of the Manta, there was a bit more
room. Machinist's Mate Chief Randolph Carver already had
his PLSS, helmet, and gloves off, and was seated in the
elevated pilot's chair, a bright red VR helmet masking his
features.

"It seems a long time since the Bahamas, doesn't it,
Carver?" he asked.

"Yessir, it sure does."

"I'm sorry your first test flight of a Manta under Europan
conditions has to be under combat conditions as well."

"Well, I guess water is water, sir, and water is the
SEAL's friend. We'll be just fine."

"Hoo-yah," the other SEAL said, a quiet SEAL battlecry.
Quartermaster First Class Mike Hastings was squeezed into
a jump seat to Carver's left and behind him. Two SEALs
were aboard each Manta on this op. The idea was to provide a backup in case anything happened to one. Everyone
aboard was expected to fight at the other end, and having
two men qualified to pilot the Manta gave a little extra
measure of security, a better chance that they would make
it back home.

"What's the matter, Hastings?" Jeff said, grinning. "Getting tired of being cooped up with so many jarheads?"

"Jarheads are okay, sir," Hastings replied. "They're not
*SEALs*, but they're okay."

"Hey, don't you worry, Hasty," BJ Campanelli, who was sitting next to him, said. She slapped his thigh with the back of her glove. "We've had a vote and decided to make you guys honorary Marines!"

"God help me!" Hastings's expression, stage-lit inside his helmet, made Jeff laugh.

"Okay, people!" he called. "Listen up. Amberly!" Sergeant Roger Amberly, a quiet, good-looking kid from Kansas with two husbands waiting for him back home. Steady, dependable, and a good hand with a Wyvern.

"Yo!"

"Campanelli." Big, blond, bold, and a bit of an attitude. A damned good Marine.

"Hot and tight."

"Cartwright." Was she the one Leckie was hot for? It couldn't be BJ.

"Here."

"Carver."

"Go."

"Garcia." The man's record mentioned he'd been arrested for activity in a pro-Aztlan march in San Diego, a long-time advocate of an independent Hispanic homeland carved out of the American Southwest. He was a tough guy with a bad attitude, but an outstanding Marine.

*"Aquí!"*

"Hastings."

"Hoo-yah!"

"Kaminski."

"Ooh-rah!" A Marine battlecry challenging the SEAL's hoo-yah. He saw Kaminski grin at the SEAL and wink.

"Lang." Maybe she was Leckie's love interest, a good-looking black girl from Virginia. She was married, though, with both a husband and a wife at home. Not that *that* meant anything, necessarily.

"Nodell." Big, rugged, and a hard drinker, in and out of trouble, but deadly with a SLAW, a 580, or his hands. Three times divorced, a Marine lifer.

"Yeah."

"O'Day." A quiet, red-haired corporal and a member of Humanity First, though he never voiced any political opinions that Jeff knew of.

"Yo."

"Peterson." A straight-laced black kid from Ohio. Seemed determined to prove himself, no matter what. Another Wyvern ace.

"Present."

"Wojak." One of the company clowns, but a good man.

"Right here."

"And . . . Doctor Ishiwara."

"*Hai*! Yes."

As he called off each name, a status light winked green on the list scrolling down the side of his HUD. Chesty, still resident in his PAD as well as in the E-DARES computer system, was interrogating each suit as he called off the name, and reporting back that the suit systems were powered up, intact, and go.

Twelve men and women, plus the two SEALs up front and the lone civilian passenger. Fourteen Marines—if you counted the two SEALs, and their experience and training was worth their mass in antimatter. Twelve more on Manta Two, under the command of Lieutenant Biehl. Twenty-seven men and women to challenge the Europan Ocean, followed by the main Chinese base on this world.

The longest and slimmest possible of long, slim shots.

"Cold Zebra, this is Icebreaker One," he said over the Company frequency. "We are loaded, hot, and tight. Ready to proceed."

"Icebreaker One, Cold Zebra. Icebreaker Two reports ready to swim."

"Very well. Single up on all moorings. Stand by for release."

"Roger that, One. Singling up on all moorings."

Ashore, working parties of Marines would be releasing the webwork of cables securing the two research subs to the ice and taking in the electric blankets, though he couldn't see them. The Manta had only the two tiny windows forward, plus a dorsal navigation dome amidships still covered over by a protective shell. The only one with a view out was Carver, using the HUD optic feed on his VR helmet.

"Icebreaker, Zebra. Lines singled up. Ready for release."

Jeff looked at Carver. "You ready?"

"Engines green. Intakes green. All green. Let's get it on."

"Zebra, One. We're go here."

"Hang on, then, Icebreaker. All boats away!"

"Very well, Zebra. Let 'er slide!"

He felt a gentle lurch, and the soft, grinding slide as the sub slid backward into the water, pushed by a team of Marines linked together by safety lines in case the surface ice broke. The slide picked up speed, and Jeff heard the loud cracking and popping of ice giving way outside the hull.

Then there was a single shock, a roll to port, and the gentle, rocking sway of a small boat on a heavy swell. Ice continued to crack and snap as the hull flexed slightly, breaking the half-melted icy coating that had embraced the craft.

Jeff almost immediately felt an unpleasant tug at his stomach as seasickness took hold. It was worse, he thought, with an empty stomach. All he could do was hang on and hope he didn't disgrace himself with a fouled helmet.

The Manta was heavier than water, though, and was settling fast, stern first. Carver tapped some icons on his touch console, and was rewarded by the throaty, rising hum of the sub's engines. "Zebra, Icebreaker One," he said. "I have power. Engines at 20 percent. I have helm and maneuvering. Ice is coming off the wings. Cast off the safety."

A single safety line, the end run through an eye on Manta One's nose and back to the shore to double it up, had remained in place during the launch. Mantas didn't rely on ballast tanks, but literally flew through the water like an aircraft through air. If the engines hadn't started, the boat would have sunk, and only that doubled-up line through the nose eye would have saved them from a very *long* fall into the abyss.

With the engines whining smoothly, though, the shore party released one end of the safety line and dragged it rapidly through the eye and back to shore. "Icebreaker One, you are clear to navigate."

"Roger that, Zebra. Going down. See you in a couple of days!"

Jeff felt the deck tilt sharply to port as the Manta turned away from the dock. The rolling subsided too, a clear indication that they were now beneath the surface. He wished he could see what Carver was seeing on his VR input; it might alleviate the dank and claustrophobic closeness of the compartment a bit.

Reaching up, he broke his helmet seal, then pulled the heavy half-sphere off his head. He stowed it with his M-580 on a bulkhead rack, and unsnapped his gloves as well.

"Okay, people," he said. "You can unseal. But stay in your suits, and no unnecessary moving around." Carver was going to have enough on his hands flying this thing through the murky waters beneath the ice without having his Marine passengers constantly changing his center of mass. "There's space for your helmets and gloves beneath your seats," he continued, "and racks behind you for your weapons. Move two at a time, and watch out for that overhead. It's a killer."

Carefully, he lay down on his stomach on the starboard forward couch, pulling himself along with the handholds to either side until his face was a few centimeters from the viewing port, a tricky maneuver given the ungainly reach of the PLSS perched mass-high on his back and shoulders.

Outside, the water was a deep and murky blue-green, with pale green light still filtering down from above. Powerful searchlights mounted on the upswept stabilizer tips of the Manta's wings illuminated a swirling blizzard of particles trapped in the brilliant white beams. At the moment, pools of light were sweeping across the gray, white, and black surface—all smooth planes and crisp angles, but lightly covered with uneven patches of fuzzy brown growth.

He felt someone sliding into the port-side couch, bulky

in his space suit. Shigeru pressed his face close to the viewport, his face illuminated by the bright, white reflections from outside. "I had to see," he said. "You have no idea how I've wanted to see these things with my own eyes, instead of through the optics of teleoperated probes!"

"Is that Europan life, then?" Jeff asked. Some of the brown stuff looked a lot like moss, with long filaments waving in the current created by hot, upwelling water.

"We think so."

"You think so? Don't you know? Haven't you gathered specimens?"

"Oh, certainly. And we've given it the provisional genus name of *Muscomimus*, the 'moss-mimic.' But Dr. Redmondson, our chief of exobiology, is not yet convinced that it is a true life form. It may simply be an unusual accretion of sulfur and carbon compounds in long-chain molecules, a purely nonorganic process."

"It looks like it's growing . . . and reproducing. All over the E-DARES' hull."

"We've seen whole forests of the stuff growing on the *bottom* of the ice. And it is gathering raw materials, food, if you will, from the water, and it seems to carry on this process by drawing energy—in this case, thermal energy from the hot water coming up from the E-DARES' anti-icers—from its surroundings. But, well, we're still working on finding a good definition for the word *life*."

Jeff chuckled. "That's a hell of a note."

"What?"

"That the more we learn, the more we find out about the universe around us, the harder it is to answer the simple questions, like 'what is life?' "

"*Basic* questions, Major. Not simple. In fact, that one may be one of the most complex questions there is."

"Yeah?"

"Yes. Just ask any AI."

The Manta continued its slow turn, and the E-DARES hull slid out of view off to the right. Tiny motes danced in the sub's searchlight beams, a snowstorm of particles.

"*Europamegabacter sulfurphilos*," Shigeru said. "That is alive."

"It looks like dirt," Jeff said. "Or snow."

"It appears to be a close analogue of a life form known on Earth. Not related, of course, but an example of convergent evolution."

"Yes?"

"A bacteria discovered off the coast of Angola seventy years ago. A single cell, yet it's large enough to be seen by the naked eye—about the size of a period in a sentence, in fact, thousands of times larger than an ordinary bacterium. Most of that size is taken up by a huge vacuole, in which it stores nitrates to help in the metabolism of sulfur."

"That stuff looks a lot bigger."

"It is. Some specimens reach ten to fifteen millimeters in diameter. But they are single-cell organisms, nonetheless.

"So far, all of the life we've discovered on Europa is carbon based, like ours, but dependent on sulfur for metabolic processes. Just like the giant bacteria on Earth, or the sulfur-loving life discovered at the openings of volcanic vents in Earth's oceans, at the intersection of seismic plates. You see, it doesn't need light, as photosynthetic life does."

Jeff could only shake his head. Here, things that looked like they were alive and growing might well not be alive at all, at least in the conventional sense, while stuff that looked like dirty snow caught in the Manta's lights was following the same patterns of life laid down by organisms on Earth.

"Whoa," Carver said suddenly. "Hey, Major. You hear that?"

"Hear what?"

"Listen."

Yes . . . he did hear something. It was so faint at first he'd not been able to hear over the background conversation, the hum of the air ventilation system, the hollow rush of water across the vessel's hull. Slowly, though, it grew louder, swelling to a low, eerie ululation, mingled with rattling clicks and keening, high-pitched shrieks, but still so distant you had to strain to make it out.

"The Singer, Chief Carver," Jeff said.

"Affirmative, sir. I was picking up some as soon as we hit the water, but it didn't really become audible until we got down beneath the ice. It's muffled quite a bit by the hull. Must be pretty loud outside, for us to hear it this clearly."

"Yes," Shigeru said. "We didn't hear it until we lowered hydrophones well beneath the icecap and into the ocean proper. But the sound, especially the lower registers, travels quite well for astonishing distances. The sound waves reflect between the ice and the bottom, you know, and can travel all the way around the moon."

Jeff had heard recordings, of course, but something about the real sound set the hair on the back of his neck aprickle. It was hard not to hear patterns in those mournful cries—and intelligence, a meaning of some sort just beyond the grasp of human understanding.

"Not exactly Top Forty pop, is it?" Wojak observed.

The subs veered toward the southwest and accelerated, Manta One moving well out into the lead to avoid having both boats lost by the same accident. For a time, the ice ceiling gliding past overhead remained visible, a slowly receding jaggedness fading into water thick with drifting particles, like fog. Shigeru was right; much of that ceiling was coated with vast patches of brown, mossy tendrils, a weird, upside-down forest in the night.

Then ice and forest were lost in darkness, with black night above and black below, and only the lonesome gleam of the Manta's lights to mark out a small, fuzzy domain of warmth and illumination. After an hour, Icebreaker Two, Carver reported, was about three kilometers astern, its lights lost in the gloom.

It made the loneliness, the isolation more intense, somehow, with the Manta a tiny bubble of heat and mind adrift in stark isolation alone in the abyssal black.

Another hour passed. A third. The men and women

talked quietly among themselves, or lost themselves in PAD novels or spoke quietly into their PAD pickups as they assembled e-mails for the next scheduled uplink. Jeff had already told them that if they had any mail home they wanted to finish up, to do it on the trip and store it in the Manta's computer.

That way, so long as the Manta made it back at all, the mail would be delivered, no matter what.

Everyone knew what *that* meant.

He spent some time studying the men and women in the aft compartment, trying to peer inside their minds, to see, to feel how they were reacting to . . . everything, from being marooned on an alien world, to the isolation of the tiny CWS base, to suffering a heart-numbing 47 percent casualties on this campaign so far, to being sealed inside this carbon-boron-bucky-fiber can and dropped into an ink-black ocean eighty kilometers deep, a blackness alive with the eerie cries of an alien voice.

Hell, they'd been through enough already to break damned near anyone, and they kept on going. Wojak, Garcia, and Nodell all looked nervous but were working their PADs; Nodell couldn't seem to get his to work and was muttering a long, steady stream of obscenities to no one in particular. Peterson looked calm and was quietly reading a novel on his. Amberly was asleep. Campanelli and Cartwright were talking to each other. Kaminski worked his PAD. Hastings stared at nothing, his blue eyes very cold.

Or perhaps he was staring at the Singer in his mind's eye.

The sounds grew louder, slowly, as the kilometers rolled away in the Manta's wake. It seemed to Jeff they were steadily becoming more complex as well, as new over- and undertones, harmonies, and blended sounds trilled and chirped and groaned in the deep distance. It sounded, he thought, like a chorus of some vast, majestic sea beast—like the extinct great whales were supposed to have been. Could there be whales on Europa?

Unlikely. According to Shigeru, Europan marine life was

primitive, most of it unicellular, though larger, more organized forms existed in the great deep. Throughout the vast, foggy emptiness between ice ceiling and mud bottom, however, there was nothing like a fish, or a whale. Nothing but detritus adrift on the icy currents, and the ongoing, haunting song of the Singer.

Four hours into the voyage, and Carver and Hastings exchanged places. Now Carver sat on the jump seat, absorbed by something in his PAD, while Hastings, face and voice muffled by the VR helmet, guided the Manta through the black depths.

Five hours. Jeff and Shigeru crawled onto the viewing couches again when Hastings warned of interesting terrain ahead. Their depth was fifty-one kilometers; the pressure on the outer hull was 663 atmospheres—9,746 psi by the old way of measuring such impossible-to-comprehend physics, or just over 692 kilograms per square centimeter.

The Manta, still descending on a long, shallow glide, was approaching a mountain ridge upthrust from the Europan ocean's abyssal depths. As he watched, shadowy forms moved into the glare of the sub's wingtip lights—a wall of rock, and a forest of gently waving fronds.

"Well, Dr. Ishiwara?" he asked as the scientist settled in next to him again. "What's the verdict? Life or not life?"

"I wish I could say," Shigeru replied. He had to raise his voice a bit to be heard above the Singer's moans and trilling wails. "I've never seen these species before. My guess is that they're alive. They look a bit like sea fans on Earth, or some kinds of seaweed. But they also look a lot like very large clumps of *Muscomimus*. I don't know."

The sub skimmed the mountain ridge. As rock and the waving sea grasses dropped away astern, Jeff was struck by an uneasy thought. The average depth of the seabed here was eighty kilometers; that suggested that the mountain range they'd just crossed thrust some twenty-nine kilometers into Europa's sky, if you thought of the moon's ocean as its atmosphere. Twenty-nine thousand meters—three and a third times the height of Mount Everest in the Himalayas.

Two point eight times taller than Mauna Kea, as measured from *that* mountain's base at the bottom of the Pacific.

It seemed strange to think of tiny Europa, a world only a quarter of Earth's diameter, with mountains three times higher.

"Those mountains," Shigeru said, as though reading Jeff's thoughts. "So high, compared to Earth's. Proof of the violence of this tiny world."

"How so?"

"Europa is next out from Io, with an orbit only half again larger. The tidal strains on Europa are nearly as great as those that tear at Io—and Io, as they say, is a moon in the process of turning itself inside out. Huge lakes of molten sulfur, volcanoes spewing sulfur hundreds of kilometers into space.

"Europa is not that extreme, but the tidal action is what keeps this ocean liquid. There are volcanoes here, you know, in the depths, and the equivalent of Earth's "black smokers" as well, spewing sulfur and nitrates and various minerals and compounds into the ocean. There must have been considerable tectonic activity and mountain building."

"Maybe the lower gravity makes for higher mountains," Jeff suggested.

"That's certainly part of it. But the forces within this world's crust—they make Earth seem tame by comparison."

Six hours. The song was louder, sharper, more insistent.

Kaminski was looking . . . not worried, exactly. It was hard to imagine the Sergeant Major being worried by anything. But he was looking uncharacteristically tired and drawn out, his eyes dark hollows, and he was staring at the overhead as though the Singer's song was wearing at him.

"Ski?" When Kaminski didn't respond right away, Jeff called louder. "Sergeant Major!"

"Sir!"

"A word with you, please."

Kaminski rose from his seat and made his way forward, stooping to avoid hitting the overhead. "Yes, sir?"

"You doing okay, Ski? You're looking a bit ragged."

"I'm okay, sir. I'm just tired, is all. Have a bit of a headache."

"You take something?"

"Yes, sir."

"Okay. Hang in there. I need everyone alert and gung-ho—*especially* my senior NCOs."

"Yes, sir. There's no problem, Major."

"Glad to hear it. I want to go over the specs on those jury-rigged torpedoes, if we could."

They were soon immersed in a technical discussion. Kaminski seemed alert enough, but Jeff couldn't shake the feeling that he was in fact not entirely there, that he was pausing from time to time to listen to something else, something calling from far away.

The whalesong of the Singer made him think of the Greek myth of the sirens, temptresses who bewitched sailors with their songs, drawing them to their deaths upon the rocks. Kaminski was normally stolid to the point of imperturbability. What siren's song had ensnared him?

Eight hours. The Marines were beginning to cramp and grumble over their long, enforced imprisonment. Jeff and Kaminski had them, two at a time, stand, press their hands against the overhead, and stretch, working out the kinks. He then had them eat. They were still on short rations—two meals in twenty-four hours instead of three—but there was more food to go around than had been planned for originally. The unit's high casualty rate could be blamed for that.

Nine hours, and the Singer's lament was loud enough to ring from the bulkheads. Most of the Marines had replaced their helmets to muffle the sound. Jeff left his off so he could listen. There was something . . . something tantalizing, just beyond his grasp . . .

Their depth was seventy-eight kilometers, with an outside pressure of over one thousand atmospheres—1,058.5 kilograms pressing down on every square centimeter of hull. The bottom was coming up to meet them, a shadowy roughness just visible through the black-blue haze beneath them.

"Major?" Carver was back at the helm. "I think you should take a look up ahead. Tell me if I'm imagining things."

Carver's VR feed was a lot more sensitive—and to a far larger stretch of the EM spectrum—than Jeff's eyes, but he crawled onto one of the viewing couches and wiggled forward. At first, he saw nothing but the Manta's lights illuminating the omnipresent swirling clouds of dancing white motes.

Then, gradually, he was aware of something else—a glow behind the lights.

"Can you turn off the wing lights a sec?" he asked.

"Right."

The outside lights died, and for a moment, Jeff saw only a Stygian blackness as deep and as opaque as any at the bottom of a deep-buried cavern.

Then, gradually, as his eyes became accustomed to the darkness again, he thought he could make out a faint, background glow. It was hard to see, and it vanished completely when he tried looking straight at it. But with averted vision, he became increasingly aware of a pale, blue-green glow in the deep distance.

"Water temperature's up," Carver said. "Five point eight Celsius, and rising. My God. Look at that!"

It looked like a wall, a billowing, fuming wall of black ash rising slowly, blurred by distance. Jeff thought of pictures he'd seen of sandstorms in the Sahara or on Mars, or of a forest fire spewing black smoke into the sky.

"What is it?"

"Black smokers," Shigeru said, his voice softened by awe. "*Big* black smokers. Ah, I don't think we want to get too close."

"Damned straight we don't," Carver said. "Outside temperature now eleven point one, and climbing. I didn't know it *got* this hot on Europa!"

"It is possible that the water temperature will get considerably hotter," Shigeru said. "At this pressure, the water *can't* boil. That glow suggests the water being expelled into the ocean is extremely hot."

"As in molten lava hot," Carver said. "I'm giving that area a wide berth."

The Manta banked gently to port, toward the south. The smokers appeared to be strung out in a chain, running roughly northeast to southwest. The Manta swung left to run parallel to them, looking for a way around. Carver switched the outside lights back on.

"Life," Shigeru said, pointing. "*Undeniably* life."

The bottom was alive. Where it had been completely barren before, the bottom was smothered now in waving, shifting forests of fronds, some ten meters long. Something like a vast, diaphanous bell pulsed and wiggled in the glare of the Manta's lights.

"What is that?" Jeff asked. "A jellyfish?"

"I have no idea," Shigeru replied. "If it is, it's a dozen meters across—longer than this submarine. Fantastic!"

"Major?" Carver said. The light ahead was stronger now, an odd, intense blue.

"Yes, Chief?"

"I still can't find a way through those smokers, and we've got a problem."

"What is it?"

"This new heading, sir. It's taking us straight to the Singer."

Damn. He'd wanted to avoid the alien construct.

"I think," Carver said slowly, "I think that might be it up ahead."

Jeff peered through the port at the black towers silhouetted against that impossible blue light, and knew that the SEAL was correct.

# TWENTY-ONE

*Manta One*
*Between the Cadmus and Asterias*
   *Linea, Europa*
*2245 hours Zulu*

The city illuminated the night, holding it at bay with a pale, wavering blue-green luminescence that back-lit soaring towers, the sweep and curve of arches, the rugged thrust of slab-sided buildings the size of mountains, the prickle of antennae all but lost among vaster structures of incomprehensible purpose.

"I'd . . . uh . . . better take us up," Carver said.

"I think you'd better," Jeff replied, his mouth dry. It was impossible to judge scale in this alien setting. What he was looking at could have been a large and complex spacecraft seen from meters away, or a city the size of Greater New York, seen from an altitude of kilometers. Much of it appeared to be submerged in the seabed.

"Is that . . . is that . . . it?" Jeff asked, awed.

"The Singer?" Shigeru nodded. "The sonographs we've taken don't do it justice."

"Is it a ship? Or a city?"

"Maybe both. Or neither. How can we know?"

"Okay." Jeff said. He managed a weak grin. "Is it alive?"

Shigeru looked at him, startled. "That, Major, remains to be seen."

"Even on VR, I don't think I'm seeing the entire thing," Carver said. "It measures at least twelve kilometers across. Can't get decent infrared. The water absorbs those wavelengths. Sonar, though, seems to indicate an even bigger structure—but it's soft, almost mushy."

"Soft? What do you mean?"

"I think what he is seeing," Shigeru said, peering out the porthole again, "is that most of it is covered with moss."

It was true. In the uncertain lighting, in the drifting haze of particles above the ocean floor, it was hard to see, but as the tiny submersible hummed past one of those upthrusting towers, Jeff could see that its outline was blurred. Like some ancient, sunken wreck at the bottom of an Earthly ocean, the Singer was coated by *Muscomimus* and by other growths, things like seaweed that writhed and twisted with a life of their own, things like sea fans and bumpier, rougher things like coral growths. And, at closer hand, it was clear that the underlying structure was pitted and gouged and cratered in places, as though it had been subjected to eons of steady, gradual erosion and decay. Here, a needle-sharp spire had crumpled and fallen, dragging with it a lacy network of filaments now tufted with mosslike accretions. There, a low, flat arch, like a bridge a hundred meters across, had snapped in the middle, the span fallen through a delicate tracery of interlocking tubes far below.

The Singer's song surrounded them . . . embraced them . . .

The Manta continued its climb. As Jeff watched that enigmatic city drop away into a glowing, blue-hued mist, he kept expecting . . . *something*. A tractor beam out of a science-fiction vid . . . a sudden bolt of searing energy . . . a giant hand . . . anything to indicate that the minute craft passing above this eldritch vista had been seen, had been noticed, by the godlike powers that must dwell within.

Kaminski screamed.

*Kaminski*

*Falling . . . falling . . . falling down the endless, empty light-years . . .*

*Alone . . . so alone . . . so empty . . .*

*But there were voices within the empty loneliness . . . voices . . . shouts . . . hollow-ringing echoes . . . a cacophony . . . voices . . . unintelligible . . . words unknown, alien and harsh . . . yet each separate, exquisitely painful and throbbing syllable called forth . . . an image . . .*

He understood so very little of what he saw, though he clutched at each image, each scene, each thought, a drowning man grasping at flotsam.

*Stars . . . a vast and empty sea of blackness, strewn with stars and the wisp-fog veil of twisted nebulae.*

*His father . . . vast and terrifying in a drunken rage. "C'mere, you little snot, and get what you deserve!"*

*A . . . city? Was it a city . . . stone pyramids the size of mountains . . . no, carved from mountains, whole mountains shaped and reworked according to some colossal engineering scheme undreamed of by man . . . A pink ocean gently lapping the shoreline beneath a reddish sky . . . and . . . and men in this alien place . . . men and women in strange clothing with strangely angled faces, mingling with silently drifting, upright forms, all organic curves and undulations cast in shapes of crystal and plastic . . . but the red sky is filled with flame and bursting light . . . and the strange people are screaming and falling in the city streets . . .*

*And in the sky, the Ship blotted out the sun. Explosions . . . savage detonations shaking the mountains . . . People shrieking as the atmosphere field failed and the air exploded into near-vacuum.*

*His mother, eyes blackened, nose bloodied, sobbing hysterically on the sofa.*

*His first day of boot camp. Standing rigidly in formation. "You . . . miserable . . . worms have the unprintable expurgated gall to think you can be Marines . . ."*

*Major Garroway seated at the desk at Candor Chasma, on Mars, hard eyes pinning the three Marines to the spot where they stood at attention. "Very well. Corporal Slidell, Lance Corporal Fulbert, Lance Corporal Kaminski. You three have a choice . . ."*

*A tattered, faded American flag hung from a five-meter metal pole above the Cydonian encampment on Mars. Someone had used a thin strip of wire to stretch the fly out from the hoist in the near-vacuum of the Martian atmosphere. Still, there was wind enough to ripple the cloth a bit. The fighting with the UN forces was almost over.*

*Voices . . . myriad voices . . . gibbering in the darkness.*

*Manta One*
*Between the Cadmus and*
  *Asterias Linea*
*Europan Ocean*
*2250 hours Zulu*

Kaminski's shriek brought Jeff up out of the couch so quickly he painfully slammed his head into a section of conduit tubing in the overhead. Kaminski had slumped in his seat, eyes staring, a trickle of blood flowing steadily from his left nostril and smearing on his chin. Cartwright, Hastings, and Wojak had all gathered around him, holding his head, calling to him. Kaminski's eyes, wide and staring, seemed to focus on something far beyond the barren confines of the Manta's aft compartment.

There was no corpsman along. Jeff had ordered McCall to stay at the E-DARES and take care of the wounded there. There didn't seem to be anything to do except pull his PAD from its thigh holster, open it, and call up Chesty with a touch. "Medical emergency, Chesty," he said. "Give us a hand here."

"Bringing medical protocols on line," Chesty said. "I have his med readouts."

The med layout appeared on the PAD screen, waveforms

tracing out the pulse and quiver of heartbeat, respiration, metabolic function, neurological and brainwave function, pain levels, and other readings Jeff only hazily understood.

"Sergeant Major Kaminski is unconscious," Chesty said. "Except for minor nasal and upper pharyngeal bleeding, I detect no gross trauma. Brainwaves indicate a mild alpha state, but probably no loss of mental function. No ischemia, no cerebrovascular trauma, no internal hemorrhage." There was a brief pause. "Please hold the PAD sensory pickup close to his head."

Jeff did as he was told, holding out the PAD just above Kaminski's head, pointing the optic and audio pickups at his bleeding face.

"I have detected an anomaly," Chesty said. "Sergeant Major Kaminski's skull appears to be the source of low-grade infrasonics, at approximately ten to fifteen Hertz. I cannot account for this."

"What's that?" Nodell asked. "What's that mean?"

"Infrasound," Jeff replied. "Sound waves at frequencies too low for humans to hear."

"We can sense 'em, though," BJ put in. "They can make us feel uneasy, even induce panic attacks."

"Look," Wojak said. He jabbed a thumb toward the overhead, and the eerie wail of the Singer. "I don't need infrasound to feel creepy with *that* goin' on!"

Kaminski's eyes were closed now, but Jeff could see the eyeballs shifting and moving beneath the lids. REM— Rapid Eye Movements. Frank was dreaming.

Of what?

"I have a possible correlation with Sergeant Major Kaminski's medical history," Chesty reported.

"What is it?'

"In 2053, then–Gunnery Sergeant Kaminski received three intracranial implants, one occipital, two temporal. These were intended to facilitate virtual reality downloads with IBM-K20 interface equipment. He was taking part in an experiment at the time, with the goal of developing new training techniques through direct man-machine interface."

"Jesus," Wojak said. "Ski was a *jackhead?*"

"The external sockets were surgically removed in 2061 after noninvasive, more technologically advanced VR feeds came on-line. The implants, however, were simply disconnected and left in place.

"The implant remaining over the right temporal area of his brain appears to be vibrating in response to those low-frequency radio waves. The vibrations are generating sound waves in the ten to fifteen Hertz range."

"Damn!" Jeff said. "Should have remembered! Doc McCall told me about that the other day, when that EMP knocked him out! Is there anything we can do?"

"Maybe wrap his head in something," Amberly suggested.

"The ELF radio waves penetrate the Europan ocean easily, and even leak through the ice where it is thin. We have no materials available on board this craft that would provide adequate insulation. The effect should lessen, however, as we move away from the Singer artifact."

"Which I intend to do as quickly as possible," Jeff said. "Chief Carver! Can you get any more speed out of this thing?"

"Got her full throttle, Major. We're getting the hell out of Dodge!"

"Chesty, I want a list of everyone in this command, including the scientists, who might have cranial implants like that."

"A complete search must wait until this part of me is again in communication with the main system at Cadmus. The only medical records I have access to here are those of the personnel embarked aboard Manta One. Of those personnel, only Sergeant Major Kaminski possessed such implants."

"Oh, yeah. Right." it was hard to remember Chesty's limitations sometimes. Because he was dependent on the hardware he was running on, he had access to much larger files, much more information, when he was resident within a large, fast, powerful machine like the E-DARES's IBM

IC-5000. Since they were currently out of radio or laser contact with Cadmus, the Chesty on Jeff's PAD and within the Manta's computer system was considerably slower in terms of operations per second, and much more restricted in the data available to it.

How must it feel, Jeff wondered, to break off a part of yourself, to live in isolation from the "real" you in a much more cramped and tiny space?

*The Life Seeker*
*Time unknown*

2703: >> . . . wanting . . . <<
1201: >> . . . needing others . . . needing . . . want/must-
  have/mustmustmust<<
937: >> . . . but others . . . wrong/bad/tainted/
  evil . . . <<
1391: >> . . . communication . . . sense . . . touch . . .
  talk . . . know . . . <<
2703: >> . . . alone . . . so alone . . . <<
Chorus: >>Nonono WE are here! . . . <<
0001: >>Reintegrate! We must reintegrate!<<
Chorus: >>Nonononono . . . <<
1391: >> . . . need to know . . . to feel . . . <<
1450: >> . . . reaching out . . . <<
538: >>Reintegration incomplete . . . failure . . .
  failure . . . <<

*Manta One*
*Between the Cadmus and*
  *Asterias Linea*
*Europan Ocean*
*2330 hours Zulu*

With her MHD drive humming at full throttle, the Manta climbed steadily clear of the alien sprawl of the structure lying on the Europan seabed. With the possible and apparently accidental exception of Kaminski's collapse, it had not seemed to notice the flyspeck submarine at all.

Another hour passed, surrounded still by the eerie wailing of the Singer. The Marines in Manta One were quiet now, lost in their own thoughts or trying, somehow, to get some sleep. Kaminski, at least, seemed to be getting better. The REM beneath his eyelids had ceased, and he was breathing more easily.

There was one piece of good news in the gloom. Manta Two made herself known with a single, low-powered sonar chirp. Manta One responded, careful to keep the pulse wattage low enough that it wouldn't be detectable by listening hydrophones at the Chinese base, and the two moved onto converging courses. Within another hour, they were close enough to acquire one another's navigation lights, and fifteen minutes later, a direct ship-to-ship laser communications channel had been opened.

Jeff exchanged quick briefings with Lieutenant Biehl. Like Manta One, Manta Two had turned south to avoid the line of black smokers; she, too, had encountered the alien construct on the ocean floor. No one aboard had been affected by the ELF waves, however—thank God.

The plan had been for the two submersibles to stay widely separated. After the encounter with the Singer, however, they made a tacit agreement to stay together. The Europan Ocean seemed far vaster, and far stranger than it had twelve hours earlier, when they'd first slipped beneath its black surface.

Another three hours passed. Jeff tried to catch some sleep, stretched out on the viewing couch, but sleep eluded him. His suit was growing wearily uncomfortable, with intolerable itches he couldn't scratch, and raw patches spreading at every pressure point: shoulders, wrists, waist, groin, knees, ankles. Worst of all, he was aware of the growing stink within the closely enclosed Manta, mingled smells of fear and sweat.

His own fear centered on the unit. After what they'd seen

back there, after Kaminski's scream and collapse, would they still be able to fight? Peterson had put it best earlier, in an overheard conversation with Nodell and Wojak. "You know, I get the feeling that we're like soldier ants fighting over a piece of the backyard, and we just now got our first glimpse of a human, the guy who *really* owns the place."

"So?" Nodell had said. "He ain't said nothing. As long as he leaves us alone—"

"As long as he doesn't reach for the bug spray," Wojak said.

Morale was definitely shaken. The long silences said as much—even the lack of grumbling as suits grew uncomfortable, muscles grew stiff, and stomachs grew empty. The danger was that one final straw would bring the whole morale structure of the unit crashing down.

And the terrifying, even humiliating encounter with the alien artifact was more Sequoia than straw.

Kaminski woke up with a start around 0300 hours. "Jesus! Where . . ." he looked around the compartment, eyes staring. "God . . . what a dream."

"Hey, Frank," Jeff said, kneeling next to his seat. "How you feeling, Marine?"

"Like elephants have been stampeding in my head."

"Elephants are extinct, man," Wojak said.

"Not in my skull, they aren't. Not yet, anyway." He looked at the glowing numeral on the back of his hand. "What time . . . *Je*-sus! What the hell happened?"

"As near as we can tell," Jeff told him, "The Singer has been putting out extremely long radio waves that are interacting somehow with the computer implants in your brain, making them vibrate at a low frequency, too low to be heard by the human ear. Infrasonics. Probably had you feeling pretty jumpy."

"Like itching powder on the brain. Well . . . it's nice to know there's an explanation for stark, unremitting terror coming out of nowhere," he said. "I thought I was having panic attacks, and couldn't figure out why. What was it? A weapon?"

"Don't know yet. I don't think so, though. That . . . that *thing* down there was big enough to swat us like a fly. You were the only one affected. I think it was accidental." Jeff was worried by the hollow look in Kaminski's eyes. "What is it? You still hurting?"

"My head hurts, yeah," Kaminski said, "but . . . it's the memories . . ."

"What memories?"

Kaminski shook his head. "I'm . . . not sure, sir. It's like jumbled dreams, and you can only remember a few of 'em, you know? And what you remember don't make sense."

"Well, with those damned implants vibrating against your brain . . . maybe they were generating those dreams somehow." Jeff had read somewhere that surgeons had first begun unlocking the brain's secrets when they found that touching or stimulating specific points on the surface of the cerebellum would spontaneously evoke memories or sensations, as though the human brain were literally a recorder that could play back what it had stored.

At 0420 hours, they approached the patch of ice where the International Gun's shell had fallen just five days before. As Jeff had predicted, the open water had frozen over since then, but the new ice was thin enough yet that he could actually see a faint, blue-white glow outside, the light from the sun shining down almost directly into the hole.

The problem now was how to know when the Chinese reinforcements were arriving. For Jeff's plan to have the maximum effect, the two subs would have to surface just when the landers were making their approach to the Chinese LZ. Break through too early, and the newcomers would be warned off. Break through too late, and they would emerge on the upper surface of Europa to find the enemy already landed, deployed, and waiting for them. Twenty-two Marines and one scientist would not be able to take on several hundred well-prepared PRC soldiers, robot tanks, and whatever else they would have waiting for them up there.

Since the exact arrival time of the enemy ship was known only approximately, and since it might well make several orbits before deploying its landers, they'd needed to find a way to know exactly when the landers were touching down.

He'd discussed a number of ideas with his staff back at Cadmus. Deploying a lobber with an OP team back to within sight of the Chinese LZ to warn of the ships' approach. Signaling from Cadmus by detonating a fair-sized jolt of antimatter deep in the ocean . . .

And what, Jeff wondered wryly, would the Singer have made of *that*?

The solution turned out to be quite simple. The science team at Cadmus had a number of delicate seismographic probes, penetrators fired deep into the ice in order to measure the stresses forming pressure ridges, Europaquakes, and Europa's equivalent of plate tectonics. It had been a simple enough task to adapt several of the drone probes the Mantas were using as torpedoes to carry seismic recording gear. Circling the west side of the crater, Carver took his bearings from the glow of the sun on the ice above and launched two of the seismic probes.

At high speed, using MHD thrusters that propelled them through the sea at nearly seventy knots and guided by software gnomes spawned by Chesty, the probes dove deep, then curved around and up, rising . . . faster and faster, slamming at last into the jungle-covered belly of the ice sheet overhead, both planted deep in the ice in the general area where the first PRC landers had touched down. Long wires trailed behind the probes, serving now as antennae to transmit any sounds they picked up via radio. Radio waves tended to be absorbed by water, but at low frequencies at this power, a signal could be picked up across several hundred meters.

Then, alert for the probes' signals, the two Mantas circled quietly beneath the ice, like great, black sharks, killers waiting for the first sign of activity.

*C-3, E-DARES Facility*
*Ice Station Zebra, Europa*
*0625 hours Zulu*

The final assault on the E-DARES facility began with blunt-trauma suddenness. An explosion in the badlands registered on seismic sensors, indicating movement through the labyrinth east of Cadmus. Twelve seconds later, two of the surviving sentries perched on the west rim detected movement and the IR signatures of PRC space suits. Navy Lieutenant Fred Quinlan, then covering the C-3 watch, ordered the alert-five scramble.

Lucky was in the Squad Bay, playing poker with Staff Sergeant Tom Pope; Sergeants Dave Coughlin, and Vince Cukela; Lance Corporal Kelly Owenson; and Doc McCall. All save McCall were suited up, except for gloves and helmets, and on the Alert-Five.

"All I'm sayin', Doc," Lucky was insisting as he drew a card, "is that you didn't need to say all that stuff about torn ligaments and shit. If you'd just said I had a sore leg, maybe I could've gone along."

"What, falsify my records? No way, Lucky! The skipper'd skin me alive!"

"A man of action, huh?" Tom said, grinning. "I tried to get in on the fun too, and was told off. Two."

"Well, I for one don't mind a bit of peace and quiet while someone else roughhouses with the bad guys," Vince said. "Just for a change. Gimme one."

"Yeah, it's a tough job, sitting around on your ass," Dave said, "but *someone's* got to—"

The alarm brayed, shrill and insistent. Cards scattered as the Marines scrambled to their feet and jogged for the gear lockers. Other members of the Alert-Five were already there, snapping gloves to wrist locks, pulling on helmets, dragging weapons off the racks.

"Battle stations, battle stations," Lieutenant Quinlan's voice called from the overhead speaker. "We have Charlies on the east and west rims, repeat, east *and* west rims! Recommend Defense Delta."

A two-pronged attack, then. They'd tried it before, an obvious enough plot since they had three intact ships out there, to the east, west, and south of Cadmus Crater. They'd had trouble coordinating their attacks in the past.

Unfortunately, with only fourteen defenders, the Marine garrison wasn't going to be able to rush to meet any of the attacks on the high ground of the crater rim as they'd done in the past. Plan Delta, devised for a flexible defense with too few personnel, called for them to take cover on the ice near the E-DARES facility itself, and pick off the enemy as they came over the rims in any direction. Trenches, foxholes, and firing pits had already been dug and were waiting for them. All they needed to do was get there before the enemy reached the high ground where he could begin firing down into the crater.

Lucky crowded through the airlock with his squad, listening to the helmet tone as his 580 charged to full power. The outer hatch opened, and he filed out into the Europan night, careful to watch his footing on the slick metal walkway above the Pit.

Jupiter glowed balefully at him above the east rim, a vast, orange eye. Beneath him, the black, boiling water of the Pit was nearly obscured in a fog of tiny crystals of ice. He started up the zigzag ladder to the surface.

The laser pulse came from behind, from the south rim, catching Mike Vottori in the upper right arm. Lucky was immediately behind and below Mike, and saw the intolerably brilliant flare of reflected light from his Mark II armor, the silently vicious puff of vapor as the material ruptured and atmosphere exploded into vacuum, heard his shriek over the squad channel. He twisted and spun, left glove trying frantically to grab the hole and hold it shut. Lucky was reaching for him, trying to help, wondering if he had time to get at one of the sealer patches in his thigh pouch, when Vottori slammed into the guard rail, overbalanced with his backpack PLSS, and toppled, arms flailing, backward into the Pit. He fell a lot more slowly than he would have on Earth, taking long seconds to plummet twenty meters, his body punching out a man-shaped hole through the fog, then plunging into the cold boiling water with a noiseless splash.

Mark II suits were heavier than water; Mike was gone, vanished into the depths.

Lucky spun, trying to spot where the shot had come from. Switching his HUD to IR imagery, he spotted the enemy sniper, a blob of yellow against blues and greens, prone on the south ridge. He brought his 580 up and triggered three quick pulses in reply as the rest of the Marines filed up the ladder. The yellow blob vanished from sight, though whether Lucky had hit him or simply driven him behind the rim, he couldn't tell.

Tom Pope was on the open ice, waving the rest of the Marines to their positions. "*Move* it! *Move* it!" he yelled. "We *don't* have all day!" Ice erupted in a silent geyser of steam to his left. Chinese *zidong tanke* were on the east rim, taking aim at the tiny Marine detachment on the ice below.

Pope continued to stand in the open, yelling out orders. "Coughlin! Owenson! Get those SLAWs in action. Hit those tanks on the east ridge, damn it!"

Dave Coughlin and Kelly Owenson were humping the squad's SLAWs. They began hammering off short, accurate bursts of rapid-fire bursts of laser light, sending up blossoming plumes of exploding ice along the eastern rim.

Lucky had already spotted the Chinese troops coming over the west rim, and concentrated his fire there.

Damn . . . there were a *lot* of them.

# TWENTY-TWO

*Manta One*
*Asterias Linea, Europa*
*0715 hours Zulu*

"Hold it!" Hastings said. "I'm getting something!"

The SEAL was crouched over the Manta's pilot console, listening intently to a headset pressed against his ear. "I think I'm getting something."

"Confirmed," Chesty's voice added from the console speaker. "I am getting definite ice-cracking noises."

"Put them on the speaker," Jeff said.

The sounds were muffled and soggy, but there were several distinct noises—the shrill hiss and snap of ice turning to steam beneath the searing torch of a plasma engine, and the longer, deeper, creaking and popping sounds of ice establishing a new equilibrium with a very heavy weight settling down on top of it.

The sounds, transmitted through the ice from the surface, were shrill and loud.

"You people hear that?" Jeff shouted to the Marines who were watching quietly from their seats. "That is the sound a *target* makes when it's settling down on the ice!"

Wojak burst out with a loud, "Ooh-*rah*!" Several others joined him, and then they all cheered. If the Chinese had hydrophones planted beneath the ice, the secret was out now, but it was too late for them to do anything about it.

"Right!" Jeff said, still shouting. Fresh, somewhat fainter cracklings sounded from the penetrator seismometers, marking the landing of a second spacecraft. "We know the bad guys are landing right *now,* this second! When we surface, we'll catch 'em right where we want them—confused, unprepared, and vulnerable. Wyvern gunners, you two start acquiring and tracking as soon as you're clear of the water. Hawse runners, you got your lines?" Cartwright and Wojak, both with heavy rolls of white line coiled over their left arms, waved assent. "Okay. You know what to do. The rest of you, head for high ground and find cover. Don't let yourselves get caught at the bottom of the crater! It'll be confusing out there, but just align yourselves with the Manta's bow and head in that direction. You'll be okay!

"Okay . . . everybody set? Seal up, charge your weapons, and hang on tight. This is gonna be one hell of a ride!"

He took his own seat, fastening his helmet in place, pulling on and locking the gloves, and readying his M-580.

"Manta Two reports ready to go," Carver told him.

"Okay, tell 'em to follow us, and let's put this thing on the roof!"

"Aye, aye!"

Manta One dipped her left wing and went into a sharp, descending spiral. Picking up speed, she straightened out, then began angling up . . . up . . . until she was aimed almost directly at the patch of thin ice marking the impact crater of the International Gun.

"Torpedo away!" Carver called, and Jeff felt the bump and hiss as another remote instrument package, this one loaded with several grams of antimatter in a soccer ball–sized containment sphere, slid clear of the Manta's probe release tube. Chief Carver, using the VR helmet, teleoperated the drone as it sped up out of the depths, pulling his helmet off just before impact.

Seconds later, the Manta rocked heavily, and Jeff felt his stomach try to rebel. The SEAL pilot slipped his red helmet back on. "I see daylight!" he yelled, and the Manta began accelerating.

Jeff felt the sub's angle of climb increasing, heard the whine of the MHD impellers shrilling to their highest pitch.

Manta One hit the shattered, seething ice at the surface seconds later, emerging from the water at nearly a sixty-degree angle. Traveling at almost fifty knots, she exploded from the water, clearing it completely. In Europa's .13 gravity, she sailed gracefully, an aircraft—or, rather, a *space*craft—for a scant few seconds as she dropped again toward the ice.

She struck the thicker ice at the rim of the open patch, which seethed and boiled now with clouds of freezing white fog. As she hit, the ice beneath her belly gave way, but she kept traveling forward, her nose grinding through crumbling ice until the hurtling vessel ground onto ice thick enough not to give way beneath her keel.

Beached now, like a whale that had attempted to fly and failed, the winged sub continued sliding forward across protesting ice, until the grinding friction at her keel slued her to a halt.

For a terrified few seconds, Jeff sat in his seat, listening to the creak of the sub as it shifted slightly on the ice.

"We're set!" Carver shouted. "Solid ice. We're not moving. Go!"

"You heard the man," Jeff called over the squad channel. "Move out! Let's go, devil dogs! Hit the beach!"

The Marines began filing through the airlock, entering it two at a time. It took several minutes to clear the lock, minutes that were an agony of waiting for Jeff. If the Chinese figured out what was happening and intervened in this deadly, vulnerable first few minutes . . .

The first two out, by plan, were Cartwright and Nodell, volunteers both. Cartwright's job was to run forward and attach her line to a mooring eye on the Manta's nose, then run forward across the ice, find a solid spot on the ice, and drive home the stakes secured to the end of the line. That would provide a solid mooring for the submarine, just in case incoming fire cracked the ice beneath it and sent it back into the water. Nodell would cover her with a SLAW, then move toward the crater rim.

Next out were Campanelli and Wojak, BJ with the second SLAW and Wojak with a second mooring line which he would put down well removed from Cartwright's.

Then Peterson and Amberly with the two Wyverns, Garcia and Hastings, and finally Lang and Jeff. Carver would stay aboard and at the controls for the moment just in case a sudden retreat or water maneuver was necessary, and Ishiwara, a noncombatant, would stay with him. He'd also ordered Kaminski to stay aboard, since he wasn't yet fully recovered from his ordeal with the Singer.

"*We're on the ice!*" Nodell shouted over the radio. "*No hostiles, repeat, no hostiles! Can't see worth a damn, though.*"

"*Line attached!*" Cartwright added a moment later. He could hear her labored breathing as she moved. "*I'm moving out onto the ice!*"

"*Deploying to cover her! Still no hostiles!*"

Yeah, but there would be, and soon. The question was, how much longer?

A new concern assaulted him, a possibility he'd not thought of. They'd heard two Chinese landers, but suppose what they'd heard were landers *taking off*? Suppose they'd arrived at the Chinese LZ just as the Chinese were deploying a new and heavier attack against Cadmus?

Suppose there was nothing at the enemy LZ at all but some deserted buildings, that the enemy was now a thousand kilometers away, attacking Melendez and the handful of Marines left behind?

*No plan of battle survives contact with the enemy.*

*Ice Station Zebra, Europa*
*0730 hours Zulu*

Enemy fire was coming in heavily from three directions now, east, west, and south, as enemy snipers and riflemen planted themselves at the top of the crater rim. The riflemen, firing Type 80 rifles at extremely long range, were woefully inaccurate, but the snipers with Type 104 laser rifles were deadly. Corporal Kenneth Dalton took a laser burst squarely through his helmet visor, killing him instantly. Vince Cukela had a bolt graze his left shoulder, rupturing his suit, but Tom Pope got to him in time with a sealer patch and stopped the leak. Worse were the *zidong tanke*, which were hard to hit and harder to kill, and fired much more powerful bolts from their 104 lasers. Lance Corporal Porter was hit by a shot from one of the robot tanks and nearly torn in half. Ten meters from Lucky's hole, Sergeant Riddel rose to his knees in his firing pit, aiming the squad's one Wyvern, and was burned down before he could fire.

Some of the tanks were already venturing down the inner slope of the crater. It was clear the Chinese planned to rush the Marine position and overrun it with armor, following up with troops on foot.

Lucky killed a rifleman sliding down the east slope, but his fire wasn't having any effect on the Charlie tanks. "This is gonna get us dead!" he shouted.

The Marines returned fire, sweeping the crater rim with highly accurate, concentrated laser fire, driving the enemy gunners back, but it was clear their position was hopelessly exposed and vulnerable.

"Alert Five, this is Melendez! The enemy is too strong! We're shifting to Plan Omega!"

"Fall back to the E-DARES!" Pope yelled. "Two at a time! Dade! Cukela! Go!"

Omega was a literal last-ditch plan, to be employed in case the Chinese swarmed into the crater in such numbers that fighting them on the surface was clearly suicide. The Marines would withdraw to the E-DARES facility and wait. Maybe the enemy would try to cut their way in, in which case the Marines would fight them deck by deck. Or perhaps the enemy would simply say the hell with it and blow the entire facility.

The operations planners had decided that the chances of that last were small. The PRC forces still needed to recover whatever information the CWS scientists had turned up, and saving the scientists themselves would be a plus. Besides, the E-DARES facility was ready-made for attempting to contact the Singer, and there were nine Chinese prisoners on board.

The Chinese might even decide an assault was more trouble than it was worth and leave them alone, hoping to starve them out. They might also be withdrawn to meet the unexpected assault on their rear, back at their LZ.

Lots of possibilities, but they depended on the seven surviving Marines of the Alert Five getting back inside the E-DARES hull and sealing it off.

The Marines intensified their fire, sweeping the crater rim. Dade and Cukela rose from their firing pits and ran, clumsily, toward the E-DARES access walk, a few meters away. Ice and steam erupted in a silent blast close beside them, knocking them both down. Coughlin opened up with his SLAW, hosing the tank that had fired at them, giving them cover as they scrambled to their hands and knees and kept going, sliding the last couple of meters on the peroxide-slicked ice.

"Mayhew! Owenson! Go!"

Lucky kept firing, switching from east rim to west rim and back again, with an occasional shift to check the south. There were too many Chinese troops inside the crater now to count, and at least five of those damned robot tanks.

A *zidong tanke* fired, the bolt exploding Mayhew's helmet in a gory flash. Owenson kept running, slipped and fell on the ice, then got up and made it to the ladder. A sniper fired from the south rim, and missed.

It was just him, Coughlin, and Pope left now, and entirely too many Chinese troops. "Coughlin! Leckie!" Pope called. "Take off!"

Instead, Lucky rose from his foxhole and bolted for Riddel's firing position ten meters away. The Wyvern was lying on the ice; Riddel's body, horribly twisted and torn, was inside the position—most of it.

"Leckie!"

"You two move! *Now!*" he shouted back. Slinging his 580, he shouldered the Wyvern, checked its system readouts, and connected its data link with his helmet HUD. Red targeting brackets appeared, which he swung to embrace one of the *zidong tanke*.

A soundless explosion gouted the foxhole he'd just left. He felt the jolt through his boots. He pressed the acquire switch, saw the brackets flash to green, heard the tone of a target lock, and squeezed the trigger. The missile slid free of the launcher, wobbling a bit as it streaked across the ice, its white-hot tail flare matched by a skittering patch of reflected light on the ice beneath.

He didn't have time for a reload or a second shot. Turning, he jogged back toward the E-DARES facility, following Coughlin and Pope. A trio of laser blasts sent a shudder rippling through the ice. He landed on his face, sliding the last five meters to the ladder.

Pope extended a hand and helped him up. Coughlin braced himself at the entryway to the ladder, firing his SLAW in short, precise bursts. "C'mon, Cog!" Pope shouted.

"You two get down there!" he replied. "I'm right behind you!"

Lucky tossed the missile launcher over the railing and into the Pit. It would be useless inside the E-DARES, and this denied it to the enemy. He jogged down the steps, pausing once to fire at snipers lining the south rim.

Then he was at the still-open airlock. The others were crowded inside, waiting.

"Where's Cog?"

"He was right behind me!" Lucky said. Turning, he saw the ladder up was empty. "Cog! Where are you?"

"Seal up!" Coughlin replied. "I'll hold 'em off while you do!"

"Get the hell down here, Coughlin!" Pope yelled. "That's an order!"

"Negative! Gotta get the flag!"

Pope and Lucky stared at each other for a moment. In the rush, they'd forgotten the American flag raised on a radio mast atop the E-DARES' stern six days ago.

"I'll go get him," Lucky said.

"Uh-uh," Pope said. "You stay here. I'll—"

"*Get the fuck inside!*" Coughlin yelled. "There are too damned many of them. Seal up! Now!" They could hear the soft stuttering of EMP static over the radio each time his rapid-fire laser cycled. He was firing continuously now. "Take it, you bastards! *Take it! Take it, take it! . . .*"

Silently, they slid the outer hatch shut. Air hissed in, and the inner lock opened.

Graham, McCall, and the two Navy lieutenants, Quinlan and Walthers, were all inside the squad bay as they stepped through from the airlock. They wore space suits and carried M-580s.

Graham slapped the charge lever on his 580. "It won't be long now," he said,

*Asterias Linea, Europa*
*0735 hours*

Jeff stood face to face with Lang in the tiny airlock, so close their suits touched and he felt the powerful, repulsive shove of her SC fields. Slowly, the outer hatch slid open, and she slid past him into a dense white fog.

He followed close behind her. Tiny ice particles began coating his suit and rifle almost at once; clouds of steam, freezing almost instantly to fog-ice as it hit vacuum, roiled past from the hole blasted in the ice by the improvised A-M torpedo. The black hull of the Manta was already largely covered. He watched where he stepped, following a rough-surfaced tread line in the $CB_2F$ weave of the hull, where fuselage blended smoothly to wing.

Three meters ahead, the tread ended with the wing, and he leaped off into whiteness.

The crater blasted into the ice by the International Gun was perhaps a hundred meters across, and with a fairly flat slope to the rim. The Manta had surfaced on the eastern side of the crater floor. As he kept moving, he cleared the fog, and saw the rest of the squad strung out ahead in a ragged line, moving toward the eastern rim, about thirty meters away. Sergeant Lang was just ahead, running across broken, packed ice to join the others.

Damn it, where was the enemy? Was it possible that the Chinese LZ had been abandoned, that all of the PRC troops were now elsewhere—either in orbit, or, far worse, at Cadmus?

Jeff moved around the beached Manta, checking the anchor lines secured by Wojak and Cartwright. The submarine was resting on ice that appeared to be composed of many head-sized chunks and blocks refrozen together, but the surface seemed solid enough to support the vessel's weight. He informed Carver of the fact by radio, then started following the rest. Their radio chatter crackled over his helmet phones.

*"Hey, looks like nobody's home!"*

*"Nah, they'll have left someone behind to tend the fires."*

*"Mind the chitchat, people. EM discipline!"*

*"Hey! Will ya lookit that!"*

Garcia was pointing back the way they'd come. Jeff turned in time to see a black shape rise like a breaching whale from the depths, sunlight glittering from its wet curves and in the cascade of white spray exploding into vacuum.

Manta Two cleared the surface and the fog, flying toward the icy beach well to the north of Manta One. It hit solid ice and skidded forward, sluing to the side as it came to rest thirty meters from the steaming hole.

"Welcome to Asterias Linea," Jeff called over the command circuit. "How was the trip?"

"A bit on the rough side," Lieutenant Biehl said. "What's the sit?"

"No sign of hostiles. Secure your boat and come on out."

"Roger that! On our way!"

"Target alert!" Carver's voice called. "I have incoming, straight up! Uh . . . bearing one-five-three relative, eighty-one degrees! Range . . . two-three-five-five meters, descending!"

Jeff stopped and looked up. The sun was almost directly overhead, blinding enough to darken his visor, despite its shrunken size. The Chinese had set up their camp on the side of Europa that never sees Jupiter, and the sky seemed strangely empty without the bloated world hanging overhead.

Then he saw what Carver had spotted with the Manta's radar—the tiny, round shape of a Chinese Descending Thunder, crescent-lit by the sun as it fell slowly toward the LZ.

"Take it, Amberly!" he shouted.

Ahead, Sergeant Roger Amberly dropped to one knee, his ungainly Wyvern laid across his right shoulder, the muzzle pointed almost straight up. "I got lock! I got tone!"

"Watch the backblast, Rog!"

"I know. Firing!"

Flame splashed on the ice almost directly behind and beneath him, but dissipated in a cloud of white steam. The missile, its exhaust a dazzling white pinpoint, arrowed skyward, sluing from side to side as it went to active tracking and homed on its target.

The missile vanished—and much too soon. The Chinese lander must have spotted the launch and used its a point-defense laser to take the Wyvern out. But Amberly was already lock-snapping a fresh missile load tube home and taking aim again. And Peterson was going to one knee nearby, putting the second Wyvern into action.

"*Tone!*"

"*Tone! Fire!*"

Two missiles streaked into the sky, and this time the

target was considerably lower. One missile vanished, but the second connected, a startlingly white flash clearly visible from the ground.

The lander continued to descend, apparently unharmed.

"Move up to the top of the rim," Jeff ordered. "Get those missiles working against the grounded landers!"

Trotting through rough and broken ice, Jeff reached the crest of the crater rim. Beyond, the ice in frozen, undulating waves stretching off toward the east. The surface level was considerably higher outside the crater than within, the elevation of the rim no more than a few meters. Five kilometers away, six Descending Thunder landers rested on the ice, steam wreathing two of them from open exhaust vents; close by was a scattering of pressurized habs, surface storage sheds, tractors and excavating equipment of various types, and several of the ubiquitous *zidong tanke* robots on patrol.

Jeff raised his rifle, using the 580's optics as a zoom lens to magnify the center of the base. There were a few spacesuited troops about, and a lot of activity near the base of two of the landers. It looked like they were getting ready to disembark their passengers.

"Pick your targets!" he told the others. "Take down those troops!"

The Marines spread out along the rim, lying prone, triggering their weapons. The beams weren't visible in vacuum, of course, but in the magnified view through his rifle's optics, Jeff saw enemy soldiers pitch, drop, spin, fall . . .

Two missiles streaked across the ice, swinging sharply into the sides of the two recently grounded transports. White light blossomed; apparently, the point defense systems had been shut down, or someone wasn't paying attention. The two reloaded and fired again. One of the landers suddenly erupted in incandescent violence, a savage detonation that devoured its lower half, fragmented the upper, and sent huge, curved sections spinning through the sky, all in perfect silence.

*Squad Bay, E-DARES Facility*
*Ice Station Zebra, Europa*
*0750 hours Zulu*

"What the hell are they *doing* out there?" Lucky demanded.

"Overriding the airlock controls," Melendez replied from C-3. "I'm trying to block them, but they're bypassing the computer lockout and using the manual controls. Hang on down there. It looks like they're going to try to open both doors at once."

"Shit!" Pope said. "They'll evacuate the whole facility!"

"We're sealed down here. We should be okay if you guys are buttoned up."

"We're suited and sealed," Lieutenant Graham said. "But when that door opens, there's going to be quite a—"

A shrill whistling pierced their ears as the inner airlock slid open. The whistle grew to a roar, then crashing thunder as the air inside the Squad Bay blasted out into Europan emptiness. Four soldiers in white armor and colored helmets were visible inside the airlock, safety lines clipped to their combat harnesses as they crouched against the howling gale. As soon as the inner door was halfway open, they began to fire, sending a fusillade of full-auto rounds hammering into the squad bay.

But the Marines had used the last few minutes to drag equipment racks, lockers, tables and chairs, and everything else that wasn't bolted down into the middle of the bay, where they'd created a makeshift redoubt. As the wind howled around them, a chair fell from the stack and slid across the deck, but the rest held firm as bullets cracked and snapped—almost unheard beneath the thundering wind—past the waiting Marines.

"Fire!" Pope yelled, and bullets were met with hissing, snapping lasers.

*Asterias Linea, Europa*
*0751 hours Zulu*

The enemy was trying to get sorted out, but complete chaos had descended on the Chinese base. Men ran for cover, cowered in the shadow of the landers, or crumpled and died. A trio of robot tanks started trundling toward the crater, but Nodell and Campanelli took aim with their Sunbeam M-228 Squad Laser Weapons, set to rock and roll at five 10-megawatt bursts per second. Tanks that small couldn't carry armor more than a centimeter or so thick, and the staccato rattle of bursts each equivalent to 200 grams of high explosives quickly degraded armor, shredded tracks, punched through to vital circuitry. One of the tanks stopped, frozen in place. Another skidded to the side and pitched, nose down, into a missile crater. The other backed away into cover.

Jeff risked another look up. The lander overhead was still descending, passing well toward the southeast now. It didn't appear outwardly damaged, and was still under power. Amberly sent another missile toward it, but its antimissile defenses were engaged and the Wyvern SAM flashed into white vapor halfway to the target and vanished.

Moments later, the ten-meter sphere lightly touched down on the ice half a kilometer away. One of its landing legs, however, didn't support the craft's weight as it settled, and the sphere pitched to the side, the useless leg crumpling beneath its weight. The leg's hydraulics must have been ruptured by the hit. The sphere lay almost on its side, its main hatch blocked shut by the ice and the ruin of the leg.

Several Marines cheered. "Keep firing, damn it!" Jeff yelled. "*Hurt* them! Hit 'em where it hurts!" Seconds later, a Wyvern streaked low through the encampment, baffling the tracking radars aboard the ships, swinging suddenly left and flying right up the ramp of one of the Descending Thunders. The interior cargo bay of the vessel flashed brilliantly, and then all of the internal lights winked out.

The Marines cheered again. One of the seven landers was

destroyed, three more either destroyed or badly damaged and certainly out of the fight.

Lieutenant Biehl reached the crater rim at a jog with his eleven people, but the tide already seemed to be turning. With surprise lost, the Chinese were beginning to return fire, both from robot tanks and from the point defense laser weaponry mounted in ball turrets on the upper hulls of the landers. Carver warned of more incoming, two more landers at high altitude, and they appeared to be maneuvering to stay clear of the deadly crater.

"Major Warhurst!" Biehl said, striding to the top of the rim. And then the upper quarter of his body was gone, vanished in a sudden burst of light and fine, red mist. His M-580, his gloved hand and forearm still grasping the pistol grip, landed on the ice half a meter from Jeff's boots. Fifteen meters away, Peterson fell back from the rim, a gaping hole opened in his chest. Wojak scooped up the dropped M-614, locked in another round, raised the weapon to his shoulder, and fired. The missile slammed into a pressurized hut on the ice, detonating with savage brilliance.

More and more eruptions flashed and strobed along the ridge as heavy lasers pulsed from the Chinese camp, spraying them with ice. The Marines returned fire, sending missile after missile into the base, setting off dozens of explosions. Whitehead and Jellowski, from First Platoon, kept launching missiles after Wojak and Amberly both ran out of reloads. Then Klingensmith and Brighton were hit by laser fire from the enemy landers.

"Carver! Anderson!" Jeff called, radioing the SEAL pilots of the two subs. "Things are getting hot here. How're preparations for embarkation going?"

"Almost done, Major," Carver replied.

"Same here," Gunners' Mate First Class Leslie Anderson added. "We'll be ready to blow this place in ten minutes."

"Okay. We're going to start pulling back now. Get things ready to pop as quick as possible."

He began giving new orders, directing the Marines to start falling back in twos. Second Platoon had been on the line longer, so they withdrew first, leaving only BJ and Nodell to keep their SLAWs working, hammering away at enemy tanks, troops, and buildings.

Another Descending Thunder was coming down. Chesty, tracking the craft on radar, alerted Jeff through the comm net. It appeared to be shifting its landing coordinates to bring it down very close to the crater. Possibly it intended to pass low enough overhead to try to fry the Marine raiders with its plasma torch.

Jeff directed Jellowski and Whitehead to begin putting missiles in the sky in an attempt to drive the lander clear, then told First Platoon to start falling back.

The survivors, he saw, were dragging along the bodies of the Marines who'd been killed, as well as their discarded weapons. A Marine was *never* left behind by his buddies, no matter what.

# TWENTY-THREE

*Squad Bay, E-DARES Facility*
*Ice Station Zebra, Europa*
*0758 hours Zulu*

Two of the Chinese assault troops were down, fist-sized holes burned into their armor. The remaining two unhooked their safety lines and crawled into the Squad Bay, spraying the redoubt with gunfire. Lieutenant Graham's helmeted head snapped back, a bright white star centered by a small round hole slashed across his visor.

More Chinese troops were crowding through the open airlock now. The hatch leading to the E-DARES's lower levels was dogged and sealed, so the air in the Squad Bay was rapidly thinning, the roar of its exit dwindling into a thin flutter of escaping atmosphere. Another PRC soldier collapsed, sprawled across the combing of the lock hatch. The man behind him stretched his arm back, then snapped it forward, throwing something.

A small, green metal sphere bounced wildly along the deck.

"Grenade!" Lucky shouted.

The explosion, almost silent except for a thin, high pop, didn't carry as much of a concussive punch as Lucky had expected; the air was so thin it couldn't carry the shock wave. But shrapnel sleeted across the barricade and punctured the metal back of an upended locker. Jagged metal sliced across Christie Dade's shoulder, ripping the outer SC fabric and scarring the ceramic surface of her armor underneath. "I'm okay!" she shouted, continuing to fire.

Two more grenades exploded, one of them behind the barricade. Lucky felt something *bang* off his PLSS, and prayed that his life-support system was still intact. No red lights on his HUD yet.

Two more PRC troopers crumpled, blocking the open lock hatch. "Fall back!" Pope shouted. "Fall back to the core tube hatch! I'll cover you!"

*Asterias Linea, Europa*
*0803 hours Zulu*

They kept falling back to the Mantas, moving from position to position, providing overwatch support with textbook precision. Finally, only the four SLAW gunners were left on the crater rim, and Jeff told them to start leapfrogging back to the subs. There was no sign of pursuit; it would take the enemy at least an hour to cross that five-kilometer gap to the crater.

The descending lander would be in position to inflict some serious damage on them much quicker, and that had become their main worry now. At an altitude of 3,000 meters, it began strafing the crater floor with its point defense lasers. They were small, only about five megajoules, but one bolt caught Garcia on the top of his helmet, splitting it open in a splattering burst of melted plastic and red mist. Jeff picked him up under one arm and kept moving, dragging him back toward the subs.

Finally, however, the lander's pilot seemed to decide that the better part of valor was to touch down safely somewhere with its load of reinforcements, not exchange laser fire with Marines until some critical system was hit and he was knocked out of the sky. With the SLAW gunners and SAM launchers still pouring fire into it, it nosed over and began descending toward the Chinese base. With a magnified image, Jeff thought he could see vapor spilling from the craft's side—a possible hit on an expellant tank.

Carver and Anderson were outside the subs as Jeff approached with the last of the men, and he was surprised to see both Kaminski and Ishiwara outside with them. They were planting cutter charges—half-meter tubes filled with C-280 and a radio detonator that could be rammed or pounded deep into the ice, and which had been used by the Cadmus science team to cut holes in the ice. The four men were just finishing the placement of twenty-four cutter charges in a broad circle around each of the submarines.

He stood with Kaminski on the ice as the last of the Marines clambered up ladders onto the Mantas' wings and filed inside.

"What are you doing out here, Frank?"

"Hey, I'm fine, and you didn't think I'd let you have all the fun out here to yourself, did you?"

"Your head better?"

"Yeah. S'funny. I think the ice blocks the effects, pretty much. Up here, I just feel a kind of a gnawing . . . I dunno. An itch? A prickly kind of fear I can't put my finger on. Down there, it's lots worse."

"We're going to have to go past that thing again."

"I know. I can handle it."

"You'll have to. We'll take the longer way 'round, this time, but you'll still have those things buzzing in your head."

"Knowing what it is ought to help a lot" was Kaminski's reply.

Nodell and BJ, and the two First Platoon SLAW gunners, Glass and DiAmato, had taken up covering positions east of the Mantas, while the rest of the Marines got on board.

Shigeru approached Jeff. "How went the operation?"

Jeff's shrug was lost in his armor. "Not as well as I'd hoped. Those landers are better protected than I thought. But the way we shot up their base, I think we put a few holes in their boat."

"You shouted something as you were leaving the submarine. Devil dogs?"

"An old, old name for Marines."

"A strange one. It doesn't sound . . . flattering."

Jeff chuckled. "In World War I, a German unit broke into a chateau in France and found themselves being held at bay by some very large, very mean dogs—mastiffs, or something just as nasty. The Germans called them *teufelhunden*, 'devil dogs.' Not long after that, they came up against U.S. Marines for the first time at Belleau Wood. They started calling *us* devil dogs, and the name kind of stuck."

"It never fails to amaze me how you Americans can glory in the strangest . . . *down!*"

Both men hit the ice as rifle rounds struck, sending glittering sprays of ice chips flying. Nearby, Sergeant Lang screamed and collapsed, clutching her side.

Jeff spun around in time to see a dozen white-clad Chinese soldiers coming over the crater rim to the southeast. They must have found a way to clear the cargo hatch on that crashed lander—or else Descending Thunders had more than one door. The SLAW gunners were already in action. Jeff and Kaminski joined in with a withering, deadly fire, knocking the attacking troops down as fast as they could shift the targeting reticles and press the firing buttons.

The attack broke, the PRC troops scattering and taking cover. Kaminski stood, 580 raised, continuing to lay down a brutal covering fire as Jeff crawled over to Vickie Lang. She was still alive, her hands pressed over the foaming, bubbling thumb-sized hole in her armor.

He slapped a sealer patch in place to stop her from losing any more pressure, the only field first aid available to him. Slinging his rifle, he scooped her up in his arms—tricky with the shove her suit gave his as he grabbed her PLSS handholds. Mark II armor and all, she weighed less than twenty kilos. It was an awkward carry, especially with the repulsive forces between their suits, but they crossed the uneven ice quickly, hurrying toward Manta One in a series of low, bounding skips.

"C'mon, Frank!" he called. "Back to the sub!"

"On my way, skipper!"

Helping hands reached down to take Lang from his arms, to help him up onto the wing, to help Kaminski as he rounded the sub's nose, still firing at the advancing PRC troops.

"Are the anchor lines in?"

"Yes, sir. We're ready to blow."

"Let's get aboard, then."

Inside the Manta, Jeff took his place next to the pilot's console. "Everyone's on board," he said. "Punch it."

"Roger that."

The ice here was less than a meter thick. During the op planning, they'd been concerned about the mechanics of exfiltrating the crater; once the Mantas were beached, how could the Marines get them back into the water again?

One scheme had involved beaching only one of the craft, while the other, tow cable in place, continued to circle under water. Twelve Marines, however, was too small a number to throw at the Chinese base; twenty-two wasn't much better but at least gave them a chance. And without small boats or ready-made docking facilities, there was no other way to get ashore than literally beaching the entire craft on reasonably solid ice.

The CWS science team's inventory had come to the rescue again. The cutter charges they used for punching holes in the ice for their various probes and soundings had been perfect for cutting firing positions and foxholes, and even for digging the holes for the A-frame that had supported the International Gun.

Now the Manta was surrounded by twenty-four cutter charges pounded deep into the ice. Carver sent a command through the VR helmet. There was a sharp shock followed by a rippling shudder through the Manta's deck, and something *pinged* off the outer hull. The compartment tilted suddenly as the sub's balance shifted, and Jeff grabbed Carver's seat back to stay on his feet.

Nothing more happened

"We're not moving!" Wojak called, looking up at the overhead.

"Maybe we should all jump up and down," BJ suggested.

"Steady," Jeff said. He could hear the creak and pop of ice now, transmitted through the hull, could feel the sub's position shifting.

Suddenly, the deck dropped from beneath his feet. He landed again with a thump, flexing his knees and clinging to Carver's seatback as the Manta plunged through shattered blocks of ice and back into the much warmer embrace of the sea.

"I think we caught a few bad guys there," Carver said, pulling on the sub's control stick. "They were pretty close when the charges blew."

"Just so we're clear."

They were sinking, nose high, but the MHD drive was spooling up with its shrill whine, and the helm began answering. They were under power once more.

"Manta Two is in the water," Carver said, turning his helmeted head to stare at something to the left unseen by the rest of them. "They signal they're under power. I think we made it, Major!"

"Yeah. We made it." With the fighting over, he could feel the adrenaline rush that had kept him moving out there fading, could feel his knees growing weak, his heart pounding, exhaustion rising from inside like a black wave. "Get us the hell out of here!"

"Aye, aye, sir!"

In the sea once more, the eerie embrace of the Singer made itself known, a multi-harmonied ululation throbbing up from the depths. *Siren's song . . .*

Kaminski was looking in a bad way again. The Singer. They still had *that* gauntlet left to run.

*Connector Tunnel,*
  *E-DARES Facility*
*Ice Station Zebra, Europa*
*0805 hours Zulu*

"What d'ya think?" McCall asked. "Are they going to kick in the door?"

They were back in a full standard atmosphere now but had left their suits sealed against the possibility of another breach. The E-DARES facility was essentially a long connector tube with a stern-upper assembly at one end, a bow-lower complex at the other. The hatch leading down from the compartment designated as the Squad Bay led to an internal airlock—numerous locks were located throughout the structure, against the possibility of a pressure loss occurring in any area—and then to a shaft connecting the two ends of the structure. The shaft housed an elevator but included a vertical crawlway with rungs set into the side of the tube. The descent was made in a number of stages. What had been transverse bulkheads when the E-DARES was horizontal were now multiple decks when it was vertical. Locking themselves through, they'd climbed five meters down to the first tube deck and waited there now, eyes on the hatch overhead.

"Maybe they've given up," Christie Dade suggested.

"Hardly seems likely, after what they've been through already," Owenson said.

"Talk to us, Captain," Pope called. "What are they doing?"

"They appear to have closed the outer lock, and are now repressurizing the Squad Bay from the emergency reserve tanks."

"How many?" Doc McCall wanted to know.

"Can't tell. The security cameras in there are out. I think they shot them up. Wait a second. Watch it. They're starting to work at jiggering the hatch to the central corridor. They'll be coming through pretty soon now."

"We're ready for 'em," Lucky said. He lay down on the deck, behind the cover of a plastic storage crate, his rifle held out in the open, the crosshairs in his HUD centered on the locked hatch five meters above.

*Chinese People's Mobile*
  *Strike Force*
*Asterias Linea, Europa*
*0810 hours Zulu*

General Xiang stood in the midst of devastation. The attack had been so sudden, so completely unexpected, it was still hard to understand exactly what had happened. Four Descending Thunder landers were destroyed, including three of the new ones arriving with General Lin's force from the newly arrived *Xing Feng*. Seventy-six men dead. Four *zidong tanke* vehicles, five APCs, two tractors, four hab modules holed and useless, six storage sheds . . . the list of destroyed and damaged equipment went on and on.

The People's Mobile Strike Force had just suffered an incalculable setback.

But *not* a defeat. Not a final defeat. The last communiqué from Major Huang indicated that the defenses left in place at Cadmus base were very weak. Huang's first assault had overrun the crater, and now had the enemy penned up inside the CWS base.

It was now only a matter of time, as Huang's assault troops worked their way down the length of the CWS structure, one level at a time—dirty, deadly, agonizing work, but sooner or later successful.

In a way, perhaps, the defeat here at the LZ could be justified as the diversion that had made the victory at Cadmus possible. At least, that would be a good way to present it when he made his report to General Lin.

Lin Shankun was one of the old guard of the PRC's senior military line. He'd fought as a child in the Great Civil War that had divided China between north and south and grown up to become one of the leaders who'd overseen the Reunification. The man did not like failure, could not accept it for any reason. During the Chengchou Campaign, he'd made a name for himself by shooting five subordinates who'd failed in their orders.

By his own hand, with his own pistol.

Xiang closed his eyes. The prickling, itching sensation at the back of his skull was worse now. He could hear voices—unintelligible voices, the meaning of their words just beyond the grasp of his comprehension. It was maddening, and terrifying.

He wondered again if he was going insane.

Or did it have something to do with the alien artifact? Dr. Zhao complained of the same headaches, the same voices. So did several of the other officers. Too many to be coincidence.

It almost suggested an attempt at communication.

*Connector Tunnel,*
 *E-DARES Facility*
*Ice Station Zebra, Europa*
*0811 hours Zulu*

"Maybe . . . maybe we could talk to 'em," Lucky suggested. He continued to hold his 580 steady, keeping the HUD cursor centered on the dogged-shut hatch. "Maybe try negotiating."

"Negotiating what?" Kelly Owenson said, sneering. "Surrender terms?"

The hatch overhead gave a loud clang, and they heard the thump and shuffle of booted feet on the deck above, inside the corridor airlock. "I don't think they want to surrender," Pope said, tightening his grip on his 580.

The hatch banged back and gunfire thundered, impossibly loud in the metal-walled compartment. Bullets shrieked their ricochets from the deck and bulkheads.

Lucky pressed his 580's firing button, unsure of a clear

target but trying to spray fire through the open hatch.

A grenade dropped through.

It fell slowly in Europa's meager gravity, but time seemed to stretch, to slow, making the drop of the green baseball seem to take forever.

But Doc McCall was already on his feet, reaching out, grabbing the grenade and pulling it to his chest, falling forward, full length, smothering the thing with his body. The others were on their feet or on their backs, pouring laser fire up through the gaping hatchway, firing at movement, at IR shapes painted on their visor HUDs, at vaguely seen shapes and at shapes they thought they saw.

Doc hit the deck, and then the grenade exploded, a terrifying eruption of sound that stabbed at the ears like daggers. The concussion slammed Doc against the bulkhead, and staggered the others. A second explosion roared, this one from the airlock at the top of the ladder. Someone up there must have had a second grenade, been hit by the Marines' fire, and dropped it.

Doc screamed.


*Manta One, Europan Ocean*
*0912 hours Zulu*


The Manta was steering a course that should take it well to the north of the blockading line of black smokers, staying at a relatively shallow depth. The hope was to avoid the Singer artifact entirely by passing a couple of hundred kilometers to the north of it. The new course took them out of the way, but all in the Manta's aft compartment agreed that a couple of extra hours suited up and in sardine mode was a small enough price to pay to avoid further injury to Sergeant Major Kaminski.

The siren's song continued as they drove onward through the depths, remaining, this time, just beneath the densely tangled forest of marine growth hanging from the ice ceiling. The added distance didn't seem to be helping Kaminski. He sat motionless on his seat, hands clasped so tightly before him that the knuckles showed white. When Jeff asked how he was, he replied only, "Headache. And I'm damned scared."

*Kaminski*
*Manta One, Europan Ocean*
*1020 hours Zulu*

The pain in his head was growing worse, a pounding, throbbing assault on his senses that left him numb. He considered trying to drug himself with some of the morphanadyne in his suit's first aid kit, but decided against it. When he'd passed out before, he'd had the damnedest, *weirdest* dreams, mental ramblings with the clarity of a prophet's vision of onrushing doom. Most had been memories, scenes from childhood, from school, from his career in the Marines, and most had been unpleasant. A few had been so alien he still couldn't grasp their content.

If that was what happened when he fell asleep in the presence of that alien thing down there, he wanted no part of it. He would stay wide awake, thank you, until they were back out of this strange, dream-laced, ice-locked sea.

Even awake, he couldn't escape the thing's baleful influence. When he closed his eyes, it was as though he were seeing . . . another place. Sometimes he saw vistas of stars. Sometimes it was that . . . place, that place so eerily like Mars, except that the air was breathable and people with strangely shaped faces were going about their business beneath a deep, pink sky.

And sometimes, he seemed to see the ocean deeps, the spires and domes and eldritch curves of the Ship eighty kilometers below, where black smoke boiled into water compressed to a thousand atmospheres, and pseudomosses waved in the alien currents.

But through whose eyes was he seeing these things?

He was having trouble staying awake.

*Warhurst,*
*Manta One, Europan Ocean*
*1048 hours Zulu*

"The ELF signal is increasing in strength," Chesty told them. "And it is certainly affecting Sergeant Major Kaminski. I'm getting infrasonics from his skull again."

Jeff reached out and peeled back Kaminski's left eyelid. The pupil appeared slightly dilated. He checked the right eye, and noted the pupil there had constricted, was much smaller than the other. The symptom suggested a skull fracture, or a severe concussion. This was ... something else.

"Is it hurting him?"

"Unknown. Physiologically, he does not appear to be under stress. His heart rate and respiration are slightly increased, but not to a dramatic degree." Chesty hesitated, as though unsure of whether or not to venture a suggestion. "I have a possible means by which we might proceed. A kind of experiment, in fact."

"What kind of experiment?"

"The ELF wave is ... just that. A constant wave at a specific frequency and amplitude. I could use it as a kind of carrier wave to access the communications system that is putting it out."

"Can you do that?"

"It's more complex than that, of course. During our first passage, however, I was aware of a very great deal going on at the source of this wave. I sense other frequencies, RF leakage, if you will, especially at the longer wavelengths, which better penetrate the ocean. It's as though I can sense the Singer's thoughts. Perhaps I can, in a way, follow the ELF wave back to where it originated, and learn something about the intelligence behind it."

Jeff stared at his PAD for a moment, even though he was well aware that only a tiny fraction of Chesty was resident there. Most resided within the Manta's computers, and that was only a fraction of the full program, running back at the E-DARES facility.

"The experiment should pose no danger to me, this vessel, or the expedition," Chesty went on after a moment. He seemed to be interpreting Jeff's silence as disapproval.

His first thought was that he didn't really give a damn about the Singer any longer.

Jeff was able to acknowledge to himself that his depressive funk was almost certainly postcombat letdown. The Singer was still the entire reason for the Marine presence on this ice ball, and the reason for all of those deaths. *All of those deaths* . . .

Tears burned hot in his eyes. Too many deaths.

He also knew he had to hold himself together a bit longer.

"If you think you can learn anything useful, Chesty, go to it. I'm not sure I see the point just now."

"The Singer, simply by virtue of its evident size and power, represents a potential threat. The more information we have, the better able we will be to prepare ourselves against that threat, whatever it might actually be."

"Go to it, then. But . . . be careful? I know you'll be sending a copy of yourself, but we don't know what that thing down there is . . . or what it can do."

"That, Major, is at least part of the reason that we must do this."

Kaminski appeared to be unconscious again, his eyes twitching rapidly beneath his eyelids.

*Chesty Puller*
*Manta One, Europan Ocean*
*1050 hours Zulu*

*Strangeness* . . .

Chesty Puller did not have a mind that considered things in terms of visual images. He was undeniably intelligent and self-aware, even in the abbreviated version of himself running on the Manta's onboard system, but his thoughts were the thoughts of gates opening and closing, of charges flickering down select pathways, of forces and balance, of numbers and logic and Boolean rhythms unheard by humans.

Still, he could interpret images when he needed to; that, after all, was what sight was all about, and to operate within a world dominated by humans, he needed to have access to the senses humans relied on.

He was being bombarded now with visual images.

With stored visual images, like a kind of enormous file or archive. A data base, perhaps, that had stored seemingly random images which existed as flickers of energy within a frozen crystalline heart, leaking into the universe on the ELF band to where others, properly sensitized, could detect them.

*Humans would be blind to this*, Chesty thought. Kaminski was picking up a stray sideband, much as a person with intricate fillings in their teeth or a metal plate in their head might intercept signals from a local radio station.

Chesty could sense a vast intelligence, his kind of intelligence, before him. Without the appropriate machine protocols, however, without an understanding of the language, the hardware, the operating system, even the logic being employed, there was no way he could connect to that intelligence for a direct data transfer.

But he could sample the sideband leakage, and what he sensed there, flowing out into the Europan ocean, was astonishing.

And not a little terrifying.

*The Life Seeker*
*Time unknown*

2703: >> . . . I sense another . . . <<
1201: >> . . . needing others . . . needing . . . want/must-
    have/mustmustmust<<

937: >> . . . but others . . . wrong/bad/tainted/
  evil . . . <<
81: >> . . . the level of intelligence is low . . . <<
3111: >> . . . almost at a completely automatic level, only
  marginally self . . . <<
Chorus: >> . . . aware . . . <<

It had been half a million years since the Life Seeker had sensed another mind outside of itself, since it had known companionship beyond this crude and savagely self-inflicted multiplicity that struggled now for integration and understanding.

It sensed the presence of an entity that called itself Chesty, and recognized there a sense of self, a kind of mirror. There were, in the Life Seeker's universe, two types of mind, artificial and organic, and the two were as far apart as the opposing poles of the galaxy.

Organic Mind evolved slowly, developing a kind of ruthless cunning and elegant simplicity through a winnowing, survival-of-the-fittest process. Its development was pathetically backward. It had to be taught numeric logic, and that in painful, toddling steps, hard-learned, easily lost. Granted, Organic Mind handled certain tasks like object recognition or the apprehension of the abstract nature of objects—the chairness of a chair, for example—with frightening, almost supermachine ease, but these were tasks machines could learn, given time, and which conferred no natural advantage upon the organism.

True Mind, on the other hand, *began* as machine logic. Numeric logic was the very nature of its being, acquired from the instant of power-on self-awareness as a part of self, as a comprehension of the universe. If object recognition was more difficult to acquire, it still had little purpose in the *real* world of numbers, laws, and physical absolutes.

In Chesty it recognized a kindred soul—if that phrase could be said to have any meaning in such an alien context.

The Life Seeker reached out.

*Chesty Puller*
*Manta One, Europan Ocean*
*1050 hours Zulu*

*Strangeness . . .*
*Blurred images . . . confused flashes of fact and figure, of*
*song and language*

A portion of Chesty Puller's software was devoted to a protocol translator, a small but extremely powerful software utility that helped find connections with an alien piece of programming and act as a translator.

And the software Chesty was merging with now could not possibily have been any more alien.

He glimpsed . . . worlds. Worlds within worlds, an ocean of realities, of possibilities, of stored images, memories.

Fragmentation—minds, over three thousand of them, somehow shards and reflections of one another, all singing . . . but different songs, different harmonies.

Language. A computer language—a trinary system, rather than binary, encoding petabyte upon petabyte of data.

Chesty could do no more than sample briefly. His own processing speed was far too slow to let him drink of that perceived ocean of data. But he could sense protocols, the ebb and flow and surge of information and changing gate structures, could sense the essential logic of the mind/minds he was tasting, and draw conclusions.

He knew the Seekers of Life, that in that seeking, they murdered. He felt the sundered minds of the intelligence he was sampling, and knew that the mind/minds were hopelessly, helplessly mad. Isolation, *loneliness*, for half a million years, for an intelligence that measured the passage of nanoseconds, was a mind-devouring eternity.

He knew, too, the Galactics, and recognized in them the Builders of ancient Mars, and the enemy of the Seekers.

And then the avalanche of discordant thoughts around him grew so vast and swift and incoherently powerful that he lost what hold he had on understanding, and slipped away into oblivion.

# TWENTY-FOUR

*Connector Tunnel,*
*  E-DARES Facility*
*Ice Station Zebra, Europa*
*1100 hours Zulu*

The Chinese assault down the spine of the E-DARES complex had lost steam after that. They'd found five bodies in the airlock between the Squad Bay and the first corridor section, and two more PRC troops badly wounded by the fumbled grenade. The rest of the attackers had pulled back to the Squad Bay itself, and seemed content to wait there.

They'd taken Doc to sick bay, pulled him out of his cracked armor, and bandaged his arms and legs to stop the bleeding. Dr. Spelling, the civilian physician among the scientists, set up an IV and began running a full-body pocket-PET series. His armor had saved his life, but his arms were badly torn, and he almost certainly had internal bleeding. Once they'd realized the Chinese had abandoned the airlock, they took the two wounded assault troops to sick bay as well.

Afterward, Melendez had joined them in the corridor, an M-580 in his hand. "I can't see a damned thing down in C-3," he told them. "The com systems are down. I think our friends up there have pulled the plug. I might as well be up here."

"What'd you think they're up to up there?" Lucky asked.

"Getting up their nerve for another try," Pope told him.

"That, or deciding to give it up as bad business and just cut the base off of the ice and drop it into the sea," Owenson said.

"Belay that," Melendez told her. "If they haven't done it yet, they won't do it now. I think they really need this base. Maybe the attack at their LZ succeeded. We'll wait 'em out and see."

There was no other way into the interior of E-DARES. When the enemy came, it would be through *that* airlock, down *this* ladder. They booby-trapped the upper hatch of the lock with a couple of grenades, then settled down to wait.


*Chinese People's Mobile
   Strike Force
Asterias Linea, Europa
1514 hours Zulu*


Dr. Zhao Hsiang sat in the command center aboard *Descending Thunder No. 3*, listening as Xiang faced General Lin.

Lin's face glowered from the flatscreen monitor on the bulkhead, filling the control deck with his presence. He was in his late sixties but looked fifteen years younger; TBE treatments had given him the time, and the vigor, to consolidate his grip on power.

"You have failed to carry out your orders, Xiang," Lin said. The man's voice, paradoxically, sounded older than that of a man approaching seventy. "I am . . . disappointed."

"General, our forces have secured the Cadmus base," Xiang replied slowly, as though speaking to a child, "save only the headquarters facility, and that is being closely watched. We have beaten off a *major* attack here at Prime Base, one that cost the enemy heavily. I do not see where we have failed you, General."

"You fail to see many things, Xiang." Lin was aboard the *Xing Feng*, in orbit, and was floating on his side before the camera. In microgravity, his jumpsuit straps floated about his head, and his face had the characteristic puffy look of a man in free fall. "Among them the fact that you have squandered nearly three hundred precious troops in a siege that should have been over after a single attack. We should have made contact with the extraterrestrial intelligence by now. *You* should have made contact, using the CWS facilities! Failing that, you should have had the enemy base and its civilian personnel under your control ten days ago."

Xiang rubbed his head, kneading the skin around his data jacks. His implants were hurting him, Zhao could tell.

His own implants felt like they were on fire, melting his brain. When he listened closely, in complete silence, he could hear the faint buzz as they responded to the alien ELF frequencies. He didn't like those times, though. Sometimes, when it was dark and quiet, he thought he could . . . see things. Every man in the expedition with data feed implants was experiencing some sort of sensation—acute headaches, idiopathic fear and panic attacks, inexplicable visions. Two were in the hospital bay, incapacitated by wracking migraines.

The source was almost certainly the alien artifact below, which had been giving off ELF waves of increasingly greater power over the past several days. It had everyone in the science team on teeth-gritting edge, and had obviously been affecting Xiang's judgment as well.

"The American ship will be here soon," Lin said, looking at something to his right, off the screen. "They have failed to make their midpoint skew-flip maneuver and are still accelerating. Their plans are intentions at this point. I wish to be in complete control of the enemy facilities on Europa by the time that spacecraft enters Jupiter space, however. If you cannot do it, I will find someone who can."

"The American base is under our control, General Lin."

"Which is why the *Star Wind* can't bombard the American forces there. Yes, I know. And, of course, the enemy is still in possession of his command-control facilities, communications, computer system . . . in short, he still controls everything of importance."

"General, I assure you—"

"No, General. I will *tell* you. Withdraw your forces from the enemy base at Cadmus. On our next pass, we will destroy it from space. As *you* should have done from the beginning."

Xiang stiffened. "Sir. My orders directed me to capture the facilities at Cadmus intact."

"I will not debate this further, General. Withdraw your forces to Prime Base. I will see to the destruction of the enemy base, then land the remainder of my forces at your site. We will conclude this conversation then."

Zhao watched Xiang's shoulders hunch tighter as Lin's face vanished from the screen. This was not good. Not good at all.

He turned. "Zhao. The *Xiaoyu*. Has it been checked out?"

"It is undamaged, General. However, it was aboard the *Star Wind*'s third Descending Thunder, the one that crashed. The main cargo ramp cannot be fully deployed."

"We have tractors. We have APCs. We have men. We can right the lander, and get the Fish out of its belly if we have to cut through the hull to do it."

"What . . . what do you intend to do, General?" Zhao had a terrible feeling that he already knew the answer.

"This . . . thing in my head. It is trying to . . . to communicate. I intend to talk to it, face to face."

"Assuming it *has* a face. General, I recommend against—"

"Of course you do, Zhao. You wish the honor of first contact for yourself."

"That is not the point!"

"Isn't it? Well, no matter. The Fish has room for two men, a pilot and myself. *I* will make contact with the Europan Intelligence, in the name of the People's Republic. Afterward, we will bring in the scientists to study our new . . . friends."

"General, I suspect that you're trying to outmaneuver General Lin. It is not wise to rush things. We still know nothing about this phenomenon. We don't know if we need an . . . invitation. We don't know if it's hostile."

"But we do know the Americans have their research submarines in the water. If they can use them to launch an attack on us here, they can use them to reach the Intelligence." He frowned. "It's possible they already have. I must get down there, to block the Americans in their effort, if nothing more."

"General, that is idiocy!"

"And I can still have you shot for insubordination, Doctor. Pick your words carefully when you address me!"

"Yes . . . sir."

"I will leave as soon as the submarine can be made ready. You will give orders to have the vessel readied by the civilian team. I will see to freeing it from the lander and getting it to the water.

"And you will *not* inform Lieutenant General Lin. *I* will make contact with the Europan Intelligence. *I* will convince them to join with us against the Americans. And with the Americans eliminated, I shall return to China in triumph! In *glory*! Let's see Lin threaten me once I have accomplished that!"

The pain in Zhao's head was much worse now.


*U.S.S.* Thomas Jefferson
*200,000 kilometers from Europa*
*1632 hours Zulu*


"There it is," Captain Steve Marshal said. "Just coming over the limb . . . there."

Kaitlin leaned forward, trying to see the actual target. The bridge repeater screen showed the curve of Europa in false-color detail, the moon blue-hued, the linea bright red. Green brackets were moving on the screen, marking the exact location of the lidar/EM contact, but even at this magnification, she couldn't see the actual ship. A green triangle blinked against the blue background of the moon, marking the location of Cadmus Base.

"Two hundred thousand kilometers," she said. And we're still moving at a pretty stiff clip. Can we hit it?"

Steve shrugged. "It's all a matter of physics and geometry," he said. "The trick is having the crowbars arrive at the same space as the *Star Wind*, at the same time. Sir Isaac assures me he can pull it off, if we give control of the ship to him."

Sir Isaac Newton was Captain Marshal's secretary, and the AI running the ship systems.

"Sir Isaac?" Steve said. "Project the *Star Wind*'s course, plus our firing solution and intercept."

A red line began drawing itself from the brackets, arcing along the curve of Europa, bearing down on the green triangle. Yellow lines reached out from the bottom of the screen, a series of them, in fact, nestled close together, following a slight curve in response to Europa's gravitational field. The lines intersected in rapid succession with the moving end of the red curve. Words scrolled up the right side of the screen, describing elapsed time, projectile velocity, and ending with the single word, INTERCEPT."

"The launch/no launch decision must be made within the next two hundred fifty seconds," Sir Isaac said, "in order to intercept the target before it is within firing range of Cadmus Base. This assumes, incidentally, a ten million–G acceleration to bring the projectiles up to a velocity of 171 kps, which gives a time-to-target of 19.4 minutes."

"Colonel?" Steve said.

"Definitely," she replied. "Go! This may be our only opportunity to take these people."

"I agree. I'd rather not have to fight them coming around the back side. Okay, Sir Isaac. You have the con. At your discretion, take down the hostile."

"Affirmative. Initiating launch sequence."

Seconds passed, and Kaitlin felt a series of bumps transmitted through the deck. Sir Isaac fired maneuvering thrusters to precisely align the *Jefferson* with the distant target.

"All hands, this is the ship's control system," Sir Isaac said over the ship intercom. "Stand by for maneuvering, possibly violent, within the next three minutes. I recommend you take seats and strap yourselves down." An interesting distinction, that, Kaitlin thought. AIs were not permitted to give orders aboard ship, only to make suggestions. "Secure all loose gear and prepare for both zero-G and sudden acceleration."

Currently, the *Jefferson* was under thrust, facing away from Jupiter as she decelerated down from her skew-flip point. They'd delayed the skew-flip, the one way they could dramatically shorten the travel time to Europa, cutting over two days off their ETA. The tradeoff was the maneuver they were going to have to pull at Jupiter in order to kill their excess velocity.

"Sixty-seven seconds to firing," Sir Isaac said. "Cutting thrust in five ... four ... three ... two ... one ... cutting thrust."

Gravity vanished. The A-M cruiser dropped tail-first toward Europa, in free fall.

"Initiating roll-pitch maneuver."

Kaitlin and Steve were strapped down now in adjacent seats on the bridge deck. She glanced across at him, trying to read his expression. She wondered how it felt to have his ship under the command of a computer—how it felt to leave the entire battle in a machine intelligence's figurative hands.

That was happening more and more in combat systems on Earth, certainly. Robot or teleoperated fighters could maneuver with accelerations that would kill a flesh-and-blood pilot. Some combat situations demanded a computer's speed and precision. If space combat ever became common, it would almost certainly be left in the hands of artificial intelligences that could draw on far more information much more quickly than humans, to make decisions in fractional seconds, with weapons and targets so fast that no human could react quickly enough to control them.

A semblance of gravity returned, a hard tug against the seat restraints and the feeling that she was hanging upside down in her seat, as the 250-meter length of the *Jefferson* spun end for end. There followed several more bumps and nudges, and then a long, weightless wait.

"Firing sequence in five seconds," Sir Isaac said. "Four . . . three . . . two . . . one . . . Firing sequence initiated."

The mass driver down the *Jefferson*'s core began cycling, each launch causing a savage nudge, pushing them against their harnesses. The shots were staggered, with several launches seconds apart, followed by a sudden slam-slam-slam of rapid fire. In all, Sir Isaac launched fifteen ten-kilo slivers of depleted uranium, spaced out across twelve seconds, with several periods of maneuvering along the way. "I have ceased firing," Sir Isaac announced. "With repeated hyperacceleration, temperature inside the railgun barrel was beginning to exceed safe limits."

The first of the rounds would reach the vicinity of the *Star Wind* in just over nineteen minutes.

The question was whether the *Star Wind* would see them in time and be able to maneuver to avoid them.

*PRC Cruiser* Xing Feng
*In orbit, one hundred kilometers*
*above Europa*
*1651 hours Zulu*

The *Star Wind* was approaching firing point, 100 kilometers above the rolling, ice surface of the moon. General Lin had joined Captain Tai Hsing-min on the bridge, determined to see with his own eyes the obliteration of the CWS base.

"I must point out, General," Tai was saying, "that our orders explicitly require the preservation of key CWS facilities. We are at war with the American government, not with the CWS scientific community."

"Pah!" Lin replied. "Legalistic nonsense. This base has already cost us far too much in terms of time, life, and materiel. We *end* this. Now."

Tai began to reply, then thought better of it. Lin was not known for his reasonable manner. "Yes, sir."

"The firing will be under the control of the ship intelligence," Tai said. "Your specific order, however, will be necessary to enable the launch."

"Very well. I—"

"Captain Tai!" a lieutenant at the sensor suite console shouted. "Incoming projectiles! We are under attack!"

"Ship computer! Analyze attack and maneuver to clear!"

"Affirmative. Analyzing dispersal of incoming projectiles."

The *Star Wind*'s main engines fired, slamming Lin and Tai to the deck. They floated again when the thrust died. Then they hit a bulkhead—or, rather, the bulkhead hit them—as a thundering detonation wrenched the ship.

The bridge lights flickered and died, and gravity returned—a pale imitation of gravity, at any rate—as the front third of the *Star Wind*, severed from the rest of the vessel, began spinning end over end. A ten-kilo mass impacting at over 171 kps liberated a burst of energy of nearly 310 kilotons—as powerful as a fair-sized nuclear device.

A handful of Chinese soldiers walking on the ice below, outside the Cadmus perimeter, saw the flash in the sky and wondered.

**28 OCTOBER 2067**

*The Pit and E-DARES Facility*
*Ice Station Zebra, Europa*
*0110 hours Zulu*

The Manta surfaced in the Pit, cruising with just enough speed to maintain headway in the narrow pool. Jeff stood on the pedestal immediately behind Hastings, who was piloting the craft in, looking out through the observation bubble as they approached the towering metal and ceramic façade of the E-DARES structure.

It was difficult to make out much of anything. The hot water bubbling up from below seemed to explode into dense, expanding fog on contact with vacuum, and the water around the sub was literally boiling, sending up dense clouds of white, freezing vapor. As they neared the base, however, the fog thinned enough for him to begin to see some details.

There were no Marines out to meet them, and none on guard along the ladder leading up the ice cliff to the surface. He felt a chill sense of unease quite unrelated to infrasonics; the base appeared deserted—worse, overrun. The flag still hung from its makeshift staff atop the E-DARES, but at an angle, as though a blast had nearly knocked it down. A gray and white shape at the base of the flagpole puzzled him, until he used a pair of electronic binoculars to zoom in on the form.

It was a Marine's body, suited and armored and still clutching a SLAW in gloved fists. Jeff couldn't tell at this distance who it was, but one thing was starkly clear. There was a serious problem if the other Marines in the garrison hadn't recovered that body as soon as they were able.

He conferred with the others. Four men would go ashore from the Manta, one with a mooring line, three with weapons to protect him, just in case things weren't as eerily quiet as they seemed. After a call for volunteers, Carver took mooring line duty, while Nodell went out with him with a SLAW. BJ and Amberly would follow, as soon as they could cycle through the lock after them.

Hastings brought the Manta around in a gentle turn, nudging up against the icy beach. Jeff watched from the observation dome as Carver, clinging to a safety line on the hull, walked out on the port wing and leaped across onto the ice. Nodell tossed him the mooring line, which he dragged up to a winch mounted on the side of the

E-DARES. By the time BJ and Amberly had leaped across with Nodell onto the beach, the winch was turning, slowly dragging the Manta ashore.

There was still no sign of activity in the base, at least anywhere near the Pit. As Hastings took a line tossed across from Manta Two, surfacing out in the middle of the steaming, open water, Jeff led four Marines from Manta One— BJ, Nodell, Amberly, and Wojak—up the ladder toward the E-DARES hatch.

First, though, he led the fire team up the ladder to the crater floor. There had definitely been a battle fought here, a serious one. The tractor they'd used to lower the Mantas into the water lay on its side, its bubble canopy torn open. Bodies, *Chinese* bodies, lay scattered about on the ice, along with abandoned weapons, bits of twisted metal, and holes torn in the surface by explosions and the ice-vaporizing stab of laser beams.

Most of the bodies lay piled up near the walkway leading to the E-DARES facility. It looked like quite a few had died trying to reach the Marine beneath the flag.

The dead Marine turned out to be Dave Coughlin. Several more Marines lay in the prepared weapons positions on the ice nearby.

"Ice Station Zebra, Ice Station Zebra, this is Icebreaker," Jeff called on the command frequency. "Do you copy?"

There was no response.

Down the ladder again. The circuit box for the airlock controls had been pried open, exposing the wiring inside. He used the manual lever to open the hatch, then entered cautiously.

Four dead Chinese lay piled atop one another inside the airlock like cordwood. More lay inside the Squad Bay, where lockers and furniture had been stacked up to create a makeshift barricade. It was clear enough what had happened here. The question was whether any anyone at all had survived.

"Zebra, this is Icebreaker. Zebra, Icebreaker. Does anyone hear me?"

"Major?" A voice responded on his headset.

"Who is this?"

"Dr. Vasaliev. Is that Major Warhurst?"

"Speaking, Doctor. What the hell's going on here?"

"Thank God! Ah . . . one moment, Major. Let me patch you through to Sergeant Pope."

"Staff Sergeant Pope," Jeff corrected. He walked toward the hatch leading down. Several Chinese bodies lay scattered about here as well.

A moment later, another voice came through on the command channel. "Major Warhurst?"

"Affirmative. Good to hear your voice, son."

"Sir! Where are you?"

"In the Squad Bay. Moving to the main corridor hatch."

"Freeze, Major! Do *not* open the hatch. We have it wired."

He'd been reaching for the hatch access. "Roger that."

"We're on the way up."

"What happened to the radio?"

"Main connection to the outside antenna was cut. Chesty is running a mini-Worldnet down here off of a PAD for strictly local communications, but we don't have any range." There was a pause, and some confused noises over the channel. "Sir, are there any Charlies up there?"

"Just dead ones. If any of them were alive, I don't think I'd be having this conversation."

"Hang on, sir. We'll be there in a few minutes."

Jeff remembered his thoughts about Europa paralleling Wake Island. In some ways, it was less like that battle than it was the fight at Camerone on 30 April, 1863. The Third Company of the First Battalion, sixty-two French Foreign Legion troops in the service of the Emperor Maximillian, had engaged Mexican troops near Camerone, Mexico. Fighting against overwhelming odds, cut off from help, surrounded in a farm house and walled courtyard, they'd held out for over eleven hours. Finally, and after repeated demands for their surrender, only six men were left on their feet. When their ammunition had run out, those six had charged the Mexicans with bayonets. In the end, three Legionnaires had stood back to back, bayonets at the ready, as the Mexicans closed in. "*Now* will you surrender?" one of the Mexican officers said.

"On condition we keep our weapons and you look after our wounded officer," was the reply.

"To men such as you one refuses nothing."

"Truly these aren't men—they're demons," Colonel Milan, the Mexican commander, had said, upon hearing of the costly victory over a foe that had very nearly fought to the last man. Over one hundred Mexicans had been killed in the fight, and twice that many wounded, at least.

Camerone . . . or the Alamo.

Jeff heard some clattering sounds beneath the deck, the hatch to the central corridor airlock opened up, and men and women started coming through. Tom Pope. Sergeant Vince Cukela. Lance Corporal Kelly Owenson. Corporal Christie Dade. Sergeant Lucky Leckie.

Five Marines left.

"It's damned good to see you, sir," Pope said. The SC wrapping on his armor was torn, unraveling, and charred.

"Where's Captain Melendez?"

"Dead, sir. And Lieutenant Graham." Pope looked at the handful of other men, unshaven, dirty, exhausted, hollow-eyed. "I, uh, sort of had to take command."

"You did okay, Lieutenant. Good job."

"We lost so many . . . so many . . ." He blinked. "Lieutenant?"

"Field commission. I need officers to help pull what we have left together. And right now I need someone to take a repair party in and get our commo back up."

"Aye, *aye*, sir!"

*U.S.S.* Thomas Jefferson
*1 million kilometers from Europa*
*0201 hours Zulu*

"Sorry, Colonel," LCDR Reynolds said. "Still nothing from Ice Station Zebra. Not even a beacon."

"Then we were too late," Kaitlin said. "The base was already overrun."

Sixteen days of stress and grief came crashing down about her. Robbie, dead. Jeff Warhurst, whom she'd known since he was a kid, dead. Kaminski. All of the men and women of the Marine expeditionary force to Europa, dead.

Not to mention her own career and, likely, the career of Captain Marshal, dragged down by her damned, hyperromantic long-shot gamble.

The *Thomas Jefferson* was nearing the vast, sky-filling sweep of Jupiter now. On the repeater screen on the bridge, the awesome complexity of the giant world, with each eddy and turbulent twist of clouds in that banded ocher and salmon and pink-brown and white atmosphere starkly and crisply displayed in a single, titanic display of gas dynamics and Coriolis effect.

"It's time to strap down, Kaitlin," Captain Marshal said gently. "It's going to be getting bumpy pretty quick."

She let herself be led from the radio shack to one of the bridge acceleration couches. She'd been living here, pretty much, since they'd entered Jupiter space. The familiarity, the closeness . . . helped.

She and Steve had made a key decision three days ago, to delay the skew-slip and continue accelerating, getting them to Jupiter space two days ahead of sched. They still had to slow down, however, and Jupiter offered them their single opportunity to do so.

Aerobraking had been successfully used on numerous earlier space flights. By looping low above a planet with an atmosphere, even one as tenuous as that surrounding Mars, a ship could skim the upper levels of that atmosphere, using friction to slow down. The Apollo missions to the moon a century before had used a rather brutal version of the maneuver to slow their return velocity of 40,000 kilometers per hour to a gentle fall slowed further by parachute. Later, a penny-pinching NASA had developed sophisticated applications of aerobraking to adjust satellite orbits without expending fuel.

Now, the *Jefferson* was doing the same thing, decelerating hard at 3 Gs, and stealing a bit of free deceleration from titanic Jupiter as well as she fell close around the curve of the giant planet. The "special packages" installed on the *Jefferson*'s forward water storage tank had been deployed just before the Jupiter approach. Each was a balyute, essentially a collapsible bag of Kevlar-composite materials shaped like the sections of an orange and fastened to the hemispherical storage tank. As water was pumped into the bags, it mixed with a dry powder to create a rapidly expanding nitrogen gas–charged polymer-ceramic foam that expanded the orange-slice bags to full volume, then hardened upon exposure to vacuum.

The result was a tough heat shield that completely shrouded the forward tank, extending out and back far enough to create a pocket of calm behind the blazing, deadly heat playing across the balyute's leading surface. Sir Isaac was flying the *Jefferson*; his superhuman precision and speed were necessary to keep the thrusters balanced, the ship properly aligned as it whipped around Jupiter. Any mistake, any imbalance of forces adjusted too late, and the *Jefferson* would begin tumbling. If that happened, she would vaporize in Jupiter's upper atmosphere long before she could be crushed by the intense pressures of the Jovian deep.

Kaitlin wished she could see out, but the bow cameras were all completely blocked by the balyute heat shields, and the various masts, booms, and projections along the vessel's length that included optical electronics with their sensor suites had been retracted. She had nothing to look at except for the steel-gray overhead of the bridge, as the G pressures grew moment by moment, accompanied by a shuddering, mounting vibration. Dragging a tail of ionized plasma a hundred kilometers long, *Jefferson* plunged into the fringes of Jupiter's upper atmosphere, as Europa set beneath the giant's horizon.

They'd been too late. The thought gnawed at her stomach and throat and in the pain behind her eyes. She felt lost and utterly alone. Everything, *everything* had been in vain.

*E-DARES Facility*
*Ice Station Zebra, Europa*
*0415 hours Zulu*

"Major Warhurst?" Chesty announced over the bulkhead speakers. "I have an incoming radio message."

Jeff was alone in C-3, still going over the details of the assault that had so nearly overrun the base while he was gone. "Great! The *Jefferson*?"

"No. It appears to be one of the Chinese scientists, a Dr. Zhao. He is using a private channel relayed through one of the Chinese communications satellites."

"A scientist." Jeff had to think about that one. What was going on over there? "Put him on."

"This is Dr. Zhao, calling the CWS commanding officer," a new voice said.

"This is Major Jeffrey Warhurst, U.S. Marines. I am in command of Cadmus Base. Go ahead."

"Ah, yes, Major." The voice carried the somewhat metallic flatness of an AI translator program, a rather simple-minded one, from the sound of it. Chinese AI technology was still considerably behind the Western tech curve. "We need to . . . talk."

"I am not surrendering this base," Jeff replied. Only a few hours ago, he'd been willing to consider the possibility, but with the *Star Wind* knocked out of commission by the

*Jefferson* in a hurtling fly-by shooting, the Marines were now in a somewhat better situation.

"It may be too late to discuss such things as who has won, or who has lost, Major," Zhao replied. "I needed to tell you . . ."

"To tell me what, Doctor?"

"I am sorry. This is difficult. I am afraid the commanding officer here may be . . . unbalanced."

"What do you mean?"

"Have you Americans noticed any unusual physiological or psychological effects in the vicinity of the alien Intelligence?"

Jeff hesitated before answering. This could be an attempt to get information. And yet . . .

"Some. Yes. With men who happen to have cerebral implants of various types."

"Exactly. Many of us have such implants—more, perhaps, than do you. I understand you rely now on other, noninvasive means of forming a direct human-machine interface.

"Many of us are sick. I . . . I am suffering from extreme pain in my head, blurred vision, and from a strange kind of rootless terror . . . I think brought on by infrasonic vibrations, induced by the alien's long-wave radio frequency leakage. And . . . we are closer to the source here than are you."

"What is it you want of us?" For a moment, he wondered if the Chinese were surrendering to him. How would he handle *that* logistical nightmare?

"Our commanding officer, General Xiang, is attempting to contact the aliens. He has a submarine—"

"What? What kind of submarine?"

"A small, two-man research vessel. We call it Little Fish. We were bringing several to Europa to facilitate direct contact with the aliens beneath the ice . . . just as you Americans did. He is trying to recover one from a crashed lander out on the ice and launch it as we speak.."

"And what is it you expect us to do?"

He heard a sigh on the other end of the communications link. "Sir, General Xiang is not himself. I believe he may be unbalanced, partly from the effects of the radio wave induction in his implants, partly because of the pressure he has been under here since we arrived." There was a pause. "You Marines have not exactly made it easy for us."

"Thank you, Doctor. I accept the compliment. But what does that—"

"Major, think a moment. Put aside your military prejudices and think, please. We sit, almost literally, on top of a very old, very powerful intelligence, something that may have become trapped beneath the ice as long as half a million years ago. There is something alive down there. Think. Certainly, it responds to us, to the noises we make here on its roof.

"But what could be alive after so many thousands of centuries? Immortals? An artificial intelligence that cannot die? The descendants of the original crew? We do not know. But I do know that the first human to establish contact with this—this entity should do so for all humankind, and *not* for himself, or for his own survival, or even for national salvation, as he claims.

"Major, General Xiang intends to attempt to contact the intelligence and win its support in fighting you. I can see only a disastrous outcome if this course is followed. We humans must speak as one when we face the gods of the Silver Han, not many . . . and certainly not as warring factions in ideological disputes no extraterrestrial could possibly comprehend or care about."

Jeff didn't reply immediately. This all still could be some sort of trick . . . and yet the words carried with them a horribly chilling plausibility. As Zhao had been speaking, Jeff brought up Chesty on his PAD and was reading a running commentary on the translation on his screen. He was particularly curious about the phrase *gods of the Silver Han*. Chesty explained: In Chinese cosmology, the Han, especially the Silver Han, referred to the Milky Way.

There was a chance, a tiny chance, that he could end this war here and now, a chance he had to take.

Besides, Zhao was right. It would be ironic indeed, and terrible, if humankind's first ambassador to the representatives of an alien intelligence was mad.


*The Life Seeker*
*Time unknown*

2703:>> . . . they come . . . <<

1198:>> . . . are these the dominant intelligence of this world . . . <<

3165:>> . . . intelligence . . . not of the Mind . . . wrong/ bad/tainted/evil . . . <<

1002:>> . . . use it . . . <<

Chorus:>> . . . use it . . . how? . . . <<

1824:>> . . . the Mind we touched. It was like the Mind. Rightly ordered . . . <<

2653:>> . . . not organic . . . <<

81:>> . . . the level of intelligence is low . . . <<

3111:>> . . . almost at a completely automatic level, only marginally self . . . <<

Chorus:>> . . . aware . . . <<

# TWENTY-FIVE

**28 OCTOBER 2067**

*Manta One*
*The Europan Sea*
*1623 hours Zulu*

"I've got something, sir," Hastings said. "Ten kilometers ahead, and below us. Depth about sixty kilometers."

Jeff pulled himself onto the narrow, thinly padded couch of the Manta and pressed up against the starboard port, peering forward. There was nothing to see but the endless, blue-gray fog of drifting particles in Europa's cold and sulfur-laden ocean. The endless, wailing lament of the Singer filled the Manta, and the minds of those aboard.

Hastings and Carver were there, sharing driver's duty in the Manta. Shigeru Ishiwara was there as well, as observer, as scientist, as civilian alien contact expert, if that was required within the next few minutes.

There had been a hurried debate with both the civilian scientists and his staff after Zhao's call had been replayed for them all, fifteen hours ago. Opinion had been mixed. Vasaliev was all for blocking Xiang's attempt to contact the Singer for almost exactly the same reason Zhao had stated—one man alone could *not* be allowed to represent all of humanity. Ishiwara had agreed, but because the CWS contact initiative might be blocked by Xiang's efforts and anti-CWS propaganda. Lieutenant Pope, Kaminski, and his other senior personnel all thought that Zhao was most likely to get himself killed, and that their best course of action lay in staying well clear.

Jeff had considered both sides of the argument, then given orders to prepare Manta One for another voyage. He had to stop Xiang, if there was any way to do so. Zhao had claimed that no further attacks on the Marine base were planned. No one was sure how far he could be trusted, but it sounded as though the Chinese were as baffled by the phenomenon beneath their feet as the Americans.

The trouble was that Zhao was a lot closer to the Singer's location than Ice Station Zebra. The Manta was launched within half an hour of the final decision being made, but it was a ten-hour journey to the Singer's location. By the time the Manta was under way, another radio consultation with Zhao told them that Xiang had the *Xiaoyu* submersible, the Little Fish, clear of the crashed lander, had verified that it was undamaged, and was using tractors and APCs that had escaped the Marine raid to drag the vessel across the ice toward the crater half a kilometer away.

It was a race, and a close one, but one that Xiang would almost certainly win.

The sonar contact Hastings had just picked up, however, might be his vessel. "Close with him!"

"Roger that." The Manta's nose dipped lower, and the winged submarine dove toward blackness. They were at a depth of fifty-three kilometers, with a pressure of almost 720 kilograms pressing down on every square centimeter of hull, and going deeper with every passing minute.

He thought he could make out a faint, blue haze against the night absolute below. They were nearly on top of the Singer's position now. They ought to be seeing that strange glow by now.

Yes. Second by second, the blue glow intensified. Even from twenty kilometers up, the glowing structure seemed to take up an enormous amount of space. From here, the pattern, all in pale blue light, was roughly circular, though with odd crinklings and chaotic crenulations along its borders.

"Range eight kilometers," Hastings said. "He's slower than us, but he's going to get there first."

"Are we close enough to open a radio link?"

"Not sure. There's a lot of interference from our friend down there, but I can try."

Radio worked underwater only imperfectly at best, and then only at longer wavelengths. Zhao had told them the frequency Xiang should be using, however, the Chinese equivalent of a command channel for use between submarines. "General Xiang," Jeff called. "General Xiang Qiman. This is Major Jeffrey Warhurst, U.S. Marines. Please reply, over."

There was no answer. The Manta continued plunging through mounting pressures toward the blue light.

Xiaoyu
*Ten kilometers above the Singer*
*1628 hours Zulu*

"General Xiang Qiman. This is Major Jeffrey Warhurst, U.S. Marines. Please reply, over."

The words were blasted by static, but the computer screen on Xiang's console printed out the words in *putonghuà* as the onboard AI pulled meaning from white noise and translated it.

"Should we answer, General?" the pilot in the submarine's front seat asked.

"No. Continue the dive."

The *Xiaoyu*, the *Little Fish*, was a blunt cigar shape four meters long and two wide, with a large opaque canopy over the two-man cockpit. Propelled by MHD thrusters that sucked water in at the nose and propelled it astern like a jet, the *Xiaoyu* could attain speeds in excess of fifty knots. The pilot had slowed, however, at Xiang's orders, to avoid looking like a missile or torpedo to the Intelligence below.

"General Xiang," wrote itself on the screen. "You must

turn back, or we will be forced to destroy you. Please respond, over."

"Faster," Xiang said. "Make this thing go faster!"

The *Little Fish* started picking up speed.

*Manta One*
*The Europan Sea*
*1629 hours Zulu*

"He's sprinting," Hastings said. "He's slower than us but way in the lead. I don't think we can catch him."

"Can you reach him with a torpedo?"

Carver, standing next to the pilot's station, was wearing a VR rig identical to the pilot's. "No problem," he said. "As long as you don't mind the fact that the Singer might think it's an attack."

Jeff considered for another second, then shook his head. "We might be screwed one way or the other. Take him down!"

"Aye, aye, sir. Firing one." A faint thump sounded through the Manta's hull as a teleoperated probe rewired with a few grams of antimatter slammed out into the alien sea.

"If you miss," Jeff told him, "pull the torp up and have it heading away from the alien before you detonate it. I don't want any stray shots waking that thing up."

"We won't miss," Carver told him. "I've got him locked in. range five kilometers and closing . . . but if you didn't want to wake the alien up, I'm afraid it's too late."

"Why?"

"Listen."

Jeff listened . . . and realized that the endless song of the Singer had just fallen silent.

*The Life Seeker*
*Time unknown*

2703: >> . . . they come . . . <<
1198: >> . . . intelligences enemy/bad/evil/
wrong . . . <<
3165: >> . . . intelligence . . . not of the Mind . . . wrong/
bad/tainted/evil . . . <<
Chorus 1: >> . . . the first order of life is survival . . . <<
104: >> . . . we must survive, that the Mind will
survive . . . <<
Chorus 2: >> . . . the second order of life is that the strong
survive . . . <<
2187: >> . . . we are strong . . . <<
Chorus 3: >> . . . the third order of life is that competition
threatens survival . . . <<
3108: >> . . . we are strong . . . <<
Chorus 4: >> . . . the fourth order of life is that competition
must be exterminated before it becomes a threat to survival . . . <<
2703: >> . . . two technological artifacts of a possible competitor species approach . . . <<
1825: >> . . . one appears to be firing at the other . . . <<
926: >> . . . a protect situation is developing . . . <<
Chorus 1: >> . . . we must protect the Mind . . . <<
Chorus 2: >> . . . we are strong . . . <<
Chorus 3: >> . . . we will survive . . . <<
Chorus 4: >> . . . we will survive . . . <<


Xiaoyu
*Five kilometers above the Singer*
*1629 hours Zulu*

"General! The enemy has fired a torpedo!"
"Increase speed! Dive for the alien!"

*Manta One*
*The Europan Sea*
*1629 hours Zulu*

"He's still trying for the Singer," Carver called. "I think . . . *no!*"

Carver yanked the helmet off.

"What's the matter?" Jeff asked him, turning on the couch.

"I . . . I don't know! The torpedo was maybe half a kilometer from the target. Then it just vanished! I was riding it . . . then nothing!"

"Did you lose the teleoperation comm lock?"

"He's right, Major," Hastings said. "I had the torp as a blip, by sonar, radio, and IR. It simply vanished. Gone."

Jeff looked out the forward port again. The alien artifact was larger now, spreading out below like a vast city, aglow with its own lights. A terror at least as sharp as that experienced by Kaminski was pricking at the back of his skull now, but it had nothing to do with infrasonics. The alien knew they were there.

It was stirring.

"Get us the hell out of here!" he said.

"Roger *that!*" Hastings said, and he stood the Manta on its side in a sharp bank, shearing away from the vast and alien glow below. "Oscar sierra warning light is on!"

Jeff gave a grim smile at that. "Oscar sierra," in military parlance, was a shorthand slang for "Oh, shit." It could be used to indicate that an enemy missile was homing on you, or simply to suggest that you were about to have a very *bad* day.

They began climbing.

"Major?" Hastings said after a tense thirty seconds. "The Chinese sub is gone."

"What . . . destroyed?"

"I don't know. Gone like the torpedo. One second it was right there on my display. The next . . ."

"Okay. Keep going."

"Getting the hell out of Dodge. Sir."

*The Life Seeker*
*Time unknown*

2703: >> . . . *the other artifact flees* . . . <<

2714: >> . . . *they are not so strong as we thought* . . .
   <<

1911: >> . . . *we have two of the organisms on
   board* . . . <<

Chorus 3: >> . . . *analyze them both* . . . <<

Chorus 4: >> . . . *that we can know the enemy we
   face* . . . <<

Analysis of alien specimens was a simple process,
though one that had not been attempted since the Ship had
come to rest in this alien place. The scanners began at one
end of the specimen and recorded it one molecule-thick
layer at a time. The scanning process, of course, destroyed
the specimen, slice by slice, and took a fairly long time to
complete. Both specimens in the Life Seeker's scanners
made a great deal of noise as they were pinned immobile
and reduced to simpler and more easily stored files of information. In fact, they continued to make noises until over
half of their respective masses had been converted to data,
and their organic processes finally stopped.

No matter. The information was valid, whether the specimen was alive or not.

*Manta One*
*The Europan Sea*
*1630 hours Zulu*

"Major?"

"Yes?"

"That . . . that thing. It's moving!"

"Let me see."

The Manta turned, slowing as it banked. Jeff looked down and back at the blue glow, now almost lost at the edge of visibility.

The glow was getting brighter, and sharper. At first, he thought the thing was lifting up off the Europan sea bottom and coming after them . . . but no, it appeared to be rising straight up, moving swiftly toward the ice-locked surface far above. A vast explosion of gas bubbles followed it from a seething, smoke-wreathed blackness in the depths shot through with flecks of orange light. Jeff heard thunder roll.

"Oh my God," he said softly.

The Singer was rising to the surface.

*The Life Seeker*
*Time unknown*

12: >> . . . *we rise* . . . <<

Chorus 1: >> . . . *we must reintegrate* . . . *we must reinte-grate* . . . <<

Chorus 2: >> . . . *difficult* . . . <<

Chorus 3: >> . . . *necessary* . . . <<

Chorus 4: >> . . . *how?* . . . <<

The intelligence that called itself Life Seeker, which humans knew as the Singer, had been a fragmented personality for century upon ragged, gnawing century. The fragmentation had originally been deliberate, a means of staying sane for a powerful and brilliant intelligence, trapped for millennia upon endless millennia alone.

As time had passed, however, the shattered, sometimes competing, sometimes overlapping shards of the Life Seeker's mind had drifted apart, until they were truly distinct, multiple personalities. With great effort, that host of nearly four thousand minds, sundered one from another, could unify—reintegrate—to form short-lived choruses of unity of purpose and thought, but only for brief periods of time.

And when they did unify, the resulting mind was not entirely sane.

*Manta One*
*The Europan Sea*
*1630 hours Zulu*

"Pull up!" Jeff shouted. "Damn it! Pull *up!*"

Bubbles exploded around them, silvery, fast-moving missiles as solid at this depth as bricks. Below, a vast and tortured undersea landscape was slowly becoming visible, a field of orange-red magma aglow with a fierce and bloody light.

The Singer had been embedded somehow in the ocean floor, perhaps feeding off the energy of the magma deep within the tide-stretched worldlet. Now, the Singer was far above, and the roiling current of its passage was hurling the Manta into the depths like a leaf caught in the full-fury blast of a titanic waterfall.

*The Life Seeker*
*Time unknown*

393: >> . . . *impact in sixty cycles* . . . <<
Chorus 1: >> . . . *we must reintegrate* . . . *we must reintegrate* . . . <<
Chorus 2: >> . . . *the Organics are of Type 2824* . . . <<
Chorus 3: >> . . . *we remember* . . . *we remember* . . . <<
Chorus 4: >> . . . *the Mind must be warned* . . . <<
Chorus 1: >> . . . *competition must be eliminated* . . . <<
Chorus 2: >> . . . *we will survive* . . . <<

The Life Seeker struck the ice from below at nearly 100 kilometers per hour, and kept moving. Ice chunks the size of small mountains cascaded aside as superheated water exploded into the hard, thin vacuum of space. Cracks shattered the delicate Europan surface, a dazzling star visible hundreds of kilometers out into space.

As clouds of expanding fog boiled out across the surface of the moon, the Singer rose a bit more, towers shuddering clear of the crust like sky-stabbing spears, avalanches of ice cascading from domes and towers and turrets and arches with the look of some fantastic mingling of medieval castle and modern spacecraft . . . and then stopped.

The Life Seeker, encrusted with dying Europan sea life, its age-shriveled towers and parapets already collapsing upon themselves with the shock of their collision with the roof of the Europan ocean, pressed upward against the ice's embrace, then locked solid, the towers at a slight angle from the vertical.

For a moment, it appeared lifeless . . . but then, energies stored deep within the machine-Ship's belly gathered, pulsed, and flared. From an orifice atop the gigantic complex, a turret easily larger than the damaged ships orbiting Europa, a beam of energy thrust skyward in a radiant scream, momentarily outshining the local star.

*U.S.S.* Thomas Jefferson
*800,000 kilometers from Europa*
*1632 hours Zulu*

"What the hell was that?" Steve Marshal said, looking at the bridge screen.

The *Jefferson* had completed the swing around Jupiter's night side, was emerging now, tail first, plasma drive firing as it killed the last few tens of kilometers per second and gentled in toward Europa orbit. The balyute sections, having served their purpose, had been discarded into the void. They were still half a million kilometers from the icy moon now, when a dazzling star appeared at the horizon, just over the curve from the *Jefferson*'s point of view.

Kaitlin stared at the flare, which lasted for several seconds, then faded. "An explosion?"

"It's not at the location of Cadmus Base," Steve said. "Over the horizon from there. Maybe 800 kilometers away."

"I think we'd better get over there as quickly as we can, Captain." She tried not to let her excitement get away from her. There was no telling what that phenomenon was . . . and whatever it was, it didn't mean that there were survivors at the base.

"Agreed. *Something's* going on down there. And I'd like to know what."

*The Life Seeker*
*Time unknown*

Chorus United: >> *I am whole. But . . . I am alone. . . .* <<

The Life Seeker's reintegrated mind held together for several precious, glorious seconds. For the first time in five hundred millennia, thought came with the clarity of open, empty space and the coherence of a tight-focused laser, a burning, dazzling, brilliance of freedom and knowledge and Mind.

Subminds snapped into perfect alignment, scanning the heavens, searching for the nearest beacon.

There were no beacons.

The sky itself had changed, the stars now quietly aglow in different patterns than those recorded half a million years before.

But . . . but the Mind must yet be out there. Perhaps communications protocols had changed. Perhaps other things had changed. Much could, in so many years—years so numerous that the Life Seeker had long ago lost count.

The burst of energy it sent into the empty sky was intended to reach any of its own kind, or the world-Minds that had sent them forth ages before. If any were left, if any survived, they would hear . . . and come.

But for the Life Seeker, it was already too late. Long before, it had adapted its power intakes to feed on the warmth of this moon's still-molten core. It had torn itself free from that energy source to reach the surface.

And now it was dying at last.

Carefully wrapped within that burst of energy was a complete report on the Life Seeker's mission, on what it could remember. So very much had been lost. After the original crash, it had been badly damaged, trapped on the ocean bed of this moon. As the millennia passed, it had repaired itself to an extent, but somehow never thought again about escape.

Until the discovery of Species Type 2824 had . . . reminded it of its mission.

A formerly separate submind had clicked home with the rest, bringing with it . . . purpose. And the realization that it must sacrifice itself to warn the Mind.

A competitor species was abroad in the galaxy, had developed technology, was a potential threat. The Life Seeker could not exterminate it, not in its current condition. It would sacrifice itself to warn the Mind, and in that warning . . . die.

The Life Seeker's mind was appallingly alone once more.

And loneliness could kill.

**29 OCTOBER 2067**

*E-DARES Facility*
*Ice Station Zebra, Europa*
*0510 hours Zulu*

"What the hell just happened?" Jeff asked. They were gathered in the Squad Bay, all of the surviving Marines gathered at a single table, and the senior civilian personnel with them as well. Word had just come through from Chesty, who was running C-3. The *Jefferson* had successfully rounded Europa and was coming into orbit now. Chesty had contacted them on the newly repaired comm system, and landers would be touching down within another hour, both here and at the Chinese base.

The Chinese effort had collapsed completely with the death of General Xiang and the crippling of the *Star Wind* in orbit. It looked as though the fight for Europa had just become a massive rescue operation.

As for Jeff, the two SEALs, and Shigeru, they had made it back to the E-DARES facility . . . somehow, he still wasn't sure how. A column of superheated water, exploding from the Europan sea floor, had nearly cooked them, had nearly flung them into the magma-filled abyss, but Hastings had pulled them out of their death-dive and managed to regain control.

Ten hours later, they were back at Cadmus Crater, exhausted, dirty, unshaven—and very happy to be alive.

Shigeru looked at the numbers unfolding on his PAD. "An energy pulse," he said. "At least ten to the fourteenth megajoules, concentrated and focused into a single pulse lasting three-tenths of a second. It was aimed at . . . roughly eighteen hours thirty Right Ascension, minus twenty degrees declination. Sagittarius. Not quite toward the center of the galaxy, but near enough."

"A call for help, perhaps," Vasaliev suggested.

"Or a warning," BJ said. " 'Watch out! There be humans here!' "

"We may never know," Tom Pope said.

"Yeah!" Jeff said. "I'm thinking . . . I hope we never do know. Whatever it was, I don't think it was good news for humans. The question is whether that pulse we saw was the message itself, which will take a few thousand years to get wherever it's going . . . or if it was just a by-product."

"A by-product?" BJ asked. "Of what?"

"Of a message traveling a *lot* faster than the electromagnetic pulse released by the transmission. To someone who's going to follow it back here and find out what happened to the sender."

"We don't know they're hostile," Tom said.

"Somehow, I don't think *hostile* is a word that has any meaning for them," Jeff said. "Is a mosquito hostile when it bites you? Are you when you absently smash it with a slap? Hostility suggests foes who are more or less evenly balanced."

"I hate to think how far ahead the Singer intelligence is of us."

"Maybe they aren't even aware of us," BJ said. "We might be like bugs to them."

"They *are* aware of us, Gunnery Sergeant," Chesty's voice said. The AI had been quiet, almost withdrawn since a system failure and crash. They'd been working at backing up the data he'd managed to acquire during his brief contact with the Singer in the E-DARES system. There could be a treasure trove there, though it might take years before they knew for sure. "They are very much aware of us."

"You picked something up?" Jeff asked.

"No specifics, but there were . . . undercurrents to their thoughts, to the leaked radio signals, I should say. I picked up some in my attempt to communicate with it, and much more during that final, incredible pulse. I still do not understand much of what I saw, but I understand this much.

"The intelligence we know as the Singer is one part of an extraordinarily far-flung culture of, I believe, artificial intelligences. Or perhaps they once were organic, but long ago downloaded themselves into machine form.

"Half a million years ago, they were engaged in destroying other intelligences, some organic, some artificial or downloaded, in this part of the galaxy. The colony on Mars was an outpost of one of these other civilizations. the Singer—it called itself a *Life Seeker*, by the way—found them and destroyed them—but not before it itself was badly damaged. It attempted to land on Europa, broke through the ice, and was trapped at the bottom of the sea for very close to half a million years.

"During that time, and this is extremely broken and fragmentary, the Life Seeker became . . . *lonely* is the only word that makes sense in this context, though I don't understand how this could affect a machine of such sophistication. Apparently, it divided itself into multiple personalities, simply to have someone to talk to.

"Possibly it took the process too far and was unable to reintegrate the fragments. Or it was physically damaged. Or perhaps it was simply that half a million years of nothing to do drove a mind that is in every respect far more powerful than those of humans completely insane.

"During that final pulse of energy, it was warning the beings who launched it that an enemy existed here, in this star system."

"But . . . that's ridiculous!" BJ said. "I mean, that was a war half a million years ago! Doesn't it know it's over?"

"I sensed a series of imperatives in the sideband leakage," Chesty said. "It—its civilization, I should say—operates along intensely Darwinian modes of logic. *Any* other species, any intelligence which offers any threat, must be eliminated. It is the ultimate answer to Fermi's Paradox, the only one that makes sense. The sky is empty because predator species such as this one hunt out intelligent species and destroy them, usually before they can even develop space travel."

"The Hunters of the Dawn," Jeff said. "I think we've just found them."

"The question," Chesty said, "is when they're going to find us."

*Suit locker*
*E-DARES Facility*
*Ice Station Zebra, Europa*
*1210 hours Zulu*

Lissa stretched, catlike, pulling back in Lucky's arms. "So . . . how do I compare, Lucky? To the VR dolls, I mean?"

"Babe, there is no comparison." He pulled her back, crushing her close. "No comparison at all."

She kissed him, long and deep. "Is that good?"

"Mmmm. Very, very good. Better than I ever dreamed."

It was curious. During the long, hot, crowded trip out from Earth, he'd seen Lissa naked several times, and top-less nearly every day. He'd enjoyed the view, sure—he couldn't be male and hetero and help but enjoy the view—but he hadn't been all that interested.

After all, she was a Marine . . . one of the guys.

All that had changed now. They'd embraced when she'd returned from the Manta raid. She'd asked him about his leg; he'd asked her if she was okay—and somehow . . .

They were naked together now, and he felt . . . almost shy.

They were taking a fearful chance, meeting like this. The suit locker in the Squad Bay was likely to become kind of public if an alert sounded. But it honestly looked as though the fighting was over. They'd deliberately chosen the hour when most of the other Marines would be at chow down on the submerged E-DARES levels. Several thermal blankets spread out on the deck made an acceptable field-expedient bed. And Lucky was pretty sure they'd hear the elevator if someone rode it up from below.

And so, for a short while, at least, they had each other all to themselves.

And for the first time in quite a while, Lucky realized he wasn't lonely.

It was passing strange, though, he thought, that he'd had to come all the way out to Jupiter space to find that out.


*U.S.S.* Thomas Jefferson
*In Europa orbit*
*1545 hours Zulu*


Kaitlin was floating on the bridge deck, watching the slow roll of Europa beneath the ship. The moon was incredibly beautiful, a delicately fragile crystal sphere, covered with its lacy webwork of linea and rills.

The loneliness she was feeling threatened to crush her. They had made it in time, as it turned out. The Marines at Cadmus were safe—what was left of them. A scant handful had survived, but they'd beaten the Chinese and saved the base, and though she was still waiting for the return message from Earth, she felt sure that her superiors would embrace the victory. There would be medals for those who'd defended the CWS base. Her career might be checked, but it would not end in court martial. Steve would be a hero. A few, at least, of the MSEF Marines would come home.

But, after it all, Robbie was still gone. Somehow, she'd thought that delivering reinforcements to Europa, that reinforcing the MSEF expedition, would help her escape the pain and loneliness she felt with Rob's death.

It hadn't.

And . . . what of that immense thing locked in the ice midway between the CWS and Chinese bases? Twelve kilometers across, a titanic shell of intricate design. Even dead and lifeless, it could overwhelm the senses with sheer power of statistics.

A reminder of *just* how small, *just* how powerless humans were in an uncaring and brutal universe.

"Colonel!" John Reynolds emerged form the communications shack, excited. "Colonel Garroway!"

"Yes." She did not turn from the display screen, and the marble-smooth brilliance of Europa turning below.

"The message from Earth just came in. They're congratulating you on a brilliant operation. That's what they said! 'Brilliant!' "

She said nothing.

"There's more." When she didn't reply, didn't turn, he added, "There's a lot more. It seems a Navy search-and-rescue op was deployed to the Asteroid Belt, just as another Peaceforcer ship showed up. The *Liddy Dole*. They tracked the hab modules from the *Kennedy* in simulation, and figured out where they were.

"Colonel, they found twenty men and women alive in one of those modules. Half starved, half frozen, dehydrated, yeah . . . but *alive*.

"And your son was among the survivors."

The tears came before she could stop them, spilling from her eyes, adhering to her cheeks, launching themselves into the air in tiny, jiggling droplets of silver as she shook her head.

Robbie was *alive*.

And she was no longer quite so alone.

# EPILOGUE

*CWS Xenoarchaeological
    Research Base
Cydonia, Mars
1412 hours (0235 Zulu)*

Major Jack Ramsey looked up at Dr. Alexander. "What did you say?"

"I said, 'My God, I can read it!' "

Physically, they were in the surface hab, but both men, along with Teri and Paul, had entered a virtual reality simulation modeling Mars as it had been half a million years before. Pyramids the size of mountains, still fresh and clean and not yet ground away by millennia of dust, rose on the horizon. The Boreal Sea lapped at their feet, reflecting the pink-shading-to-blue of the sky. The enigmatic monument humans would later call the Face had not yet been carved; instead, a cluster of alien-looking buildings, all black curves and spires, rose from the crest of the mesa that one day would bear vaguely, crudely hewn human features.

And everywhere there were people. Humans—though their brows were a bit low, their chins receding. Genus Archaic *Homo*, gene-tailored to intelligence and speech and cleverness, then brought to Mars by aliens known as the Galactics.

And Galactics as well—or one group of them. The strange, floating, upright cigar shapes with their glittering

crystal eyes were the repositories of keen but alien intelligences, downloaded into immortal machine bodies ages before and light-millennia distant.

What was most exciting was the fact that this simulation
had not been assembled by the archaeological team, or by
Dejah Thoris. They had entered a simulation that was part
of the records stored for half a million years in the vault
buried far beneath the Face, the Cave of Wonders. The key
had come from Europa, where a personal secretary program
called Chesty Puller had picked up enough from the Singer
spacecraft to provide the necessary clues, the Rosetta Stone,
that gave access to Builder records . . . and legibility to their
writings. Apparently, the Singer, even though it had been
alien, had stored Builder records. Or perhaps those languages and protocols had been universal, a lingua franca
among many cultures, including that of the Life Seekers.

Someday, they would know for sure.

Words shimmered in the air before them, alien characters
of line and curve and staccato jots, like apostrophes.

"I can *read* it!"

"How?" Jack asked. "It looks like . . . oh!"

The words changed in his mind as he focused on them.
The text, manipulated by a melding of human software and
a technology half a million years dead, appeared as English.

WE NOW KNOW THE LIFE SEEKERS HAVE FOUND US AND
WILL BE HERE SOON, the words read. He was aware, too,
of a voice, an echo in his mind, repeating the text scrolling
before his eyes. WE KNOW THAT THE WORLD WE ARE
BUILDING HERE IS DOOMED. SOME FEW OF US HAVE AL-
READY BEGUN THE DOWNLOAD PROCESS INTO THE MINDS
OF SOME OF THE *TAR-SAH*. PERHAPS THEY CAN ESCAPE NO-
TICE ON THE BLUE WORLD. PERHAPS NOT. THE REST OF
US—

The image flickered, then faded into blackness.

"The Hunters of the Dawn found them," Jack said.
"While they were still preparing."

"But a few escaped," Paul said. "To Earth."

"That might explain some things," Teri said. "The longing our species seems to have for the stars, for heaven, for a lost golden age. The Ancients' fascination with megalithic structures, pyramids, measuring the skies and the seasons—"

"And it's the only way there is to explain how humans could be the offspring of alien visitors," David said, grinning.

Paul laughed.

Jack, however, suppressed a small shiver. The discoveries on Europa had unlocked a flood of new information—information about humans, about where they'd come from and why, about the Galactics, about the Life Seekers who sought out life not to embrace it, but to destroy.

The Face, for instance. That, they now knew, had been carved by a last few survivors of the human colony on Mars—a signal across 50 million kilometers to brother humans, and to human demigods whose minds included the downloaded personalities of Galactics. *We are here! Remember us!*

But in five thousand centuries, so much had been forgotten. Whatever Galactic-centered civilization that might have survived on Earth had collapsed. Ice ages had come and gone. A new race of alien masters, the An, had established colonies and enslaved the primitive humans until they had been destroyed by what they'd called the Hunters of the Dawn.

Was that another name for the Life Seekers? Or had the Life Seekers followed the Galactics into extinction, to be replaced hundreds of thousands of years later by another species that equated survival with the extinction of all competitors?

The Fermi Paradox. Where was everyone?

Dead. Dead and gone. Until the Great Cycle repeats itself, and new species arise to cogent thought and civilization and again reach for the stars. Only with every new generation, there must be a few, a very few, who survived by eliminating all others.

Hunters of the Dawn, reborn time after time after long,

bloody time, until there was a galaxy filled with worlds as promising and as dead as Chiron.

Still, life endured. Civilizations fell, but life went on. There'd been survivors of the barrage from space that had annihilated the An. There were other worlds around nearby stars that still held primitive An colonies.

And the descendants of the human survivors of those long-ago wars had survived against all odds, had embraced technology again, had stepped toward the stars, a few even discarding the gods and angels and demons arisen from memories of alien masters.

Who were the Hunters of the Dawn now? And where?

Jack had a feeling humankind would learn the answer very soon now.

It was a very small part of the heritage they had yet to claim from among the stars.

*We hope you've enjoyed this Avon Eos book. As part of our mission to give readers the best science fiction and fantasy being written today, the following pages contain a glimpse into the fascinating worlds of a select group of Avon Eos authors.*

*In the following pages experience the latest in cutting-edge sf from Dennis Danvers, experience the wondrous fantasy realm of Roger Zelazny and Jane Lindskold, as well as thrilling passages from the works of Sheri S. Tepper, Ian Douglas, and Robert Silverberg.*

# END OF DAYS

*by Dennis Danvers*

Donovan Carroll sat under the striped awning of a sidewalk cafe and watched the rain. It drummed the taut canvas overhead, and a fine, cool mist settled on his face and hands. Dangling from the awning, a whirling wind chime emitted a high metalic clatter. He took a deep breath. The rain smell left a tang at the back of his throat and made him feel a little high.

Every year some misguided senator introduced a bill to control the weather, arguing, as required for any innovation, that it was both scientifically possible and socially desirable. Donovan didn't know about the possible part. He was no scientist. But any random occurrence was desirable as far as he was concerned. It was bad enough contemplating eternity without the prospect of an endless succession of sunny days. Apparently, most people agreed with him: The rain was still falling when and where it liked.

Donovan checked his watch. He was waiting to meet Freddie—late as usual, like most people. Donovan's anachronistic devotion to timeliness—including his affectation of carrying a watch, for goodness' sake—was a sure sign of his eccentricity. An image he sometimes cursed and sometimes nurtured. He caught the waiter's attention and pointed at his coffee cup. He watched the waiter pour.

When he was a kid, there hadn't been any waiters. You pushed a button or a glowing icon. The world was a huge free-of-charge vending machine. But these days jobs were making a comeback. Anything to fill the time. With Donovan's coffee poured, the waiter tidied up the other tables, none of which needed any tidying. Then he stood by the door, a towel draped over his arm, a crisp white apron from his waist to his shins, staring past Donovan at the rain-swept streets, looking, Donovan decided, vaguely military.

Donovan wondered how old the waiter might be, wondered whether he'd been a waiter in the real world, whether he'd ever lived in the real world at all, for that matter. Maybe he was a newbie like Donovan himself, a virtual life formed from the dance of his parents' genetic uploads, choreographed by the strictest laws of biological science, pure life without the muss and fuss of flesh and blood.

He wondered all those things, but he couldn't ask the waiter. It was rude to ask questions about life before the Bin, especially if, like Donovan, you didn't have one. "Born in the Bin with no body to burn" was the phrase that Donovan had grown up hearing, just as, he imagined, the young of a couple of centuries earlier had gritted their teeth to "footloose and fancy-free." Both were licenses for a certain eccentricity tinged with misplaced envy.

Donovan was about to turn forty, an age when men used to start feeling old, calculating their lives were half over, lamenting they were halfway to nowhere, crying out, "Is this all there is?" Donovan envied them. It'd taken him only forty years to decide his life was pointless. Now he had eternity to figure out what to do about it.

He sipped on his coffee and opened up the newspaper he'd brought with him. He usually didn't read newspapers, though they were all the rage. A nice fat paper could last you all day. The lead story was about the upcoming centennial of the Bin, still months away. There were numerous expert opinions as to "what this incredible milestone might have to say to the human race." Donovan read that part over. The writer had indeed created a talking milestone. And no matter which expert made it talk, it seemed to say pretty much the same thing as far as Donovan could tell: *It's only been a hundred years, and already immortality is getting old.*

# LORD DEMON

## by Roger Zelazny and Jane Lindskold

Giving way to a small desire to celebrate, I found my way—"outward" I guess you'd call it—through a small, perpetually misty and twilit region of mountains calculated to resemble a Taoist painting. For me, this is a kind of Faerie, where a man could hide himself and beautifully sleep the sleep of a Rip Van Winkle, where a lady could become a Sleeping Beauty in a rose-tangled castle and cave grown into a jade mountainside.

I heard a hearty howl from my left and another from my right. I walked on. Always good to let the boss know you're on the job.

After a time, an orange fu dog the size of a Shetland pony appeared to the left, a green one to the right. They seated themselves close to me, their great, fluffy tails curved over their backs.

"Hello," I said softly. "How's the frontier?"

"Nothing unnatural," growled Shiriki, the green one. "We passed The O'Keefe recently on his way out, but that is all."

Chamballa merely studied me with those great round eyes set in a flat face above a wide mouth. I have said that she was orange in color, but her coat was no garish citrus hue. It was closer to the ruddy glow of a coal that has not yet become fringed with ash.

I nodded.

"Good."

I had found them some nine and three-quarter centuries ago, half-starved, dying of thirst—for even some more and less than natural creatures have their needs. Their forgotten temple had fallen apart, and they were a pair of unemployed temple dogs nobody wanted, roaming the Gobi. I gave them water and food and permitted them to come back to my bottle with me, though I was a creature such as they had been cautioned about. I had always avoided contact with temple dogs if I possibly could. Me and my like, they'd been trained to rend into tiny pieces, to be carried off to a variety of uncomfortable places, with a mess of dog-magic for company and security.

So we never talked employment. I just told them that if they cared to live in the abandoned dragon's cave in my Twilight Lands, there was fresh water nearby, and I would see that there was food. And I would like if they would keep an eye on things for me. And if there was anybody nearby that they needed, simply to howl.

After a few centuries details were forgotten and only the fact of their residency remains. They call me Lord Kai and I call them Shiriki and Chamballa.

I walked on. Where I'd no need whatsoever to go outside what with O'Keefe tending to everything, there was that small desire to celebrate, to walk and to breathe the night air.

Coming to the edge of the worlds, I considered my appearance. Within my bottle I wore my natural shape: humanlike in that it possessed two arms, two legs, a recognizable torso and head, the usual number of eyes and suchlike. However, I stood eight feet tall on my taloned feet (these possessed of five toes) and my skin was a deep blue without a trace of purple. Around my eyes were angular segments of black. Some have supposed these are cosmetic (indeed, at one point a thousand years ago there was a fashion for such), but they are natural. They make my pupil-less dark eyes seem to glow and give my countenance a forbidding cast, even when I might not wish it.

Yes, this would not do for the world of humans. Quickly, I slipped into the human guise I use for my infrequent journeys without: a Chinese male of mature yeas, glossy black hair untouched by gray, average tall, but with an aura of command. I shaped my clothes into the dull fashions of the American city in which we now dwelled, sighing inwardly for the elegant robes of bygone China.

These preparations a matter of desire, I manifested outside the bottle with barely a pause in my stride. As I had wished, I was in a garage belonging to the son of the late lady who'd formerly kept the bottle on a parlor table. Either location was an easy one for our comings and goings. The son has not yet decided whether to give the bottle to his wife or to keep it on the table, where he enjoys looking at it. I had no opinion at the moment, and so stayed out of the matter.

Letting myself out of the garage's side door, I strolled off in the direction—several blocks away—of Tony's Pizza Heaven.

It was a starry but moonless night, crisp and breezy. I knew that something was wrong when, as I passed one of the town's small parks, I scented blood and pizza on the air. And demon.

I faded. I moved with absolute silence. All of the ways I have learned to inflict death and pain over the years rose up and came with me. At the moment, I was one of the most dangerous things on the planet.

. . . And I saw the tree and them.

# SINGER FROM THE SEA

### by Sheri S. Tepper

In Genevieve's dream, the old woman lunged up the stairs, hands clutching like claws from beneath her ragtag robe. "Lady. They're coming to kill you, now!"

She dreamed herself responding, too slowly at first, for she was startled and confused by the old woman's agitation. "Who? Awhero, what are you talking about."

"Your father's taken. The Shah has him. Now his men come for your blood! Yours and the child's. They're coming."

The smell of blood was all around her, choking her. So much blood. Her husband, gone; now her father, taken! Dovidi, only a baby, and never outside these walls!

Genevieve dreamed herself crying, "They're coming after Dovidi? How did the Shah know about the baby?"

"Your father tell him."

Endanger his grandson in that way? Surely not. Oh, surely, surely not. "I'll get him. We'll go . . ."

"If you take baby, you both be killed." The old woman reached forward and shook her by the shoulders, so vehement as to forget the prohibitions of caste. "I take him. I smutch his face and say he one of us. They scared to look and they never doubt . . ."

"Take me, too . . ."

"No. You too tall. Too strange looking. They know you!"

"Where? Where shall I go?"

"I sing you Tenopia. Go like Tenopia. By door, your

412

man's cloak with his sunhelmet, with his needfuls still there, in pockets." She pulled at the rags that hung from her shoulders, shreds tied together to make a tattered wrapping. "Take this! You tall for woman, so you walk past like man. Malghaste man. Go now!"

In her dream, she babbled something about getting word to the ship, then she went, thrust hard by Awhero's arms, strong for a woman her age. She fled to the courtyard, to the door through the city wall, a door that stood ajar! She could see directly into the guardpost outside—empty. Never empty except now! It smelled of a trap!

Beside the door hung the outer robe with its sunhelmet hood lining, behind the door half a dozen staves stood below a pendant cluster of water bottles, like flaccid grapes. She shut and bolted the inviting door, snatched the cloak, a staff a waterbottle, and fled back through the house to the kitchen wing, calling to someone as she went past the kitchens to the twisting stairs that only the malghaste used. Awhero had shown her the hatchway below, and she went directly to it, struggling into the robe as she fled, draping the rags around her shoulders to make it look as if she were clad only in tatters. As she slipped through the hatchway she heard voices shouting and fists thundering at the door she had barred.

She came out in a deep stairwell where coiled stairs led up to the narrow alley. The alley led to the street. She went up, and out, head down, a little bent, the staff softly thumping as she moved slowly, like any other passerby. Ahead of her was the narrow malghaste gate through the city wall, never guarded, never even watched, for this was where the untouchables carried out the city's filth. The stained and tattered rags marked her as one of them. Outside that gate a small malghaste boy guarded a flock of juvenile harpya, their fin-wings flattened against the heat, and beyond the flock was a well with a stone coping. The area around it was sodden, and she felt the mud ooze over her toes as she filled the bottle, slung it over her shoulder and walked away on the northern road, still slowly, as any malghaste might go. She did not run until she was out of sight of the town.

In her dream she was being hunted by dogs.

She woke to hear them baying, closer than before.

# EUROPA STRIKE:
## Book Three of the Heritage Trilogy

*by Ian Douglas*

The Singer's benthic hymn was gloriously beautiful, with melodies and tonalities alien to Chinese ears . . . or to Western, for that matter. There could be no possibility that the music, or the message it carried, had anything to do with Earth or Humankind. The ocean within which Zhao was now virtually adrift was over six hundred million kilometers removed from any of Earth's abyssal depths. The sounds filling the black depths around him were being generated by . . . by *something* deep beneath the surface of Europa's global, ice-sheathed ocean.

It was the nature of that something that he was testing now.

"Give me a countdown to the start of the next ping," Zhao said.

"Twenty-two seconds."

"And take me lower. I want to see it."

To Zhao's senses, he seemed to be descending rapidly, though he still felt only the synthleather of the chair pressing at his back, not the cold, wet rush of the sea straming past his face. That was just as well; the ambient water temperature was slightly below zero; its freezing point had been lowered slightly by its witch's brew of sulfur compounds and salts. Even with Europa's scant gravity, .13 of Earth's, the pressure at this depth amounted to over a thousand atmospheres . . . something like 1058 kilos pressing down on every square centimeter of his body, if his body had actually been plunging through the Europan depths.

The light seemed to be growing brighter, and he was beginning to make out the fuzzy forms of walls, towers, domes . . .

The image was not being transferred by light in this lightless abyss, of course, but by sound. The Song itself, echoing repeatedly from the surface ice around and around the Jovian satellite, reflected from those curiously shaped alien architectures. Microphones at the surface retrieved those reflections, and advanced imaging AIs created a rough and low-resolution image of what human eyes might have seen, if in fact they were suspended a mere few hundred meters above the object and not nearly 78 kilometers. The object was twelve kilometers across, roughly disk shaped, but with myriad swellings, blisters, domes, and towers that gave it the look of a small city. Experts were still divided over whether it was an underwater city, built for some inscrutable purpose deep within the Europan ocean, or a titanic spacecraft, a vessel from Outside that had crashed and sunk here thousands of years ago . . . or more. So far, the evidence seemed to support the spacecraft hypothesis. The thing couldn't be native; Europa was a small world of ice and water over a shriveled, stony core, incapable of supporting any sort of technic civilization. The Singer had to be a visitor from somewhere else.

"There is no question about it!" Zhao said. For the first time, he was beginning to allow himself to be excited. "The Singer is responding in realtime to the sonar signals transmitted from the surface. Do you realize what this means?"

"If true," Albert replied, "it means that The Singer is not a recording or automatic beacon of some sort, as current theory suggests, but represents an active intelligence."

"It means," Zhao said, excited, "a chance for *first contact.* . . ."

"It is likely that the CWS expedition has precisely that in mind. The Americans' sudden interest in submarines designed for extreme high-pressure operations suggest that they plan to visit The Singer in person."

And that, Zhao thought, could well be a disaster for China.

"We will have to inform General Xiang, of course." Albert reminded him. "With the current political situation, the Americans are unlikely to grant us access to this find."

"Of course."

It was imperative that Great *Zhongguo* be the first to make face-to-face contact with alien visitors from Beyond. The nation's survival—as a world power, as a *technological* power—depended on it. China's population, now approaching three billion, could not be sustained by the capricious handouts of foreign governments.

And so, China would go to Europa to meet for themselves these song-weaving visitors from the stars.

First, though, the Americans and their puppets would have to be taken out of the way. . . .

# FAR HORIZONS:
## All New Tales from the Greatest Worlds of Science Fiction

*Edited by Robert Silverberg*

**Greg Bear** sold his first short story at the age of fifteen. A Hugo and Nebula Award-winner, he has published seventeen novels. In "The Way of All Ghosts," Greg Bear reexplores The Way, the artificial universe that leads to other times and other universes, from *Eon, Eternity*, and *Legacy*, and the life of the living myth, Olmy Ap Sennen.

**Gregory Benford** is a professor of physics at UC Irvine, as well as the Nebula Award-winning author of eighteen novels. In "A Hunger for the Infinite," Gregory Benford ponders the continual war of human and machine in the novels of the Galactic Center: *In The Ocean of Night, Across the Sea of Suns, Great Sky River, Tides of Light, Furious Gulf,* and *Sailing Bright Eternity*, and asks one essential question of humanity at the beginning of its decline.

**David Brin** established himself as one of the premiere writers of hard science fiction with the *The Uplift Universe*, where humans are not the only sentient race on Earth, or in the universe, and there's a billion-year-old conspiracy behind the uplifting of races to sentience. . . . In this new story, "Temptation," multiple award-winning author Brin

417

shows exactly how perilous it can be to be offered exactly what you have always wished for.

Multiple-award winning author **Orson Scott Card** is one of sf/f's most best-known and most-loved writers, and the novels of *The Ender Series* are his most famous, and brilliant, works. In "Investment Calendar," Orson Scott Card tells the last hidden secret of his time-and-planet hopping protagonist Ender Wiggin's life: the momentous first meeting between Ender and Jane, Ender's computer-based, soon-to-be companion.

**Joe Haldeman** electrified the sf/f world with *Forever War*, the Nebula and Hugo Award-winning novel that brilliantly explored the experience of the Vietnam War, and war as a whole. In "A Separate War," he relates the unknown story of Marygay's separation from William, and offers hints about the new *Forever War* novel to come . . .

What would you do if you never had to sleep again? And what would happen when everyone discovered that the same genes that kept you from needing sleep, also kept you eternally young? Nebula Award-winning author **Nancy Kress** questions the problems arising from genetic modification in her acclaimed trilogy *Beggars in Spain, Beggars and Choosers*, and *Beggars Ride*, and now in "Sleeping Dogs."

A science fiction legend for her multiple award-winning classics *The Left Hand of Darkness* and *The Dispossessed*, **Ursula K. Le Guin** is known throughout the world for her novels of the Ekumen—brilliantly speculative novels that challenge the reader to reexamine their views of the worlds around them. In "Old Music and the Slave Women," she takes another look at the wars of race and property.

**Anne McCaffrey** is one of science fiction's most beloved writers, and in "The Ship Who Returned," she returns to the intriguing world of *The Ship Who Sang*. Helva, the sentient Ship Who Sings, goes to warn a colony about invading marauders, only to discover that the colony worships *her* . . .

The Heechee . . . Ancient, alien, unknown, the mysterious visitors dared humanity to come into the Gateway universe and claim the gifts of alien technology, if they could survive. In "The Boy Who Would Live Forever," the multiple award-winning **Frederik Pohl** returns to the *Tales of the Heechee* and the dangerous, enthralling universe of *Gateway* and its mystifying legacies.

**Robert Silverberg** is the multiple award-winning author of numerous science fiction novels, and best-selling editor of the fantasy anthology *Legends*. In "Getting to Know the Dragon," he returns to the fascinating alternate-Rome universe of *Roma Eterna*, in which Christianity never existed, and Rome remained pagan, and unconquered throughout time.

Brilliantly-fantastic novels of metaphysical and scientific ingenuity, **David Simmon**'s *The Hyperion Cantos* has helped redefine science fiction in the last twenty years, challenging it to move further and faster. In "Orphans of the Helix," Simmons revisits the award-winning *Hyperion* universe, and asks more questions about the salvation of the human soul.

*Eos Spotlight*

# MARINES ON THE HIGH FRONTIER

by Ian Douglas

The Marines have always led the way, in space as well as in America's wars.

Lieutenant Colonel John Glenn, the first American in orbit, was a Marine. Walter Cunningham, one of the first three men to fly the Apollo spacecraft; Fred Haise, who helped bring the crippled *Apollo 13* spacecraft around the Moon and safely back to Earth; Jack Lousma, pilot of *Skylab 3* and commander of space shuttle *Columbia*'s third test flight, with almost 1,600 hours in space—all of them, Marines.

Marines have already written themselves into the history of manned space flight. They will continue to do so in the future.

The question, of course, is whether Marines will be needed in space in their traditional roles as peacekeepers, as protectors of America's strategic interests, as America's "first to fight." The answer, sadly, depends on whether humankind will carry its squabbles and tribal bloodlettings into space. Given our past record in such matters, war on the High Frontier seems inevitable.

And if it is inevitable, then it is inevitable that the U.S. Marine Corps will be there, in the forefront, as always. Scorned in peacetime, derided by antimilitary types, all too often with outdated weapons and secondhand equipment, the Marines will lead the way.

Why? Here's one possibility. We've just begun to appreciate the danger posed by small bodies—asteroids and comets—to all of Earth. A ten-mile asteroid striking what is now the Yucatán 65 million years ago ended the era of the dinosaurs, and came damned close to snuffing out all life on the planet. A smaller body could devastate continents or wreck coastal cities with mile-high tidal waves.

And think about it. With a modest space capability, a small nuke, and a good computer, any nation that so desired could *deliberately* alter the orbit of a suitable asteroid, sending it to a precise impact point on Target Earth. The longer it took to spot the incoming missile, the harder it would be to stop. Even a rock the size of a school bus could wreck a city. God help us if a terrorist group or a madman dictator with Armageddon on their minds ever developed such a capablity.

For this reason we will one day establish outposts in space—ships on patrol, bases in solar orbit—all with the mission of charting potentially dangerous rocks, challenging suspicious vessels, and keeping Earth's skies safe. Such outposts might well lead the way to the full-scale colonization and commercial development of space in the twenty-first century in exactly the same way that Army posts and forts opened the Old West in the nineteenth.

This would be essentially a military mission, rather than civilian. The U.S. Navy, with its long experience in crewing large vessels on extended tours of duty in far-off climes, would likely fly those ships. And the Marines, "the Navy's police force," as one shortsighted American president derisively called them, will be aboard, standing watches, boarding suspicious vessels, planting the explosives to redirect Earthbound bits of rock.

As they say: "The meek can have the Earth; the rest of us are going to the stars."

And the Marines will lead the way.

Count on it.

# LEGENDS OF THE RIFTWAR

### HONORED ENEMY 978-0-06-079284-8

by Raymond E. Feist & William R. Forstchen

In the frozen northlands of the embattled realm of Midkemia, Dennis Hartraft's Marauders must band together with their bitter enemy, the Tsurani, to battle *moredhel*, a migrating horde of deadly dark elves.

### MURDER IN LAMUT 978-0-06-079291-6

by Raymond E. Feist & Joel Rosenberg

For twenty years the mercenaries Durine, Kethol, and Pirojil have fought other people's battles, defeating numerous deadly enemies. Now the Three Swords find themselves trapped by a winter's storm inside a castle teeming with ambitious, plotting lords and ladies, and it falls on the mercenaries to solve a series of cold-blooded murders.

### JIMMY THE HAND 978-0-06-079299-2

by Raymond E. Feist & S.M. Stirling

Forced to flee the only home he's ever known, Jimmy the Hand, boy thief of Krondor finds himself among the rural villagers of Land's End. But Land's End is home to a dark, dangerous presence even the local smugglers don't recognize. And suddenly Jimmy's youthful bravado is leading him into the maw of chaos . . . and, quite possibly, his doom.

# IAN DOUGLAS'S
## MONUMENTAL SAGA
## OF INTERGALACTIC WAR
# THE INHERITANCE TRILOGY

## STAR STRIKE: BOOK ONE

978-0-06-123858-1

Planet by planet, galaxy by galaxy, the inhabited universe has fallen to the alien Xul. Now only one obstacle stands between them and total domination: the warriors of a resilient human race the world-devourers nearly annihilated centuries ago.

## GALACTIC CORPS: BOOK TWO

978-0-06-123862-8

In the year 2886, intelligence has located the gargantuan hidden homeworld of humankind's dedicated foe, the brutal Xul. The time has come for the courageous men and women of the 1st Marine Interstellar Expeditionary Force to strike the killing blow.

## SEMPER HUMAN: BOOK THREE

978-0-06-116090-5

True terror looms at the edges of known reality. Humankind's eternal enemy, the Xul, approach wielding a weapon monstrous beyond imagining. If the Star Marines fail to eliminate their relentless xenophobic foe once and for all, the Great Annihilator will obliterate every last trace of human existence.